cigarettes. The remaining furniture of the room was simple and poor: a neat camp bedstead, a boot-jack, and a round mirror, not more than four inches in diameter; a tin tub and an iron washing-stand; a much battered old "schläger," with the colours at the hilt all in rags, hung over the iron stove; and that was all the room contained besides books and the working-table and chair. It would be impossible to live more simply, and yet everything was neat and clean, and stamped, too, with a certain cachet of individuality. There were probably hundreds of student-rooms in the town of Heidelberg which boasted no more adornment or luxury than this, and yet there was not one that looked like it. A student's room, as he grows up, is a reflection of himself; it is a kind of dissolving view, in which the one set of objects and books fades gradually away as his opinions form themselves, and as he collects about him the works that are really of interest to him, as distinguished from those with which he has been obliged to occupy himself prior to taking his academic steps. Then, as in the human frame every particle of bone and sinew is said to change in seven years, the student one day looks about him and recognises that hardly a book or a paper is there of all the store over which he was busied in those months before he took his degree, or sustained his disputation. When a man has entered on his career, if he enters on it with a will, he soon finds that all books and objects not essential as tools for his work creep stealthily into the dusty corner, or to the inaccessible top shelf of the bookcase,—or if he is very poor, to the second-hand bookshop. He cannot afford to be hampered by any dead weight.

Now Dr. Claudius had gone through many changes of thought and habit since he came to Heidelberg ten years ago. But he had never changed his quarters; for he loved the garret window and the isolation from visits and companions that he gained by his three flights of stairs. The camp-bed in the corner was the same whereon he had lain after his first duel, with a bag of ice on his head and his bosom friend by his side, with a long pipe. At that very table he had drawn his first caricature of Herr Professor Winkelnase, which had been framed and hung up in the "Kneipe"—the drinking-hall of his corps; at the same board he had written his thesis for his doctorate, and here again he had penned the notes for his first lecture. Professor Winkelnase was dead; not one of his old corps-brothers remained in Heidelberg, but still he clung to the old room. The learned doctors with whom he drank his wine or his beer of an evening, when he sallied forth from his solitude, wondered at his way of living; for Dr. Claudius was not poor, as incomes go in South Germany. He had a modest competence of his own to begin with, and his lectures brought him in something, so that he might have had a couple of rooms "parterre"—as the Germans call the rez-de-chaussée—and could have been as comfortable as he pleased. But no one ever attempted to account for Dr. Claudius at all. He was a credit to the University, where first-rate men are scarce,—for Heidelberg is not a seat of very great learning; and no one troubled to inquire why he did not return to his native country when he had obtained his "Phil.D." Only, if he meant to spend the rest of his life in Heidelberg, it was high time he married and settled down to genuine "Philisterleben"—at least so Dr. Wiener had said to Dr. Wurst over the second "schoppen" every night for a year past.

But Claudius did not marry, nor did he even allow his blue eyes to rest contemplatively on black-eyed Fräulein Wiener, or red-cheeked Fräulein Wurst. He would indeed occasionally accept an invitation to drink coffee at his colleagues' houses, but his talk was little and his manner a placid blank. He had been wild enough ten years before, when his yellow hair and tall straight presence were the admiration of every burgher's daughter in the Hirschgasse or the Langestrasse; but years and study had brought out the broad traits of his character, his uniformly quiet manner, his habits of regularity, and a certain deliberateness of gait and gesture which well became his towering figure and massive strength. He was utterly independent in all his ways, without the least trace of the arrogance that hangs about people whose independence is put on, and constantly asserted, in order to be beforehand with the expected opposition of their fellow-men.

Dr. Claudius was a Swede by birth and early education, and finding himself at twenty free to go where he would, he had wandered to Heidelberg in pursuit of the ideal student-life he had read so much of in his Northern home. Full of talent, independent and young, he cared little for the national enmities of Scandinavians and Germans, and, like all foreigners who behave sensibly, he was received with open arms by the enthusiastic students, who looked upon him as a sort of typical Goth, the prototype of the Teutonic races. And when they found how readily he learned to handle schläger and sabre, and that, like a true son of Odin, he could drain the great horn of brown ale at a draught, and laugh through the foam on his yellow beard, he became to them the embodiment of the student as he should be. But there was little of all that left now, and though the stalwart frame was stronger and tougher in its manly proportions, and the yellow beard grown long and curly, and the hair as thick as ever, the flush of youth was gone; and Dr. Claudius leaned out of his high window and smelled the river breeze, and said to himself it was not so sweet as it used to be, and that, for all he only had thirty summers behind him, he was growing old—very old; and that was why he did not care to spend more than half-an-hour of an evening with Dr. Wiener and Dr. Wurst.

In truth it was an unnatural life for a man just reaching his prime, and full of imagination and talent and love for the beautiful. But he had fallen into the philosophical groove of study which sooner or later seems to absorb so many gifted minds, only to lay them waste in nine cases out of ten. A brilliant mathematician, he had taken his doctorate without difficulty, and his thesis had even attracted some attention. From the higher speculations of modern mathematics to the study of philosophy is but a step, and Claudius had plunged into the vast sea of Kant, Spinoza, and Hegel, without, perhaps, having any very definite idea of what he was doing, until he found himself forced to go forward or to acknowledge himself baffled and beaten. This he was not willing to do, and so he had gone on and on, until one day, some six months ago, he had asked himself what it all led to? why he had laboured so hard for years over such things? whether the old free life and ready enjoyment were not better than this midnight prowling among other people's thoughts, which, whatever they might have been when spoken, never seemed quite clear on paper? Or would it not be better to leave the whole thing and go back to his Northern home? He might find plenty of adventure there, and breathe in fresh youth and vitality in the cold bright life of the Norwegian fisheries or of some outlying Swedish farm. And yet he could not make up his mind to move, or to acknowledge that he had laboured in vain. It was in vain, though, he said, as he looked out at the flowing river. Had he gained a single advantage either for his thoughts or his deeds by all his study of philosophy? In his weariness he said to himself that he had not; that he had been far better able to deal with questions of life, so long as he had only handled the exact sciences, than he was now, through all this uncertain saturation of foggy visions and contradictory speculations. Questions of life—but did questions of life ever arise for him? He had reduced it all to its simplest expression. His little store of money was safely invested, and he drew the income four times a year. He possessed no goods or chattels not stowed away in his garret chamber. He owed no man anything; he was not even a regular professor, tied to his University by a fixed engagement. In a word, he was perfectly free and untrammelled. To what end? He worked on from force of habit; but work had long ceased to amuse him. When had he laughed last? Probably not since his trip on foot to the Bavarian Highlands, where he had met a witty journalist from Berlin, with whom he had walked for a couple of days.

This evening he was more weary than usual. He almost thought he would go away if he could think of any place to go to where life might be more interesting. He had no relations excepting an uncle, who had emigrated to America when Claudius was a baby, and who wrote twice a year, with that regular determination to keep up his family ties which characterises the true Northman. To this uncle he also wrote regularly at stated intervals, telling of his quiet student-life. He knew that this solitary relation was in business in New York, and he inferred from the regular offers of assistance which came in every letter that he was in good circumstances,—but that was all. This evening he fell

Doctor Claudius: A True Story by F. Marion Crawford

Francis Marion Crawford was born on August 2nd, 1854 at Bagni di Lucca, Italy. An only son and a nephew to Julia Ward Howe, the American poet and writer of 'The Battle Hymn of the Republic'.

His education began at St Paul's School, Concord, New Hampshire, then to Cambridge University; University of Heidelberg; and the University of Rome.

In 1879 Crawford went to India, to study Sanskrit and then edited The Indian Herald. In 1881 he returned to America to continue his Sanskrit studies at Harvard University.

At this time in Boston he lived at his Aunt Julia house and in the company of his Uncle, Sam Ward. His family was concerned about his employment prospects. After a singing career as a baritone was ruled out, he was encouraged to write.

In December 1882 his first novel, 'Mr Isaacs', was an immediate hit which was amplified by 'Dr Claudius' in 1883.

In October 1884 he married Elizabeth Berdan. They went on to have two sons and two daughters.

Encouraged by his excellent start to a literary career he returned to Italy with Elizabeth to make a permanent home, principally in Sant' Agnello, where he bought the Villa Renzi that then became Villa Crawford.

In the late 1890s, he began to write his historical works: 'Ave Roma Immortalis' (1898), 'Rulers of the South' (1900) and 'Gleanings from Venetian History' (1905). The Saracinesca series is perhaps his best work. 'Saracinesca' was followed by 'Sant' Ilario' in 1889, 'Don Orsino' in 1892 and 'Corleone' in 1897, that being the first major treatment of the Mafia in literature.

Francis Marion Crawford died at Sorrento on Good Friday 1909 at Villa Crawford of a heart attack.

Index of Contents

CHAPTER I

"I believe I am old," said the Doctor, pushing his straight-backed wooden chair from the table, and turning from his books to look out of his small window. "Yes, I am certainly very old," he said again, rapping absently on the arm of the chair with the pen he held. But the fingers that held the instrument were neither thin nor withered, and there was no trembling in the careless motion of the hand. The flaxen hair, long and tangled, was thick on the massive head, and the broad shoulders were flat and square across. Whatever Dr. Claudius might say of himself, he certainly did not look old.

And yet he said to himself that he was, and he probably knew. He said to himself, as he had said every day for many long months, that this was the secret of the difference he felt between his life and the life of his companions—such companions as he had, between his thoughts and their thoughts, between his ways and their ways. Of late the fancy had gained a stronger hold on his imagination, excited by solitude and an undue consumption of the midnight oil, and as he turned his face to the evening light, an observer, had there been one, might have felt half inclined to agree with him. His face was pale, and the high aquiline nose looked drawn. Moreover, the tangled hair and beard contrasted strangely with his broad, spotless collar, and his dressing-gown of sober black. The long habit of neatness in dress survived any small vanity of personal looks.

He rose, and throwing the pen impatiently on the table, went to the little window and looked out. His shoulders overlapped the opening on both sides as he thrust his yellow head out into the evening sunshine, and Master Simpelmayer, the shoemaker down in the street, glanced up, and seeing that the Herr Doctor was taking his evening sniff of the Neckar breeze, laid down his awl and went to "vespers,"—a "maas" of cool beer and a "pretzel." For the Herr Doctor was a regular man, and always appeared at his window at the same hour, rain or shine. And when Simpelmayer mended the well-worn shoes that came to him periodically from across the way, he was sure that the flaxen-haired student would not call over to know if they were finished until the sun was well down and the day far spent. On this particular evening, however, there was no mending in hand for the Herr Doctor, and so the crooked little shoemaker filled himself a pipe, and twisted his apron round his waist, and stumped leisurely down the street to the beer-shop at the corner, where he and his fellows took their pots and their pipes, undisturbed by the playful pranks of the students.

But the Doctor remained at his window, and neither vouchsafed look nor greeting to Master Simpelmayer. He was not thinking of shoes or shoemakers just then, though, to judge by his face, he was thinking very intently of something. And well he might, for he had been reading serious stuff. The walls of his little chamber were lined with books, and there was a small sliding-rack on the table, presumably for those volumes he immediately required for his work. A rare copy of Sextus Empiricus, with the Greek and Latin side by side, lay open on an inclined desk at one end, and the table was strewn with papers, on which were roughly drawn a variety of mathematical figures, margined all around with odd-looking equations and algebraically-expressed formulæ. Well-thumbed volumes of mathematical works in English, German, and French, lay about, opened in various places, and there was a cracked old plate, half full of tobacco ashes and the ends of to thinking about him. The firm was "Barker and Lindstrand," he remembered. He wondered what Mr. Barker was like. By the by it would soon be midsummer, and he might expect the half-yearly letter at any time. Not that it would interest him in the least when it came, but yet he liked to feel that he was not utterly alone in the world. There was the postman coming down the street in his leisurely, old-fashioned way, chatting with the host at the corner and with the tinman two doors off, and then—yes, he was stopping at Dr. Claudius's door.

The messenger looked up, and, seeing the Doctor at his window, held out a large envelope.

"A letter for you, Herr Doctor," he cried, and his red nose gleamed in the evening glow, strongly foreshortened to the Doctor's eye.

"Gleich," replied Claudius, and the yellow head disappeared from the window, its owner descending to open the door.

As he mounted the dingy staircase Claudius turned the great sealed envelope over and over in his hand, wondering what could be the contents. It was postmarked "New York," but the hand was large and round and flourished, not in the least like his uncle's sexagenarian crabbedness of hieroglyphic. In the corner was the name of a firm he did not know, and the top of the letter was covered with a long row of stamps, for it was very thick and heavy. So he went into his room, and sat down on the window-sill to see what Messrs. Screw and Scratch of Pine Street, New York, could possibly want of Claudius, Phil.D. of Heidelberg.

His curiosity soon gave way to very considerable surprise. The first part of the letter contained the formal announcement of the sudden decease of Gustavus Lindstrand, of the firm of Barker and Lindstrand of New York. Claudius laid down the letter and sighed. His one relation had not been much to him. He had no recollection even of the old gentleman's appearance, but the regular correspondence had given him a feeling of reliance, a sensation of not being absolutely alone. He was alone now. Not a relation of any description in the world. Well, he would read the remainder of the letter. He turned over the page.

"We enclose a copy of the will," the lawyer continued, "for your inspection. You will see that Mr. Screw of our firm is appointed joint executor with Mr. Silas B. Barker, and we await your further instructions. In view of the large fortune you inherit," . . .

Claudius looked up suddenly and gazed blankly out of the window; then he went on—

. . . "by the aforesaid will of your uncle, the late Mr. Gustavus Lindstrand, it might be well if, at your convenience, you could pay a visit to this country."

Here Claudius thought it was time to look at the will itself. Unfolding the document, which was very short, he acquainted himself with the contents. There were a few legacies to old servants, and one or two to persons who were probably friends. Everything else was devised and bequeathed "to my nephew, the son of my sister, Claudius, privat-docent in the University of Heidelberg, Grand Duchy of Baden, Germany." And it appeared that the surplus, after deducting all legacies and debts, amounted to about one million and a half of dollars.

Claudius carefully reread the papers without betraying the smallest emotion. He then put them back in the envelope, and opening a small iron cash-box, which stood on a shelf of the book-case, locked up will, letter, power of attorney, and all. Then he shook his long limbs, with a sigh, and having rolled a thick cigarette, lighted it, and sat down in his chair to think. The shadows were deepening, and the smoke of his tobacco showed white against the gloom in the room. The news he had just received would have driven some men crazy, and certainly most people would experience some kind of vivid sensation at finding themselves suddenly endowed with immense wealth from a quarter where they did not even suspect it existed. Moreover, old Lindstrand's will was perfectly unequivocal, and contained none of those ill-natured restrictions about marrying or not marrying, or assuming the testator's name, or anything which could put the legatee to the slightest inconvenience. But Claudius experienced no sensation of pleasure at finding himself sole master of a million and a half.

It was not that he was foolish enough to despise money, or even to pretend to, as some people do. He would have felt keenly the loss of his own little store, and would have hated to work for money instead of working for work's sake. But he had enough, and had always had enough, for his small wants. He loved beautiful things intensely, but he had no desire to possess them; it was enough that he might see them, and carry away the remembrance. He loved books, but he cared not a jot for rare editions, so long as there were cheap ones published in Leipzic. That old copy of Sextus Empiricus, on the desk there, he had bought because he could not get an ordinary edition; and now that he had read it he did not care to keep it. Of course it contained a great deal that was good, but he had extracted the best of it, and meant to sell the volume to the first bidder—not that he wanted the money, but because it was in the way; if he allowed things to accumulate, there would be no turning round in his little den. So he leaned back in his straight-backed chair and wondered what in the world he should do with "all that money." He might travel. Yes, but he preferred to travel with a view of seeing things, rather than of reaching places. He would rather walk most of the way. The only way in which he could possibly live up to such an income must be by changing his entire mode of life—a house, somewhere in a great city, horses, servants, and even a wife—Claudius laughed for the first time in many months, a deep Homeric laugh—they would all help him to get rid of his money. But then, a life like that—pshaw! impossible. He was sick of it before beginning, then what would he feel after a month of it?

The problem faced him in the dark, like an unsolved equation, staring out black and white before his eyes, or like an unfinished game of chess when one goes to bed after five or six hours' play. Something he must decide, because it was his nature to decide always, before he left a subject, on some course of thought. Meanwhile he had been so little disturbed by the whole business that, in spite of his uncle's death, and a million and a half of money, he was hungry and thirsty. So he struck a match and lit his study-lamp, and found his coat and hat and stick. Then he paused. He did not want to meet Dr. Wiener and Dr. Wurst that evening; he would fetch himself something to eat and drink, and be quiet. So he slung a heavy stone jug on his arm, and, turning his lamp down to save the oil, trudged down the stairs and out into the street. He made for the little inn at the corner, and while the fat old landlord filled his jug with the best Markgräfler, he himself picked out a couple of smoked sausages from the great pile on the counter, and wrapping them up with half a dozen pretzels, transferred the package to his capacious pocket. Then he took the jug from the innkeeper, and having paid half a gulden for the whole supply of eatables and wine, he departed to consume them in solitude. It was his usual supper. He had done the same thing for ten years, off and on, whenever he was not inclined for company.

"But I suppose it is incongruous," he soliloquised, "that, being a millionaire, I should fetch my own supper." Once more he laughed aloud in the crowded street, for it was warm and the people were sitting in front of their houses, Simpelmayer the shoemaker, and Blech the tinman, and all the rest, each with his children and his pot of beer. As the Doctor laughed, the little boys laughed too, and Blech remarked to Simpelmayer that the Herr Doctor must have won the great prize in the Hamburg lottery, for he had not heard him laugh like that in three years.

"Freilich," returned the crooked shoemaker, "but he was used to laugh loud enough ten years ago. I can remember when he first moved in there, and his corps-fellows locked him in his room for a jest, and stood mocking in the street. And he climbed right down the woodwork and stepped on the signboard of the baker and jumped into the street, laughing all the while, though they were holding in their breath for fear he should break his neck. Ja, he was a right student; but he is changed now— the much reading, lieber Blech, the much reading." And the old fellow looked after Claudius as he disappeared into the dark doorway.

The Doctor mounted his three flights with even tread, and, turning up his light, proceeded leisurely to eat his twisted rolls and sausages. When he had done that, he took the great stone jug in his hand, as if it had been a wine-glass, and set it to his lips and drank a long draught.

The result of his cogitations, assisted by the soothing influence of supper, was to be foreseen. In the first place, he reflected that the problem was itself a myth. No one could require of him that he should use his money unless he liked. He might let it accumulate without any trouble to himself; and then, why should he tell any one of his inheritance? Surely he might go on living as he was living now for an indefinite period, and nobody would be the wiser. Besides, it would be a novel sensation to feel that while living like a simple student he possessed a great power, put away, as it were, on the shelf, whereby he could, if he liked, at any moment astonish the whole country. Very novel, indeed, and considering the importance of the question of the disposal of his income, he could well afford to give it six months' consideration. And he might move undisturbed about the University and eat his supper with Dr. Wiener and Dr. Wurst without being the object of general interest, which he would at once become if it were known that he, a simple privat-docent, with his decent black coat and his twice-mended shoes, was the richest man in the Grand Duchy of Baden.

These reflections of Dr. Claudius, strange as they must seem in the eyes of men of the world, were only what were to be expected from a man of his education and character. He had travelled after a fashion, it is true, and had frequented society when he was younger; for the Heidelberg student is a lover of the dance, and many of the wild young burschen become the brilliant officers of the crack regiments of the first army in the world. He had been in Paris and Vienna and Rome for a few weeks, and, being of a good family in the North, had received introductions through the diplomatic representatives of his country. His striking personality had always attracted attention, and he might have gone everywhere had he chosen. But he had only cared enough for society and its life to wish to see it now and then, and he fancied that he understood it at a glance—that it was all a sham and a glamour and vanity of vanities. There was, of course, a potent reason for all this. In his short peregrinations into the world of decorations and blue ribbons and cosmopolitan uniforms he had never come across a woman that interested him. He had a holy reverence for woman in the abstract, but he had not met one to whom he could do homage as the type of the ideal womanhood he worshipped. Perhaps he expected too much, or perhaps he judged too much by small and really insignificant signs. As no man living or dead has ever understood any woman for five minutes at a time, he was not to be blamed. Women are very like religion—we must take them on faith, or go without.

Moreover, Dr. Claudius had but an indifferent appreciation of the value of money; partly because he had never cared for what it would buy, and had therefore never examined its purchasing power, and partly because he had never lived intimately with people who spent a great deal. He knew nothing of business, and had never gambled, and he did not conceive that the combination of the two could be of any interest. Compared with the questions that had occupied his mind of late, it seemed to make no more difference whether a man were rich or poor than whether he had light hair or dark. And if he had seriously asked himself whether even those great problems which had occupied the minds of the mightiest thinkers led to any result of importance, it was not likely that he would bestow a thought on such a trivial matter as the question of pounds, shillings, and pence.

So, before he went to bed, he took out a sheet of paper and an envelope—he never bought but one package of envelopes a year, when he sent his New Year's card to the other doctors of the University—and wrote a short letter to Messrs. Screw and Scratch of Pine Street, New York. He acknowledged the receipt of their communication, deplored the death of his only relation, and requested that they would look after his money for him, as he had no use whatever for it at present. He objected, he said, to signing a power of attorney as yet, for as there was no hurry they might consult him by letter or telegraph as often as they liked. When Messrs. Screw and Scratch read this epistle they opened their eyes wide, wondering what manner of man Claudius, Phil.D., might be. And it took them some time to find out. But Claudius put out his light when he had signed and sealed the missive, and slept the sleep of the strong and the just, undisturbed by the possession of a fortune or by any more doubts as to the future.

Before receiving this letter he had thought seriously of going away. Now that a move was almost thrust upon him, he found that he did not want to make it. A professor he would live and die. What could be more contemptible, he reflected, than to give up the march of thought and the struggle for knowledge, in order to sit at ease, devising means of getting rid of so much cash? And he straightened his great limbs along the narrow camp-bed and was asleep in five minutes.

CHAPTER II

When Claudius awoke at daybreak he had a strong impression that he had been dreaming. His first action was to open his iron box and read the will over again. That being done, he reflected that his determination to keep his fortune a secret was a wise one, and that for the present he would abide by it. So he went out and got a notary to attest his signature to the letter, and posted it to Messrs. Screw and Scratch, and returned to his books. But the weather was intensely hot, and the sun beat down fiercely on the roof over his head, so that after two or three hours he gave it up and sallied forth to seek coolness abroad. His steps turned naturally upwards towards the overhanging castle where he was sure of a breeze and plenty of shade; and as he passed the famous old "Wirthshaus zum faulen Pelz" on the ascent, he turned in and took a drink of the cool clear ale and a pretzel, an operation termed in Germany the "Frühschoppen," or "early glass," and as universal a practice as the early tea in the tropics before the sun is up, or the "vermouth" of the Italian before the evening meal. Having offered this customary libation to the summer deities, the Doctor leisurely climbed the hill and entered the precincts of the Schloss. Sure enough, there was a breeze here among the ruins, and shade in abundance wherein to lie and read all through the summer day, with an occasional shift of position as the sun rose and sank in the blazing sky.

Claudius stretched himself out near the great ruined tower under a bit of wall, and, pulling out a book, began to read. But the book did not interest him, and before long he let it drop and fell to thinking. The light wind stirred the broad green foliage over him, and the sun struck fiercely down beyond the border of shade; but then, again, beyond there were more trees and more shade. The nameless little crickets and flies and all manner of humming things panted musically in the warm air; the small birds chirped lazily now and then in desultory conversation, too hot to hop or fly; and a small lizard lay along the wall dazed and stupid in the noontide heat. The genius loci was doubtless cooling himself in the retirement of some luxurious hole among the ruins, and the dwarf Perkéo, famous in song and toast, had the best of it that day down in the cellar by the great tun.

But Claudius was of a tough nature, and minded neither heat nor cold; only when a large bluebottle fly buzzed round his nose he whisked his broad hat to drive the tormentor away, and said to himself that summer had its drawbacks even in Germany, though there were certainly more flies and mosquitoes and evil beasts on the wing in Sweden during the two months' heat there. On the whole, he was pretty comfortable among the ruins on this June day, though he ought to begin considering where his summer foot tour was to take him this year. It might be as well, certainly. Where could he go? There was the Black Forest, but he knew that thoroughly; Bohemia—he had been there; Switzerland; the Engadine—yes, he would go back to Pontresina and see what it had grown into since he was there six years ago. It used to be a delightful place then, as different from St. Moritz as anything could well be. Only students and artists and an occasional sturdy English climber used to go to Pontresina, while all Europe congregated at St. Moritz half a dozen miles away. He would go there as he went everywhere, with a knapsack and a thick stick and a few guldens in his pocket, and be happy, if so be that he had any capacity for enjoyment left in him.

"It is absurd," said Claudius to himself, argumentatively. "I am barely thirty years old, as strong as an ox, and I have just inherited more money than I know what to do with, and I feel like an old cripple of ninety, who has nothing left to live for. It must be morbid imagination or liver complaint, or something."

But it was neither liver nor imagination, for it was perfectly genuine. Tired of writing, tired of reading, of seeing, of hearing, and speaking; and yet blessed with a constitution that bid fair to carry him through another sixty years of life. He tried to argue about it. Was it possible that it came of living in a foreign country with whose people he had but a fancied sympathy? There are no folk like our own folk, after all; and there is truly a great gulf between Scandinavians and every other kind of people. But it seemed to Claudius that he loved the Germans and their ways—and indeed he did; but does not everyday experience show that the people we admire, and even love, the most are not necessarily those with whom we are most in sympathy or with whom it is best for us to live? He would have been better among his own Northern people; but that did not strike him, and he determined he would go to the Engadine to-morrow or next day.

The Doctor, having made up his mind, shifted his position and sat up, pulling a pipe from his pocket, which he proceeded to fill and to light. The flame of the match was white and transparent in the mid-day glare, and the smoke hung lazily about as he puffed at the ungainly instrument of enjoyment.

Before he had half finished his pipe he heard footsteps on the path. He looked up idly and saw a lady—two ladies—coming leisurely towards him. Beyond the fact that it was an unusual hour for strangers to visit the Schloss—and they evidently were strangers—there was nothing unusual in the apparition; and Claudius merely rose to his feet and moved slowly on, not from any desire to get out of the way, but merely because he was too well bred to remain seated by the path while a lady passed, and having risen, he could not very well stand still. So he moved on till he stood by the broken tower, and seeing that by climbing down he could reach a more secure resting-place, with the advantage of a view, he let himself drop easily on to a projecting ledge of masonry and resumed his pipe with philosophic indifference. Before long he heard voices above him, or more properly a voice, for one of the parties confined her conversation strictly to yea and nay, while the other spoke enthusiastically, and almost as if soliloquising, about the scene.

It was a deep-strung voice, that would have been masculine if it had been the least harsh; but it was not—it was only strong and large and smooth, a woman's voice with the gift of resonance that lends interest where there might otherwise seem to be none. There is a certain kind of voice in woman that seems to vibrate in a way especially its own. Whether it be that under certain conditions of the vocal organs harmonic sounds are produced as they may be upon a stringed instrument or upon an organ pipe; or whether, again, the secret lies deeper, depending on the subtile folding and unfolding of new-shaped waves of sound to which our ordinary ears are not used—who can tell? And yet there are voices that from the first produce upon us a strange impression unlike anything else in the world. Not that we necessarily become interested in the possessor of the voice, who may remain for ever utterly indifferent to us, for the magic lies in the tone merely, which seems to have a power of perpetuating itself and rebounding among the echoes of our recollections. Barely, very rarely, singers possess it, and even though their powers be limited there comes a strange thrill into their singing which fixes it indelibly on the memory.

Such a voice it was that Claudius heard as he lay on his ledge of masonry some ten feet below, and listened to the poetic flow of the strange lady's thoughts on Heidelberg and the scene at her feet. He did not move, for he was sure she had not seen him; and he supposed she would go away in a few minutes. He was destined to be seen, however. She stopped talking, and was apparently lost in thought; but in a moment there was a small cry.

"O mon Dieu!" and a dainty lace-covered parasol fell over the edge, and, striking the platform where Claudius was lying, went straight to the bottom of the ruin, some twenty feet farther.

"What a nuisance," said the thrilling voice from above, "I can never get it back now; and there are no gardeners or people about."

"Permit me, Madam," said Claudius, stepping as far out as he dared, and looking up to catch a glimpse of a beautiful woman in black and white staring down at the unlucky parasol in a rather helpless fashion. "Do not be disturbed, Madam; I will get it for you in a moment." And he began to descend.

The fair unknown protested—Monsieur must not trouble himself; Monsieur would certainly break his neck—enfin, it was very obliging on the part of Monsieur to risk himself in such a terrible gulf, etc. etc. But "Monsieur," when once he had caught sight of those dark eyes, climbed steadily down to the bottom, and had reached the lost parasol before the string of polite protestations had ceased. The ascent was quickly accomplished, and he stood at the summit, hat in hand, to return the object of his search to its rightful owner. There was not a trace of embarrassment on his face; and he looked the foreign lady boldly in the eyes as he bowed. She could not express her thanks sufficiently, and would probably have wished to continue expressing them for some time longer to the handsome and herculean young man, who had apparently started out of space to her assistance; but when Claudius had taken a good look he simply answered—

"Il n'y a pas de quoi, Madame," and bowing low walked off. Perhaps the least contraction of curiosity was in his eyes; and he would have liked to know who the lady was who had the crown and the large M carved in the ivory of her parasol stick. But, after all, he came to the conclusion that he did not care, and so went strolling down the path, wondering where he could hide himself if visitors were to infest the Schloss at this time of year, and in the hottest hours of the day.

"I will leave here to-morrow," he said, "and see if I cannot be more comfortable in Pontresina." He reached another part of the Schloss, and sitting down resumed his pipe, which seemed destined to interruptions.

The lady of the parasol had made an impression on Dr. Claudius, for all his apparent indifference. It was rarely, indeed, nowadays that he looked at a woman at all; and to-day he had not only looked, but he owned to himself, now it was past, that he would like to look again. If he had had any principle in avoiding women during the last few years, he would not have admitted now that he would like to see her again—just for one moment. But he had no principle in the matter. It was choice, and there it ended; and whenever he should take it into his head to associate with the fair sex again, he would consider it a sign that his youth had returned, and he would yield without the smallest struggle. But in this ease—"Pshaw!" thought the humble privat-docent, "she is some great lady, I suppose. How should I make her acquaintance? Oh! I forgot—I am a millionaire to-day; I have only to ask and it shall be opened." He smiled to himself, and, with the returning sense of the power to do what he pleased, the little undefined longing for another glimpse of the fair stranger subsided for a time.

Then he regretted it. He was sorry it was gone; for while it had been there he had felt a something telling him he was not old after all, but only very young—so young that he had never been in love. As a consequence of his wishing his little rag of sentiment back again, it came; but artificially this time, and as if expecting to be criticised. He would contemplate for a space the fair picture that had the power to rouse his weary soul, even for an instant, from the sea of indifference in which it was plunged.

Claudius lay back in the grass and crossed one leg over the other. Then he tried to recall the features of the woman who had begun to occupy his thoughts. She was certainly very beautiful. He could remember one or two points. Her skin was olive-tinted and dark about the eyes, and the eyes themselves were like soft burning amber, and her hair was very black. That was all he could recollect of her—saving her voice. Ah yes! he had seen beautiful women enough, even in his quiet life, but he had never heard anything exactly like this woman's tones. There are some sounds one never forgets. For instance, the glorious cry of the trumpeter swans in Iceland when they pass in full flight overhead in the early morning; or the sweet musical ring of the fresh black ice on the river as it clangs again to sweep of the steel skate. Claudius tried to compare the sound of that voice to something he had heard, but with little success.

Southern and Eastern born races fall in love at first sight in a way that the soberer Northener cannot understand. A face in a crowd, a glance, a droop of the lashes, and all is said. The seed of passion is sown and will grow in a day to all destroying proportions. But the Northern heart is a very different affair. It will play with its affections as a cat plays with a mouse; only the difference is, that the mouse grows larger and more formidable, like the one in the story of the Eastern sage, which successively changed its shape until it became a tiger, and the wise man was driven to take precautions for his own safety. There is never the least doubt in the mind of an Italian or an Oriental when he is in love; but an Englishman will associate with a woman for ten years, and one day will wake up to the fact that he loves her, and has loved her probably for some time past. And then his whole manner changes immediately, and he is apt to make himself very disagreeable unless indeed the lady loves him—and women are rarely in doubt in their inmost hearts as to whether they love or not.

The heart of the cold northern-born man is a strange puzzle. It can only be compared in its first awakening to a very backward spring. In the first place, the previous absence of anything like love has bred a rough and somewhat coarse scepticism about the existence of passion at all. Young Boreas scoffs at the mere mention of a serious affection, and turns up his nose at a love-match. He thinks young women no end of fun; his vanity makes him fancy himself the heartless hero of many an adventure, and if, as frequently happens, he is but an imperfect gentleman, he will not scruple to devise, imagine, and recount (to his bosom friend, of course, in strictest secrecy) some hairbreadth escape from an irate husband or an avenging father, where he has nearly lost his life, he says, in the pursuit of some woman, generally a lady of spotless reputation whom he barely knows. But put him in her society for an hour, with every opportunity of pressing his suit, and the veriest lambkin could not be more harmless. He has not yet tasted blood, though he will often smack his lips and talk as if he had.

It is generally chance that makes him fall in love the first time. He is thrown together with his fate—tall or short, dark or fair, it makes no difference—in some country house or on some journey. For a long time her society only amuses him and helps to pass the hours, for Boreas is easily bored and finds time a terrible adversary. Gradually he understands that she is a necessity to his comfort, and there is nothing he will not do to secure her on every possible opportunity for himself. Then perhaps he allows to himself that he really does care a little, and he loses some of his incrustation of vanity. He feels less sure of himself, and his companions observe that he ceases to talk of his alleged good fortunes. Very, very slowly his real heart wakes up, and whatever is manly and serious and gentle in his nature comes unconsciously to the surface. Henceforth he knows he loves, and because his love has been slow to develop itself it is not necessarily sluggish or deficient when once it is come. But Englishmen are rarely heroic lovers except in their novels. There is generally a little bypath of caution, a postern gate of mercantile foresight, by which they can slip quietly out at the right moment and forget all about the whole thing.

Claudius was not an Englishman, but a Scandinavian, and he differed from the imaginary young man described above in that he had a great broad reverence of woman and for woman's love. But it was all a theory, of which the practice to him was as yet unknown. He had soon wearied of the class of women he had met in his student-life—chiefly the daughters of respectable Heidelberg Philistines, of various degrees of south Teutonic prettiness; and the beautiful women of the world, of whom he had caught a glimpse in his travels had never seemed real enough to him to be in any way approached. He never had realised that his own personality, combined with his faultless manners, would have soon made him a favourite in what is called society, had he chosen to court it.

After all, it was very vague this passing fancy for the dark-eyed woman of the Schloss. Perhaps Dr. Claudius watched his symptoms too narrowly, and was overmuch pleased at finding that something could still rouse a youthful thrill in him, after the sensation of old age that had of late oppressed him. A man, he said to himself, is not old so long as he can love—and be loved—well, so long as he can love, say, and let the rest take care of itself. And by and by the sun went westering down the hill, and he shook himself out of his dreams, and pocketed his book and turned homeward. His day, he thought, had not amounted to much after all, and he would spend the evening in sober study, and not dream any more until bedtime. But he would be sociable this evening and eat his supper—now he thought about it, it would be dinner and supper combined—in the company of his colleagues at their favourite haunt. And he would go to-morrow, he would certainly go to the Engadine.

But to-morrow came, and the Herr Doctor looked out of his window as usual, and he did not go to Pontresina or anywhere else, nor the next day, nor the day after. Only up to the Schloss every day through the hot week, with his book and his pipe, and there he would lie and read and smoke, and say to himself, "To-morrow I will certainly go." There was something almost pathetic in Claudius, thus day after day revisiting the scene where he had experienced a momentary sensation of youth and vitality, where he had discovered, somewhat to his surprise, that he was still alive and full of strength and sanguine hope, when he thought himself so old. And lying among the ruins he called up the scene again and again, and the strange woman gradually got possession of his mind, as a cunning enchantress might, and she moulded his thoughts about her till they clung to her and burned. He did not seriously think to meet her again in the Schloss, if he thought of it at all, for he knew of course that she must have been a bird of passage, only pausing an instant on that hot day to visit some scene long familiar to her memory. And of course, like a true philosophical student, he did not attempt to explain to himself his own conduct, nor to catalogue the reasons for and against a daily visit to the old castle.

So the week passed, and another after it, and one day, late in the afternoon, Claudius descended the hill and went up as usual to his chamber above the river, to spend an hour indoors before going to supper. It was a beautiful evening, and he left his door partly open on to the landing that the breeze might blow through the room as he sat by the window. A book was in his hand before he had sat many moments, from sheer force of habit; but he did not read. The sounds of the street rose pleasantly to his ear as the little boys and girls played together across each other's doorsteps. To tell the truth, it all seemed very far off, much farther than three flights of steps from the little crowd below to the solitary nest of learning aloft where he sat; and Dr. Claudius was, in his thoughts, incalculably far away from the shoemaker's Hans and the tinman's Gretel and their eight-year-old flirtation. Claudius was flirting with his fancies, and drawing pretty pictures in the smoke, with dark eyes and masses of black hair; and then he moved uneasily, and came back to his threadbare proposition that he was old, and that it was absurd that he should be.

"Ah! what would I not give to enjoy it all—to feel I could wish one moment to remain!" He sighed and leaned back in the straight-backed chair. The door creaked slightly, he thought it was the evening wind. It creaked again; he turned his head, and his gaze remained riveted on the opening. A beautiful pair of dark eyes were fixed on him, deep and searching, and on meeting his, a great silky black head was pushed forward into the room, and a magnificent black hound stalked slowly across the floor and laid his head on the Doctor's knee with a look of evident inquiry.

Claudius was fond of animals, and caressed the friendly beast, wondering to whom he might belong, and speculating whether the appearance of the dog heralded the approach of a visitor. But the dog was not one of those that he knew by sight in the streets of Heidelberg—one of those superb favourites of the students who are as well known as the professors themselves to every inhabitant of a university town in Germany. And the Doctor stroked the beautiful head and listened for steps upon the stairs. Before long he heard an ominous stumbling, as of some one unfamiliar with the dark and narrow way, and in a moment more a young man stood in the doorway, dazzled by the flood of the evening sunshine that faced him.

"Mr. Claudius live here?" interrogated the stranger in a high and metallic, but gentlemanly voice.

"I am Dr. Claudius," said the tenant of the old chair, rising politely. "Pray be seated, sir," and he offered his one seat to his visitor, who advanced into the middle of the room.

He was a young man, dressed in the extreme of the English fashion. He was probably excessively thin, to judge by his face and neck and hands, but he was made up admirably. He removed his hat and showed a forehead of mediocre proportions, over which his dark hair was conscientiously parted in the middle. Though not in appearance robust, he wore a moustache that would not have disgraced a Cossack, his eyes were small, gray, and near together, and his complexion was bad. His feet were minute, and his hands bony.

He took the offered chair, and Claudius sat down upon the bed, which was by no means so far removed in the little room as to make conversation at that distance difficult.

"Dr. Claudius?" the stranger repeated, and the Doctor nodded gravely. "Dr. Claudius, the nephew of the late Mr. Gustavus Lindstrand of New York?"

"The same, sir. May I inquire to what good fortune I am indebted—"

"Oh! of course," interrupted the other, "I am Mr. Barker—Silas B. Barker junior of New York, and my father was your uncle's partner."

"Indeed," said Claudius, rising and coming forward, "then we must shake hands again," and his face wore a pleasant expression. He thought nothing of first impressions, and was prepared to offer a hearty welcome to any friend of his uncle, even of the most unprepossessing type. Mr. Barker was not exactly unprepossessing; he was certainly not handsome, but there was a look of action about him that was not unpleasing. Claudius felt at once, however, that the American belonged to a type of humanity of which he knew nothing as yet. But they shook hands cordially, and the Doctor resumed his seat.

"And is it long since you received the news, Professor?" inquired Mr. Barker, with the ready Transatlantic use of titles.

"I heard of my uncle's death about three weeks ago—rather less."

"Ah yes! And the news about the will—did you hear that?"

"Certainly," said the Doctor; "I received the intelligence simultaneously."

"Well," said the American, "do you propose to continue living here?"

Claudius looked at his visitor. He was as yet unfamiliar with New World curiosity, and thought the question a rather strange one. However, he reflected that Mr. Barker's father might have some moral claim to know what his old partner's heir meant to do with his money; so he answered the question categorically.

"I was, as perhaps you may imagine, greatly surprised at the intelligence that I had inherited a great fortune. But you will hardly understand, with your tastes,"—the Doctor glanced at Mr. Barker's faultless costume,—"that such abundant and unexpected wealth may not be to me a wholly unalloyed blessing." Claudius proceeded to explain how little he cared for the things that his money might bring him, and announced his intention of continuing his present mode of life some time longer. Mr. Silas B. Barker junior of New York opened his small eyes wider and wider, as his host set forth his views.

"I should think you would be bored to death!" he said simply.

"Ennui, in the ordinary sense, does not exist for a man whose life is devoted to study. What corresponds to it is a very different thing. I sometimes feel oppressed with a sense of profound dissatisfaction with what I am doing—"

"I should think so," remarked Mr. Barker. Then, checking himself, he added, "I beg your pardon, don't misunderstand me. I can hardly conceive of leading such a life as yours. I could never be a professor."

Claudius judged the statement to be strictly true. Mr. Barker did not look like a professor in the least. However, the Doctor wanted to be civil.

"Have you just arrived? Have you seen our sights?"

"Came last night from Baden-Baden. I have been here before. You had better come around to my hotel, and take dinner with me. But first we will drive somewhere and get cool."

Claudius put on his best coat and combed his hair, apologising to Mr. Barker for the informality. Mr. Barker watched him, and thought he would make a sensation in New York.

"We might go up to the castle," said the American, when they were seated in the carriage. So to the castle they went, and, leaving their carriage at the entrance, strolled slowly through the grounds till they reached the broken tower.

"If they had used dynamite," said Mr. Barker, "they would have sent the whole thing flying across the river."

"It would have been less picturesque afterwards," said Claudius.

"It would have been more effective at the time."

Claudius was thinking of the dark woman and her parasol, and how he had climbed down there a few weeks before. To show to himself that he did not care, he told his companion the incident as graphically as he could. His description of the lady was so graphic that Mr. Barker screwed up his eyes and put out his jaw, so that two great lines circled on his sallow face from just above the nostril, under his heavy moustache to his chin.

"I could almost fancy I had seen her somewhere," said he.

"Where?" asked Claudius eagerly.

"I thought he would give himself away," was the American's terse inward reflection; but he answered coolly—

"I don't know, I am sure. Very likely I am mistaken. It was pretty romantic though. Ask me to the wedding, Professor."

"What wedding?"

"Why, when you marry the fascinating creature with the parasol."

Claudius looked at Mr. Barker with some astonishment.

"Do you generally manage things so quickly in your country?"

"Oh, I was only joking," returned the American. "But, of course, you can marry anybody you like, and why not the dark lady? On the whole, though, if I were you, I would like to astonish the natives before I left. Now, you might buy the castle here and turn it into a hotel."

"Horrible!" ejaculated Claudius.

"No worse than making a hotel of Switzerland, which is an older and more interesting monument than the castle of Heidelberg."

"Epigrammatic, but fallacious, Mr. Barker."

"Epigrams and proverbs are generally that."

"I think," said Claudius, "that proverbs are only fallacious when they are carelessly applied."

"Very likely. Life is too short to waste time over weapons that will only go off in some singular and old-fashioned way. When I start out to do any shooting, I want to hit."

So they went to dinner. Claudius found himself becoming gayer in the society of his new acquaintance than he had been for some time past. He could not have said whether he liked him or thought him interesting, but he had a strong impression that there was something somewhere, he could not tell what, which Mr. Barker understood thoroughly, and in which he might show to great advantage. He felt that however superficial and unartistic the American might be, he was nevertheless no fool. There was something keen and sharp-edged about him that proclaimed a character capable of influencing men, and accustomed to deal boldly and daringly with life.

They dined as well as could be expected in a country which is not gastronomic, and Mr. Barker produced a rare brand of cigars, without which, he informed his guest, he never travelled. They were fat brown Havanas, and Claudius enjoyed them.

"Let us go to Baden-Baden," said Barker, sucking at his weed, which protruded from his immense moustache like a gun under the raised port-hole of an old-fashioned man-of-war.

"If I were seeking innocent recreation from my labours, that is not exactly the spot I would choose to disport myself in," replied Claudius. "The scenery is good, but the people are detestable."

"I agree with you; but it is a nice place for all that. You can always gamble to pass the time."

"I never play games of chance, and there is no play in Baden now."

"Principle or taste, Professor?"

"I suppose I must allow that it is principle. I used to play a little when I was a student; but I do not believe in leaving anything to fortune. I would not do it in anything else."

"Well, I suppose you are right; but you miss a great deal of healthy excitement. You have never known the joys of being short of a thousand N.P. or Wabash on a rising market."

"I fear I do not understand the illustration, Mr. Barker."

"No? Well, it is not to be wondered at. Perhaps if you ever come to New York you will take an interest in the stock market."

"Ah—you were referring to stocks? Yes, I have read a little about your methods of business, but that kind of study is not much in my line. Why do you say Baden, though, instead of some quiet place?"

"I suppose I like a crowd. Besides, there are some people I know there. But I want you to go with me, and if you would rather not go to Baden-Baden, we can go somewhere else. I really think we ought to become better acquainted, and I may prevail on you to go with me to New York."

Claudius was silent, and he blew a great cloud of smoke. What sort of a travelling companion would Mr. Barker be for him? Could there be a greater contrast to his own nature? And yet he felt that he would like to observe Mr. Barker. He felt drawn to him without knowing why, and he had a presentiment that the American would drag him out of his quiet life into a very different existence. Mr. Barker, on the other hand, possessed the showman's instinct. He had found a creature who, he was sure, had the elements of a tremendous lion about town; and having found him, he meant to capture him and exhibit him in society, and take to himself ever after the credit of having unearthed the handsome, rich, and talented Dr. Claudius from a garret in Heidelberg. What a story that would be to tell next year, when Claudius, clothed and clipped, should be marrying the girl of the season, or tooling his coach down the Newport avenue, or doing any of the other fashionable and merry things that Americans love to do in spring and summer!

So Mr. Barker insisted on driving Claudius back to his lodging, though it was only five minutes' walk, and exacted a promise that the Doctor should take him on the morrow to a real German breakfast at the Fauler Pelz, and that they would "start off somewhere" in the afternoon.

Claudius said he had enjoyed a very pleasant evening, and went up to his room, where he read an elaborate article on the vortex theory by Professor Helmholtz, with which, having dipped into transcendental geometry, he was inclined to find fault; and then he went calmly to bed.

CHAPTER III

Claudius told his old landlord—his philister, as he would have called him—that he was going away on his customary foot tour for a month or so. He packed a book and a few things in his knapsack and joined Mr. Barker. To Claudius in his simplicity there was nothing incongruous in his travelling as a plain student in the company of the exquisitely-arrayed New Yorker, and the latter was far too much a man of the world to care what his companion wore. He intended that the Doctor should be introduced to the affectionate skill of a London tailor before he was much older, and he registered a vow that the long yellow hair should be cut. But these details were the result of his showman's intuition; personally, he would as readily have travelled with Claudius had he affected the costume of a shoeblack. He knew that the man was very rich, and he respected his eccentricity for the present. To accomplish the transformation of exterior which he contemplated, from the professional and semi-cynic garb to the splendour of a swell of the period, Mr. Barker counted on some more potent influence than his own. The only point on which his mind was made up was that Claudius must accompany him to America and create a great sensation.

"I wonder if we shall meet her," remarked Mr. Barker reflectively, when they were seated in the train.

"Whom?" asked Claudius, who did not intend to understand his companion's chaff.

But Mr. Barker had shot his arrow, and started cleverly as he answered—

"Did I say anything? I must have been talking to myself."

Claudius was not so sure. However, the hint had produced its effect, falling, as it did, into the vague current of his thoughts and giving them direction. He began to wonder whether there was any likelihood of his meeting the woman of whom he had thought so much, and before long he found himself constructing a conversation, supposed to take place on their first encounter, overleaping such trifles as probability, the question of an introduction, and other formalities with the ready agility of a mind accustomed to speculation.

"The scenery is fine, is it not?" remarked Claudius tritely as they neared Baden.

"Oh yes, for Europe. We manage our landscapes better in America."

"How so?"

"Swivels. You can turn the rocks around and see the other side."

Claudius laughed a little, but Barker did not smile. He was apparently occupied in inventing a patent transformation landscape on wheels. In reality, he was thinking out a menu for dinner whereby he might feed his friend without starving himself. For Mr. Barker was particular about his meals, and accustomed to fare sumptuously every day, whereas he had observed that the Doctor was fond of sausages and decayed cabbage. But he knew such depraved tastes could not long withstand the blandishments and caressing hypersensualism of Delmonico, if he ever got the Doctor so far.

Having successfully accomplished the business of dining, Mr. Barker promised to return in an hour, and sallied out to find the British aristocracy, whom he knew. The British aristocracy was taking his coffee in solitude at the principal café, and hailed Mr. Barker's advent with considerable interest, for they had tastes in common.

"How are you, Duke?"

"Pretty fit, thanks. Where have you been?"

"Oh, all over. I was just looking for you."

"Yes?" said the aristocracy interrogatively.

"Yes. I want you to introduce me to somebody you know."

"Pleasure. Who?"

"She has black eyes and dark hair, very dark complexion, middling height, fine figure; carries an ivory-handled parasol with a big M and a crown." Mr. Barker paused for a look of intelligence on the Englishman's face.

"Sure she's here?" inquired the latter.

"I won't swear. She was seen in Heidelberg, admiring views and dropping her parasol about, something like three weeks ago."

"Oh! ah, yes. Come on." And the British aristocracy settled the rose in his button-hole and led the way. He moved strongly with long steps, but Mr. Barker walked delicately like Agag.

"By the by, Barker, she is a countrywoman of yours. She married a Russian, and her name is Margaret."

"Was it a happy marriage?" asked the American, taking his cigar from his mouth.

"Exceedingly. Husband killed at Plevna. Left her lots of tin."

They reached their destination. The Countess was at home. The Countess was enchanted to make the acquaintance of Monsieur, and on learning that he was an American and a compatriot, was delighted to see him. They conversed pleasantly. In the course of twenty minutes the aristocracy discovered he had an engagement and departed, but Mr. Barker remained. It was rather stretching his advantage, but he did not lack confidence.

"So you, too, Countess, have been in Heidelberg this summer?"

"About three weeks ago. I am very fond of the old place."

"Lovely, indeed," said Barker. "The castle, the old tower half blown away in that slovenly war—"

"Oh, such a funny thing happened to me there," exclaimed the Countess Margaret, innocently falling into the trap. "I was standing just at the edge with Miss Skeat—she is my companion, you know—and I dropped my parasol, and it fell rattling to the bottom, and suddenly there started, apparently out of space—"

"A German professor, seven or eight feet high, who bounded after the sunshade, and bounded back and bowed and left you to your astonishment. Is not that what you were going to say, Countess?"

"I believe you are a medium," said the Countess, looking at Barker in astonishment. "But perhaps you only guessed it. Can you tell me what he was like, this German professor?"

"Certainly. He had long yellow hair, and a beard like Rip van Winkle's, and large white hands; and he was altogether one of the most striking individuals you ever saw."

"It is evident that you know him, Mr. Barker, and that he has told you the story. Though how you should have known it was I—"

"Guess-work and my friend's description."

"But how do you come to be intimate with German professors, Mr. Barker? Are you learned, and that sort of thing?"

"He was a German professor once. He is now an eccentricity without a purpose. Worth millions, and living in a Heidelberg garret, wishing he were poor again."

"What an interesting creature! Tell me more, please."

Barker told as much of Claudius's history as he knew.

"Too delightful!" ejaculated the Countess Margaret, looking out of the window rather pensively.

"Countess," said the American, "if I had enjoyed the advantage of your acquaintance even twenty-four hours I would venture to ask leave to present my friend to you. As it is—" Mr. Barker paused.

"As it is I will grant you the permission unasked," said the Countess quietly, still looking out of the window. "I am enough of an American still to know that your name is a guarantee for any one you introduce."

"You are very kind," said Mr. Barker modestly. Indeed the name of Barker had long been honourably known in connection with New York enterprise. The Barkers were not Dutch, it is true, but they had the next highest title to consideration in that their progenitor had dwelt in Salem, Massachusetts.

"Bring him in the morning," said the Countess, after a moment's thought.

"About two?"

"Oh no! At eleven or so. I am a very early person. I get up at the screech of dawn."

"Permit me to thank you on behalf of my friend as well as for myself," said Mr. Barker, bending low over the dark lady's hand as he took his departure.

"So glad to have seen you. It is pleasant to meet a civilised countryman in these days."

"It can be nothing to the pleasure of meeting a charming countrywoman," replied Mr. Barker, and he glided from the room.

The dark lady stood for a moment looking at the door through which her visitor had departed. It was almost nine o'clock by this time, and she rang for lights, subsiding into a low chair while the servant brought them. The candles flickered in the light breeze that fanned fitfully through the room, and, finding it difficult to read, the Countess sent for Miss Skeat.

"What a tiny little world it is!" said Margaret, by way of opening the conversation.

Miss Skeat sat down by the table. She was thin and yellow, and her bones were on the outside. She wore gold-rimmed eyeglasses, and was well dressed, in plain black, with a single white ruffle about her long and sinewy neck. She was hideous, but she had a certain touch of dignified elegance, and her face looked trustworthy and not unkind.

"Apropos of anything especial?" asked she, seeing that the Countess expected her to say something.

"Do you remember when I dropped my parasol at Heidelberg?"

"Perfectly," replied Miss Skeat.

"And the man who picked it up, and who looked like Niemann in Lohengrin?"

"Yes, and who must have been a professor. I remember very well."

"A friend of mine brought a friend of his to see me this afternoon, and the man himself is coming to-morrow."

"What is his name?" asked the lady-companion.

"I am sure I don't know, but Mr. Barker says he is very eccentric. He is very rich, and yet he lives in a garret in Heidelberg and wishes he were poor."

"Are you quite sure he is in his right mind, dear Countess?"

Margaret looked kindly at Miss Skeat. Poor lady! she had been rich once, and had not lived in a garret. Money to her meant freedom and independence. Not that she was unhappy with Margaret, who was always thoughtful and considerate, and valued her companion as a friend; but she would rather have lived with Margaret feeling it was a matter of choice and not of necessity, for she came of good Scottish blood, and was very proud.

"Oh yes!" answered the younger lady; "he is very learned and philosophical, and I am sure you will like him. If he is at all civilised we will have him to dinner."

"By all means," said Miss Skeat with alacrity. She liked intelligent society, and the Countess had of late indulged in a rather prolonged fit of solitude. Miss Skeat took the last novel—one of Tourguéneff's—from the table and, armed with a paper-cutter, began to read to her ladyship.

It was late when Mr. Barker found Claudius scribbling equations on a sheet of the hotel letter-paper. The Doctor looked up pleasantly at his friend. He could almost fancy he had missed his society a little; but the sensation was too novel a one to be believed genuine.

"Did you find your friends?" he inquired.

"Yes, by some good luck. It is apt to be the other people one finds, as a rule."

"Cynicism is not appropriate to your character, Mr. Barker."

"No. I hate cynical men. It is generally affectation, and it is always nonsense. But I think the wrong people have a way of turning up at the wrong moment." After a pause, during which Mr. Barker lighted a cigar and extended his thin legs and trim little feet on a chair in front of him, he continued:

"Professor, have you a very strong and rooted dislike to the society of women?"

Assailed by this point-blank question, the Doctor put his bit of paper inside his book, and drumming on the table with his pencil, considered a moment. Mr. Barker puffed at his cigar with great regularity.

"No," said Claudius at last, "certainly not. To woman man owes his life, and to woman he ought to owe his happiness. Without woman civilisation would be impossible, and society would fall to pieces."

"Oh!" ejaculated Mr. Barker.

"I worship woman in the abstract and in the concrete. I reverence her mission, and I honour the gifts of Heaven which fit her to fulfil it."

"Ah!" exclaimed Mr. Barker.

"I think there is nothing made in creation that can be compared with woman, not even man. I am enthusiastic, of course, you will say, but I believe that homage and devotion to woman is the first duty of man, after homage and devotion to the Supreme Being whom all different races unite in describing as God."

"That will do, thank you," said Mr. Barker, "I am quite satisfied of your adoration, and I will not ask her name."

"She has no name, and she has all names," continued Claudius seriously. "She is an ideal."

"Yes, my feeble intelligence grasps that she cannot be anything else. But I did not want a confession of faith. I only asked if you disliked ladies' society, because I was going to propose to introduce you to some friends of mine here."

"Oh!" said Claudius, and he leaned back in his chair and stared at the lamp. Barker was silent.

The Doctor was puzzled. He thought it would be very rude of him to refuse Mr. Barker's offer. On the other hand, in spite of his protestations of devotion to the sex, he knew that the exalted opinion he held of woman in general had gained upon him of late years, since he had associated less with them. It was with him a beautiful theory, the outcome of a knightly nature thrown back on itself, but as yet not fixed or clearly defined by any intimate knowledge of woman's character, still less by any profound personal experience of love. Courtesy was uppermost as he answered.

"Really," he said at last, "if you are very desirous of presenting me to your friends, of course I—"

"Oh, only if it is agreeable to you, of course. If it is in any way the reverse—" protested the polite Mr. Barker.

"Not that—not exactly disagreeable. Only it is some time since I have enjoyed the advantage of an hour's conversation with ladies; and besides, since it comes to that, I am here as a pedestrian, and I do not present a very civilised appearance."

"Don't let that disturb you. Since you consent," went on Mr. Barker, briskly taking everything for granted, "I may tell you that the lady in question has expressed a wish to have you presented, and that I could not do less than promise to bring you if possible. As for your personal appearance, it is not of the least consequence. Perhaps, if you don't mind a great deal, you might have your hair cut. Don't be offended, Professor, but nothing produces an appearance of being dressed so infallibly as a neatly-trimmed head."

"Oh, certainly, if you think it best, I will have my hair cut. It will soon grow again."

Mr. Barker smiled under the lambrikin of his moustache. "Yes," thought he, "but it sha'n't."

"Then," he said aloud, "we will go about eleven."

Claudius sat wondering who the lady could be who wanted to have him presented. But he was afraid to ask; Barker would immediately suppose he imagined it to be the dark lady. However, his thoughts took it as a certainty that it must be she, and went on building castles in the air and conversations in the clouds. Barker watched him and probably guessed what he was thinking of; but he did not want to spoil the surprise he had arranged, and fearing lest Claudius might ask some awkward question, he went to bed, leaving the Doctor to his cogitations.

In the morning he lay in wait for his friend, who had gone off for an early walk in the woods. He expected that a renewal of the attack would be necessary before the sacrifice of the yellow locks could be accomplished, and he stood on the steps of the hotel, clad in the most exquisite of grays, tapering down to the most brilliant of boots. He had a white rose in his buttonhole, and his great black dog was lying at his feet, having for a wonder found his master, for the beast was given to roaming, or to the plebeian society of Barker's servant. The American's careful attire contrasted rather oddly with his sallow face, and with the bony hand that rested against the column. He was a young man, but he looked any age that morning. Before long his eye twinkled and he changed his position expectantly, for he saw the tall figure of Claudius striding up the street, a head and shoulders above the strolling crowd; and, wonderful to relate, the hair was gone, the long beard was carefully clipped and trimmed, and the Doctor wore a new gray hat!

"If he will black his boots and put a rose in his coat, he will do. What a tearing swell he will be when he is dressed," thought Mr. Barker, as he looked at his friend.

"You see I have followed your advice," said Claudius, holding out his hand.

"Always do that, and you will yet taste greatness," said the other cheerfully. "You look like a crown prince like that. Perfectly immense."

"I suppose I am rather big," said Claudius apologetically, not catching the American idiom. Mr. Barker, however, did not explain himself, for he was thinking of other things.

"We will go very soon. Excuse the liberty, Professor, but you might have your boots blacked. There is a little cad down the backstairs who does it."

"Of course," answered Claudius, and disappeared within. A small man who was coming out paused and turned to look after him, putting up his eyeglass. Then he took off his hat to Mr. Barker.

"Pardon, Monsieur," he began, "if I take the liberty of making an inquiry, but could you inform me of the name of that gentleman, whose appearance fills me with astonishment, and whose vast dimensions obscure the landscape of Baden?"

Mr. Barker looked at the small man for a moment very gravely.

"Yes," said he pensively, "his royal highness is a large man certainly." And while his interlocutor was recovering enough to formulate another question, Mr. Barker moved gently away to a flowerstand.

When Claudius returned his friend was waiting for him, and himself pinned a large and expensive rose in the Doctor's buttonhole. Mr. Barker surveyed his work—the clipped head, the new hat, the shiny boots and the rose—with a satisfied air, such as Mr. Barnum may have worn when he landed Jumbo on the New York pier. Then he called a cab, and they drove away.

CHAPTER IV

The summer breath of the roses blew sweetly in through the long windows of the Countess's morning-room from the little garden outside as Barker and Claudius entered. There was an air of inhabited luxury which was evidently congenial to the American, for he rubbed his hands softly together and touched one or two objects caressingly while waiting for the lady of the house. Claudius glanced at the table and took up a book, with that singular student habit that is never lost. It was a volume of English verse, and in a moment he was reading, just as he stood, with his hat caught between the fingers that held the book, oblivious of countesses and visits and formalities.

There was a rustle and a step on the garden walk, and both men turned towards the open glass door. Claudius almost dropped the vellum-covered poet, and was very perceptibly startled as he recognised the lady of his Heidelberg adventure—the woman who had got, as by magic, a hold over his thoughts, so that he dreamed of her and wondered about her, sleeping and waking.

Dark-eyed Countess Margaret, all clad in pure white, the smallest of lace fichus just dropped over her heavy hair, moved smoothly up the steps and into the room.

"Good morning, Mr. Barker, I am so glad you have come," said she, graciously extending her hand in the cordial Transatlantic fashion.

"Permit me to present my friend, Professor Claudius," said Barker. Claudius bowed very low. The plunge was over, and he recovered his outward calm, whatever he might feel.

"Mr. Barker flatters me, Madam," he said quietly. "I am not a professor, but only a private lecturer."

"I am too far removed from anything learned to make such distinctions," said the Countess. "But since good fortune has brought you into the circle of my ignorance, let me renew my thanks for the service you did me in Heidelberg the other day."

Claudius bowed and murmured something inaudible.

"Or had you not realised that I was the heroine of the parasol at the broken tower?" asked Margaret smiling, as she seated herself in a low chair and motioned to her guests to follow her example. Barker selected a comfortable seat, and arranged the cushion to suit him before he subsided into repose, but the Doctor laid hands on a stern and solid-looking piece of carving, and sat upright facing the Countess.

"Pardon me," said he, "I had. But it is always startling to realise a dream." The Countess looked at Claudius rather inquiringly; perhaps she had not expected he was the sort of man to begin an acquaintance by making compliments. However, she said nothing, and he continued, "Do you not always find it so?"

"The bearded hermit is no duffer," thought Mr. Barker. "He will say grace over the whole barrel of pork."

"Ah! I have few dreams," replied the Countess, "and when I do have any, I never realise them. I am a very matter-of-fact person."

"What matters the fact when you are the person, Madam?" retorted Claudius, fencing for a discussion of some kind.

"Immense," thought Mr. Barker, changing one leg over the other and becoming interested.

"Does that mean anything, or is it only a pretty paradox?" asked the lady, observing that Claudius had thrown himself boldly into a crucial position. Upon his answer would probably depend her opinion of him as being either intelligent or banal. It is an easy matter to frame paradoxical questions implying a compliment, but it is no light task to be obliged to answer them oneself. Claudius was not thinking of producing an effect, for the fascination of the dark woman was upon him, and the low, strange voice bewitched him, so he said what came uppermost.

"Yes," said he, "there are persons whose lives may indeed be matters of fact to themselves—who shall say?—but who are always dreams in the lives of others."

"Charming," laughed the Countess, "do you always talk like that, Professor Claudius?"

"I have always thought," Mr. Barker remarked in his high-set voice, "that I would like to be the dream of somebody's life. But somehow things have gone against me."

The other two laughed. He did not strike one as the sort of individual who would haunt the love-sick dreams of a confiding heart.

"I would rather it were the other way," said Claudius thoughtfully.

"And I," rejoined the American, "would drink perdition to the unattainable."

"Either I do not agree with you, Mr. Barker," said the Countess, "or else I believe nothing is unattainable."

"I implore you to be kind, and believe the latter," he answered courteously.

"Come, I will show you my garden," said Margaret rising. "It is pleasanter in the open air." She led the way out through the glass door, the men walking on her right and left.

"I am very fond of my garden," she said, "and I take great care of it when I am here." She stopped and pulled two or three dead leaves off a rosebush to illustrate her profession of industry.

"And do you generally live here?" asked Claudius, who was as yet in complete ignorance of the Countess's name, title, nationality, and mode of life, for Mr. Barker had, for some occult reason, left him in the dark.

Perhaps the Countess guessed as much, for she briefly imparted a good deal of information.

"When Count Alexis, my husband, was alive, we lived a great deal in Russia. But I am an American like Mr. Barker, and I occasionally make a trip to my native country. However, I love this place in summer, and I always try to be here. That is my friend, Miss Skeat, who lives with me."

Miss Skeat was stranded under a tree with a newspaper and several books. Her polished cheekbones and knuckles glimmered yellow in the shade. By her side was a long cane chair, in which lay a white silk wrap and a bit of needlework, tumbled together as the Countess had left them when she went in to receive her visitors. Miss Skeat rose as the party approached. The Countess introduced the two men, who bowed low, and they all sat down, Mr. Barker on the bench by the ancient virgin, and Claudius on the grass at Margaret's feet. It was noonday, but there was a light breeze through, the flowers and grasses. The conversation soon fell into pairs as they sat.

"I should not have said, at first sight, that you were a very imaginative person, Dr. Claudius," said the Countess.

"I have been dreaming for years," he answered. "I am a mathematician, and of late I have become a philosopher in a small way, as far as that is possible from reading the subject. There are no two branches of learning that require more imagination than mathematics and philosophy."

"Philosophy, perhaps," she replied, "but mathematics—I thought that was an exact science, where everything was known, and there was no room for dreaming."

"I suppose that is the general impression. But do you think it requires no imagination to conceive a new application of knowledge, to invent new methods where old ones are inadequate, to lay out a route through the unknown land beyond the regions of the known?"

"Ordinary people, like me, associate mathematics with measurement and figures and angles."

"Yes," said Claudius, "but it is the same as though you confused religion with its practical results. If the religion is true at all, it would be just as true if man did not exist, and if it consequently had no application to life."

"I understand the truth of that, though we might differ about the word. So you have been dreaming for years—and what were your dreams like?" The Countess looked down earnestly at Claudius, who in his turn looked at her with a little smile. She thought he was different from other men, and he was wondering how much of his dreams he might tell her.

"Of all sorts," he answered, still looking up into her face. "Bitter and sweet. I have dreamed of the glory of life and of mind-power, of the accomplishment of the greatest good to the greatest number; I have believed the extension of science possible 'beyond the bounds of all imaginable experience' into the realms of the occult and hidden; I have wandered with Hermes by the banks of the Nile, with Gautama along the mud-flats of the Ganges. I have disgusted myself with the writings of those who would reduce all history and religion to solar myths, and I have striven to fathom the meaning of those whose thoughts are profound and their hearts noble, but their speech halting. I have dreamed many things, Countess, and the worst is that I have lived to weary of my dreams, and to say that all things are vanity—all save one," he added with hesitation. There was a momentary pause.

"Of course," Mr. Barker was saying to Miss Skeat, with a fascinating smile, "I have the greatest admiration for Scotch heroism. John Grahame of Claver-house. Who can read Macaulay's account—"

"Ah," interrupted the old gentlewoman, "if you knew how I feel about these odious calumnies!"

"I quite understand that," said Barker sympathetically. He had discovered Miss Skeat's especial enthusiasm.

Margaret turned again to the Doctor.

"And may I ask, without indiscretion, what the one dream may be that you have refused to relegate among the vanities?"

"Woman," answered Claudius, and was silent.

The Countess thought the Doctor spoke ironically, and she laughed aloud, half amused and half annoyed. "I am in earnest," said Claudius, plucking a blade of grass and twisting it round his finger.

"Truly?" asked she.

"Foi de gentilhomme!" he answered.

"But Mr. Barker told me you lived like a hermit."

"That is the reason it has been a dream," said he.

"You have not told me what the dream was like. What beautiful things have you fancied about us?"

"I have dreamed of woman's mission, and of woman's love. I have fancied that woman and woman's love represented the ruling spirit, as man and man's brain represent the moving agent, in the world. I have drawn pictures of an age in which real chivalry of word and thought and deed might be the only law necessary to control men's actions. Not the scenic and theatrical chivalry of the middle age, ready at any moment to break out into epidemic crime, but a true reverence and understanding of woman's supreme right to honour and consideration; an age wherein it should be no longer coarsely said that love is but an episode in the brutal life of man, while to woman it is life itself. I have dreamed that the eternal womanhood of the universe beckoned me to follow."

The Countess could not take her eyes off Claudius. She had never met a man like him; at least she had never met a man who plunged into this kind of talk after half an hour's acquaintance. There was a thrill of feeling in her smooth deep voice when she answered: "If all men thought as you think, the world would be a very different place."

"It would be a better place in more ways than one," he replied.

"And yet you yourself call it a dream," said Margaret, musing.

"It is only you, Countess, who say that dreams are never realised."

"And do you expect to realise yours?"

"Yes—I do." He looked at her with his bold blue eyes, and she thought they sparkled.

"Tell me," she asked, "are you going to preach a crusade for the liberation of our sex? Do you mean to bring about the great change in the social relations of the world? Is it you who will build up the pedestal which we are to mount and from which we shall survey countless ranks of adoring men?"

"Do you not see, as you look down on me from your throne, from this chair, that I have begun already?" answered Claudius, smiling, and making a pretence of folding his hands.

"No," said the Countess, overlooking his last speech; "if you had any convictions about it, as you pretend to have, you would begin at once and revolutionise the world in six months. What is the use of dreaming? It is not dreamers who make history."

"No, it is more often women. But tell me, Countess, do you approve of my crusade? Am I not right? Have I your sanction?"

Margaret was silent. Mr. Barker's voice was heard again, holding forth to Miss Skeat.

"In all ages," he said, with an air of conviction, "the aristocracy of a country have been in reality the leaders of its thought and science and enlightenment. Perhaps the form of aristocracy most worthy of admiration is that time-honoured institution of pre-eminent families, the Scottish clan, the Hebrew tribe—"

Claudius overheard and opened his eyes. It seemed to him that Barker was talking nonsense. Margaret smiled, for she knew her companion well, and understood in a moment that the American had discovered her hobby, and was either seeking to win her good graces, or endeavouring to amuse himself by inducing her to air her views. But Claudius returned to the charge.

"What is it to be, Countess?" he asked. "Am I to take up arms and sail out and conquer the universe, and bring it bound to your feet to do you homage; or shall I go back to my turret chamber in Heidelberg?"

"Your simile seems to me to be appropriate," said Margaret. "I am sure your forefathers must have been Vikings."

"They were," replied Claudius, "for I am a Scandinavian. Shall I go out and plunder the world for your benefit? Shall I make your universality, your general expression, woman, sovereign over my general expression, man?"

"Considering who is to be the gainer," she answered, laughing, "I cannot well withhold my consent. When will you begin?"

"Now."

"And how?"

"How should I begin," said he, a smile on his face, and the light dancing in his eyes, "except by making myself the first convert?"

Margaret was used enough to pretty speeches, in earnest and in jest, but she thought she had never heard any one turn them more readily than the yellow-bearded student.

"And Mr. Barker," she asked, "will you convert him?"

"Can you look at him at this moment, Countess, and say you really think he needs it?"

She glanced at the pair on the bench, and laughed again, in the air, for it was apparent that Mr. Barker had made a complete conquest of Miss Skeat. He had led the conversation about tribes to the ancient practices of the North American Indians, and was detailing their customs with marvellous fluency. A scientific hearer might have detected some startling inaccuracies, but Miss Skeat listened with rapt attention. Who, indeed, should know more about Indians than a born American who had travelled in the West?

The Countess turned the conversation to other subjects, and talked intelligently about books. She evidently read a great deal, or rather she allowed Miss Skeat to read to her, and her memory was good. Claudius was not behind in sober criticism of current literature, though his reading had been chiefly of a tougher kind. Time flew by quickly, and when the two men rose to go their visit had lasted two hours.

"You will report the progress of your conquest?" said the Countess to Claudius as she gave him her hand, which he stooped to kiss in the good old German fashion.

"Whenever you will permit me, Countess," he said.

"I am always at home in the middle of the day. And you too, Mr. Barker, do not wait to be asked before you come again. You are absolutely the only civilised American I know here."

"Don't say that, Countess. There is the Duke, who came with me yesterday."

"But he is English."

"But he is also American. He owns mines and prairies, and he emigrates semi-annually. They all do now. You know rats leave a sinking ship, and they are going to have a commune in England."

"Oh, Mr. Barker, how can you!" exclaimed Miss Skeat.

"But I am only joking, of course," said he, and pacified her. So they parted.

Mr. Barker and Claudius stood on the front door-step, and the former lit a cigar while the carriage drove up.

"Doctor," said he, "I consider you the most remarkable man of my acquaintance."

"Why?" asked Claudius as he got into the carriage.

"Well, for several reasons. Chiefly because though you have lived in a 'three pair back' for years, and never seen so much as a woman's ear, by your own account, you nevertheless act as if you had never been out of a drawing-room during your life. You are the least shy man I ever saw."

"Shy?" exclaimed Claudius, "what a funny idea! Why should I be shy?"

"No reason in the world, I suppose, after all. But it is very odd." And Mr. Barker ruminated, rolling his cigar in his mouth. "Besides," he added, after a long pause, "you have made a conquest."

"Nonsense. Now, you have some right to flatter yourself on that score."

"Miss Skeat?" said Mr. Barker. "Sit still, my heart!"

They drove along in silence for some time. At last Mr. Barker began again,—

"Well, Professor, what are you going to do about it?"

"About what?"

"Why, about the conquest. Shall you go there again?"

"Very likely." Claudius was annoyed at his companion's tone of voice. He would have scoffed at the idea that he loved the Countess at first sight; but she nevertheless represented his ideal to him, and he could not bear to hear Mr. Barker's chaffing remarks. Of course Barker had taken him to the house, and had a right to ask if Claudius had found the visit interesting. But Claudius was determined to check any kind of levity from the first. He did not like it about women on any terms, but in connection with the Countess Margaret it was positively unbearable. So he answered curtly enough to show Mr. Barker he objected to it. The latter readily understood and drew his own inferences.

A different conversation ensued in the Countess's garden when the visitors were gone.

"Well, Miss Skeat," said Margaret, "what do you think of my new acquaintances?"

"I think Mr. Barker is the most agreeable American I ever met," said Miss Skeat. "He has very sound views about social questions, and his information on the subject of American Indians is perfectly extraordinary."

"And the Doctor? what do you think of him?"

"He dresses very oddly," said the lady companion; "but his manners seem everything that could be desired, and he has aristocratic hands."

"I did not notice his dress much. But he is very handsome. He looks like a Scandinavian hero. You know I was sure I should meet him again that day in Heidelberg."

"I suppose he really is very good-looking," assented Miss Skeat.

"Shall we have them to dinner some day? I think we might; very quietly, you know."

"I would certainly advise it, dear Countess. You really ought to begin and see people in some way besides allowing them to call on you. I think this solitude is affecting your spirits."

"Oh no; I am very happy—at least, as happy as I can be. But we will have them to dinner. When shall it be?"

"To-morrow is too soon. Say Thursday, since you ask me," said Miss Skeat.

"Very well. Shall we read a little?" And Tourguéneff was put into requisition.

It was late in the afternoon when the Countess's phaeton, black horses, black liveries, and black cushions, swept round a corner of the drive. Claudius and Barker, in a hired carriage, passed her, coming from the opposite direction. The four people bowed to each other—the ladies graciously, the men with courteous alacrity. Each of the four was interested in the others, and each of the four felt that they would all be thrown together in the immediate future. There was a feeling among them that they had known each other a long time, though they were but acquaintances of to-day and yesterday.

"I have seldom seen anything more complete than that turn-out," said Mr. Barker. "The impression of mourning is perfect; it could not have been better if it had been planned by a New York undertaker."

"Are New York undertakers such great artists?" asked Claudius.

"Yes; people get buried more profusely there. But don't you think it is remarkably fine?"

"Yes. I suppose you are trying to make me say that the Countess is a beautiful woman," answered Claudius, who was beginning to understand Barker. "If that is what you want, I yield at once. I think she is the most beautiful woman I ever saw."

"Ah!—don't you think perhaps that Miss Skeat acts as an admirable foil?"

"Such beauty as that requires no foil. The whole world is a foil to her."

"Wait till you come to America. I will show you her match in Newport."

"I doubt it. What is Newport?"

"Newport is the principal watering-place of our magnificent country. It is Baden, Homburg, Bigorre, and Biarritz rolled into one. It is a terrestrial paradise, a land of four-in-hands and houris and surf-bathing and nectar and ambrosia. I could not begin to give you an idea of it; wait till you get there."

"A society place, I suppose, then?" said Claudius, not in the least moved by the enthusiastic description.

"A society place before all things. But you may have plenty of solitude if you like."

"I hardly think I should care much for Newport," said Claudius.

"Well, I like it very much. My father has a place there, to which I take the liberty of inviting you for the season, whenever you make up your mind to enjoy yourself."

"You are very good, I am sure; and if, as you say, I ever go to America, which seems in your opinion paramount to enjoying myself, I will take advantage of your kind invitation."

"Really, I hope you will. Shall we go and dine?"

CHAPTER V

On the following day Claudius and Mr. Barker received each a note. These communications were in square, rough envelopes, and directed in a large feminine handwriting. The contents intimated that the Countess Margaret would be glad to see them at dinner at half-past seven on Thursday.

"That is to-morrow," said Mr. Barker pensively.

Claudius, who was generally the calmest of the calm, made a remark in German to the effect that he fervently desired a thousand million bushels of thunder-weather to fly away with him that very instant.

"Did you say anything, Professor?" inquired Mr. Barker blandly.

"I did. I swore," answered Claudius. "I have half a mind to swear again."

"Do it. Profanity is the safety-valve of great minds. Swear loudly, and put your whole mind to it."

Claudius strode to the window of their sitting-room and looked out.

"It is extremely awkward, upon my word," he said.

"What is awkward, Professor? The invitation?"

"Yes—very."

"Why, pray? I should think you would be very much pleased."

"Exactly—I should be: but there is a drawback."

"Of what nature? Anything I can do?"

"Not exactly. I cannot wear one of your coats."

"Oh! is that it?" said Mr. Barker; and a pleasant little thrill of triumph manifested itself, as he pushed out his jaw and exhibited his circular wrinkle. "Of course—how stupid of me! You are here as a pedestrian, and you have no evening dress. Well, the sooner we go and see a tailor the better, in that case. I will ring for a carriage." He did so, remarking internally that he had scored one in putting the Doctor into a position which forced him to dress like a Christian.

"Do you never walk?" asked Claudius, putting a handful of cigarettes into his pocket.

"No," said the American, "I never walk. If man were intended by an all-wise Providence to do much walking he would have four legs."

The tailor promised upon his faith as a gentleman to make Claudius presentable by the following evening. Baden tailors are used to providing clothes at short notice; and the man kept his word.

Pending the event, Barker remarked to Claudius that it was a pity they might not call again before the dinner. Claudius said in some countries he thought it would be the proper thing; but that in Germany Barker was undoubtedly right—it would not do at all.

"Customs vary so much in society," said Barker; "now in America we have such a pretty habit."

"What is that?"

"Sending flowers—we send them to ladies on the smallest provocation."

"But is not the Countess an American?" asked Claudius.

"Yes, certainly. Old Southern family settled north."

"In that case," said Claudius, "the provocation is sufficient. Let us send flowers immediately." And he took his hat from the table.

Thought Mr. Barker, "My show Doctor is going it;" but he translated his thoughts into English.

"I think that is a good idea. I will send for a carriage."

"It is only a step," said Claudius, "we had much better walk."

"Well, anything to oblige you."

Claudius had good taste in such things, and the flowers he sent were just enough to form a beautiful ensemble, without producing an impression of lavish extravagance. As Mr. Barker had said, the sending of flowers is a "pretty habit,"—a graceful and gentle fashion most peculiar to America. There is no country where the custom is carried to the same extent; there is no other country where on certain occasions it is requested, by advertisement in the newspapers, "that no flowers be sent." Countess Margaret was charmed, and though Miss Skeat, who loved roses and lilies, poor thing, offered to arrange them and put them in water, the dark lady would not let her touch them. She was jealous of their beauty.

The time seemed long to Claudius, though he went in the meanwhile with Barker and the British aristocracy to certain races. He rather liked the racing, though he would not bet. The Duke lost some money, and Barker won a few hundred francs from a Russian acquaintance. The Duke drank curaçao and potass water, and Mr. Barker drank champagne, while Claudius smoked innumerable cigarettes. There were a great many bright dresses, there was a great deal of shouting, and the congregation of the horse-cads was gathered together.

"It does not look much like Newmarket, does it?" said the Duke.

"More like the Paris Exposition, without the exposition," said Barker.

"Do you have much racing in America?" asked Claudius.

"Just one or two," answered Barker, "generally on wheels."

"Wheels?"

"Yes. Trotting. Ag'd nags in sulkies. See how fast they can go a mile," explained the Duke. "Lots of shekels on it too, very often."

At last the evening came, and Claudius appeared in Barker's room arrayed in full evening-dress. As Barker had predicted to himself, the result was surprising. Claudius was far beyond the ordinary stature of men, and the close-fitting costume showed off his athletic figure, while the pale, aquiline features, with the yellow heard that looked gold at night, contrasted in their refinement with the massive proportions of his frame, in a way that is rarely seen save in the races of the far north or the far south.

The Countess received them graciously, and Miss Skeat was animated. The flowers that Claudius had sent the day before were conspicuously placed on a table in the drawing-room. Mr. Barker, of course, took in the Countess, and Miss Skeat put her arm in that of Claudius, inwardly wondering how she could have overlooked the fact that he was so excessively handsome. They sat at a round table on which were flowers, and a large block of ice in a crystal dish.

"Do you understand Russian soups?" asked Margaret of Claudius, as she deposited a spoonful of a wonderful looking pâté in the middle of her consommé.

"Alas" said the Doctor, "I am no gastronome. At least my friend Mr. Barker tells me so, but I have great powers of adaptation. I shall follow your example, and shall doubtless fare sumptuously."

"Do not fear," said she, "you shall not have any more strange and Cossack things to eat. I like some Russian things, but they are so tremendous, that unless you have them first you cannot have them at all."

"I think it is rather a good plan," said Barker, "to begin with something characteristic. It settles the plan of action in one's mind, and helps the memory."

"Do you mean in things in general, or only in dinner?" asked the Countess.

"Oh, things in general, of course. I always generalise. In conversation, for instance. Take the traditional English stage father. He always devotes himself to everlasting perdition before he begins a sentence,—and then you know what to expect."

"On the principle of knowing the worst—I understand," said Margaret.

"As long as people understand each other," Claudius put in, "it is always better to plunge in medias res from the first."

"Yes, Dr. Claudius, you understand that very well;" and Margaret turned towards him as she spoke.

"The Doctor understands many things," said Barker in parenthesis.

"You have not yet reported the progress of the crusade," continued the Countess, "I must know all about it at once."

"I have been plotting and planning in the spirit, while my body has been frequenting the frivolities of this over-masculine world," answered the Doctor. At this point Miss Skeat attacked Mr. Barker about the North American Indians, and the conversation paired off, as it will under such circumstances.

Claudius was in good spirits and talked wittily, half in jest, one would have thought, but really in earnest, about what was uppermost in his mind, and what he intended should be uppermost in the world. It was a singular conversation, in the course of which he sometimes spoke very seriously; but the Countess did not allow herself the luxury of being serious, though it was an effort to her to laugh at the enthusiasm of his language, for he had a strong vitality, and something of the gift which carries people away. But Margaret had an impression that Claudius was making love, and had chosen this attractive ground upon which to open his campaign. She could not wholly believe him different from other men—at least she would not believe so soon—and her instinct told her that the fair-haired student admired her greatly.

Claudius, for his part, wondered at himself, when he found a moment to reflect on what he had been saying. He tried to remember whether any of these thoughts had been formulated in his mind a month ago. He was, indeed, conscious that his high reverence for women in the abstract had been growing in him for years, but he had had no idea how strong his belief had grown in this reverence as an element in social affairs. Doubtless the Doctor had often questioned why it was that women had so little weight in the scale, why they did so little of all they might do, and he had read something of their doings across the ocean. But it had all been vague, thick, and foggy, whereas now it was all sharp and clean-edged. He had made the first step out of his dreams in that he had thought its realisation possible, and none but dreamers know how great and wide that step is. The first faint dawning, "It may be true, after all," is as different from the remote, listless view of the shadowy thought incapable of materialisation, as a landscape picture seen by candle-light is different from the glorious reality of the scene it represents. Therefore, when Claudius felt the awakening touch, and saw his ideal before him, urging him, by her very existence which made it possible, to begin the fight, he felt the blood run quickly in his veins, and his blue eyes flashed again, and the words came flowing easily and surely from his lips. But he wondered at his own eloquence, not seeing yet that the divine spark had kindled his genius into a broad flame, and not half understanding what he felt.

It is late in the day to apostrophise love. It has been done too much by people who persuade themselves that they love because they say they do, and because it seems such a fine thing. Poets and cynics, and good men and bad, have had their will of the poor little god, and he has grown so shy and retiring that he would rather not be addressed, or described, or photographed in type, for the benefit of the profane. He is chary of using pointed shafts, and most of his target practice is done with heavy round-tipped arrows that leave an ugly black bruise where they strike, but do not draw the generous blood. He lurks in out-of-the-way places and mopes, and he rarely springs out suddenly on unwary youth and maid, as he used to in the good old days before Darwin and La Rochefoucauld destroyed the beauty of the body and the beauty of the soul,—or man's belief in them, which is nearly the same. Has not the one taught us to see the animal in the angel, and the other to detect the devil in the saint? And yet we talk of our loves as angels and our departed parents as saints, in a gentle, commonplace fashion, as we talk of our articles of faith. The only moderns who apostrophise love with any genuine success are those who smack their lips sensuously at his flesh and blood, because they are too blind to see the lovely soul that is enshrined therein, and they have too little wit to understand that soul and body are one.

Mr. Barker, who seemed to have the faculty of carrying on one conversation and listening to another at the same time, struck in when Claudius paused.

"The Professor, Countess," he began, "is one of those rare individuals who indulge in the most unbounded enthusiasm. At the present time I think, with all deference to his superior erudition, that he is running into a dead wall. We have seen something of the 'woman's rights' question in America. Let us take him over there and show him what it all means."

"My friend," answered Claudius, "you are one of those hardened sceptics for whom nothing can be hoped save a deathbed repentance. When you are mortally hit and have the alternative of marriage or death set before you in an adequately lively manner, you will, of course, elect to marry. Then your wife, if you get your deserts, will rule you with a rod of iron, and you will find, to your cost, that the woman who has got you has rights, whether you like it or not, and that she can use them."

"Dollars and cents," said Barker grimly, "that is all."

"No, it is not all," retorted Claudius. "A wise Providence has provided women in the world who can make it very uncomfortable for sinners like you, and if you do not reform and begin a regular course of worship, I hope that one of them will get you."

"Thanks. And if I repent and make a pilgrimage on my knees to every woman I know, what fate do you predict? what countless blessings are in store for me?"

The Countess was amused at the little skirmish, though she knew that Claudius was right. Barker, with all his extreme politeness and his pleasant speeches, had none of the knightly element in his character.

"You never can appreciate the 'countless blessings' until you are converted to woman-worship, my friend," said Claudius, evading the question. "But," he added, "perhaps the Countess might describe them to you."

But Margaret meant to do nothing of the kind. She did not want to continue the general conversation on the topic which seemed especially Claudius's own, particularly as Mr. Barker seemed inclined to laugh at the Doctor's enthusiasm. So she changed the subject, and began asking the American questions about the races on the previous day.

"Of course," she said, "I do not go anywhere now."

The dinner passed off very pleasantly. Miss Skeat was instructed in the Knickerbocker and Boston peerage, so to speak, by the intelligent Mr. Barker, who did not fail, however, to hint at the superiority of Debrett, who does not hesitate to tell, and boldly to print in black and white, those distinctions of rank which he considers necessary to the salvation of society; whereas the enterprising compilers of the "Boston Blue Book" and the "New York List" only divide society up into streets, mapping it out into so many square feet and so much frontage of dukes, marquesses, generals, and "people we don't know." Miss Skeat listened to the disquisition on the rights of birth with rapt attention, and the yellow candle-light played pleasantly on her old corners, and her ancient heart fluttered sympathetically. Margaret, on the other side, made Claudius talk about his youth, and took infinite pleasure in listening to his tales of the fresh Northern life he had led as a boy. The Doctor had the faculty of speech and told his stories with a certain vigour that savoured of the sea.

"I hope you will both come and see me," said the Countess, as the two men took their departure; but as she spoke she looked at Barker.

Half an hour later they sat in their sitting-room at the hotel, and Barker sipped a little champagne while Claudius smoked cigarettes, as usual. As usual, also, they were talking. It was natural that two individuals endowed with the faculty of expressing their thoughts, and holding views for the most part diametrically opposed, should have a good deal to say to each other. The one knew a great deal, and the other had seen a great deal; both were given to looking at life rather seriously than the reverse. Barker never deceived himself for a moment about the reality of things, and spent much of his time in the practical adaptation of means to ends he had in view; he was superficial in his knowledge, but profound in his actions. Claudius was an intellectual seeker after an outward and visible expression of an inward and spiritual truth which he felt must exist, though he knew he might spend a lifetime in the preliminary steps towards its attainment. Just now they were talking of marriage.

"It is detestable," said Claudius, "to think how mercenary the marriage contract is, in all civilised and uncivilised countries. It ought not to be so—it is wrong from the very beginning."

"Yes, it is wrong of course," answered Barker, who was always ready to admit the existence and even the beauty of an ideal, though he never took the ideal into consideration for a moment in his doings. "Of course it is wrong; but it cannot be helped. It crops up everywhere, as the question of dollars and cents will in every kind of business; and I believe it is better to be done with it at first. Now you have to pay a Frenchman cash down before he will marry your daughter."

"I know," said Claudius, "and I loathe the idea."

"I respect your loathing, but there it is, and it has the great advantage that it is all over, and there is no more talk about it. Now the trouble in our country is that people marry for love, and when they get through loving they have got to live, and then somebody must pay the bills. Supposing the son of one rich father marries the daughter of another rich father; by the time they have got rid of the novelty of the thing the bills begin to come in, and they spend the remainder of their amiable lives in trying to shove the expense off on to each other. With an old-fashioned marriage contract to tie them up, that would not happen, because the wife is bound to provide so many clothes, and the husband has to give her just so much to eat, and there is an end of it. See?"

"No, I do not see," returned Claudius. "If they really loved each other—"

"Get out!" interrupted Barker, merrily. "If you mean to take the immutability of the human affections as a basis of argument, I have done."

"There your cynicism comes in," said the other, "and denies you the pleasure and profit of contemplating an ideal, and of following it up to its full development."

"Is it cynical to see things as they are instead of as they might be in an imaginary world?"

"Provided you really see them as they are—no," said Claudius. "But if you begin with an idea that things, as they are, are not very good, you will very soon be judging them by your own inherent standard of badness, and you will produce a bad ideal as I produce a good one, farther still from the truth, and extremely depressing to contemplate."

"Why?" retorted Barker; "why should it be depressing to look at everything as it is, or to try to? Why should my naturally gay disposition suffer on making the discovery that the millennium is not begun yet? The world may be bad, but it is a merry little place while it lasts."

"You are a hopeless case," said Claudius, laughing; "if you had a conscience and some little feeling for humanity, you would feel uncomfortable in a bad world."

"Exactly. I am moderately comfortable because I know that I am just like everybody else. I would rather, I am sure."

"I am not sure that you are," said Claudius thoughtfully.

"Oh! not as you imagine everybody else, certainly. Medieval persons who have a hankering after tournaments and crawl about worshipping women."

"I do not deny the softer impeachment," answered the Doctor, "but I hardly think I crawl much."

"No, but the people you imagine do—the male population of this merry globe, as you represent it to the Countess."

"I think Countess Margaret understands me very well."

"Yes," said Barker, "she understands you very well." He did not emphasise the remark, and his voice was high and monotonous; but the repetition was so forcible that Claudius looked at his companion rather curiously, and was silent. Barker was examining the cork of his little pint bottle of champagne—"just one square drink," as he would have expressed it—and his face was a blank.

"Don't you think, Professor," he said at last, "that with your views about the rights of women you might make some interesting studies in America?"

"Decidedly."

"You might write a book."

"I might," said Claudius.

"You and the Countess might write a book together."

"Are you joking?"

"No. What I have heard you saying to each other this evening and the other day when we called would make a very interesting book, though I disagree with you both from beginning to end. It would sell, though."

"It seems to me you rather take things for granted when you infer that the Countess would be willing to undertake anything of the kind."

Barker looked at the Doctor steadily, and smiled.

"Do you really think so? Do you imagine that if you would do the work she would have any objection whatever to giving you the benefit of her views and experience?"

"In other words," Claudius said, "you are referring to the possibility of a journey to America, in the company of the charming woman to whom you have introduced me."

"You are improving, Professor; that is exactly what I mean. Let us adjourn from the bowers of Baden to the wind-swept cliffs of Newport—we can be there before the season is over. But I forgot, you thought you would not like Newport."

"I am not sure," said Claudius. "Do you think the Countess would go?"

"If you will call there assiduously, and explain to her the glorious future that awaits your joint literary enterprise, I believe she might be induced."

Claudius went to bed that night with his head full of this new idea, just as Mr. Barker had intended. He dreamed he was writing with the Countess, and travelling with her and talking to her; and he woke up with the determination that the thing should be done if it were possible. Why not? She often made a trip to her native country, as she herself had told him, and why should she not make another? For aught he knew, she might be thinking of it even now.

Then he had a reaction of despondency. He knew nothing of her ties or of her way of life. A woman in her position probably made engagements long beforehand, and mapped out her year among her friends. She would have promised a week here and a month there In visits all over Europe, and the idea that she would give up her plans and consent, at the instance of a two days' acquaintance, to go to America was preposterous. Then again, he said to himself, as he came back from his morning walk in the woods, there was nothing like trying. He would call as soon as it was decent after the dinner, and he would call again.

Mr. Barker was a man in whom a considerable experience of men supplemented a considerable natural astuteness. He was not always right in the judgments he formed of people and their aims, but he was more often right than wrong. His way of dealing with men was calculated on the majority, and he knew that there are no complete exceptions to be found in the world's characters. But his standard was necessarily somewhat low, and he lacked the sympathetic element which enables one high nature to understand another better than it understands its inferiors. Barker would know how to deal with the people he met; Claudius could understand a hero if he ever met one, but he bore himself toward ordinary people by fixed rules of his own, not caring or attempting to comprehend the principles on which they acted.

If any one had asked the Doctor if he loved the Countess, he would have answered that he certainly did not. That she was the most beautiful woman in the world, that she represented to him his highest ideal, and that he was certain she came up to that ideal, although he knew her so little, for he felt sure of that. But love, the Doctor thought, was quite a different affair. What he felt for Margaret bore no resemblance to what he had been used to call love. Besides, he would have said, did ever a man fall in love at such short notice? Only in books. But as no one asked him the question, he did not ask it of himself, but only went on thinking a great deal of her, and recalling all she said. He was in an unknown region, but he was happy and he asked no questions. Nevertheless his nature comprehended hers, and when he began to go often to the beautiful little villa, he knew perfectly well that Barker was mistaken, and that the dark Countess would think twice and three times before she would be persuaded to go to America, or to write a book, or to do anything in the world for Claudius, except like him and show him that he was welcome. She would have changed the subject had Claudius proposed to her to do any of the things he seemed to think she was ready to do, and Claudius knew it instinctively. He was bold with women, but he never transgressed, and his manner allowed him to say many things that would have sounded oddly enough in Mr. Barker's mouth. He impressed women with a sense of confidence that he might be trusted to honour them and respect them under any circumstances.

The Countess was accustomed to have men at her feet, but she had never treated a man unjustly, and if they had sometimes lost their heads it was not her fault. She was a loyal woman, and had loved her husband as much as most good wives, though with an honest determination to love him better; for she was young when they married, and she thought her love stronger than it really was. She had mourned him sincerely, but the wound had healed, and being a brave woman, with no morbid sensitiveness of herself, she had contemplated the possibility of marrying again, without, however, connecting the idea with any individual. She had liked Claudius from the first, and there had been something semi-romantic about their meeting in the Schloss at Heidelberg. On nearer acquaintance she liked him better, though she knew that he admired her, and by the time a fortnight had passed Claudius had become an institution. They read together and they walked together, and once she took him with her in the black phaeton, whereupon Barker remarked that it was "an immense thing on wheels."

Mr. Barker, seeing that his companion was safe for the present, left Baden for a time and lighted on his friend the Duke at Como, where the latter had discovered some attractive metal. The Duke remarked that Como would be a very decent place if the scenery wasn't so confoundedly bad. "I could beat it on my own place in the west," he added.

The British aristocracy liked Mr. Barker, because he was always inventing original ways of passing the time, and because, though he was so rich, he never talked about money except in a vague way as "lots of shekels," or "piles of tin." So they said they would go back to Baden together, which they did, and as they had talked a good deal about Claudius, they called on the Countess the same afternoon, and there, sure enough, was the Swede, sitting by the Countess's side in the garden, and expounding the works of Mr. Herbert Spencer. Barker and the Duke remained half an hour, and Claudius would have gone with them, but Margaret insisted upon finishing the chapter, so he stayed behind.

"He's a gone 'coon, Duke," remarked Barker, beginning to smoke as soon as he was in the Victoria.

"I should say he was pretty hard hit, myself. I guess nothing better could have happened." The Duke, in virtue of his possessions in America, affected to "guess" a little now and then when none of those horrid people were about.

"Come on, Duke," said Barker, "let us go home, and take them with us."

"I could not go just now. Next month. Autumn, you know. Glories of the forest and those sort of things."

"Think they would go?"

"Don't know," said the Duke. "Take them over in the yacht, if they like."

"All right. We can play poker while they bay the moon."

"Hold on, though; she won't go without some other woman, you know. It would be in all the papers."

"She has a lady-companion," said Barker.

"That won't do for respectability."

"It is rather awkward, then." There was silence for a few moments.

"Stop a bit," said the Duke suddenly. "It just strikes me. I have got a sister somewhere. I'll look her up. She is never ill at sea, and they have sent her husband off to Kamtchatka, or some such place."

"That's the very thing," said Barker. "I will talk to Claudius. Can you manage the Countess, do you think? Have you known her long?"

"Rather. Ever since she married poor Alexis."

"All right, then. You ask her." And they reached their hotel.

So these two gentlemen settled things between them. They both wanted to go to America, and they were not in a hurry, so that the prospect of a pleasant party, with all the liberty and home feeling there is on board of a yacht, was an immense attraction. Barker, of course, was amused and interested by his scheme for making Claudius and the Countess fall in love with each other, and he depended on the dark lady for his show. Claudius would not have been easily induced to leave Europe by argument or persuasion, but there was little doubt that he would follow the Countess, if she could be induced to lead. The Duke, on the other hand, thought only of making up a well-arranged party of people who wanted to make the journey in any case, and would not be on his hands after he landed. So two or three days later he called on the Countess to open the campaign. It was not altogether new ground, as they had crossed together once before. The Duke was not very good at leading the conversation up to his points, so he immediately began talking about America, in order to be sure of hitting somewhere near the mark.

"I have not been over since the autumn," he said, "and I really ought to go."

"When will you start?" asked Margaret.

"I meant to go next month. I think I will take the yacht."

"I wonder you do not always do that. It is so much pleasanter, and you feel as if you never had gone out of your own house."

"The fact is," said he, plunging, "I am going to take my sister, and I would like to have a little party. Will you not join us yourself, Countess, and Miss Skeat?"

"Really, Duke, you are very kind. But I was not thinking of going home just yet."

"It is a long time since you have been there. Not since—"

"Yes, I know," said Margaret gravely. "And perhaps that is why I hesitate to go now."

"But would it not be different if we all went together? Do you not think it would be much nicer?"

"Did you say your sister was going?"

"Oh yes, she will certainly go."

"Well," said the Countess after a moment's thought, "I will not say just yet. I need not make up my mind yet; need I? Then I will take a few days to think of it."

"I am sure you will decide to join us," said the Duke pressingly.

"Perhaps I ought to go, and it is so kind of you, really, to give me such a delightful chance." She had a presentiment that before long she would be on her way to join the yacht, though at first sight it seemed rather improbable, for, as Claudius had guessed, she had a great many engagements for visits. If any one had suggested to her that morning that she might make a trip to America, she would have said it was quite impossible. The idea of the disagreeable journey, the horror of being cast among an immense crowd of unknown travellers; or, still worse, of being thrown into the society of some chance acquaintance who would make the most of knowing her—it was all sufficient, even in the absence of other reasons, to deter her from undertaking the journey. But in the party proposed by the Duke it was all very different. He was a gentleman, besides being a peer, and he was an old friend. His sister was a kind-hearted gentlewoman of narrow views but broad humanity; and not least, the yacht was sure to be perfection, and she would be the honoured guest. She would be sorry to leave Baden for some reasons; she liked Claudius very much, and he made her feel that she was leading an intellectual life. But she had not entirely realised him yet. He was to her always the quiet student whom she had met in Heidelberg, and during the month past the feeling she entertained for him had developed more in the direction of intellectual sympathy than of personal friendship. She would not mind parting with him any more than she would mind laying down an interesting book before she had half read it. Still that was something, and the feeling had weight.

"Miss Skeat," she said, when they were alone, "you have never been in America?"

"No, dear Countess, I have never been there, and until lately I have never thought I would care to go."

"Would you like to go now?"

"Oh!" exclaimed the ancient one, "I would like it of all things!"

"I am thinking of going over next month," said Margaret, "and of course I would like you to go with me. Do you mind the sea very much?"

"Oh dear, no! I used to sail a great deal when I was a girl, and the Atlantic cannot be worse than our coast."

Miss Skeat's assent was a matter of real importance to Margaret, for the old gentlewoman was sincerely attached to her, and Margaret would have been very unwilling to turn her faithful companion adrift, even for a time, besides the minor consideration that without a companion she would not go at all. The end of it was that by dinner-time she had made up her mind to write excuses to all the people who expected her, and to accept the Duke's invitation. After all, it was not until next month, and she could finish the book she was reading with Claudius before that. She postponed writing to the Duke until the following day, in order to make a show of having considered the matter somewhat longer. But her resolution did not change, and in the morning she despatched a friendly little note to the effect that she found her engagements would permit her, etc. etc.

When Margaret told Miss Skeat that they were going in one of the finest yachts afloat, with the Duke and his sister, her companion fairly crackled with joy.

CHAPTER VI

The Duke was away during the day, and did not receive the Countess's note until late in the evening. To tell the truth, he was very glad to find that she was going; but he felt there might be difficulties in the way; for, of course, he was bound to let her know the names of his remaining guests. She might hesitate when she heard that Claudius and Barker were to be of the party. After all, Barker was the companion whom the Duke wanted. He knew nothing about Claudius, but he had met enough men of all types of eccentricity not to be much surprised at him, and as the Doctor was evidently a gentleman, there was no objection. Therefore, as soon as the Duke knew of Margaret's determination, he sallied forth, armed with her note, to find Mr. Barker. It was late, but the American was nocturnal in his habits, and was discovered by his friend in a huge cloud of tobacco smoke, examining his nails with that deep interest which in some persons betokens thought.

"It's all right," said the Duke; "she will go."

"You don't mean it?" said Barker, taking his legs off the sofa and wrinkling his face.

"There you are. Note. Formal acceptance, and all the rest of it." And he handed Margaret's letter to Barker.

"Well, that is pretty smart practice," remarked the latter; "I expected you would have difficulties."

"Said she would take some days to make up her mind. She wrote this the same evening I called, I am sure. Just like a woman."

"Well, I think it's deuced lucky, anyhow," said Barker. "Did you tell her who was going?"

"I told her about my sister. I have not mentioned you or your friend yet. Of course I will do that as soon as I am sure of you both."

"Well," said Barker, "if you don't mind, perhaps you might write a note to the Doctor. He might be shy of accepting an invitation by word of mouth. Do you mind?"

"Not in the least," said the Englishman; "give me a rag of paper and a quill, and I'll do it now."

And he accordingly did it, and directed the invitation to Claudius, Phil.D., and Barker pushed it into the crack of the door leading to the apartment where the Doctor was sleeping, lest it should be forgotten.

The next morning Claudius appeared with the Duke's note in his hand.

"What does this mean?" he asked. "I hardly know him at all, and here he asks me to cross the Atlantic in his yacht. I wish you would explain."

"Keep your hair on, my young friend," replied Mr. Barker jocosely. "He has asked you and me because his party would not be complete without us."

"And who are 'the party'?"

"Oh, very small. Principally his sister, I believe. Hold on though, Miss Skeat is going."

"Miss Skeat?" Claudius anticipated some chaff from his friend, and knit his brows a little.

"Yes; Miss Skeat and the Countess; or, perhaps I should say the Countess and Miss Skeat."

"Ah!" ejaculated Claudius, "any one else?"

"Not that I know of. Will you go?"

"It is rather sudden," said the Doctor reflectively.

"You must make up your mind one way or the other, or you will spoil the Duke's arrangements."

"Barker," said Claudius seriously, "do you suppose the Countess knows who are going?"

"My dear boy," replied the other, peeling a peach which he had impaled on a fork, "it is not likely the Duke would ask a lady to go with him without telling her who the men were to be. Be calm, however; I have observed your habits, and in two hours and twenty-three minutes your mind will be at rest."

"How so?"

"It is now thirty-seven minutes past nine. Do you mean to say you have failed once for weeks past to be at the Countess's as the clock strikes twelve?"

Claudius was silent. It was quite true; he went there daily at the same hour; for, as appeared in the beginning of this tale, he was a regular man. But he reflected just now that the Countess would not be likely to speak of the party unless she knew that he was to be one. He had not accepted his invitation yet, and the Duke would certainly not take his acceptance as a foregone conclusion. Altogether it seemed probable that he would be kept in suspense. If he then accepted without being sure of the Countess, he was binding himself to leave her. Claudius had many things to learn yet.

"If I were you," said Barker, "I would write at once and say 'Yes.' Why can't you do it now?"

"Because I have not made up my mind."

"Well, a bird in the hand is the soul of business, as the good old proverb says. I have accepted for myself, anyhow; but I would be sorry to leave you on this side."

So Claudius went to the Countess as usual, and found her in her morning-room awaiting him. He bent over her hand, but as he took it he thought it was a trifle colder than usual. It might have been imagination, but he fancied her whole manner was less cordial than before. And he said to himself, "She has heard I am going, and she is annoyed, and is not glad to see me." There was a preternatural solemnity about their conversation which neither of them could break through, and in a few minutes they both looked as though they had not smiled for years.

Now Claudius was entirely mistaken. Margaret had not heard that he was going. If she had, she would have spoken frankly, as was her nature to do always, if she spoke at all. Margaret had accepted the Duke's invitation, and intended to keep her word, and she had no suspicion whatever of who the other guests might be. She foresaw that such a journey would break up her acquaintance with Claudius, and she regretted it; and especially she regretted having allowed the Doctor so much intimacy and so many visits. Not that he had taken advantage of the footing on which he was received, for any signs of such a disposition on his part would have abruptly terminated the situation; he had been the very model of courtesy from the first. But she knew enough of men to perceive that this gentle homage clothed a more sincere admiration than lay at the root of the pushing attentions of some other men she had known. Therefore she made up her mind that as there were yet three weeks before sailing, after the expiration of which she would never be likely to see Claudius again, she would let him down easily, so to speak, that there might be no over-tender recollections on his part, nor any little stings of remorse on her own. He had interested her; they had spent a couple of pleasant months; she had given him no encouragement, and he was gone without a sigh: that was the way in which Countess Margaret hoped to remember Dr. Claudius by that time next month. And so, fearing lest she might inadvertently have been the least shade too cordial, she began to be a little more severe, on this hot morning when Claudius, full of indecision, followed her out to their favourite reading-place under the trees. It was the same spot where they had sat when Barker first brought him to see her. Margaret had no particular feeling about the little nook under the trees. It was merely the most convenient place to sit and work; that was all. But to Claudius the circle of green sward represented the temple of his soul, and Margaret was to him Rune Wife and prophetess as well as divinity. In such places, and of such women, his fair-haired forefathers, bare-armed and sword-girt, had asked counsel in trouble, and song-inspiration in peace.

Here they sat them down, she determined to do the right by him, and thinking it an easy matter; he utterly misunderstanding her. Without a smile, they set to work at their reading. They read for an hour or more, maintaining the utmost gravity, when, as luck would have it, the word "friendship" occurred in a passage of the book. Claudius paused a moment, his broad hand laid flat on the open page.

"That is one of the most interesting and one of the most singularly misunderstood words in all languages," he said.

"What word?" inquired Margaret, looking up from her work, to which she had attentively applied herself while he was reading.

"Friendship."

"Will you please define what it means?" said she.

"I can define what I myself mean by it, or rather what I think I mean by it. I can define what a dozen writers have meant by it. But I cannot tell what it really means, still less what it may ultimately come to mean."

"You will probably be best able to explain what you mean by it yourself," answered Margaret rather coldly. "Will you please begin?"

"It seems to me," Claudius began, "that the difficulty lies in the contradiction between the theory and the fact. Of course, as in all such cases, the theory loses the battle, and we are left groping for an explanation of the fact which we do not understand. Perhaps that is a little vague?" Claudius paused.

"A little vague—yes," said she.

"I will try and put it more clearly. First take the fact. No one will deny that there have occasionally in the world's history existed friendships which have stood every test and which have lasted to the very end. Such attachments have been always affairs of the heart, even between man and man. I do not think you can name an instance of a lasting friendship on a purely intellectual basis. True friendship implies the absence of envy, and the vanity of even the meanest intellect is far too great to admit of such a condition out of pure thought-sympathy."

"I do not see any contradiction, even admitting your last remark, which is cynical enough." Margaret spoke indifferently, as making a mere criticism.

"But I believe most people connect the idea of friendship, beyond ordinary liking, with intellectual sympathy. They suppose, for instance, that a man may love a woman wholly and entirely with the best kind of love, and may have at the same time a friend with whom he is in entire sympathy."

"And why not?" she asked.

"Simply because he cannot serve two masters. If he is in entire sympathy with more than one individual he must sometimes not only contradict himself, as he would rightly do for one or the other alone, but he must also contradict one in favour of the other in case they disagree. In such a case he is no longer in entire sympathy with both, and either his love or his friendship must be imperfect." Claudius looked at the Countess to see what impression he had made. She did not return his glance.

"In other words?" was her question.

"In other words," he answered in a tone of conviction, "friendship is only a substitute for love, and cannot exist beside it unless lover and friend be one and the same person. Friendship purely intellectual is a fallacy, owing to the manifest imperfections of human nature. It must, then, be an affair of the heart, whatever you may define that to be, and cannot, therefore, exist at the same time with any other affair of the heart without inevitable contradiction. How often has love separated old friends, and friendship bred discord between lovers!"

"I never heard that argument before," said Margaret, who, to tell the truth, was surprised at the result of the Doctor's discourse.

"What do you think of it?" he asked.

"I am not sure, but the point is interesting. I think you are a little vague about what an 'affair of the heart,' as you call it, really is."

"I suppose an affair of the heart to be such a situation of the feelings that the heart rules the head and the actions by the head. The prime essence of love is that it should be complete, making no reservations and allowing of no check from the reason."

"A dangerous state of things."

"Yes," said Claudius. "When the heart gets the mastery it knows neither rest nor mercy. If the heart is good the result will be good, if it is bad the result will be evil. Real love has produced incalculably great results in the lives of individuals and in the life of the world."

"I suppose so," said Margaret; "but you made out friendship to be also an 'affair of the heart,' so far as you believe in it at all. Is true friendship as uncalculating as true love? Does it make no reservations, and does it admit of no check from the reason?"

"I think, as I said, that friendship is a substitute for love, second best in its nature and second best, too, in its unselfishness."

"Many people say love is selfishness itself."

"I know," answered the Doctor, and paused as if thinking.

"Do you not want to smoke?" asked Margaret, with a tinge of irony, "it may help you to solve the difficulty."

"Thank you, no," said he, "the difficulty is solved, and it is no difficulty at all. The people who say that do not know what they are talking about, for they have never been in love themselves. Love, worth the name, is complete; and being complete, demands the whole, and is not satisfied with less than the whole any more than it is satisfied with giving less than all that it has. The selfishness lies in demanding and insisting upon having everything, while only offering rags and shreds in return; and if one may find this fault in ordinary love affairs, one may find it tenfold in ordinary friendships. Friendship may be heroic but love is godlike."

Margaret had become interested in spite of herself, though she had preserved the constrained manner she had first assumed. Now, however, as Claudius turned his flashing blue eyes to hers, she understood that she had allowed the conversation to go far enough, and she marvelled that on the very day when she was trying to be most unapproachable he should have said more to show what was next his heart than ever before. She did not know enough of exceptional natures like his to be aware that a touch of the curb is the very thing to rouse the fierce blood. True, he spoke generally, and even argumentatively, and his deep voice was calm enough, but there was a curious light in his eyes that dazzled her even in the mid-day sun, and she looked away.

"I am not sure I agree with you," she said, "but you put it very clearly. Shall we go on reading?"

Claudius was some time in finding his place in the open book, and then went on. Again he misunderstood her, for though he could not remember saying anything he regretted, he fancied she had brought the conversation to a somewhat abrupt close. He read on, feeling very uncomfortable, and longing for one of those explanations that are impossible between acquaintances and emotional between lovers. He felt also that if he ever spoke out and told her he loved her it would be in some such situation as the present. Margaret let her needlework drop and leaned back in the long chair, staring at a very uninteresting-looking tree on the other side of the garden. Claudius read in a steady determined tone, emphasising his sentences with care, and never once taking his eyes from the book. At last, noticing how quietly he was doing his work, Margaret looked at him, not furtively or as by stealth, but curiously and thoughtfully. He was good to look at, so strong and straight, even as he sat at ease with the book in his hand, and the quivering sunlight through the leaves played over his yellow beard and white forehead. She knew well enough now that he admired her greatly, and she hoped it would not be very hard for him when she went away. Somehow, he was still to her the professor, the student, quiet and dignified and careless of the world, as she had first known him. She could not realise Claudius as a man of wealth and power, who was as well able to indulge his fancies as the Duke himself,—perhaps more so, for the Duke's financial affairs were the gossip of Europe, and always had been since he came of age.

Meanwhile the Doctor reached the end of the chapter, and there was a pause. Neither spoke, and the silence was becoming awkward, when a servant came across the lawn announcing the Duke.

"Ask his Grace to come outside," said Margaret, and the representative of the aristocracy was striding over the green, hat in hand, a moment afterwards. Margaret put out her hand and Claudius rose. Each felt that the deus ex machinâ had arrived, and that the subject of the yachting excursion would be immediately broached.

"Immense luck, finding you both," remarked the Duke when he was seated.

"We have been reading. It is so pleasant here," said Margaret, to say something.

"I have come to thank you for your kind note, Countess. It is extremely good of you to go in such a party, with your taste for literature and those sort of things."

"I am sure it is I who ought to thank you, Duke. But when are we to sail?"

"About the tenth of next month, I should say. Will that be convenient?"

Margaret turned to Claudius.

"Do you think we can finish our book by the tenth, Dr. Claudius?"

"If not," broke in the Duke, "there is no reason why you should not finish it on board. We shall have lovely weather."

"Oh no!" said Margaret, "we must finish it before we start. I could not understand a word of it alone."

"Alone?" inquired the Duke. "Ah! I forgot. Thought he had told you. I have asked Dr. Claudius to give us the pleasure of his company."

"Oh, indeed!" said Margaret. "That will be very nice." She did not look as if she thought so, however. Her expression was not such as led the Duke to believe she was pleased, or Claudius to think she would like his going. To tell the truth, she was annoyed for more than one reason. She thought the Duke, although he was such an old friend, should have consulted her before making up the list of men for the party. She was annoyed with Claudius because he had not told her he was going, when he really thought she knew it, and was displeased at it. And most of all, she was momentarily disconcerted at being thus taken off her guard. Besides, the Duke must have supposed she liked Claudius very much, and he had perhaps contrived the whole excursion in order to throw them together. Her first impulse was to change her mind and not go after all.

Meanwhile Claudius was much astonished at the turn things had taken. Margaret had known nothing about the invitation to the Doctor after all, and her coldness this morning must be attributed to some other cause. But now that she did know she looked less pleased than ever. She did not want him. The Doctor was a proud man in his quiet way, and he was, moreover, in love, not indeed hopelessly as yet, for love is never wholly irrevocable until it has survived the crucial test, attainment of its object; but Claudius loved, and he knew it. Consequently his pride revolted at the idea of thrusting himself where he was not wanted, and his love forbade him to persecute the woman he worshipped. He also said to himself, "I will not go." He had not yet accepted the invitation.

"I had intended to write to you this afternoon," he said, turning to the Duke. "But since it is my good fortune to be able to thank you in person for your kind invitation, let me do so now."

"I hope you are going," said the Duke.

"I fear," answered Claudius, "that I shall be prevented from joining you, much as I would like to do so. I have by no means decided to abandon my position in Heidelberg."

Neither Margaret nor the Duke were in the least prepared for this piece of news. The Duke was taken aback at the idea that any human being could refuse such an invitation. Following on his astonishment that Margaret should not be delighted at having the Doctor on board, the intelligence that the Doctor did not want to go at all threw the poor man into the greatest perplexity. He had made a mistake somewhere, evidently; but where or how he could not tell.

"Barker," he said to himself, "is an ass. He has made me muff the whole thing." However, he did not mean to give up the fight.

"I am extremely sorry to hear you say that, Dr. Claudius," he said aloud, "and I hope you will change your mind, if I have to send you an invitation every day until we sail. You know one does not ask people on one's yacht unless one wants them very much, and we want you. It is just like asking a man to ride your favourite hunter; you would not ask him unless you meant it, for fear he would." The Duke seldom made so long a speech, and Claudius felt that the invitation was really genuine, which gave his wounded pride a pleasant little respite from its aches. He was grateful, and he said so. Margaret was silent and plied her needle, planning how she might escape the party if Claudius changed his mind and went, and how she could with decency leave herself the option of going if he remained. She did not intend to give people any farther chance of pairing her off with Claudius or any one else whom they thought she fancied, and she blamed herself for having given people even the shadow of an idea that such officious party-making would please her.

Claudius rose to go. The position was not tenable any longer, and it was his only course. The Countess bade him good morning with more cordiality than she had displayed as yet; for, in spite of her annoyance, she would have been sorry to wound his feelings. The change of tone at first gave Claudius a thrill of pleasure, which gave way to an increased sense of mortification as he reflected that she was probably only showing that she was glad to be rid of him—a clumsy, manlike thought, which his reason would soon get the better of. So he departed.

There was silence for some minutes after he had gone, for Margaret and the Englishman were old friends, and there was no immediate necessity for making conversation. At last he spoke with a certain amount of embarrassment.

"I ought to have told you before that I had asked those two men."

"Who is the other?" she inquired without looking up.

"Why, Barker, his friend."

"Oh, of course! But it would have been simpler to have told me. It made it rather awkward, for of course Dr. Claudius thought I knew he was asked and wondered why I did not speak of it. Don't you see?" she raised her eyes as she put the question.

"It was idiotic of me, and I am very sorry. Please forgive me."

"As he is not going, it does not make any difference, of course, and so I forgive you."

Considering that Barker had suggested the party, that it was Barker whom the Duke especially wanted to amuse him on the trip, that Barker had proposed Margaret and Claudius, and that, finally, the whole affair was a horrid mess, the Duke did not see what he could have done. But he knew it was good form to be penitent whenever it seemed to be expected, and he liked Margaret well enough to hope that she would go. He did not care very much for the society of women at any time. He was more or less married when he was at home, which was never for long together, and when he was away he preferred the untrammelled conversational delights of a foreign green-room to the twaddle of the embassies or to the mingled snobbery and philistinism produced by the modern fusion of the almighty dollar and the ancienne noblesse.

And so he was in trouble just now, and his one idea was to submit to everything the Countess might say, and then to go and "give it" to Mr. Barker for producing so much complication. But Margaret had nothing more to say about the party, and launched out into a discussion of the voyage. She introduced a cautious "if" in most of her sentences. "If I go I would like to see Madeira," and "if we join you, you must take care of Miss Skeat, and give her the best cabin," etc. etc. The Duke wisely abstained from pressing his cause, or asking why she qualified her plans. At last he got away, after promising to do every conceivable and inconceivable thing which she should now or at any future time evolve from the depths of her inventive feminine consciousness.

"By the way, Duke," she called after him, as he went over the, lawn, "may I take old Vladimir if I go?"

"If you go," he answered, moving back a step or two, "you may bring all the Imperial Guards if you choose, and I will provide transports for those that the yacht won't hold."

"Thanks; that is all," she said laughing, and the stalwart peer vanished through the house. The moment he was gone Margaret dropped her work and lay back in her long chair to think. The heavy lids half closed over her dark eyes, and the fingers of her right hand slowly turned round and round the ring she wore upon her left. Miss Skeat was upstairs reading Lord Byron's Corsair in anticipation of the voyage. Margaret did not know this, or the thought of the angular and well-bred Scotchwoman bounding over the glad waters of the dark blue sea would have made her smile. As it was, she looked serious.

"I am sorry," she thought to herself. "It was nice of him to say he would not go."

Meanwhile the strong-legged nobleman footed it merrily towards Barker's hotel. It was a good two miles, and the Duke's ruddy face shone again under the August sun. But the race characteristic was strong in him, and he liked to make himself unnecessarily hot; moreover he was really fond of Barker, and now he was going to pitch into him, as he said to himself, so it was indispensable to keep the steam up. He found his friend as usual the picture of dried-up coolness, so to say. Mr. Barker never seemed to be warm, but he never seemed to feel cold either, and at this moment, as he sat in a half-lighted room, clad in a variety of delicate gray tints, with a collar that looked like fresh-baked biscuit ware, and a pile of New York papers and letters beside him, he was refreshing to the eye.

"Upon my word, Barker, you always look cool," said the Duke, as he sat himself down in an arm-chair, and passed his handkerchief round his wrists. "I would like to know how you do it."

"To begin with, I do not rush madly about in the sun in the middle of the day. That may have something to do with it."

The Duke sneezed loudly, from the mingled dust and sunshine he had been inhaling.

"And then I don't come into a cold room and catch cold, like you. Here I sit in seclusion and fan myself with the pages of my newspapers as I turn them over."

"You have got us all into the deuce of a mess with your confounded coolness," said the Duke after a pause, during which he had in vain searched all his pockets for his cigar-case. Barker had watched him, and pushed an open box of Havanas across the table. But the Duke was determined to be sulky, and took no notice of the attention. The circular wrinkle slowly furrowed its way round Barker's mouth, and his under jaw pushed forward. It always amused him to see sanguine people angry. They looked so uncomfortable, and "gave themselves away" so recklessly.

"If you won't smoke, have some beer," he suggested. But his Grace fumed the redder.

"I don't understand how a man of your intelligence, Barker, can go and put people into such awkward positions," he said. "I think it is perfectly idiotic."

"Write me down an ass, by all means," said Barker calmly; "but please explain what you mean. I told you not to buy in the Green Swash Mine, and now I suppose you have gone and done it, because I said it might possibly be active some day."

"I have been to see the Countess this morning," said the Duke, beating the dust from his thick walking-boot with his cane.

"Ah!" said Barker, without any show of interest. "Was she at home?"

"I should think so," said the Duke. "Very much at home, and Dr. Claudius was there too."

"Oh! so you are jealous of Claudius, are you?" The ducal wrath rose.

"Barker, you are insufferably ridiculous."

"Duke, you had much better go to bed," returned his friend.

"Look here, Barker—"

"Do not waste your vitality in that way," said the American. "I wish I had half of it. It quite pains me to see you. Now I will put the whole thing clearly before you as I suppose it happened, and you shall tell me if it is my fault or not, and whether, after all, it is such a very serious matter. Countess Margaret did not know that Claudius was going, and did not speak of the trip. Claudius thought she was angry, and when you arrived and let the cat out of the bag the Countess thought you were trying to amuse yourself by surprising her, and she was angry too. Then they both made common cause and would have nothing more to do with you, and told you to go to the devil, and at this moment they are planning to remain here for the next forty or fifty years, and are sending off a joint telegram to Professor Immanuel Spencer, or whatever his name is, to hurry up and get some more books ready for them to read. I am glad you have not bought Green Swash, though, really." There was a pause, and the Duke glared savagely at the cigar-box.

"Is your serene highness satisfied that I know all about it?" asked Barker at last.

"No, I am not. And I am not serene. She says she will go, and Claudius says he won't. And it is entirely your fault."

"It is not of any importance what he says, or whether it is my fault or not. If you had bestirred yourself to go and see her at eleven before Claudius arrived it would not have happened. But he will go all the same; never fear. And the Countess will persuade him too, without our doing anything in the matter."

"You would not have thought so if you had seen the way she received the news that he was invited," grumbled the Duke.

"If you associated more with women you would understand them better," replied the other.

"I dare say." The Englishman was cooler, and at last made up his mind to take one of Mr. Barker's cigars. When he had lit it, he looked across at his friend. "How do you expect to manage it?" he inquired.

"If you will write a simple little note to the Countess, and say you are sorry there should have been any misunderstanding, and if you and I leave those two to themselves for ten days, even if she invites us to dinner, they will manage it between them, depend upon it. They are in love, you know perfectly well."

"I suppose they are," said the Duke, as if he did not understand that kind of thing. "I think I will have some curaçao and potass;" and he rang the bell.

"That's not half a bad idea," he said when he was refreshed. "I begin to think you are not so idiotic as I supposed."

"Waal," said Barker, suddenly affecting the accents of his native shore, "I ain't much on the drivel this journey anyhow." The Duke laughed; he always laughed at Americanisms.

"I guess so," said the Duke, trying ineffectually to mimic his friend. Then he went on in his natural voice, "I have an idea."

"Keep it," said Barker; "they are scarce."

"No; seriously. If we must leave them alone, why—why should we not go down and look at the yacht?"

"Not bad at all. As you say, we might go round and see how she looks. Where is she?"

"Nice."

So the one went down and the other went round, but they went together, and saw the yacht, and ran over to Monte Carlo, and had a good taste of the dear old green-table, now that they could not have it in Baden any longer. And they enjoyed the trip, and were temperate and well dressed and cynical, after their kind. But Claudius stayed where he was.

CHAPTER VII

The daily reading proceeded as usual after Barker's departure, but neither Margaret nor Claudius mentioned the subject of the voyage. Margaret was friendly, and sometimes seemed on the point of relapsing into her old manner, but she always checked herself. What the precise change was it would be hard to say. Claudius knew it was very easy to feel the difference, but impossible to define it. As the days passed, he knew also that his life had ceased to be his own; and, with the chivalrous wholeness of purpose that was his nature, he took his soul and laid it at her feet, for better for worse, to do with as she would. But he knew the hour was not come yet wherein he should speak; and so he served her in silence, content to feel the tree of life growing within him, which should one day overshadow them both with its sheltering branches. His service was none the less whole and devoted because it had not yet been accepted.

One evening, nearly a week after they had been left to themselves, Claudius was sitting over his solitary dinner in the casino restaurant when a note was brought to him, a large square envelope of rough paper, and he knew the handwriting. He hesitated to open it, and, glancing round the brilliantly-lighted restaurant, involuntarily wondered if any man at all those tables were that moment in such suspense as he. He thought it was probably an intimation that she was going away, and that he was wanted no longer. Then, for the first time in many days, he thought of his money. "And if she does," he said half aloud, "shall I not follow? Shall not gold command everything save her heart, and can I not win that for myself?" And he took courage and quietly opened the note.

"MY DEAR DR. CLAUDIUS—As the time is approaching, will you not do me a favour? I want you to make a list of books to read on the voyage—that is, if I may count on your kindness as an expounder. If not, please tell me of some good novels.

"Sincerely yours,"

—and her full name signed at the end. The hot blood turned his white forehead red as Claudius finished reading. He could not believe his eyes, and the room swam for a moment; for he was very much in love, this big Swede. Then he grew pale again and quite calm, and read the note over. Novels indeed! What did he know about novels? He would ask her plainly if she wanted his company on the yacht or no. He would say, "Shall I come? or shall I stay behind?" Claudius had much to learn from Mr. Barker before he was competent to deal with women. But then Claudius would have scorned the very expression "to deal" with them; theirs to command, his to obey—there was to be no question of dealing. Only in his simple heart he would like to know in so many words what the commands were; and that is sometimes a little hard, for women like to be half understood before they speak, and the grosser intellect of man seldom more than half understands them after they have spoken.

A note requires an answer, and Claudius made the usual number of failures. When one has a great deal more to say than one has any right to say, and when at the same time one is expected to say particularly little, it is very hard to write a good note. All sorts of ideas creep in and express themselves automatically. A misplaced plural for a singular, a superlative adjective where the vaguer comparative belongs; the vast and immeasurable waste of weary years that may lie between "dear" and "dearest," the gulf placed between "sincerely yours, John Smith," and "yours, J.S.," and "your J.," until the blessed state is reached wherein the signature is omitted altogether, and every word bears the sign-manual of the one woman or one man who really exists for you. What a registering thermometer of intimacy exists in notes, from the icy zero of first acquaintance to the raging throb of boiling blood-heat! So Claudius, after many trials, arrived at the requisite pitch of absolute severity, and began his note, "My dear Countess Margaret," and signed it, "very obediently yours," which said just what was literally true; and he stated that he would immediately proceed to carry out the Countess's commands, and make a list in which nothing should be wanting that could contribute to her amusement.

When he went to see her on the following day he was a little surprised at her manner, which inclined more to the severe coldness of that memorable day of difficulties than to the unbending he had expected from her note. Of course he had no reason to be disappointed, and he showed his inexperience. She was compensating her conscience for the concession she had made in intimating that he might go. It was indeed a concession, but to what superior power she had yielded it behoves not inquisitive man to ask. Perhaps she thought Claudius would enjoy the trip very much, and said to herself she had no right to make him give it up.

They read together for some time, and at last Claudius asked her, in connection with a point which arose, whether she would like to read a German book that he thought good.

"Very much," said she. "By the by, I am glad you have been able to arrange to go with us. I thought your engagements were going to prevent you."

Claudius looked at her, trying to read her thoughts, in which he failed. He might have been satisfied, but he was not. There was a short silence, and then he closed the book over his hand and spoke.

"Countess, do you wish me to go or not?"

Margaret raised her dark eyebrows. He had never seen her do that before. But then he had never said anything so clumsy before in his whole life, and he knew it the moment the words were out of his mouth, and his face was white in sunshine. She looked at him suddenly, a slight smile on her lips, and her eyes just the least contracted, as if she were going to say something sarcastic. But his face was so pitifully pale. She saw how his hand trembled. A great wave of womanly compassion welled up in her soul, and the smile faded and softened away as she said one word.

"Yes." It came from the heart, and she could not help it if it sounded kindly.

"Then I will go," said Claudius, hardly knowing what he said, for the blood came quickly back to his face.

"Of course you will, I could have told you that ever so long ago," chirped a little bullfinch in the tree overhead.

A couple of weeks or more after the events last chronicled, the steam yacht Streak was two days out on the Atlantic, with a goodly party on board. There were three ladies—the Duke's sister, the Countess, and Miss Skeat, the latter looking very nautical in blue serge, which sat tightly over her, like the canvas cover sewn round a bicycle when it is sent by rail. Of men there were also three—to wit, the owner of the yacht, Mr. Barker, and Dr. Claudius.

The sea has many kinds of fish. Some swim on their sides, some swim straight, some come up to take a sniff of air, and some stay below. It is just the same with people who go to sea. Take half a dozen individuals who are all more or less used to the water, and they will behave in half a dozen different ways. One will become encrusted to the deck like a barnacle, another will sit in the cabin playing cards; a third will spend his time spinning yarns with the ship's company, and a fourth will rush madly up and down the deck from morning till night in the pursuit of an appetite which shall leave no feat of marine digestion untried or unaccomplished. Are they not all stamped on the memory of them that go down to the sea in yachts? The little card-box and the scoring-book of the players, the deck chair and rugs of the inveterate reader, the hurried tread and irascible eye of the carnivorous passenger, and the everlasting pipe of the ocean talker, who feels time before him and the world at his feet wherein to spin yarns—has any one not seen them?

Now, the elements on board of the Streak were sufficiently diverse to form a successful party, and by the time they were two days out on the long swell, with a gentle breeze just filling the trysails, and everything stowed, they had each fallen into the groove of sea life that was natural to him or to her. There were Barker and the Duke in the pretty smoking-room forward with the windows open and a pack of cards between them. Every now and then they stopped to chat a little, or the Duke would go out and look at the course, and make his rounds to see that every one was all right and nobody sea-sick. But Barker rarely moved, save to turn his chair and cross one leg over the other, whereby he might the more easily contemplate his little patent leather shoes and stroke his bony hands over his silk-clad ankles; for Mr. Barker considered sea-dressing, as he called it, a piece of affectation, and arrayed himself on board ship precisely as he did on land. The Duke, on the other hand, like most Englishmen when they get a chance, revelled in what he considered ease; that is to say, no two of his garments matched or appeared to have been made in the same century; he wore a flannel shirt, and was inclined to go about barefoot when the ladies were not on deck, and he adorned his ducal forehead with a red worsted cap, price one shilling.

Margaret, as was to be expected, was the deck member, with her curiously-wrought chair and her furs and her portable bookcase; while Miss Skeat, who looked tall and finny, and sported a labyrinthine tartan, was generally to be seen entangled in the weather-shrouds near by. As for the Duke's sister, Lady Victoria, she was plain, but healthy, and made regular circuits of the steamer, stopping every now and then to watch the green swirl of the foam by the side, and to take long draughts of salt air into her robust lungs. But of all the party there was not one on whom the change from the dry land to the leaping water produced more palpable results than on Claudius. He affected nothing nautical in dress or speech, but when the Duke saw him come on deck the first morning out, there was something about his appearance that made the yachtsman say to Barker—

"That man has been to sea, I am positive. I am glad I asked him."

"All those Swedes are amphibious," replied Barker; "they take to the water like ducks. But I don't believe he has smelled salt water for a dozen years."

"They are the best sailors, at all events," said the Duke. "I have lots of them among the men. Captain a Swede too. Let me introduce you." They were standing on the bridge. "Captain Sturleson, my friend Mr. Barker." And so in turn the captain was made known to every one on board; for he was an institution with the Duke, and had sailed his Grace's yachts ever since there had been any to sail, which meant for about twenty years. To tell the truth, if it were not for those beastly logarithms, the Duke was no mean sailing-master himself, and he knew a seaman when he saw one; hence his remark about Claudius. The Doctor knew every inch of the yacht and every face in the ship's company by the second day, and it amused the Countess to hear his occasional snatches of the clean-cut Northern tongue that sounded like English, but was yet so different.

Obedient to her instructions, he had provided books of all sorts for the voyage, and they began to read together, foolishly imagining that, with the whole day at their disposal, they would do as much work as when they only met for an hour or two daily to accomplish a set purpose. The result of their unbounded freedom was that conversation took the place of reading. Hitherto Margaret had confined Claudius closely to the matter in hand, some instinct warning her that such an intimacy as had existed during his daily visits could only continue on the footing of severe industry she had established from the first. But the sight of the open deck, the other people constantly moving to and fro, the proper aspect of the lady-companion, just out of earshot, and altogether the appearance of publicity which the sea-life lent to their tête-à-tête hours, brought, as a necessary consequence, a certain unbending. It always seemed such an easy matter to call some third party into the conversation if it should grow too confidential. And so, insensibly, Claudius and Margaret wandered into discussions about the feelings, about love, hate, and friendship, and went deep into those topics which so often end in practical experiment. Claudius had lived little and thought much; Margaret had seen a great deal of the world, and being gifted with fine intuitions and tact, she had reasoned very little about what she saw, understanding, as she did, the why and wherefore of most actions by the pure light of feminine genius. The Doctor theorised, and it interested his companion to find facts she remembered suddenly brought directly under a neat generalisation; and before long she found herself trying to remember facts to fit his theories, a mode of going in double harness which is apt to lead to remarkable but fallacious results. In the intervals of theorising Claudius indulged in small experiments. But Barker and the Duke played poker.

Of course the three men saw a good deal of each other—in the early morning before the ladies came on deck, and late at night when they sat together in the smoking-room. In these daily meetings the Duke and Claudius had become better acquainted, and the latter, who was reticent, but perfectly simple, in speaking of himself, had more than once alluded to his peculiar position and to the unexpected change of fortune that had befallen him. One evening they were grouped as usual around the square table in the brightly-lighted little room that Barker and the Duke affected most. The fourfold beat of the screw crushed the water quickly and sent its peculiar vibration through the vessel as she sped along in the quiet night. The Duke was extended on a transom, and Claudius on the one opposite, while Barker tipped himself about on his chair at the end of the table. The Duke was talkative, in a disjointed, monosyllabic fashion.

"Yes. I know. No end of a queer sensation, lots of money. Same thing happened to me when I came of age."

"Not exactly the same thing," said Claudius; "you knew you were going to have it."

"No," put in Barker. "Having money and being likely to have it are about the same as far as spending it goes. Particularly in England."

"I believe the whole thing is a fraud," said the Duke in a tone of profound reflection. "Never had a cent before I came of age. Seems to me I never had any since."

"Spent it all in water-melon and fire-crackers, celebrating your twenty-first birthday, I suppose," suggested Barker.

"Spent it some way, at all events," replied the Duke. "Now, here," he continued, addressing Barker, "is a man who actually has it, who never expected to have it, who has got it in hard cash, and in the only way in which it is worth having—by somebody else's work. Query—what will Claudius do with his millions?" Exhausted by this effort of speech, the Duke puffed his tobacco in silence, waiting for an answer. Claudius laughed, but said nothing.

"I know of one thing he will do with his money. He will get married," said Barker.

"For God's sake, Claudius," said the Duke, looking serious, "don't do that."

"I don't think I will," said Claudius.

"I know better," retorted Barker, "I am quite sure I shall do it myself some day, and so will you. Do you think if I am caught, you are going to escape?"

The Duke thought that if Barker knew the Duchess, he might yet save himself.

"You are no chicken, Barker, and perhaps you are right. If they catch you they can catch anybody," he said aloud.

"Well, I used to say the mamma was not born who could secure me. But I am getting old, and my nerves are shaken, and a secret presentiment tells me I shall be bagged before long, and delivered over to the tormentors."

"I pity you if you are," said the Duke. "No more poker, and very little tobacco then."

"Not as bad as that. You are as much married as most men, but it does not interfere with the innocent delights of your leisure hours, that I can see."

"Ah, well—you see—I am pretty lucky. The Duchess is a domestic type of angel. Likes children and bric-à-brac and poultry, and all those things. Takes no end of trouble about the place."

"Why should not I marry the angelic domestic—the domestic angel, I mean?"

"You won't, though. Doesn't grow in America. I know the sort of woman you will get for your money."

"Give me an idea." Barker leaned back in his chair till it touched the door of the cabin, and rolled his cigar in his mouth.

"Of course she will be the rage for the time. Eighteen or nineteen summers of earthly growth, and eighteen or nineteen hundred years of experience and calculation in a former state."

"Thanks, that sounds promising. Claudius, this is intended for your instruction."

"You will see her first at a ball, with a cartload of nosegays slung on her arms, and generally all over her. That will be your first acquaintance; you will never see the last of her."

"No—I know that," said Barker gloomily.

"She will marry you out of hand after a three months' engagement. She will be married by Worth, and you will be married by Poole. It will be very effective, you know. No end of wedding presents, and acres of flowers. And then you will start away on your tour, and be miserable ever after."

"I am glad you have done," was Barker's comment.

"As for me," said Claudius, "I am of course not acquainted with the peculiarities of American life, but I fancy the Duke is rather severe in his judgment."

It was a mild protest against a wholesale condemnation of American marriages; but Barker and the Duke only laughed as if they understood each other, and Claudius had nothing more to say. He mentally compared the utterances of these men, doubtless grounded on experience, with the formulas he had made for himself about women, and which were undeniably the outcome of pure theory. He found himself face to face with the old difficulty, the apparent discord between the universal law and the individual fact. But, on the other hand, he could not help comparing himself with his two companions. It was not in his nature to think slightingly of other men, but he felt that they were of a totally different mould, besides belonging to a different race. He knew that however much he might enjoy their society, they had nothing in common with him, and that it was only his own strange fortune that had suddenly transported him into the very midst of a sphere where such characters were the rule and not the exception.

The conversation languished, and Claudius left the Duke and Barker, and went towards his quarters. It was a warm night for the Atlantic, and though there was no moon, the stars shone out brightly, their reflection moving slowly up and down the slopes of the long ocean swell. Claudius walked aft, and was going to sit down for a few minutes before turning in, when he was suddenly aware of a muffled female figure leaning against the taffrail only a couple of paces from where he was. In spite of the starlight he could not distinguish the person. She was wrapped closely in a cloak and veil, as if fearing the cold. As it must be one of the three ladies who constituted the party, Claudius naturally raised his cap, but fearing lest he had chanced on the Duke's sister, or still worse, on Miss Skeat, he did not speak. Before long, however, as he leaned against the side, watching the wake, the unknown remarked that it was a delightful night. It was Margaret's voice, and the deep musical tones trembled on the rise and fall of the waves, as if the sounds themselves had a distinct life and beating in them. Did the dark woman know what magic lay in her most trivial words? Claudius did not care a rush whether the night were beautiful or otherwise, but when she said it was a fine evening, it sounded as if she had said she loved him.

"I could not stay downstairs," she said, "and so when the others went to bed I wrapped myself up and came here. Is it not too wonderful?"

Claudius moved nearer to her.

"I have been pent up in the Duke's tabagie for at least two hours," he said, "and I am perfectly suffocated."

"How can you sit in that atmosphere? Why don't you come and smoke on deck?"

"Oh! it was not only the tobacco that suffocated me to-night, it was the ideas."

"What ideas?" asked Margaret.

"You have known the Duke a long time," said he, "and of course you can judge. Or rather, you know. But to hear those two men talk is enough to make one think there is neither heaven above nor hell beneath." He was rather incoherent.

"Have they been attacking your favourite theories," Margaret asked, and she smiled behind her veil; but he could not see that, and her voice sounded somewhat indifferent.

"Oh! I don't know," he said, as if not wanting to continue the subject; and he turned round so as to rest his elbows on the taffrail. So he stood, bent over and looking away astern at the dancing starlight on the water. There was a moment's silence.

"Tell me," said Margaret at last.

"What shall I tell you, Countess?" asked Claudius.

"Tell me what it was you did not like about their talk."

"It is hard to say, exactly. They were talking about women, and American marriages; and I did not like it, that is all." Claudius straightened himself again and turned towards his companion. The screw below them rushed round, worming its angry way through the long quiet waves.

"Barker," said Claudius, "was saying that he supposed he would be married some day—delivered up to torture, as he expressed it—and the Duke undertook to prophesy and draw a picture of Barker's future spouse. The picture was not attractive."

"Did Mr. Barker think so too?"

"Yes. He seemed to regard the prospects of matrimony from a resigned and melancholy point of view. I suppose he might marry any one he chose in his own country, might he not?"

"In the usual sense, yes," answered Margaret.

"What is the 'usual sense'?" asked the Doctor.

"He might marry beauty, wealth, and position. That is the usual meaning of marrying whom you please."

"Oh! then it does not mean any individual he pleases?"

"Certainly not. It means that out of half a dozen beautiful, rich, and accomplished girls it is morally certain that one, at least, would take him for his money, his manners, and his accomplishments."

"Then he would go from one to the other until he was accepted? A charming way of doing things, upon my word!" And Claudius sniffed the night air discontentedly.

"Oh no," said Margaret. "He will be thrown into the society of all six, and one of them will marry him, that will be the way of it."

"I cannot say I discover great beauty in that social arrangement either, except that it gives the woman the choice."

"Of course," she answered, "the system does not pretend to the beautiful, it only aspires to the practical. If the woman is satisfied with her choice, domestic peace is assured." She laughed.

"Why cannot each satisfy himself or herself of the other? Why cannot the choice be mutual?"

"It would take too long," said she; and laughed again.

"Very long?" asked Claudius, trying not to let his voice change. But it changed nevertheless.

"Generally very long," she answered in a matter-of-fact way.

"Why should it?"

"Because neither women nor men are so easily understood as a chapter of philosophy," said she.

"Is it not the highest pleasure in life, that constant, loving study of the one person one loves? Is not every anticipated thought and wish a triumph more worth living for than everything else in the wide world?" He moved close to her side. "Do you not think so too?" She said nothing.

"I think so," he said. "There is no pleasure like the pleasure of trying to understand what a woman wants; there is no sorrow like the sorrow of failing to do that; and there is no glory like the glory of success. It is a divine task for any man, and the greatest have thought it worthy of them." Still she was silent; and so was he for a little while, looking at her side face, for she had thrown back the veil and her delicate profile showed clearly against the sea foam.

"Countess," he said at last; and his voice came and went fitfully with the breeze—"I would give my whole life's strength and study for the gladness of foreseeing one little thing that you might wish, and of doing it for you." His hand stole along the taffrail till it touched hers, but he did not lift his fingers from the polished wood.

"Dr. Claudius, you would give too much," she said; for the magic of the hour and place was upon her, and the Doctor's earnest tones admitted of no laughing retort. She ought to have checked him then, and the instant she had spoken she knew it; but before she could speak again he had taken the hand he was already touching between both of his, and was looking straight in her face.

"Margaret, I love you with all my soul and heart and strength." Her hand trembled in his, but she could not take it away. Before she had answered he had dropped to his knee and was pressing the gloved fingers to his lips.

"I love you, I love you, I love you," he repeated, and his strength was as the strength of ten in that moment.

"Dr. Claudius," said she at last, in a broken and agitated way, "you ought not to have said this. It was not right of you." She tried to loose her hand, but he rose to his feet still clasping it.

"Forgive me," he said, "forgive me!" His face was almost luminously pale. "All the ages cannot take from me this—that I have told you."

Margaret said never a word, but covered her head with her veil and glided noiselessly away, leaving Claudius with his white face and staring eyes to the contemplation of what he had done. And she went below and sat in her stateroom and tried to think it all over. She was angry, she felt sure. She was angry at Claudius and half angry at herself—at least she thought so. She was disappointed, she said, in the man, and she did not mean to forgive him. Besides, in a yacht, with a party of six people, where there was absolutely no escape possible, it was unpardonable. He really ought not to have done it. Did he think—did he flatter himself—that if she had expected he was going to act just like all the rest of them she would have treated him as she had? Did he fancy his well-planned declaration would flatter her? Could he not see that she wanted to consider him always as a friend, that she thought she had found at last what she had so often dreamed of—a friendship proof against passion? It was so common, so commonplace. It was worse, for it was taking a cruel advantage of the narrow limits within which they were both confined. Besides, he had taken advantage of her kindness to plan a scene which he knew would surprise her out of herself. She ought to have spoken strongly and sharply and made him suffer for his sin while he was yet red-handed. And instead, what had she done? She had merely said very meekly that "it was not right," and had sought safety in a hasty retreat.

She sighed wearily, and began to shake out the masses of her black hair, that was as the thickness of night spun fine. And as she drew out the thick tortoise-shell pins that bore it up, it rolled down heavily in a soft dark flood and covered her as with a garment. Then she leaned back and sighed again, and her eyes fell on a book that lay at the corner of her dressing-table, where she had left it before dinner. It was the book they had been reading, and the mark was a bit of fine white cord that Claudius had cunningly twisted and braided, sailor fashion, to keep the place. Margaret rose to her feet, and taking the book in her hand, looked at it a moment without opening it. Then she hid it out of sight and sat down again. The action had been almost unconscious, but now she thought about it, and she did not like what she had done. Angry with him and with herself, she was yet calm enough to ask why she could not bear the sight of the volume on the table. Was it possible she had cared enough about her friendship for the Doctor to be seriously distressed at its sudden termination? She hardly knew—perhaps so. So many men had made love to her, none had ever before seemed to be a friend.

The weary and hard-worked little sentiment that we call conscience spoke up. Was she just to him? No. If she had cared even as much as that action showed, had he no right to care also? He had the right, yes; but he had been wanting in tact. He should have waited till they were ashore. Poor fellow! he looked so white, and his hands were so cold. Was he there still, looking out at the ship's wake? Margaret, are you quite sure you never thought of him save as a friendly professor who taught you philosophy? And there was a little something that would not be silenced, and that would say—Yes, you are playing tricks with your feelings, you care for him, you almost love him. And for a moment there was a fierce struggle in the brave heart of that strong woman as she shook out her black hair and turned pale to the lips. She rose again, and went and got the book she had hidden, and laid it just where it had lain before. Then she knew, and she bowed her head till her white forehead touched the table before her, and her hands were wet as they pressed her eyelids.

"I am very weak," she said aloud, and proceeded with her toilet.

"But you will be kind to him, Margaret," said the little voice in her heart, as she laid her head on the pillow.

"But it is my duty to be cold. I do not love him," she argued, as the watch struck eight bells.

Poor Saint Duty! what a mess you make of human kindness!

Claudius was still on deck, and a wretched man he was, as his chilled hands clung to the side. He knew well enough that she was angry, though she had reproached herself with not having made it clear to him. He said to himself he ought not to have spoken, and then he laughed bitterly, for he knew that all his strength could not have kept back the words, because they were true, and because the truth must be spoken sooner or later. He was hopeless now for a time, but he did not deceive himself.

"I am not weak. I am strong. And if my love is stronger than I what does that prove? I am glad it is, and I would not have it otherwise. It is done now and can never be undone. I am sorry I spoke to-night. I would have waited if I could. But I could not, and I should despise myself if I could. Love that is not strong enough to make a man move in spite of himself is not worth calling love. I wonder if I flattered myself she loved me? No, I am quite sure I did not. I never thought anything about it. It is enough for me that I love her, and live, and have told her so; and I can bear all the misery now, for she knows. I suppose it will begin at once. She will not speak to me. No, not that, but she will not expect me to speak to her. I will keep out of her way; it is the least I can do. And I will try and not make her life on board disagreeable. Ah, my beloved, I will never hurt you again or make you angry."

He said these things over and over to himself, and perhaps they comforted him a little. At eight bells the Swedish captain turned out, and Claudius saw him ascend the bridge, but soon he came down again and walked aft.

"God afton, Captain," said Claudius.

"It is rather late to say good evening, Doctor," replied the sailor.

"Why, what time is it?"

"Midnight."

"Well, I shall turn in."

"If you will take my advice," said the captain, "you won't leave any odds and ends lying about to-night. We shall have a dance before morning."

"Think so?" said Claudius indifferently.

"Why, Doctor, where are your eyes? You are a right Svensk sailor when you are awake. You have smelled the foam in Skager Rak as well as I."

"Many a time," replied the other, and looked to windward. It was true; the wind had backed to the north-east, and there was an angry little cross sea beginning to run over the long ocean swell. There was a straight black belt below the stars, and a short, quick splashing, dashing, and breaking of white crests through the night, while the rising breeze sang in the weather rigging.

Claudius turned away and went below. He took the captain's advice, and secured his traps and went to bed. But he could not sleep, and he said over and over to himself that he loved her, that he was glad he had told her so, and that he would stand by the result of his night's work, through all time,—ay, and beyond time.

CHAPTER VIII

Lady Victoria was not afraid of the sea. No indeed, and if her brother would go with her she would like nothing better. And Miss Skeat, too, would she like to come? Such a pity poor Margaret had a headache. She had not even come to breakfast.

Yes, Miss Skeat would come, and the boatswain would provide them both with tarpaulins and sou'-westers, and they would go on deck for a few minutes. But Mr. Barker was so sorry he had a touch of neuralgia, and besides he knew that Claudius was on deck and would be of more use to the ladies than he could ever be. Mr. Barker had no idea of getting wet, and the sudden headache of the Countess, combined with the absence of Claudius from her side, interested him. He meant to stay below and watch the events of the morning. Piloted by the Duke, the strong English girl and the wiry old Scotch lady made their way up the companion, not without difficulty, for the skipper's prediction was already fulfilled, and the Streak was ploughing her way through all sorts of weather at once.

The deck was slippery and sloppy, and the sharp spray was blowing itself in jets round every available corner. The sky was of an even lead colour, but it was hard to tell at first whether it was raining or not. The Duke's face gleamed like a wet red apple in the wind and water as he helped his sister to the leeward and anchored her among the shrouds.

"Hullo, Claudius, you seem to like this!" he sang out, spying the tall Swede near the gangway. Claudius came towards them, holding on by the pins and cleats and benches. He looked so white that Lady Victoria was frightened.

"You are not well, Dr. Claudius. Please don't mind me, my brother will be back in a moment. Go below and get warm. You really look ill."

"Do I? I do not feel ill at all. I am very fond of this kind of weather." And he put one arm through the shrouds and prepared for conversation under difficulties. Meanwhile the Duke brought out Miss Skeat, who rattled inside her tarpaulin, but did not exhibit the slightest nervousness, though a bit of a sea broke over the weather-bow just as she appeared.

"Keep your eye peeled there, will you?" the Duke shouted away to the men at the wheel; whereat they grinned, and luffed a little, just enough to let the lady get across.

"Steady!" bawled the Duke again when Miss Skeat was made fast; and the men at the wheel held her off once more, so that the spray flew up in a cloudy sheet.

Claudius was relieved. He had expected to see Margaret come up the companion, and he had dreaded the meeting, when he would almost of necessity be obliged to help her across and touch her hand; and he inwardly blessed her wisdom in staying below. The others might have stayed there too, he thought, instead of coming up to get wet and to spoil his solitude, which was the only thing left to him to-day.

But Claudius was not the man to betray his ill-temper at being disturbed; and after all there was something about these two women that he liked—in different ways. The English girl was so solidly enthusiastic, and the Scotch gentlewoman so severely courageous, that he felt a sort of companionable sympathy after he had been with them a few minutes.

Lady Victoria, as previously hinted, was married, and her husband, who was in the diplomatic service, and who had prospects afterwards of coming into money and a peerage, was now absent on a distant mission. They had not been married very long, but his wife was always ready to take things cheerfully, and, since she could not accompany him, she had made up her mind to be happy without him; and the trip with her brother was "just the very thing." Mr. Barker admired what he called her exuberant vitality, and expressed his opinion that people with a digestion like that were always having a good time. She was strong and healthy, and destined to be the mother of many bold sons, and she had a certain beauty born of a good complexion, bright eyes, and white teeth. To look at her, you would have said she must be the daughter of some robust and hardworking settler, accustomed from her youth to face rain and snow and sunshine in ready reliance on her inborn strength. She did not suggest dukes and duchesses in the least. Alas! the generation of those ruddy English boys and girls is growing rarer day by day, and a mealy-faced, over-cerebrated people are springing up, who with their children again, in trying to rival the brain-work of foreigners with larger skulls and more in them, forget that their English forefathers have always done everything by sheer strength and bloodshed, and can as easily hope to accomplish anything by skill as a whale can expect to dance upon the tight rope. They would do better, thought Lady Victoria, to give it up, to abandon the struggle for intellectual superiority of that kind. They have produced greater minds when, the mass of their countrymen were steeped in brutality, and Elizabethan surfeit of beef and ale, than they will ever produce with a twopenny-halfpenny universal education. What is the use? Progress. What is progress? Merely the adequate arrangement of inequalities—in the words of one of their own thinkers who knows most about it and troubles himself least about theories. What is the use of your "universal" education, to which nine-tenths of the population submit as to a hopeless evil, which takes bread out of their mouths and puts bran into their heads; for might they not be at work in the fields instead of scratching pothooks on a slate? At least so Lady Victoria thought.

"You look just like a sailor," said she to Claudius.

"I feel like one," he answered, "and I think I shall adopt the sea as a profession."

"It is such a pity," said Miss Skeat, sternly clutching the twisted wire shroud. "I would like to see you turn pirate; it would be so picturesque—you and Mr. Barker." The others laughed, not at the idea of Claudius sporting the black flag—for he looked gloomy enough to do murder in the first degree this morning—but the picture of the exquisite and comfort-loving Mr. Barker, with his patent-leather shoes and his elaborate travelling apparatus, leading a band of black-browed ruffians to desperate deeds of daring and blood, was novel enough to be exhilarating; and they laughed loudly. They did not understand Mr. Barker; but perhaps Miss Skeat, who liked him with an old-maidenly liking, had some instinct notion that the gentle American could be dangerous.

"Mr. Barker would never do for a pirate," laughed Lady Victoria; "he would be always getting his feet wet and having attacks of neuralgia."

"Take care, Vick," said her brother, "he might hear you."

"Well, if he did? I only said he would get his feet wet. There is no harm in that, and it is clear he has neuralgia, because he says it himself."

"Well, of course," said the Duke, "if that is what you mean. But he will wet his feet fast enough when there is any good reason."

"If you make it 'worth his while,' of course," said Lady Victoria, "I have no doubt of it." She turned up her nose, for she was not very fond of Mr. Barker, and she thought poorly of the Duke's financial enterprises in America. It was not a bit like a good old English gentleman to be always buying and selling mines and stocks and all sorts of things with queer names.

"Look here, Vick, we won't talk any more about Barker, if you please."

"Very well, then you can talk about the weather," said she.

"Yes," said Claudius, "you may well do that. There is a good deal of weather to talk about."

"Oh, I like a storm at sea, of all things!" exclaimed Lady Victoria, forgetting all about Mr. Barker in the delicious sense of saltness and freedom one feels on the deck of a good ship running through a lively sea. She put out her face to catch the fine salt spray on her cheek. Just then a little water broke over the side abaft the gangway, and the vessel rose and fell to the sweep of a big wave. The water ran along over the flush deck, as if hunting for the scuppers, and came swashing down to the lee where the party were standing, wetting the ladies' feet to the ankle. The men merely pulled themselves up by the ropes they held, and hung till the deck was clear again.

"I don't suppose it hurts you to get wet," said the Duke to his sister, "but you would be much better under hatches while this sort of thing is going on."

"I think, if you will help me, I will go down and see how the Countess is," said Miss Skeat; and Claudius detached her from the rigging and got her down the companion, but the Duke stayed with his sister, who begged for a few minutes more. Once below, Claudius felt how near he was to Margaret, who was doubtless in the ladies' cabin. He could reach his own quarters without entering that sanctum, of course, but as he still held Miss Skeat's arm to steady her to the door, he could not resist the temptation of putting his head through, for he knew now that she must be there. It was a large sitting-room, extending through the whole beam, with big port-holes on each side. Miss Skeat entered, and Claudius looked in.

There was Margaret, looking much as usual, her face turned a little from him as she lay in a huge arm-chair. She could not see him as she was, and his heart beat furiously as he looked at the face he loved best of all others.

Margaret spoke to Miss Skeat without turning her head, for she was working at some of her eternal needlework.

"Have you had a good time? How did you get down?"

"Such an airing," answered the lady-companion, who was divesting herself of her wraps, "and Dr Claudius—"

The last was lost to the Doctor's ear, for he withdrew his head and beat a hasty retreat. Miss Skeat also stopped speaking suddenly, for as she mentioned his name she looked naturally towards the door, supposing him to be standing there, and she just saw his head disappear from between the curtains. Margaret turned her eyes and saw Miss Skeat's astonishment.

"Well, what about Dr. Claudius?" she asked.

"Oh, nothing," said Miss Skeat, "you asked me how I got down, and I was going to say Dr. Claudius gave me his arm, and I thought he had come in here with me."

Neither Miss Skeat nor Claudius had noticed Mr. Barker, who was ensconced on a corner transom, with his nails and a book to amuse himself with. He saw the whole thing: how the Doctor put his white face and dripping beard through the curtains, and suddenly withdrew it at the mention of his name, and how Miss Skeat held her peace about having seen it too. He reflected that something had happened, that Miss Skeat knew all about it, and that she was a discreet woman. He wondered what it could be. Claudius would not look like that unless something were wrong, he thought, and he would certainly come back in five minutes if everything were right. He had not seen him at breakfast. He took out his watch softly and let it drop on his book, face upwards. Meanwhile he talked to the two ladies about the weather, and listened to Miss Skeat's rapturous account of the spray and the general slipperiness of the upper regions. When five minutes were elapsed he put his watch back and said he thought he would try it himself, as he fancied the fresh air would do him good. So he departed, and obtained a pair of sea-boots and an oilskin, which he contemplated with disgust, and put on with resolution. He wanted to find the Duke, and he wanted to see Claudius; but he wanted them separately.

Mr. Barker cautiously put his head out of the cuddy door and espied the Duke and his sister. This was not exactly what he wanted, and he would have retired, but at that moment Lady Victoria caught sight of him, and immediately called out to him not to be afraid, as it was much smoother now. But Mr. Barker's caution had proceeded from other causes, and being detected, he put a bold face on it, stepped on the deck and slammed the door behind him. Lady Victoria was somewhat surprised to see him tread the slippery deck with perfect confidence and ease, for she thought he was something of a "duffer." But Barker knew how to do most things more or less, and he managed to bow and take off his sou'wester with considerable grace in spite of the rolling. Having obtained permission to smoke, he lighted a cigar, crooked one booted leg through the iron rail, and seated himself on the bulwark, where, as the steamer lurched, he seemed to be in a rather precarious position. But there was a sort of cat-like agility in his wiry frame, that bespoke unlimited powers of balancing and holding on.

"I thought there were more of you," he began, addressing Lady Victoria. "You seem to be having quite a nice time here."

"Yes."

"I wish I had come up sooner; the atmosphere downstairs is very oppressive."

"I thought you had neuralgia," said Lady Victoria.

"So I had. But that kind of neuralgia comes and goes very suddenly. Where is the giant of the North?"

"Dr. Claudius? He went down with Miss Skeat, and when he came up again he said he would go forward," answered she, giving the nautical pronunciation to the latter word.

"Oh, I see him," cried Barker, "there he is, just going up the bridge. By Jove! what a height he looks."

"Yes," put in the Duke, "he is rather oversparred for a nor'-easter, eh? Rather be your size, Barker, for reefing tawpsels;" and the Englishman laughed.

"Well," said Barker, "when I first knew him he used to wear a balustrade round his neck to keep from being dizzy. I wouldn't care to have to do that. I think I will go and have a look too." And leaving his companions to laugh at his joke, Mr. Barker glided easily from the rail, and began his journey to the bridge, which he accomplished without any apparent difficulty. When he had climbed the little ladder he waved his hand to the Duke and his sister, who screamed something complimentary in reply; and then he spoke to Claudius who was standing by the skipper, his legs far apart, and both his hands on the railing.

"Is that you, Barker?" asked Claudius; "you are well disguised this morning."

"Claudius," said the other, "what on earth is the row?" The captain was on the other side of the Doctor, and could not hear in the wind.

"What row?" asked Claudius. Barker knew enough of his friend by this time to be aware that roundabout methods of extracting information were less likely to be successful than a point-blank question.

"Don't pretend ignorance," said he. "You look like a ghost, you are so pale, and when you put your head through the curtains a quarter of an hour ago, I thought you were one. And you have not been near the Countess this morning, though you have never been away from her before since we weighed anchor. Now, something has happened, and if I can do anything, tell me, and I will do it, right away." It is a good old plan, that one of trying to satisfy one's curiosity under pretence of offering assistance. But Claudius did not trouble himself about such things; he wanted no help from any one, and never had; and if he meant to tell, nothing would prevent him, and if he did not mean to tell, no power would make him.

"Since you have found it out, Barker, something has happened, as you say; and thanks for your offer of help, but I cannot tell you anything more about it."

"I think you are unwise."

"Perhaps."

"I might help you a great deal, for I have some natural tact."

"Yes."

"Besides, you know I am as secret as the grave."

"Quite so."

"I introduced you to the Countess, too."

"I know it."

"And I should be very sorry indeed to think that my action should have had any evil consequences."

"I am sure you would."

"Then, my dear fellow, you must really take me a little more into your confidence, and let me help you," said Barker, in the tone of an injured man.

"Perhaps I ought," said Claudius.

"Then why will you not tell me what has happened now?"

"Because I won't," said Claudius, turning sharply on Barker, and speaking in a voice that seemed to make the railings shake. He was evidently on the point of losing his temper, and Barker repented him too late of his attempt to extract the required information. Now he changed his tone.

"Excuse me, Claudius, I did not mean to offend you."

"You did not offend me at all, Barker. But please—do not ask me any more questions about it." Claudius was perfectly calm again.

"No indeed, my dear fellow, I would not think of it;—and I don't seem to think that I should advise anybody else to," he added mentally. He made up his mind that it must be something very serious, or Claudius, who was so rarely excited, would hardly have behaved as he had done. He made a few remarks about the weather, which had certainly not improved since morning; and then, resolving that he would find out what was the matter before he was much older, he glided down the ladder and went aft. Lady Victoria had disappeared, and her brother was trying to light a short black pipe.

"Duke," Barker began, "what the deuce is the matter with Claudius this morning?"

"Don't know, I'm sure. My sister thinks it is very odd."

"Well, if you don't know, I don't either, but I can make a pretty good guess."

The Duke's vesuvian was sputtering in the spray and wind, and he got a good light before he answered.

"I'll take six to four he marries her, at all events."

"I don't go in for playing it as low down as that on my friends," said Barker virtuously, "or I would take you in hundreds. You must be crazy. Can't you see he has shown up and is sold? Bah! it's all over, as sure as you're born."

"Think that's it?" said the other, much interested. "You may be right. Glad you would not bet, anyhow."

"Of course that's it. The idiot has proposed to her here, on board, and she has refused him, and now he has to face the fury of the elements to keep out of her way."

"Upon my soul, it looks like it," said the Duke. "He won't stay on the bridge much longer if this lasts, though."

"You had best ask your sister," answered Barker. "Women always know those things first. What do you say to a game? It is beastly dirty weather to be on the deck watch." And so they pushed forward to the smoking-room, just before the bridge, and settled themselves for the day with a pack of cards and a box of cigars.

As Margaret had not put in an appearance at breakfast, which was a late and solid meal on board, and as there was no other regular congregation of the party until dinner, for each one lunched as he or she pleased, it was clear that the Countess and Claudius would not be brought together until the evening. Margaret was glad of this for various reasons, some definable and others vague. She felt that she must have misjudged Claudius a little, and she was glad to see that her exhibition of displeasure on the previous night had been sufficient to keep him away. Had he been as tactless as she had at first thought, he would surely have sought an early opportunity of speaking to her alone, and the rest of the party were so much used to seeing them spend their mornings together that such an opportunity would not have been lacking, had he wished it. And if he had misunderstood her words and manner—well, if he had not thought they were meant as a decisive check, he would have followed her there and then, last night, when she left him. She felt a little nervous about his future conduct, but for the present she was satisfied, and prepared herself for the inevitable meeting at dinner with a certain feeling of assurance. "For," said she, "I do not love him in the least, and why should I be embarrassed?"

Not so poor Claudius, who felt the blood leave his face and rush wildly to his heart, as he entered the saloon where the party were sitting down to dinner. The vessel was rolling heavily, for the sea was running high under the north-easter, and dinner would be no easy matter. He knew he must sit next to her and help her under all the difficulties that arise under the circumstances. It would have been easy, too, for them both to see that the eyes of the other four were upon them, had either of them suspected it. Claudius held himself up to the full of his great height and steadied every nerve of his body for the meeting. Margaret belonged to the people who do not change colour easily, and when she spoke, even the alert ear of Mr. Barker opposite could hardly detect the faintest change of tone. And yet she bore the burden of it, for she spoke first.

"How do you do, Dr. Claudius?"

"Thank you, well. I was sorry to hear you had a headache to-day. I hope you are better."

"Thanks, yes; much better." They all sat down, and it was over.

The conversation was at first very disjointed, and was inclined to turn on small jokes about the difficulty of dining at an angle of forty-five degrees. The weather was certainly much heavier than it had been in the morning, and the Duke feared they would have a longer passage than they had expected, but added that they would be better able to judge to-morrow at twelve. Claudius and Margaret exchanged a few sentences, with tolerable tact and indifference; but, for some occult reason, Mr. Barker undertook to be especially lively and amusing, and after the dinner was somewhat advanced he launched out into a series of stories and anecdotes which served very well to pass the time and to attract notice to himself. As Mr. Barker was generally not very talkative at table, though frequently epigrammatic, his sudden eloquence was calculated to engage the attention of the party. Claudius and Margaret were glad of the rattling talk that delivered them from the burden of saying anything especial, and they both laughed quite naturally at Barker's odd wit. They were grateful to him for what he did, and Claudius entertained some faint hope that he might go on in the same strain for the rest of the voyage. But Margaret pondered these things. She saw quickly that Barker had perceived that some embarrassment existed, and was spending his best strength in trying to make the meal a particularly gay one. But she could not understand how Barker could have found out that there was any difficulty. Had Claudius been making confidences? It would have been very foolish for him to do so, and besides, Claudius was not the man to make confidences. He was reticent and cold as a rule, and Barker had more than once confessed to the Countess that he knew very little of Claudius's previous history, because the latter "never talked," and would not always answer questions. So she came to the conclusion that Barker only suspected something, because the Doctor had not been with her during the day. And so she laughed, and Claudius laughed, and they were well satisfied to pay their social obolus in a little well-bred and well-assumed hilarity.

So the dinner progressed, in spite of the rolling and pitching; for there was a good deal of both, as the sea ran diagonally to the course, breaking on the starboard quarter. They had reached the dessert, and two at least of the party were congratulating themselves on the happy termination of the meal, when, just as the Duke was speaking, there was a heavy lurch, and a tremendous sea broke over their heads. Then came a fearful whirring sound that shook through every plate and timber and bulkhead, like the sudden running down of mammoth clock-work, lasting some twenty seconds; then everything was quiet again save the sea, and the yacht rolled heavily to and fro.

Every one knew that there had been a serious accident, but no one moved from the table. The Duke sat like a rock in his place and finished what he was saying, though no one noticed it. Miss Skeat clutched her silver fruit-knife till her knuckles shone again, and she set her teeth. Mr. Barker, who had a glass of wine in the "fiddle" before him, took it out when the sea struck and held it up steadily to save it from being spilled; and Lady Victoria, who was not the least ashamed of being startled, cried out—

"Goodness gracious!" and then sat holding to the table and looking at her brother.

Margaret and Claudius were sitting next each other on one side of the table. By one of those strange, sympathetic instincts, that only manifest themselves in moments of great danger, they did the same thing at the same moment. Claudius put out his left hand and Margaret her right, and those two hands met just below the table and clasped each other, and in that instant each turned round to the other and looked the other in the face. What that look told man knoweth not, but for one instant there was nothing in the world for Margaret but Claudius. As for him, poor man, he had long known that she was the whole world to him, his life and his death.

It was very short, and Margaret quickly withdrew her hand and looked away. The Duke was the first to speak.

"I do not think it is anything very serious," said he. "If you will all sit still, I will go and see what is the matter." He rose and left the saloon.

"I don't fancy there is any cause for anxiety," said Barker. "There has probably been some slight accident to the machinery, and we shall be off again in an hour. I think we ought to compliment the ladies on the courage they have shown; it is perfectly wonderful." And Mr. Barker smiled gently round the table. Lady Victoria was palpably scared and Miss Skeat was silent. As for Margaret, she was confused and troubled. The accident of her seizing Claudius's hand, as she had done, was a thousand times more serious than any accident to the ship. The Doctor could not help stealing a glance at her, but he chimed in with Barker in praising the coolness of all three ladies. Presently the Duke came back. He had been forward by a passage that led between decks to the engine-room, where he had met the captain. The party felt reassured as the ruddy face of their host appeared in the doorway.

"There is nothing to fear," he said cheerfully. "But it is a horrid nuisance, all the same."

"Tell us all about it," said Lady Victoria.

"Well—we have lost our means of locomotion. We have carried away our propeller."

"What are you going to do about it?" asked Barker.

"Do? There is nothing to be done. We must sail for it. I am dreadfully sorry."

"It is not your fault," said Claudius.

"Well, I suppose not. It happens even to big steamers."

"And shall we sail all the way to New York?" asked his sister, who was completely reassured. "I think it will be lovely." Miss Skeat also thought sailing much more poetic than steaming.

"I think we must hold a council of war," said the master. "Let us put it to the vote. Shall we make for Bermuda, which is actually nearer, but which is four or five days' from New York, or shall we go straight and take our chance of a fair wind?"

"If you are equally willing to do both, why not let the ladies decide?" suggested Barker.

"Oh no," broke in the Countess, "it will be much more amusing to vote. We will write on slips of paper and put them in a bag."

"As there are five of you I will not vote," said the Duke, "for we might be three on a side, you know."

So they voted, and there were three votes for New York and two for Bermuda.

"New York has it," said the Duke, who counted, "and I am glad, on the whole, for it is Sturleson's advice." Barker had voted for New York, and he wondered who the two could have been who wanted to go to Bermuda. Probably Miss Skeat and Lady Victoria. Had the Countess suspected that those two would choose the longer journey and out-vote her, if the decision were left to the ladies?

Meanwhile there had been heavy tramping of feet on the deck, as the men trimmed the sails. She could only go under double-reefed trysails and fore-staysail for the present, and it was no joke to keep her head up while the reefs were taken in. It was blowing considerably more than half a gale of wind, and the sea was very heavy. Soon, however, the effect of the sails made itself felt; the yacht was a good sea-boat, and when she fairly heeled over on the port-tack and began to cut the waves again, the ladies downstairs agreed that sailing was much pleasanter and steadier than steam, and that the next time they crossed in a yacht they would like to sail all the way. But in spite of their courage, and notwithstanding that they were greatly reassured by the explanations of Mr. Barker, who made the nature of the accident quite clear to them, they had been badly shaken, and soon retired to their respective staterooms. In the small confusion of getting to their feet to leave the cabin it chanced that Claudius found himself helping Margaret to the door. The recollection of her touch and look when the accident happened was strong in him yet and gave him courage.

"Good-night, Countess," he said; "shall I have the pleasure of reading with you to-morrow?"

"Perhaps," she answered; "if it is very fine. Fate has decreed that we should have plenty of time." He tried to catch a glance as she left his arm, but she would not, and they were parted for the night. Barker had gone into the engine-room, now quiet and strange; the useless machinery stood still as it had been stopped when the loss of the propeller, relieving the opposition to the motor-force, allowed it to make its last frantic revolutions. The Duke and Claudius were left alone in the main cabin.

"Well," said the Duke, "we are in for it this time, at all events."

"We are indeed," said Claudius; "I hope the delay will not cause you any serious inconvenience, for I suppose we shall not reach New York for a fortnight at least."

"It will not inconvenience me at all. But I am sorry for you—for you all, I mean," he added, fearing he had been awkward in thus addressing Claudius directly, "because it will be so very disagreeable, such an awful bore for you to be at sea so long."

"I have no doubt we shall survive," said the other, with a smile. "What do you say to going on deck and having a chat with Sturleson, now that all is quiet?"

"And a pipe?" said the Duke, "I am with you." So on deck they went, and clambered along the lee to the smoking-room, without getting very wet. Sturleson was sent for, and they reviewed together the situation. The result of the inquiry was that things looked much brighter to all three. They were in a good sea-boat, well manned and provisioned, with nothing to fear from the weather, and if they were lucky they might make Sandy Hook in a week. On the other hand, they might not; but it is always well to take a cheerful view of things. People who cross the Atlantic in yachts are very different from the regular crowds that go backwards and forwards in the great lines. They are seldom in a hurry, and have generally made a good many voyages before. Perhaps the Duke himself, in his quality of host, was the most uncomfortable man on board. He did not see how the Countess and the Doctor could possibly survive being shut up together in a small vessel, for he was convinced that Barker knew all about their difficulty. If he had not liked Claudius so much, he would have been angry at him for daring to propose to this beautiful young friend of his. But then Claudius was Claudius, and even the Duke saw something in him besides his wealth which gave him a right to aspire to the highest.

"I can't make out," the Duke once said to Barker, "where Claudius got his manners. He never does anything the least odd; and he always seems at his ease."

"I only know he came to Heidelberg ten years ago, and that he is about thirty. He got his manners somewhere when he was a boy."

"Of course, there are lots of good people in Sweden," said the Duke; "but they all have titles, just as they do in Germany. And Claudius has no title."

"No," said Barker pensively, "I never heard him say he had a title."

"I don't know anything about it," answered the Duke. "But I have been a good deal about Sweden, and he is not in the least like a respectable Swedish burgher. Did you not tell me that his uncle, who left him all that money, was your father's partner in business?"

"Yes, I remember once or twice hearing the old gentleman say he had a nephew. But he was a silent man, though he piled up the dollars."

"Claudius is a silent man too," said the Duke.

"And he has sailed into the dollars ready piled."

But this was before the eventful day just described; and the Duke had forgotten the conversation, though he had repeated the reflections to himself, and found them true. To tell the truth, Claudius looked more like a duke than his host, for the sea air had blown away the professorial cobwebs; and, after all, it did not seem so very incongruous in the Englishman's eyes that his handsome guest should fall in love with the Countess Margaret. Only, it was very uncomfortable; and he did not know exactly what he should do with them for the next ten days. Perhaps he ought to devote himself to the Countess, and thus effectually prevent any approaches that Claudius might meditate. Yes—that was probably his duty. He wished he might ask counsel of his sister; but then she did not know, and it seemed unfair, and altogether rather a betrayal of confidence or something—at all events, it was not right, and he would not do it. Barker might be wrong too. And so the poor Duke, muddle-headed and weary with this storm in his tea-cup, and with having his tea-cup come to grief in a real storm into the bargain, turned into his deck-cabin to "sleep on it," thinking the morning would bring counsel.

Claudius had many things to think of too; but he was weary, for he had slept little of late, and not at all the night before; so he lay down and went over the scenes of the evening; but soon he fell asleep, and dreamed of her all the night long.

But the good yacht Streak held on her course bravely, quivering in the joy of her new-spread wings. For what hulk is so dull and pitifully modern as not to feel how much gladder a thing it is to bound along with straining shrouds and singing sails and lifting keel to the fierce music of the wind than to be ever conscious of a burning sullenly-thudding power, put in her bosom by the unartistic beast, man, to make her grind her breathless way whither he would, and whither she would not? Not the meanest mud-scow or harbour tug but would rather have a little mast and a bit of canvas in the fresh salt breeze than all the hundreds of land-born horse-powers and fire-driven cranks and rods that a haste-loving generation can cram into the belly of the poor craft. How much more, then, must the beautiful clean-built Streak have rejoiced on that night when she felt the throbbing, gnashing pain of the engines stop suddenly in her breast, and was allowed to spread her beautiful wings out to be kissed and caressed all over by her old lover, the north-east wind?

And the grand crested waves came creeping up, curling over their dark heads till they bristled with phosphorescent foam; and some of them broke angrily upward, jealous that the wind alone might touch those gleaming sails. But the wind roared at them in his wrath and drove them away, so that they sank back, afraid to fight with him; and he took the ship in his strong arms, and bore her fast and far that night, through many a heaving billow, and past many a breaking crest—far over the untrodden paths, where footsteps are not, neither the defiling hand of man.

But within were beating hearts and the breathings of life. The strong man stretched to his full length on his couch, mighty to see in his hard-earned sleep. And the beautiful woman, with parted lips and wild tossing black hair; dark cheeks flushed with soft resting; hands laid together lovingly, as though, in the quiet night, the left hand would learn at last what good work the right hand has wrought; the fringe of long eyelashes drooping with the lids, to fold and keep the glorious light safe within, and— ah yes, it is there!—the single tear still clinging to its birthplace—mortal impress of immortal suffering. Is it not always there, the jewelled sign-manual of grief?

But the good yacht Streak held on her course bravely; and the north-easter laughed and sang as he buffeted the waves from the path of his love.

CHAPTER IX

The Duke was the first to be astir in the morning, and as soon as he opened his eyes he made up his mind that the weather was improving. The sea was still running high, but there was no sound of water breaking over the bulwarks. He emerged from his deck-cabin, and took a sniff of the morning air. A reef had been shaken out of the trysails, and the fore-topsail and jib were set. He went aft, and found the mate just heaving the patent log.

"Nine and a half, your Grace," said the officer with a chuckle, for he was an old sailor, and hated steamers.

"That's very fair," remarked the owner, skating off with his bare feet over the wet deck. Then he went back to his cabin to dress.

Presently Mr. Barker's neat person emerged from the cuddy. He looked about to see if any one were out yet, but only a party of red-capped tars were visible, swabbing the forward deck with their pendulum-like brooms, and working their way aft in a regular, serried rank. The phalanx moved with an even stroke, and each bare foot advanced just so many inches at every third sweep of the broom, while the yellow-haired Norse 'prentice played the hose in front of them. Mr. Barker perceived that they would overtake him before long, and he determined on flight, not forward or aft, but aloft; and he leisurely lifted himself into the main-shrouds, and climbing half-way, hooked his feet through the ratlines. In this position he took out a cigar, lighted it with a vesuvian, and, regardless of the increased motion imparted to him at his greater elevation, he began to smoke. The atmosphere below must have been very oppressive indeed to induce Mr. Barker to come up before breakfast—in fact, before eight o'clock—for the sake of smoking a solitary cigar up there by the catharpings. Mr. Barker wanted to think, for an idea had struck him during the night.

In ten minutes the parade of deck-swabbers had passed, and Claudius also appeared on deck, looking haggard and pale. He did not see Barker, for he turned, seaman-like, to the weatherside, and the try-sail hid his friend from his sight. Presently he too thought he would go aloft, for he felt cramped and weary, and fancied a climb would stretch his limbs. He went right up to the crosstrees before he espied Barker, a few feet below him on the other side. He stopped a moment in astonishment, for this sort of diversion was the last thing he had given the American credit for. Besides, as Barker was to leeward, the rigging where he was perched stood almost perpendicular, and his position must have been a very uncomfortable one. Claudius was not given to jocularity as a rule, but he could not resist such a chance for astonishing a man who imagined himself to be enjoying an airy solitude between sky and water. So he gently swung himself into the lee rigging and, leaning far down, cautiously lifted Mr. Barker's cap from his head by the woollen button in the middle. Mr. Barker knocked the ash from his cigar with his free hand, and returned it to his mouth; he then conveyed the same hand to the top of his head, to assure himself that the cap was gone. He knew perfectly well that in his present position he could not look up to see who had played him the trick.

"I don't know who you are," he sang out, "but I may as well tell you my life is insured. If I catch cold, the company will make it hot for you—and no error."

A roar of laughter from below saluted this sally, for the Duke and Sturleson had met, and had watched together the progress of the joke.

"I will take the risk," replied Claudius, who had retired again to the crosstrees. "I am going to put it on the topmast-head, so that you may have a good look at it."

"You can't do it," said Barker, turning himself round, and lying flat against the ratlines, so that he could look up at his friend.

"What's that?" bawled the Duke from below.

"Says he will decorate the maintruck with my hat, and I say he can't do it," Barker shouted back.

"I'll back Claudius, level money," answered the Duke in stentorian tones.

"I'll take three to two," said Barker.

"No, I won't. Level money."

"Done for a hundred, then," answered the American.

It was an unlikely thing to bet on, and Barker thought he might have given the Duke odds, instead of asking them, as he had done. But he liked to get all he could in a fair way. Having arranged his bet, he told Claudius he might climb to the mast-head if he liked, but that he, Barker, was going down so as to have a better view; and he forthwith descended. All three stood leaning back against the weather bulwarks, craning their necks to see the better. Claudius was a very large man, as has been said, and Barker did not believe it possible that he could drag his gigantic frame up the smooth mast beyond the shrouds. If it were possible, he was quite willing to pay his money to see him do it.

Claudius put the woollen cap in his pocket, and began the ascent. The steamer, as has been said, was schooner-rigged, with topsail yards on the foremast, but there were no ratlines in the main topmast shrouds, which were set about ten feet below the mast-head. To this point Claudius climbed easily enough, using his arms and legs against the stiffened ropes. A shout from the Duke hailed his arrival.

"Now comes the tug of war," said the Duke.

"He can never do it," said Barker confidently.

But Barker had underrated the extraordinary strength of the man against whom he was betting, and he did not know how often, when a boy, Claudius had climbed higher masts than those of the Streak. The Doctor was one of those natural athletes whose strength does not diminish for lack of exercise, and large as he was, and tall, he was not so heavy as Barker thought. Now he pulled the cap out of his pocket and held it between his teeth, as he gripped the smooth wood between his arms and hands and legs, and with firm and even motion he began to swarm up the bare pole.

"There—I told you so," said Barker. Claudius had slipped nearly a foot back.

"He will do it yet," said the Duke, as the climber clasped his mighty hands to the mast. He would not slip again, for his blood was up, and he could almost fancy his iron grip pressed deep into the wood. Slowly, slowly those last three feet were conquered, inch by inch, and the broad hand stole stealthily over the small wooden truck at the topmast-head till it had a firm hold—then the other, and with the two he raised and pushed his body up till the truck was opposite his breast.

"Skal to the Viking!" yelled old Sturleson, the Swedish captain, his sunburnt face glowing red with triumph as Claudius clapped the woollen cap over the mast-head.

"Well done, indeed, man!" bawled the Duke.

"Well," said Barker, "it was worth the money, anyhow."

There was a faint exclamation from the door of the after-cabin; but none of the three men heard it, nor did they see a horror-struck face, stony and wide-eyed, staring up at the mast-head, where the Doctor's athletic figure swayed far out over the water with the motion of the yacht. Time had flown, and the bright sunlight streaming down into the ladies' cabin had made Margaret long for a breath of fresh air; so that when Lady Victoria appeared, in all sorts of jerseys and blue garments, fresh and ready for anything, the two had made common cause and ventured up the companion without any manly assistance. It chanced that they came out on the deck at the very moment when Claudius was accomplishing his feat, and seeing the three men looking intently at something aloft, Margaret looked too, and was horrified at what she saw. Lady Victoria caught her and held her tightly, or she would have lost her footing with the lurch of the vessel. Lady Victoria raised her eyes also, and took in the situation at a glance.

"Don't be afraid," she said, "he can take care of himself, no doubt. My brother used to be able to do it before he grew so big."

Claudius descended rapidly, but almost lost his hold when he saw Margaret leaning against the taffrail. He would not have had her see him for worlds, and there she was, and she had evidently witnessed the whole affair. Before he had reached the deck, the Duke had seen her too, and hastened to her side. She was evidently much agitated.

"How can you allow such things?" she said indignantly, her dark eyes flashing at him.

"I had nothing to say about it, Countess. But he did it magnificently."

Claudius had reached the deck, and eluding the compliments of Barker and Sturleson, hastened to the cuddy door, bowing to the ladies as he passed. He meant to beat a retreat to his cabin. But Margaret was determined to call him to account for having given her such a fright.

"Dr. Claudius," said the voice that he loved and feared.

"Yes, Countess," said he, steadying himself by the door as the vessel lurched.

"Will you please come here? I want to speak to you." He moved to her side, waiting his chance between two seas. "Do you think you have a right to risk your life in such follies?" she asked, when he was close to her. The Duke and Lady Victoria were near by.

"I do not think I have risked my life, Countess. I have often done it before."

"Do you think, then, that you have a right to do such things in the sight of nervous women?"

"No, Countess, I pretend to no such brutality, and I am very sincerely sorry that you should have unexpectedly seen me. I apologise most humbly to you and to Lady Victoria for having startled you;" he bowed to the Duke's sister as he spoke, and moved to go away. He had already turned when Margaret's face softened.

"Dr. Claudius," she called again. He was at her side in a moment. "Please do not do it again—even if I am not there." She looked at him; he thought it strange. But he was annoyed at the whole business, and really angry with himself. She had spoken in a low tone so that the others had not heard her.

"Countess," said he in a voice decidedly sarcastic, "I pledge myself never in future to ascend to the mast-head of any vessel or vessels without your express permission."

"Very well," said she coldly; "I shall keep you to your word." But Claudius had seen his mistake, and there was no trace of irony in his voice as he looked her steadfastly in the eyes and answered.

"Believe me, I will keep any promise I make to you," he said earnestly, and went away. Lady Victoria, who was not without tact, and had guessed that Margaret had something to say to the Doctor, managed meanwhile to keep her brother occupied by asking him questions about the exploit, and he, falling into the trap, had begun to tell the story from the beginning, speaking loud, by way of showing Claudius his appreciation. But Claudius, recking little of his laurels, went and sat in his cabin, pondering deeply. Barker, from a distance, had witnessed the conversation between Margaret and the Doctor. He came up murmuring to himself that the plot was thickening. "If Claudius makes a corner in mast-heads, there will be a bull market," he reflected, and he also remembered that just now he was a bear. "In that case," he continued his train of thought, "no more mast-heads."

"Good morning, Countess; Lady Victoria, good morning," he said, bowing. "I would take off my hat if I could, but the Doctor has set the cap of liberty on high." Lady Victoria and the Duke laughed, but Margaret said "Good morning" without a smile. Barker immediately abandoned the subject and talked about the weather, which is a grand topic when there is enough of it. It was clear by this time that they had passed through a violent storm, which had gone away to southward. The sea was heavy of course, but the wind had moderated, and by twelve o'clock the yacht was running between nine and ten knots, with a stiff breeze on her quarter and all sails set.

The Duke was extremely attentive to Margaret all that day, rarely leaving her side, whether she was below or on deck; bringing her books and rugs, and adjusting her chair, and altogether performing the offices of a faithful slave and attendant. Whenever Claudius came within hail the Duke would make desperate efforts to be animated, lengthening his sentences with all the vigorous superlatives and sledge-hammer adverbs he could think of, not to mention any number of "you knows." His efforts to be agreeable, especially when there appeared to be any likelihood of Claudius coming into the conversation, were so palpable that Margaret could not but see there was a reason for the expenditure of so much energy. She could not help being amused, but at the same time she was annoyed at what she considered a bit of unnecessary officiousness on the part of her host. However, he was such an old friend that she forgave him. But woman's nature is impatient of control. Left to herself she would have avoided Claudius; forcibly separated from him she discovered that she wanted to speak to him. As the day wore on and the Duke's attentions never relaxed, she grew nervous, and tried to think how she could send him away. It was no easy matter. If she asked for anything, he flew to get it and returned breathless, and of course at that very moment Claudius was just out of range. Then she called Miss Skeat, but the Duke's eloquence redoubled, and he talked to them both at once; and at last she gave it up in despair, and said she would lie down for a while. Once safe in her stateroom, the Duke drew a long breath, and went in search of Mr. Barker. Now Mr. Barker, in consequence of the idea that had unfolded itself to his fertile brain in the darkness of night, had been making efforts to amuse Claudius all day long, with as much determination as the Duke had shown in devoting himself to the Countess, but with greater success; for Barker could be very amusing when he chose, whereas the Duke was generally most amusing when he did not wish to be so. He found them in the smoking cabin, Claudius stretched at full length with a cigarette in his teeth, and Barker seated apparently on the table, the chair, and the transom, by a clever distribution of the various parts of his body, spinning yarns of a high Western flavour about death's-head editors and mosquitoes with brass ribs.

The Duke was exhausted with his efforts, and refreshed himself with beer before he challenged Barker to a game.

"To tell the truth, Duke," he answered, "I don't seem to think I feel like winning your money to-day. I will go and talk to the ladies, and Claudius will play with you."

"You won't make much headway there," said the Duke. "The Countess is gone to bed, and Miss Skeat and my sister are reading English history."

"Besides," put in Claudius, "you know I never play."

"Well," said Barker, with a sigh, "then I will play with you, and Claudius can go to sleep where he is." They cut and dealt. But Claudius did not feel at all sleepy. When the game was well started he rose and went out, making to himself the same reflection that Margaret had made, "Why is my friend so anxious to amuse me to-day?" He seldom paid any attention to such things, but his strong, clear mind was not long in unravelling the situation, now that he was roused to thinking about it. Barker had guessed the truth, or very near it, and the Duke and he had agreed to keep Claudius and Margaret apart as long as they could.

He went aft, and descended to the cabin. There sat Miss Skeat and Lady Victoria reading aloud, just as the Duke had said. He went through the passage and met the steward, or butler, whom he despatched to see if the Countess were in the ladies' cabin. The rosy-cheeked, gray-haired priest of Silenus said her ladyship was there, "alone," he added with a little emphasis. Claudius walked in, and was not disappointed. There she sat at the side of the table in her accustomed place, dark and beautiful, and his heart beat fast. She did not look up.

"Countess," he began timidly.

"Oh, Doctor Claudius, is that you? Sit down." He sat down on the transom, so that he could see the evening light fall through the port-hole above him on her side face, and as the vessel rose and fell the rays of the setting sun played strangely on her heavy hair.

"I have not seen you all day," she said.

"No, Countess." He did not know what to say to her.

"I trust you are none the worse for your foolish performance this morning?" Her voice was even and unmodulated, not too friendly and not too cold.

"I am, and I am not. I am unspeakably the worse in that I displeased you. Will you forgive me?"

"I will forgive you," in the same tone.

"Do you mean it? Do you mean you will forgive me what I said to you that—the other night?"

"I did not say that," she answered, a little weariness sounding with the words. Claudius's face fell.

"I am sorry," he said very simply.

"So am I. I am disappointed in you more than I can say. You are just like all the others, and I thought you were different. Do you not understand me?"

"Not entirely, though I will try to. Will you not tell me just what you mean to say?"

"I think I will," she answered, looking up, but not towards Claudius. She hesitated a moment and then continued, "We are not children, Dr. Claudius; let us speak plainly, and not misunderstand each other." She glanced round the cabin as if to see if they were alone. Apparently she was not satisfied. "Move my chair nearer to the sofa, please," she added; and he rose and did her bidding.

"I have not much to say," she went on, "but I do not want to say it before the whole ship's company. It is this: I thought I had found in you a friend, a man who would be to me what no one has ever been—a friend; and I am disappointed, for you want to be something else. That is all, except that it must not be thought of, and you must go."

An Englishman would have reproached her with having given him encouragement; an Italian would have broken out into a passionate expression of his love, seeking to kindle her with his own fire. But the great, calm Northman clasped his hands together firmly on his knee and sat silent.

"You must go—" she repeated.

"I cannot go," he said honestly.

"That is all the more reason why you should go at once," was the feminine argument with which she replied.

"Let us go back to two days ago, and be as we were before. Will you not forget it?"

"We cannot—you cannot, and I cannot. You are not able to take back your words or to deny them."

"May God forbid!" said he very earnestly. "But if you will let me be your friend, I will promise to obey you, and I will not say anything that will displease you."

"You cannot," she repeated; and she smiled bitterly.

"But I can, and I will, if you will let me. I am very strong, and I will keep my word;" and indeed he looked the incarnation of strength as he sat with folded hands and earnest face, awaiting her reply. His words were not eloquent, but they were plain and true, and he meant them. Something in the suppressed power of his tone drove away the smile from Margaret's face, and she looked toward him.

"Could you?" she asked. But the door opened, and Lady Victoria entered with her book.

"Oh!" said Lady Victoria.

"I must go and dress," said Claudius.

"We will go on with the book to-morrow," said the Countess. And he bore away a light heart.

On the following day the Duke began to take care of the Countess, as he had done yesterday, and Barker turned on the fireworks of his conversation for the amusement of Claudius. Claudius sat quite still for an hour or more, perhaps enjoying the surprise he was going to give the Duke and Barker. As the latter finished a brilliant tale, for the veracity of which he vouched in every particular, Claudius calmly rose and threw away his cigarette.

"That is a very good story," he said. "Good-bye for the present. I am going to read with the Countess." Barker was nearly "taken off his feet."

"Why—" he began, but stopped short. "Oh, very well. She is on deck. I saw the Duke bring up her rugs and things." His heavy moustache seemed to uncurl itself nervously, and his jaw dropped slowly, as he watched Claudius leave the deck-cabin.

"I wonder when they got a chance," he said to himself.

But Barker was not nearly so much astonished as the Duke. The latter was sitting by Margaret's side, near the wheel, making conversation. He was telling her such a good story about a mutual friend—the son of a great chancellor of the great empire of Kakotopia—who had gambled away his wife at cards with another mutual friend.

"And the point of the story," said the Duke, "is that the lady did not object in the least. Just fancy, you know, we all knew her, and now she is married again to—" At this point Claudius strode up, and Margaret, who did not care to hear any more, interrupted the Duke.

"Dr. Claudius, I have our book here. Shall we read?" The Doctor's face flushed with pleasure. The Duke stared.

"I will get a chair," he said; and his long legs made short work of it.

"Well, if you will believe it," said the Duke, who meant to finish his story, "it was not even the man who won her at cards that she married when she was divorced. It was a man you never met; and they are living in some place in Italy." The Duke could hardly believe his eyes when Claudius boldly marched up with his chair and planted himself on Margaret's other side. She leaned back, looking straight before her, and turning the leaves of the book absently backwards and forwards. The Duke was evidently expected to go, but he sat fully a minute stupidly looking at Margaret. At last she spoke.

"That was not a very nice story. How odd! I knew them both very well. Do you remember where we left off, Dr. Claudius?"

"Page one hundred and nineteen," answered the Doctor, who never forgot anything. This looked like business, and the Duke rose. He got away rather awkwardly. As usual, he departed to wreak vengeance on Mr. Barker.

"Barker," he began with emphasis, "you are an ass."

"I know it," said Barker, with humility. "I have been saying it over to myself for a quarter of an hour, and it is quite true. Say it again; it does me good."

"Oh, that is all. If you are quite sure you appreciate the fact I am satisfied."

"It dawned upon me quite suddenly a few minutes ago. Claudius has been here," said Barker.

"He has been there too," said the Duke. "He is there now."

"I suppose there is no doubt that we are talking about the same thing?"

"I don't know about you," said the other. "I am talking about Claudius and Countess Margaret. They never had a chance to speak all day yesterday, and now she asks him to come and read with her. Just as I was telling no end of a jolly story too." Mr. Barker's wrinkle wound slowly round his mouth. He had been able to shave to-day, and the deep furrow was clearly defined.

"Oh! she asked him to read, did she?" Then he swore, very slowly and conscientiously, as if he meant it.

"Why the deuce do you swear like that?" asked the Duke. "If it is not true that she has refused him, you ought to be very glad." And he stuffed a disreputable short black pipe full of tobacco.

"Why, of course I am. I was swearing at my own stupidity. Of course I am very glad if she has not refused him." He smiled a very unhealthy-looking smile. "See here—" he began again.

"Well? I am seeing, as you call it."

"This. They must have had a talk yesterday. He was here with me, and suddenly he got up and said he was going to read with her. And you say that she asked him to read with her when he went to where you were."

"Called out to him half across the deck—in the middle of my story, too, and a firstrate one at that."

"She does not care much for stories," said Barker; "but that is not the question. It was evidently a put-up job."

"Meaning a preconcerted arrangement," said the Duke. "Yes. It was arranged between them some time yesterday. But I never left her alone until she said she was going to lie down."

"And I never left him until you told me she had gone to bed."

"She did not lie down, then," said the Duke.

"Then she lied up and down," said Barker, savagely playful.

"Ladies do not lie," said the Duke, who did not like the word, and refused to laugh.

"Of course. And you and I are a couple of idiots, and we have been protecting her when she did not want to be protected. And she will hate us for ever after. I am disgusted. I will drown my cares in drink. Will you please ring the bell?"

"You had better drink apollinaris. Grog will go to your head. I never saw you so angry." The Duke pressed the electric button.

"I loathe to drink of the water," said Barker, tearing off the end of a cigar with his teeth. The Duke had seen a man in Egypt who bit off the heads of black snakes, and he thought of him at that moment. The steward appeared, and when the arrangements were made, the ocean in which Barker proposed to drown his cares was found to consist of a small glass of a very diluted concoction of champagne, bitters, limes, and soda water. The Duke had some, and thought it very good.

"It is not a question of language," said Barker, returning to the conversation. "They eluded us and met. That is all."

"By her wish, apparently," said the other.

"We must arrange a plan of action," said Barker.

"Why? If she has not refused him, it is all right. We have nothing more to do with it. Let them go their own way."

"You are an old friend of the Countess's, are you not?" asked the American. "Yes—very well, would you like to see her married to Claudius?"

"Upon my word," said the Duke, "I cannot see that I have anything to say about it. But since you ask me, I see no possible objection. He is a gentleman—has money, heaps of it—if she likes him, let her marry him if she pleases. It is very proper that she should marry again; she has no children, and the Russian estates are gone to the next heir. I only wanted to save her from any inconvenience. I did not want Claudius to be hanging after her, if she did not want him. She does. There is an end of it." O glorious English Common Sense! What a fine thing you are when anybody gets you by the right end.

"You may be right," said Barker, with a superior air that meant "you are certainly wrong." "But would Claudius be able to give her the position in foreign society—"

"Society be damned," said the Duke. "Do you think the widow of Alexis cannot command society? Besides, Claudius is a gentleman, and that is quite enough."

"I suppose he is," said Mr. Barker, with an air of regret.

"Suppose? There is no supposing about it. He is." And the Duke looked at his friend as if he would have said, "If I, a real, palpable, tangible, hereditary duke, do not know a gentleman when I see one, what can you possibly know about it, I would like to inquire?" And that settled the matter.

But Mr. Barker was uneasy in his mind. An idea was at work there which was diametrically opposed to the union of Claudius and Margaret, and day by day, as he watched the intimacy growing back into its old proportions, he ground his gold-filled teeth with increasing annoyance. He sought opportunities for saying and doing things that might curtail the length of those hours when Claudius sat at her side, ostensibly reading. Ostensibly? Yes—the first day or two after she had allowed him to come back to her side were days of unexampled industry and severe routine, only the most pertinent criticisms interrupting from time to time the even progress from line to line, from page to page, from paragraph to paragraph, from chapter to chapter. But soon the criticism became less close, the illustration more copious, the tongue more eloquent, and the glance less shy. The elective strength of their two hearts rose up and wrought mightily, saying, "We are made for each other, we understand each other, and these foolish mortals who carry us about in their bosoms shall not keep us apart." And to tell the truth, the foolish mortals made very little effort. Margaret did not believe that Claudius could possibly break his plighted word, and he knew that he would die rather than forfeit his faith. And so they sat side by side with the book, ostensibly reading, actually talking, most of the day. And sometimes one or the other would go a little too near the forbidden point, and then there was a moment's silence, and the least touch of embarrassment; and once Margaret laughed a queer little laugh at one of these stumbles, and once Claudius sighed. But they were very happy, and the faint colour that was natural to the Doctor's clear white skin came back as his heart was eased of its burden, and Margaret's dark cheek grew darker with the sun and the wind that she took no pains to keep from her face, though the olive flushed sometimes to a warmer hue, with pleasure—or what? She thought it was the salt breeze.

"How well those two look!" exclaimed Lady Victoria once to Mr. Barker.

"I have seen Claudius look ghastly," said Barker, for he thought they looked too "well" altogether.

"Yes; do you remember one morning—I think it was the day before, or the day after, the accident? I thought he was going to faint."

"Perhaps he was sea-sick," suggested Barker.

"Oh no, we were a week out then, and he was never ill at all from the first."

"Perhaps he was love-sick," said the other, willing to be spiteful.

"How ridiculous! To think of such a thing!" cried the stalwart English girl; for she was only a girl in years despite her marriage. "But really," she continued, "if I were going to write a novel I would put those two people in it, they are so awfully good-looking. I would make all my heroes and heroines beautiful if I wrote books."

"Then I fear I shall never be handed down to posterity by your pen, Lady Victoria," said Barker, with a smile.

"No," said she, eyeing him critically, "I don't think I would put you in my book. But then, you know, I would not put myself in it either."

"Ah," grinned Mr. Barker, "the book would lose by that, but I should gain."

"How?" asked her ladyship.

"Because we should both be well out of it," said he, having reached his joke triumphantly. But Lady Victoria did not like Mr. Barker, or his jokes, very much. She once said so to her brother. She thought him spiteful.

"Well, Vick," said her brother good-naturedly, "I daresay you are right. But he amuses me, and he is very square on settling days."

Meanwhile Lady Victoria was not mistaken—Mr. Barker was spiteful; but she did not know that she was the only member of the party to whom he ventured to show it, because he thought she was stupid, and because it was such a relief to say a vicious thing now and then. He devoted himself most assiduously to Miss Skeat, since Margaret would not accept his devotion to her, and indeed had given him little chance to show that he would offer it. The days sped fast for some of the party, slowly for others, and pretty much as they did anywhere else for the Duke, who was in no especial hurry to arrive in New York. His affairs were large enough to keep, and he had given himself plenty of time. But nevertheless his affairs were the object in view; and though he did not like to talk about those things, even with Barker, the fate of Claudius and Margaret as compared with the larger destinies of the Green Swash Mining Company were as the humble and unadorned mole-hill to the glories of the Himalaya. People had criticised the Duke's financial career in England. Why had he sold that snuffbox that Marie Thérèse gave to his ancestor when—well, you know when? Why had he converted those worm-eaten manuscripts, whereon were traced many valuable things in a variety of ancient tongues, into coin of the realm? And why had he turned his Irish estates into pounds, into shillings, yea, and into pence. Pence—just think of it! He had sold his ancestral lands for pence; that was what it came to. These and many other things the scoffers scoffed, with a right good-will. But none save the Duke could tell how many broad fields of ripening grain, and vine-clad hills, and clean glistening miles of bright rail, and fat ore lands sodden with wealth of gold and silver and luscious sulphurets—none save the Duke could tell how much of these good things the Duke possessed in that great land beyond the sea, upon which if England were bodily set down it would be as hard to find as a threepenny bit in a ten-acre field. But the Duke never told. He went about his business quietly, for he said in his heart, "Tush! I have children to be provided for; and if anything happens to the old country, I will save some bacon for them in the new, and they may call themselves dukes or farmers as far as I am concerned; but they shall not lack a few hundred thousand acres of homestead in the hour of need, neither a cow or two or a pig."

The breeze held well, on the whole, and old Sturleson said they were having a wonderful run, which was doubtless an effort on the part of nature to atone for the injury she had done. But the days flew by, and yet they were not at their voyage's end. At last, as they sat sunning themselves in the fair September weather, Sturleson came to them, his bright quadrant, with its coloured glasses sticking out in all directions, in his hand, and told the Duke he thought that by to-morrow afternoon they would sight the Hook. The party were all together, as it happened, and there was a general shout, in which, however, Claudius joined but faintly. He longed for contrary winds, and he wished that Sandy Hook and all its appurtenances, including New York and the United States, would sink gently down to the bottom of the sea. He knew, and Sturleson had told him, that with unfavourable weather they might be at sea a month, and he was one of the two who voted to go to Bermuda when the accident occurred.

That evening, as the sun was going down to his tossing bed of golden waves, all canopied with softest purple, Margaret stood leaning over the taffrail. Every stitch of canvas was out—topsails, gaff-topsails, staysails, and jibs—and the good yacht bounded with a will to the bright west. But the dark woman looked astern to where the billows rolled together, forgetting what precious burden they had borne. Claudius stole to her side and stood a moment looking at her face.

"So it is over," he said at last.

"Nearly over. It has been very pleasant," said she.

"It has been more than pleasant. It has been divine—for me."

"Hush!" said Margaret softly; "remember." There was silence, save for the rushing of the rudder through the dark-blue foam. Again Claudius spoke, softly, and it seemed to her that the voice was not his, but rather that it came up mystically from the water below.

"Are you sorry it is over?" he asked—or the voice of the mighty deep welling up with its burden of truth.

"Yes, I am very sorry," she answered, whether she would or no. The sun sank down, and the magic after-glow shone in the opposite sky, tinging ship and sails and waves.

"I am very sorry too," he said; and he sighed and looked astern eastwards, and thought of the golden hours he had spent on that broad track stretching away behind. Margaret leaned down, resting her chin on her hands, and presently she unfolded them, and her fingers stole upwards and covered her face, and she bent her head. There was a mighty beating in Claudius's breast, and a thousand voices in the air cried to him to speak and to say what was in his heart to say. But he would not, for he had given the woman at his side the promise of his faith. At last she looked up and turned toward him. They were alone on the deck in the faintness of the gathering twilight.

"Claudius, you have kept your promise truly and well. Keep it—keep it always." She held out her ungloved hand.

"Always, my queen and my lady," and he kissed the white fingers once.

"Hullo!" shouted the Duke, emerging from the cuddy. "Upon my word! Why, it's dinner time."

CHAPTER X

How they left the good yacht Streak, and how they bade a hearty farewell to that old sea lion Captain Sturleson, and how they went through the hundred and one formalities of the custom-house, and the thousand and one informalities of its officials, are matters of interest indeed, but not of history. There are moments in a man's existence when the act of conveying half a dozen sovereigns to the pocket of that stern monitor of good faith, the brass-buttoned custom-house officer with the tender conscience, is of more importance to salvation than women's love or the Thirty-nine Articles. All this they did. Nor were they spared by the great tormentor of the West, who bristleth with the fretful quill, whose ears surround us in the night-time, and whose voice is as the voice of the charmer, the reporter of the just and the unjust, but principally of the latter. And Mr. Barker made an appointment with the Duke, and took a tender farewell of the three ladies, and promised to call on Claudius in the afternoon, and departed. But the rest of the party went to a famous old hotel much affected by Englishmen, and whose chief recommendation in their eyes is that there is no elevator, so that they can run upstairs and get out of breath, and fancy themselves at home. Of course their apartments had been secured, and had been waiting for them a week, and the Countess was glad to withdraw for the day into the sunny suite over the corner that was hers. As for Miss Skeat, she went to the window and stayed there, for America was quite different from what she had fancied. Claudius descended to the lower regions, and had his hair cut; and the cook and the bar-keeper and the head "boots," or porter, as he called himself, all came and looked in at the door of the barber's shop, and stared at the huge Swede. And the barber walked reverently round him with scissors and comb, and they all agreed that Claudius must be Mr. Barnum's new attraction, except the head porter no relation of an English head porter—who thought it was "Fingal's babby, or maybe the blessed Sint Pathrick himself." And the little boy who brushed the frequenters of the barber's shop could not reach to Claudius's coat collar, so that the barber had to set a chair for him, and so he climbed up.

The Duke retired also to the depths of his apartments, and his servant arrayed him in the purple and stove-pipe of the higher civilisation. And before long each of the ladies received a large cardboard box full of fresh-cut flowers, sent by Mr. Barker of course; and the Duke, hearing of this from his man, sent "his compliments to Lady Victoria, and would she send him a rose for his coat?" So the Duke sallied forth on foot, and the little creases in his clothes showed that he had just arrived. But he did not attract any attention, for the majority of the population of New York have "just arrived." Besides, he had not far to go. He had a friend in town who lived but a few steps from the hotel, and his first move on arriving was generally to call there.

Claudius waited a short time to see whether Mr. Barker would come; but as Claudius rarely waited for anybody, he soon grew impatient, and squeezing himself into a cab, told the driver to take him to Messrs. Screw and Scratch in Pine Street. He was received with deference, and treated as his position demanded. Would he like to see Mr. Silas B. Barker senior? Very natural that he should want to make the acquaintance of his relative's old friend and partner. Mr. Screw was out, yes—but Mr. Scratch would accompany him. No trouble at all. Better "go around right off," as Mr. Barker would probably go to Newport by the boat that evening. So they went "around right away," and indeed it was a circular journey. Down one elevator, through a maze of corridors, round crowded corners, through narrow streets, Claudius ploughing his way through billows of curbstone brokers, sad and gay, messenger-boys, young clerks, fruit vendors, disreputable-looking millionaires and gentlemanly-looking scamps, newspaper-boys, drunken Irishmen, complacent holders of preferred, and scatterbrained speculators in wild-cat, an atmosphere of tobacco smoke, dust, melons, and unintelligible jargon—little Mr. Scratch clinging to his client's side, nodding furiously at every other face he saw, and occasionally shouting a word of outlandish etymology, but of magic import. Claudius almost thought it would be civil to offer to carry the little man, but when he saw how deftly Mr. Scratch got in a foot here and an elbow there, and how he scampered over any little bit of clear pavement, the Doctor concluded his new acquaintance was probably used to it. More elevators, more passages, a glass door, still bearing the names "Barker and Lindstrand," and they had reached their destination.

The office was on the second floor, with large windows looking over the street; there were several people in the room they first entered, and the first person Claudius saw was Mr. Barker junior, his friend.

"Well," said Barker, "so you have found us out. That's right. I was coming round to see you afterwards, for I did not suppose you would like to face 'the street' alone. Father," he said, turning to a thickset man with white hair and bushy eyebrows, "this is Dr. Claudius, Mr. Lindstrand's nephew."

The old gentleman looked up keenly into Claudius's face, and smiled pleasantly as he put out his hand. He said a few words of cordial welcome, and seemed altogether a sturdy, hearty, hardworking man of business—rather a contrast to his son. He hoped that Claudius would come on to Newport with Silas, as he wanted to have a long talk with him. The old gentleman was evidently very busy, and his son took Claudius in charge.

"What is that?" asked the Doctor, looking curiously at a couple of wheels that unwound unceasingly long strips of white paper. The paper passed through a small instrument, and came out covered with unintelligible signs, coiling itself in confusion into a waste-basket below.

"That has driven more men to desperation, ruin, and drink, than all the other evils of humanity put together," said Barker. "That is the ticker."

"I perceive that it ticks," said Claudius. And Barker explained how every variation in the market was instantly transmitted to every place of business, to every club, and to many private houses in New York, by means of a simple arrangement of symbols—how "Gr. S." meant Green Swash, and "N.P. pr." "North Pacific, preferred," and many other things. Claudius thought it an ingenious contrivance, but said it must be very wearing on the nerves.

"It is the pulse of New York," said Barker. "It is the croupier calling out from morning till night 'trente-sept, rouge, impair,' and then 'Messieurs faites votre jeu—le jeu est fait.' When stock goes down you buy, when it goes up you sell. That is the whole secret."

"I think it is very like gambling," said Claudius.

"So it is. But we never gamble here, though we have a ticker to see what other people are doing. Besides, it tells you everything. Horse-racing, baseball, steamers, births, deaths, and marriages; corn, wheat, tobacco, and cotton. Nobody can live here without a ticker."

And after this they went out into the street again, and Mr. Scratch took off his hat to Claudius, which is the highest token of unusual esteem and respect of which "the street" is capable, and in a moment the heels of his boots were seen disappearing into the dense crowd. Claudius and Barker walked on, and crossed Broadway; a few steps farther, and the Doctor was brought face to face with the triumph of business over privacy—the elevated railway. He had caught a glimpse of portions of it in the morning, but had supposed the beams and trestles to be scaffoldings for buildings. He stood a few moments in profound thought, contemplating and comprehending this triumph of wheels.

"It is a great invention," he said quietly. And when they were seated in the long airy car, he looked out of the window, and asked whether the people in the first stories of the houses did not find it very disagreeable to have trains running by their windows all day.

"The social and municipal economy of New York," explained Mr. Barker, "consists in one-third of the population everlastingly protesting against the outrageous things done by the other two-thirds. One-third fights another third, and the neutral third takes the fees of both parties. All that remains is handed over to the deserving poor."

"That is the reason, I suppose, why there are so few poor in New York," observed the Doctor with a smile.

"Exactly," said Barker; "they go West."

"I would like to discuss the political economy of this country with you, when I have been here six months."

"I hope you will not. And when you have been here six months you will be willing to pay a large sum rather than discuss it with any one."

And so they went up town, and Claudius watched everything with interest, and occasionally made a remark. Barker was obliged to go on, and he put Claudius out on the platform at the station nearest his hotel, and which was in fact at the same cross-street. As Claudius ascended the steps he was overtaken by the Duke, who was breathless with running.

"I—am afraid—it is too late," he panted; "come along," and he seized Claudius by the arm and dragged him to the corner of Fifth Avenue, before he could ask any questions.

"What is the matter?" asked the Doctor, looking about.

"He is gone," said the Duke, who had recovered his speech, "I knew he would, but I thought there was time. I was with a friend of mine, and I had just left him when I saw you, and as I have asked him to dinner I wanted to introduce you first. But he is always in such a hurry. Nowhere to be seen. Probably down town by this time." They turned back and went in. The Duke asked for the ladies. The Countess and her companion had gone to drive in the park, but Lady Victoria was upstairs.

"Vick, I am going to have a man to dinner—of course we will all dine together the first night ashore—a man you have heard me speak of; you will like him amazingly."

"Who is he?"

"He is the uncle of the whole human race."

"Including the peerage?" laughed Lady Victoria.

"Peerage? I should think so. The whole of Debrett and the Almanach de Gotha. Nobility and gentry, the Emperor of China and the North American Indians."

"That will suit Miss Skeat. She is always talking about the North American Indians. I think I know who it is."

"Of course you do, and now he is coming." There was a pause. "Vick, may I smoke?"

"Oh yes, if you like." His Grace lit a cigarette.

"Vick, I am afraid you have had a dreadfully stupid time of it on this trip. I am so sorry. Those people turned out rather differently from what I had expected." The Duke was fond of his sister, though she was much younger than he, and he began to reflect that she had been poorly provided for, as he had engaged Barker most of their time.

"Not at all. You know I am so fond of the sea and the open air, and I have enjoyed it all so much. Besides—"

"It is awfully good of you to say so, my dear, but I don't believe a word of it. 'Besides'—you were going to say something."

"Was I? Oh yes. Besides, you could not have had another man, you know, because it would have spoiled the table."

"No, but I was so selfish about Barker, because he can play cards, and Claudius would not, or could not."

"I am not sorry for that, exactly," said Lady Victoria. "You remember, we talked about him once. I do not like Mr. Barker very much."

"Oh, he is no end of a good fellow in his way," said her brother. "Have you—a—any reason for not liking him, Vick?"

"I think he is spiteful. He says such horrid things."

"Does he? What about?" said the Duke indifferently, as he tore a bit of charred paper from the end of his cigarette, which had burned badly. She did not answer at first. He inspected the cigarette, puffed it into active life again, and looked up.

"What about, Vick?"

"About his friend—about Doctor Claudius. I like Doctor Claudius." Lady Victoria smoothed her rebellious brown hair at the huge over-gilt pier-glass of the little drawing-room which she and Margaret had in common.

"I like him too," said the Duke. "He is a gentleman. Why don't you do your hair like the American women—all fuzzy, over your eyes? I should think it would be much less trouble."

"It's not neat," said her ladyship, still looking into the glass. Then suddenly, "Do you know what I think?"

"Well?"

"I believe Mr. Barker would like to marry Margaret himself."

"Pshaw! Victoria, don't talk nonsense. Who ever heard of such a thing! The Duke rose and walked once up and down the room; then he sat down again in the same place. He was not pleased at the suggestion.

"Why is it such nonsense?" she asked.

"Any number of reasons. Besides, she would not have him."

"That would not prevent him from wishing to marry her."

"No, of course not, but—well, it's great stuff." He looked a little puzzled, as if he found it hard to say exactly why he objected to the idea.

"You would be very glad if Claudius married her, would you not?" asked his sister.

"Glad—I don't know—yes, I suppose so."

"But you pretend to like Mr. Barker a great deal more than you like Doctor Claudius," said she argumentatively.

"I know him better," said the Duke; "I have known Barker several years."

"And he is rich—and that, and why should he not think of proposing to Margaret?"

"Because—well I don't know, but it would be so deuced inappropriate," in which expression the honest-hearted Englishman struck the truth, going for it with his head down, after the manner of his people.

"At first he was very nice," said Lady Victoria, who had gained a point, though for what purpose she hardly knew; "but after a while he began to say disagreeable things. He hinted in all sorts of ways that Claudius was not exactly a gentleman, and that no one knew where he came from, and that he ought not to make love to Margaret, and so on, till I wanted to box his ears;" and she waxed warm in her wrath, which was really due in great part to the fact that Mr. Barker was personally not exactly to her taste. If she had liked him she would have thought differently of the things he said. But her brother was angry too by this time, for he remembered a conversation he had had with Barker on the same topic.

"I told Barker once that Claudius was a gentleman, every inch of him, and I should think that was enough. As if I did not know—it's too bad, upon my word!" And the ducal forehead reddened angrily. The fact was that both he and his sister had taken an unaccountable fancy to this strange Northman, with his quiet ways and his unaffected courtesy, and at the present moment they would have quarrelled with their best friends rather than hear a word against him. "My guest, too, and on my yacht," he went on; and it did his sister good to see him angry—"it's true he brought him, and introduced him to me." Then a bright idea struck him. "And if Claudius were not a gentleman, what the deuce right had Barker to bring him to me at all, eh? Wasn't it his business to find out? My word! I would like to ask him that, and if I find him I will." Lady Victoria had no intention of making mischief between her brother and Mr. Barker. But she did not like the American, and she thought Barker was turning the Duke into a miner, or a farmer, or a greengrocer, or something—it was not quite clear. But she wished him out of the way, and fate had given her a powerful weapon. It was just that sort of double-handedness that the Duke most hated of all things in the earth. Moreover, he knew his sister never exaggerated, and that what she had told him was of necessity perfectly true.

Woe to Mr. Silas B. Barker junior if he came in the Duke's way that evening!

"I suppose he is coming to dinner?" said the Duke after a pause, during which his anger had settled into a comfortable ferocity.

"No," said Lady Victoria; "he sent some flowers and a note of regret."

"Well—I am glad of that. Would you like to go for a drive, Vick?"

"Yes, of all things. I have not been here since I was married"—which was about eighteen months, but she had already caught that matronly phrase—"and I want to see what they have been doing to the Park."

"All right. We'll take Claudius, if he is anywhere about the place."

"Of course," said Lady Victoria. And so the brother and sister prepared to soothe their ruffled feelings by making much of the man who was "a gentleman." But they were right, for Claudius was all they thought him, and a great deal more too, as they discovered in the sequel.

Having driven in the Park, the Duke insisting that Claudius should sit in the place of honour with Lady Victoria, and having criticised to their satisfaction the few equipages they met—for it was too early for New York—they went back to their hotel, and dispersed to dress for dinner. The Duke, as he had told his sister, had invited his friend to dine. They all sat together waiting his arrival. Punctual to the moment, the door opened, and Mr. Horace Bellingham beamed upon the assembled party. Ay, but he was a sight to do good to the souls of the hungry and thirsty, and of the poor, and in misery!

He requires description, not that any pen can describe him, but no one ever saw him who did not immediately wish to try. He was short, decidedly; but a broad deep chest and long powerful arms had given him many an advantage over taller adversaries in strange barbarous lands. He was perfectly bald, but that must have been because Nature had not the heart to cover such a wonderful cranium from the admiring gaze of phrenologists. A sweeping moustache and a long imperial of snowy white sat well on the ruddy tan of his complexion, and gave him an air at once martial and diplomatic. He was dressed in the most perfect of London clothes, and there were superb diamonds in his shirt, while a priceless sapphire sparkled, in a plain gold setting, on his broad, brown hand. He is the only man of his time who can wear precious stones without vulgarity. He moves like a king and has the air of the old school in every gesture. His dark eyes are brighter than his diamonds, and his look, for all his white beard and seventy years, is as young and fresh as the rose he wears in his coat.

There are some people who turn gray, but who do not grow hoary, whose faces are furrowed but not wrinkled, whose hearts are sore wounded in many places, but are not dead. There is a youth that bids defiance to age, and there is a kindness which laughs at the world's rough usage. These are they who have returned good for evil, not having learned it as a lesson of righteousness, but because they have no evil in them to return upon others. Whom the gods love die young, and they die young because they never grow old. The poet, who at the verge of death said this, said it of, and to, this very man.

The Duke went through the introductions, first to the Countess, then to Miss Skeat, then to his sister, and last of all to Claudius, who had been intently watching the newcomer. Mr. Bellingham paused before Claudius, and looked up in a way peculiarly his own, without raising his head. He had of course heard in New York of the strange fortune that had befallen Claudius on the death of the well-known Mr. Lindstrand, and now he stood a minute trying to take the measure of the individual before him, not in the least overcome by the physical proportions of the outer man, but struck by the intellectual face and forehead that surmounted such a tower of strength.

"I was in Heidelberg myself—a student," said he, his face lighting up with coming reminiscences, "but that was long before you were born, fifty years ago."

"I fancy it is little changed," said Claudius.

"I would like to go back to the Badischer Hof. I remember once—" but he broke off short and turned to the Countess, and sat down beside her. He knew all her people in America and her husband's people abroad. He immediately began telling her a story of her grandmother, with a verve and graphic spirit that enchanted Margaret, for she liked clever old men. Besides he is not old. It is not so long since—well, it is a long story. However, in less than one minute the assembled guests were listening to the old-time tale of Margaret's ancestress, and the waiter paused breathless on the threshold to hear the end, before he announced dinner.

There are two very different ways of dining—dining with Mr. Bellingham, and dining without him. But for those who have dined with him, all other prandial arrangements are an empty sham. At least so Claudius said to Margaret in an aside, when they got to the fruit. And Margaret, who looked wonderfully beautiful with a single band of gold through her black hair, laughed her assent, and said it was hopeless for the men of this day to enter the lists against the veterans of the ancien régime. And Claudius was not in the least hurt by the comparison, odious though it would have been to Mr. Barker, had he been there. Claudius had plenty of vanity, but it did not assume the personal type. Some people call a certain form of vanity pride. It is the same thing on a larger scale. Vanity is to pride what nervousness is to nerve, what morbid conscience is to manly goodness, what the letter of the law is to the spirit.

Before they rose from the table, Mr. Bellingham proposed that they should adjourn to Newport on the following day. He said it was too early to be in New York and that Newport was still gay; at all events, the weather promised well, and they need not stay more than twenty-four hours unless they pleased. The proposition was carried unanimously, the Duke making a condition that he should be left in peace and not "entertained in a handsome manner by the élite of our Newport millionaires"— as the local papers generally have it. Lady Victoria would not have objected to the operation of "being entertained" by Newport, for it amused her to see people, but of course she would enjoy herself very well without it. She always enjoyed herself, even when she went for a walk in the rain on a slippery Yorkshire road, all bundled up in waterproofs and hoods and things for her poor people—she enjoyed it all.

As for Claudius, he knew that if he went to Newport he must of necessity stay with the Barkers, but as he had not yet learned to look at Mr. Barker in the light of a rival, he thought this would be rather convenient than otherwise. The fact that he would be within easy reach of Margaret was uppermost in his mind.

During the last two days his relations with her had been of the happiest. There was an understanding between them, which took the place of a great deal of conversation. Claudius felt that his error in speaking too boldly had been retrieved, if not atoned for, and that henceforward his position was assured. He was only to be a friend, it was true, but he still felt that from friendship to love was but a step, and that the time would come. He thought of the mighty wooings of the heroes of his Northern home, and he felt in him their strength and their constancy. What were other men that he should think of them? He was her accepted friend of all others. She had said she hoped to find in him what she had never found before; and were not her words "always, always!" still ringing in his ears? She had found it then in him, this rare quality of friendship; she had found more,—a man who was a friend and yet a lover, but who could curb the strong passion to the semblance and docility of the gentler feeling. And when at last she should give the long-desired sign, the single glance that bids love speak, she would find such a lover as was not even dreamt of among the gods of the Greeks, nor yet among berserk heroes of ice and storm and battle. He felt to-day that he could endure to the end, for the end was worthy all endurance.

And now he sat by her side and looked down into her face when she spoke, and they laughed together. Verily was Claudius the proudest man in all earth's quarters, and his blue eyes flashed a deep fire, and his nostrils expanded with the breath of a victory won. Mr. Bellingham, on the other side of the table, sparkled with a wit and grace that were to modern table-talk what a rare flagon of old madeira, crusted with years, but brimming with the imperishable strength and perfume of eternal youth, might be to a gaudily-ticketed bottle of California champagne, effervescent, machine-made, cheap, and nasty. And his glance comprehended the pair, and loved them. He thought they were like a picture of the North and of the South; and the thought called up memories in his brave old breast of a struggle that shook the earth to her foundations, and made him think of problems yet unsolved. He sat in his place silent for some minutes, and the broad brown hand stroked the snowy beard in deep thought, so that the conversation flagged, and the Duke began to talk about the voyage. But Mr. Bellingham took his brimming glass, filled with the wine that ripened in the sun when he himself was but a little boy, and he held it a moment to the light; the juice was clearer now than it had been that day sixty years, and the hand that held the goblet was as a hand of iron for strength and steadiness, though the dark fingers might have plucked the grapes on the day they were pressed. And with an old-time motion he carried it to his lips, then paused one instant, then drank it slowly, slowly to the last drop. It was a toast, but the speech was unspoken, and none knew to whom or to what he drained the measure. In a little time he began to speak again; the conversation turned upon mutual friends in England, and the dinner was at an end.

But all through the evening Claudius never left Margaret's side. He felt that he was bridging over the difference between life at sea and life on land—that he was asserting his right to maintain in a drawing-room the privileges he had gained on the deck of the Streak. And Margaret, moreover, was especially friendly to-night, for she too felt the difference, and recognised that, after all, life on shore is the freer. There are certain conventionalities of a drawing-room that a man is less likely to break through, more certain to remember, than the unwritten rules of cruising etiquette. Most men who have led a free life are a little less likely to make love under the restraint of a white tie than they are when untrammelled by restraints of dress, which always imply some restraint of freedom.

At least Margaret thought so. And Claudius felt it, even though he would not acknowledge it. They talked about the voyage; about what they had said and done, about the accident, and a hundred other things. There is a moment in acquaintance, in friendship, and in love, when two people become suddenly aware that they have a common past. Days, weeks, or months have been spent in conversation, in reading, perhaps in toil and danger, and they have not thought much about it. But one day they wake up to the fact that these little or great things bind them, as forming the portion of their lives that have touched; and as they talk over the incidents they remember they feel unaccountably drawn to each other by the past. Margaret and Claudius knew this on the first evening they spent together on shore. The confusion of landing, the custom-house, the strange quarters in the great hotel—all composed a drop-curtain shutting off the ocean scene, and ending thus an episode of their life-drama. A new act was beginning for them, and they both knew how much might depend on the way in which it was begun, and neither dared plan how it should end. At all events, they were not to be separated yet, and neither anticipated such a thing.

Little by little their voices dropped as they talked, and they recked little of the others, as the dark cheek of the woman flushed with interest, and the blue light shone in the man's eyes. Their companions on the voyage were well used to seeing them thus together, and hardly noticed them, but Mr. Bellingham's bright eyes stole a glance from time to time at the beautiful pair in their corner, and the stories of youth and daring and love, that he seemed so full of this evening, flashed with an unwonted brilliancy. He made up his mind that the two were desperately, hopelessly, in love, and he had taken a fancy to Claudius from the first. There was no reason why they should not be, and he loved to build up romances, always ending happily, in his fertile imagination.

But at last it was "good-night." Mr. Bellingham was not the man to spend the entire evening in one house, and he moved towards Margaret, hating to disturb the couple, but yet determined to do it. He rose, therefore, still talking, and, as the Duke rose also, cleverly led him round the chairs until within speaking distance of Margaret, who was still absorbed in her conversation. Then, having finished the one thread, he turned round.

"By the by, Countess," he said, "I remember once—" and he told a graceful anecdote of Margaret's grandmother, which delighted every one, after which he bowed, like a young lover of twenty, to each of the three ladies, and departed.

The party dispersed, the Duke and Claudius for half an hour's chat and a cigar, and the ladies to their rooms. But Claudius and Margaret lingered one moment in their corner, standing.

"Has it been a happy day for you?" he asked, as she gave her hand.

"Yes, it has been happy. May there be many like it!" she answered.

"There shall be," said Claudius; "good-night, Countess."

"Good-night—good-night, Claudius."

The Duke waited fully ten minutes for the Doctor. It was the second time she had spoken his name without the formality of a prefix, and Claudius stood where she left him, thinking. There was nothing so very extraordinary in it, after all, he thought. Foreign women, especially Russians, are accustomed to omit any title or prefix, and to call their intimate friends by their simple names, and it means nothing. But her voice was so wonderful. He never knew his name sounded so sweet before—the consonants and vowels, like the swing and fall of a deep silver bell in perfect cadence. "A little longer," thought Claudius, "and it shall be hers as well as mine." He took a book from the table absently, and had opened it when he suddenly recollected the Duke, put it down and left the room.

Soon a noiseless individual in a white waistcoat and a dress-coat put his head in at the door, advanced, straightened the chairs, closed the book the Doctor had opened, put the gas out and went away, shutting the door for the night, and leaving the room to its recollections. What sleepless nights the chairs and heavy-gilt glasses and gorgeous carpets of a hotel must pass, puzzling over the fragments of history that are enacted in their presence!

CHAPTER XI

Mr. Barker's urgent engagement up town that evening must have been to meet some one; but considering that the individual he might be supposed to be awaiting did not come, he showed a remarkable degree of patience. He went to a certain quiet club and ordered, with the utmost care, a meal after his own heart—for one; and though several members hailed him and greeted him on his return, he did not seem particularly interested in what they had to say, but sat solitary at his small square table with its exquisite service; and when he had eaten, and had finished his modest pint of Pommery Sec, he drank his coffee and smoked his own cigars in undisturbed contemplation of the soft-tinted wall-paper, and in calm, though apparently melancholy, enjoyment of the gentle light that pervaded the room, and of the sweet evening breeze that blew in from the trees of Madison Square, so restful after the dust and discomfort of the hot September day.

Whoever it was that he awaited did not come, and yet Mr. Barker exhibited no sign of annoyance. He went to another room, and sat in a deep arm-chair with a newspaper which he did not read, and once he took a scrap of paper from his pocket and made a short note upon it with a patent gold pencil. It was a very quiet club, and Mr. Barker seemed to be its quietest member. And well he might be, for he had made up his mind on a grave point. He had determined to marry.

He had long known it must come, and had said to himself more than once that "to every man upon this earth death cometh, soon or late;" but being human, he had put off the evil day, having always thought that it must, of necessity, be evil. But now it was different. What he had said to the Duke, and what the Duke had said to him, that evening on the yacht when they were talking about marriage, was exactly what he had always expected to occur. The day, he said, must come when the enterprising mamma will get the better of Silas B. Barker junior. The girl of the season, with her cartload of bouquets slung all over her, her neat figure, her pink-and-white complexion and her matchless staying powers in a ballroom, will descend upon the devoted victim Barker, beak and talons, like the fish-hawk on the poor, simple minnow innocently disporting itself in the crystal waters of happiness. There will be wedding presents, and a breakfast, and a journey, and a prospect of everlasting misery. All these things, thought he, must come to every man in time, unless he is a saint, or an author, or has no money, and therefore they must come to me; but now it was different. If there is to be any fishing, he thought, I will be the hawk, and the minnow may take its chance of happiness. Why should the minnow not be happy? I am a hawk; well—but I am a very good hawk.

But these reflections were not what occupied his mind as he sat with his second cigar in the reading-room of his quiet club. These things he had elaborated in his brain at least three days ago, and they had now taken the form of a decision, against which there could be no appeal, because it was pleasant to the ego of Mr Barker. Judgments of that sort he never reversed. He had fully determined to be the hawk, he had picked out his minnow, and he was meditating the capture of his prey. A great many people do as much as that, and discover too late that what they have taken for a minnow is an alligator, or a tartar, or a salamander, or some evil beast that is too much for their powers. This was what Mr. Barker was afraid of, and this was what he wished to guard against. Unfortunately he was a little late in the selection of his victim, and he knew it. He had determined to marry the Countess Margaret.

He knew perfectly well that Claudius had determined upon the very same thing, and he knew that Claudius was intimate, to say the least of it, with the woman he loved. But Barker had made up his mind that Claudius had been refused, and had accepted the Platonic position offered him by the Countess, merely because he had not the strength to leave her. "Just like the vanity of a fellow like that," he argued, "not to be willing to believe himself beaten." He had drawn the whole situation in his mind entirely to his own satisfaction. If Claudius could only be removed, any other man would have as good a chance. The other man is Barker—therefore, remove Claudius at once. Remove him! Away with him! Let his place know him no more!

Mr. Barker sat unmoved in his chair; but he contemplated the nail on the middle finger of his left hand with absorbed interest, even bringing it nearer the light in order to obtain a better view.

He was one of those men who are seldom altogether unprepared. His mind was of the Napoleonic order, on a very small scale; with him to think of the end was to plan the means, and in the days that had followed the memorable night wherein the idea had struck him that he might marry the Countess in the teeth of Dr. Claudius, a project had grown up in his mind whereby he hoped now to effect his purpose. Perhaps the scheme had developed unconsciously, as often happens with persons whose lives are spent in planning. Perhaps he fondly hoped—for he was not without vanity—that he might yet win the Countess fairly, and had only contemplated his plot as a possibility. Be that as it may, from the moment he realised that a plan of action was necessary he also realised that the plan was ready, and he determined to put it into execution. It was an unfair plan he meditated, bad from the root up, and he knew it; but he did not hesitate on that account. Silas B. Barker junior had not enough conscience to make it an object for him to deceive himself as to the morality of his actions. A year or two since he would perhaps have defended himself in a general way by saying it was arrogance for a man to set himself up as any better than his surroundings. But between a year or two ago and this September evening there was set a gulf, represented by a couple of transactions in the "street," over which there was small joy in heaven and very little on earth.

Fair or unfair, it would be so much easier if Claudius were out of the way. It would simplify Mr. Barker's campaign so much; and, besides, it was so easy a matter to remove him, for a time at least. How? Why, simply by asserting that Claudius was not Claudius, that he was not the late Mr. Lindstrand's nephew, that he had no right to the fortune, and that if he wished to save himself trouble he had better return immediately to Heidelberg and resume his duties as a private lecturer in the University. It was easy enough! Who was there to show that Claudius was Claudius? There was nothing but the attestation of a wretched Heidelberg notary, who might easily have been persuaded to swear a little in consideration of a large bribe.

Besides, reflected Mr. Barker, the real Dr. Claudius was dead. He died about eight months ago; no doubt it was in the newspapers at the time, and a newspaper could certainly be found which should contain a notice of his death. Therefore, if the real Dr. Claudius were dead this Dr. Claudius was a sham, an impostor, a man obtaining money by personating the dead—in short, a criminal. However, it might not be necessary to proceed with all the rigour of the law, and he might be quietly sent back to Germany.

Of course Mr. Barker was responsible in some measure for having introduced this villain to the Countess and to the Duke. But how could Mr. Barker, a creature of sunny, lamb-like innocence, be expected to know an impostor at first sight? Claudius had acted his part so very well, you know, and Barker had been deceived by his apparent frankness; he had not even made any inquiries in Heidelberg, but had simply gone to the address his father had given him. Of course, also, the pretender had adopted the obvious expedient of taking the dead man's lodgings; had installed himself there, and called himself "Dr. Claudius." Nobody in America had ever seen the real Dr. Claudius; none of the yachting party had any means of knowing whether he were what he pretended to be or not; the only person who vouched for him was Silas B. Barker junior. And if Silas B. Barker junior would not vouch for him any longer, who would, pray? Obviously, no one.

"Dukes are very pretty things," said Mr. Barker; "and to know them intimately is a special grace. But they cannot swear to what they do not know anything about, any more than other people." And he lit another cigar, and looked at the clock, an old-fashioned black-marble timepiece with gilded hands. It wanted half an hour of midnight, and Mr. Barker's solitude had lasted since seven or thereabouts. Some one entered the room, bidding good-night to some one else at the door. Mr. Barker turned his eyes, and, recognising a friend, he smiled a wrinkled smile.

"Well, Mr. Screw, how goes it?" he said. "It is some time since we met."

"Happy to meet you, sir; glad to see you," replied the lawyer, putting out a long hand towards the part of the room where Mr. Barker was standing.

Mr. Screw was Mr. Scratch's partner. Mr. Screw was very tall, very thin, and exceedingly yellow. He had thick yellow hair, streaked with gray. His face seemed bound in old parchment, and his eyes were like brass nails driven very deep, but bright and fixed when he spoke. He had a great abundance of teeth of all sizes and shapes; his face was clean shaven; and he wore a stand-up collar, with a narrow black tie neatly adjusted in a bow. His feet and hands were of immense size. He was in evening-dress. He doubled up a few of his joints and deposited himself in a deep arm-chair—the twin of Barker's—on the other side of the fireplace.

"I thought very likely you would be here before the evening was out," said Mr. Barker. "Yes," he continued after a pause, "that is the reason I came here. I wanted to see you on business, and I missed you to-day down town."

"Oh! business, did you say?" inquired the other, rubbing his bony nose and looking at the empty grate.

"Yes, rather important to you—more than to myself, though it concerns me too. You have a new client, I believe; the nephew of our old partner Mr. Lindstrand."

"Dr. Claudius?" asked the lawyer, looking up.

"He calls himself so, at any rate," said Barker.

"What do you mean?" asked Mr. Screw quickly, shifting his position.

"Do you think you have taken all the necessary steps towards ascertaining that he is the heir—the right man—the real Dr. Claudius?"

"Great heavens!" exclaimed the lawyer, surprised and terribly frightened by Barker's insinuation, "you don't mean to say there is any doubt about it, do you?"

"I am inclined to think there is doubt—yes, decidedly. It is a very serious matter, and I thought it best to speak to you about it before talking to my father. You see, though the loss might fall on us, indirectly, the moral responsibility is yours, since you are the lawyers in the case."

"But your father is one of the executors, Mr. Barker," said Mr. Screw, who felt obliged to say something, and wanted to gain time.

"My father—yes," and Barker smiled disagreeably. "Yes, he is one of the executors. But you yourself are the other, Mr. Screw. And as far as any intelligence in the matter is concerned, you might be alone." Barker was willing to flatter the lawyer at the expense of his fond parent. Screw would be of more use to him than many fathers in this matter. Mr. Screw relapsed into silence, and sat for some minutes, hooking one leg behind the other, and thrusting as much of his hands into his pockets as those receptacles would contain. After a time he changed his position, heaved a species of sigh that sounded like the sudden collapse of a set of organ-bellows, and ran his fingers through his thick hair.

Barker thought he was going to speak. But he was mistaken; Mr. Screw was too much taken aback to speak yet. Then Barker spoke for him.

"Well," said he, caressing his foot and looking at the ceiling, "what are you going to do about it?"

"I shall do what is proper in such cases. I will stop his drawing any more money, and investigate the matter. If this is not the real Claudius, the real Claudius must be somewhere, and can be found."

"Perhaps he is dead," suggested Barker.

"It is about as easy to find a dead man as a live man," said Screw. "It is a surer thing, on the whole. A dead man can't change his clothes, and get his beard shaved off, and cavoort around the corner."

"Not generally speaking," said the other, "no well-regulated corpse would do it, anyhow. Besides, if he is dead, there must have been some notice of it in the Heidelberg papers. He belonged to the University, and they always put those things in the local sheet in Germany."

"That's so," said the lawyer. "Do you know anybody in Heidelberg who would look the matter up, Mr. Barker?"

Mr. Barker did know some one in Heidelberg—the very man, in fact. He would write immediately, and set the inquiry on foot. Meanwhile there were other things to be settled. After the first shock the lawyer was not inclined to let Barker off so easily for having indorsed a man he suspected of being a humbug. Barker retorted that he had found Claudius in possession of the documents transmitted by Messrs. Screw and Scratch, and that it was not his fault if he supposed that those astute gentlemen had taken proper precautions to ascertain the identity of their client. He went into many details, explaining how his suspicions had been aroused by degrees in the course of many conversations. He was expecting a question from Mr. Screw. At last it came.

"Mr. Barker," said Screw, fixing his brass-headed eyes intently on his companion—for Mr. Screw was no fool—"Mr. Barker, you brought this man over here, and you know him better than any one else. Now, what I want to know is this. He may be the right man, after all. What we are going to do is entirely precautionary. Do you want to appear or not?" Barker had not expected the question to be put so directly, but he was perfectly prepared for it.

"I am sure I do not care," he said, with a fine indifference. "I have no objection. It is a mere question of expediency; do not consider me in the matter. Do what you think is right," he added, emphasising the last word, and meeting Screw's glance boldly enough. Screw looked at him for a moment or two in silence, and then turned his eyes away. There was the faintest reflection of a smile on his yellow face, and the expression became him well. Screw was astute, sharp as a ferret, relentless as a steel-corkscrew, crushing its cruel way through the creaking cork; but Screw was an honest man, as the times go. That was the difference between him and Barker. Screw's smile was his best expression, Barker's smile was of the devil, and very wily. Screw smiled because he was amused. Barker smiled when he was successful.

"I think for the present," said Mr. Screw, "that unless you positively wish to appear, it would be as well that you should not. If we are mistaken, and the Doctor is really what he pretends to be, it will be very unpleasant for you afterwards to have been concerned in an inquiry into the validity of his rights."

"Do you think so?" asked Barker, looking languidly across at Mr. Screw. "Very well, in that case you may conduct the inquiry, and I will not appear. I shall meet him just as if nothing had happened, and let him tell me what you have done. Of course he will tell me, the first thing. Besides, as you say, he may be the right man, after all."

"Exactly," said Mr. Screw. He knew perfectly well that Barker would not want Claudius to know the part he had played, in case all turned out to be right, though he did not know that Barker was deceiving him. He supposed that Barker really had serious doubts about Claudius, and as there was no one else to vouch for the latter, he was very honestly frightened. He reviewed the situation in his own mind, and he came to the conclusion that he had really been remiss in the performance of his duties as executor. It had not seemed in the least probable that any deception could be practised, and yet, when all was said, there was only the Heidelberg notary's attestation of the signature to support the claimant of Mr. Lindstrand's fortune. This reflection comforted Mr. Screw a little. At all events, he would be perfectly justified in calling on Claudius and stating his difficulty, requesting him to give what assistance was in his power towards a speedy identification of himself. In the meantime he set himself to cross-examine Mr. Barker, endeavouring to extract all the information he could. But extracting information from Mr. Barker was no easy task, as he very soon found, and as the hands of the clock pointed to one, he rose slowly, as by stages, from the depths of his arm-chair, and made up his mind that Barker did not know very much about the matter, though he knew more than any one else, and that the only thing to be done was to go straight to Claudius and state the case. No honest man ever had much difficulty in proving who he was, thought Mr. Screw, and if he is an impostor, he will very likely not show fight at all, but make off to parts unknown, where he can very easily be caught.

Barker rose from his seat too, and took leave of the lawyer, well pleased with the result of his evening's work. It was very satisfactory. He had produced exactly the impression on Mr. Screw's mind which he had intended to produce; and having set that engine of the law in motion, he knew that he could fold his hands and proceed to enjoy himself after his manner. He knew that everything would be done which could contribute to annoy and mortify Claudius, and that it would be done in such a way, with such paraphernalia of legal courtesy and mercantile formality, that the unhappy Doctor could not complain. Barker had shrewdly calculated the difficulties Claudius would have to surmount in identifying himself in a strange country, without friends, and against the prejudices of Mr. Screw, his uncle's executor. Moreover, if, after countless efforts and endless trouble, Claudius succeeded, as he probably would, in obtaining his fortune, Barker would be no worse off than before. He would have done nothing assailable, and he would have gained all the advantages of the time Claudius lost, not to mention the cloud of suspicion which must inevitably rest on the Doctor, until he should succeed in clearing himself before the world. With skill, courage, and money, there was no telling what progress Barker might make in his suit for the Countess, before Claudius was himself again. With such an advantage, if he could not outdo the Swede, he did not deserve to.

So saying, Mr. Barker, left once more alone in the sitting-room, paced slowly twice round the table, looked at himself in the glass, twisted his heavy moustache into shape, and smoothed his hair. Then he took his hat and went out. There was a cab at the door of the club, and in a minute more he was spinning along Fifth Avenue, in the direction of his father's house.

The machinery was wound up, and he had nothing more to do. To-morrow morning Claudius would pass a bad quarter of an hour with Mr. Screw, and in the afternoon Barker would call upon him and offer such consolation as was in his power; and when he had called on Claudius, he would call on the Countess Margaret and tell her what sad sceptics these legal people were, everlastingly pestering peaceable citizens in the hope of extracting from them a few miserable dollars. And he would tell her how sorry he was that Claudius should be annoyed, and how he, Barker, would see him through—that is, he hoped so; for, he would add, of course, such men as Mr. Screw and his own father would not make so much trouble if they did not at least think they had some cause for anxiety; and so forth, and so on. And he would leave the Countess with a most decided impression that there was something wrong about Claudius. Oh yes! something not quite clear about his antecedents, you know. Of course it would come right in the end—no doubt of that; oh dear, no.

It was a happy night for Mr. Barker; but Claudius slept ill. He had an evil dream.

CHAPTER XII

When Mr. Screw called at Claudius's hotel the next day, the Doctor had gone out. Mr. Screw said he would wait, and sat down with a book to pass the time, for he was fond of reading in his leisure moments, few as they were. Claudius had left the house early in the morning, and had gone to find the spot where his uncle had been buried—no easy matter, in the vast cemetery where the dead men lie in hundreds of thousands, in stately avenues and imposing squares, in houses grand and humble, high and low, but all closed and silent with the grandeur of a great waiting. Claudius was not sentimental in this pilgrimage; it was with him a matter of course, a duty which he performed naturally for the satisfaction of his conscience. He could not have told any other reason, though, if he had been called upon to analyse the feeling which impels most men to do the same thing, under the same circumstances, he would have replied that a scientific explanation of the fact could only be found in the ancient practices of "ancestor worship," of which some trace remains unto this day. But he would have added that it was a proper mark of reverence and respect for the dead, and that man naturally inclines to fulfil such obligations, unless deterred by indolence or the fear of ridicule. At any rate, he went alone; and it was late in the afternoon before he came back.

When at last he returned, he was not surprised to find Mr. Screw awaiting him. He had not found that gentleman on his first visit to Pine Street; and it seemed very natural that his uncle's executor should call upon him. He was cordial and courteous to his visitor, who took the Doctor's measure, and looked into his honest eyes, and realised that this claimant to Lindstrand's money was undoubtedly a very fine fellow indeed. Mr. Screw felt that it would be hard to tell such a man to his face that he was not altogether satisfied of his identity. But then, as the lawyer reflected, swindlers are generally fine fellows; indeed, their imposing appearance is often their whole capital and stock-in-trade. Mr. Screw had a profound knowledge of mankind, and he immediately determined upon his course of action, which should be cautious, but at the same time honest and straightforward. After a preliminary exchange of civilities, he opened fire.

"I have come on very delicate business, Dr. Claudius," said he; and he hooked one leg behind the other as he sat and ran his hands through his hair. Claudius settled himself in his chair and waited, not having any idea what the business might be.

"You will readily understand," continued Mr. Screw, "that in my position I feel obliged to take every conceivable precaution in administering the estate of the late Mr. Lindstrand. You will, therefore, not be offended at what I am going to say. My personality has nothing to do with it, nor can any personal impression you produce upon me, no matter how favourable, be considered in the light of evidence. I have never seen you before, and I am bound to say that the little I know of you, although perfectly satisfactory as far as it goes, is not sufficient to prove in a court that you are really the person indicated in Mr. Lindstrand's will." Here Mr. Screw paused to see how Claudius would take the hint that more evidence was required.

But Claudius, the embodiment of calm strength, intellectual and physical, was not to be moved by such trifles. He showed not the slightest emotion, nor did he betray any especial interest in what the lawyer was saying. His attitude was that of attention to a matter which it was his duty to understand and to elucidate. But that was all. He wished Mr. Screw would talk a little faster, and say what he required and go; but he was too courteous to hurry him.

"My dear sir," he answered, "I fully understand your position, and any apology from you would be out of place. Pray proceed."

"I have nothing more to say," said Mr. Screw, astonished at so much indifference where a great fortune was concerned. "I like to be brief in such matters. I have nothing more to say, sir, excepting that I would be greatly obliged if you would put into my hands such documents as you may think proper for the full establishing of your rights."

"Very well," said Claudius. "If you will tell me what evidence you require I will procure it immediately." With that he rose, and lighted a cigarette.

"A properly-attested certificate of your birth would be all-sufficient," said Mr. Screw, who began to feel relieved by the conduct of the Doctor. The latter, however, suddenly stood still with the match in his fingers, and looked at the lawyer with a curious scrutiny.

"I would prefer," he said, "to give some other evidence of my identity than that, if it is the same to you."

"If you prefer it, of course," said the lawyer coldly. His suspicions were immediately roused, for he had named the simplest description of document he could think of, and it seemed odd that the Doctor should be so evidently disinclined to produce it.

"I suppose," said the Doctor, "that the formal attestation of my identity by the authorities of the University of Heidelberg would be sufficient?"

"Yes, I should think so," said Screw cautiously. "But will it not take some time to procure that?"

"Well? If it does, what then?"

"Only that—you will understand that until this matter is settled I should not feel justified in authorising you to draw upon the estate."

Claudius's sense of logic was offended.

"My dear sir," he replied, "have I drawn upon the estate for a single dollar yet?"

"No, sir, I am bound to say you have not, although you might have considered it natural to do so, and we should have put no obstacle—" Mr. Screw stopped short. He had betrayed himself, and felt extremely embarrassed. But he said enough to give Claudius an idea of the situation. Something had occurred, some one had spoken, to cast a doubt on his identity; and Mr. Screw was the chosen emissary of that "some one."

"Then, Mr. Screw," said the Doctor in measured tones, "I would admonish you to be more careful how you insinuate that I might do anything of the kind. You have inconvenienced me quite enough already. You had better not inconvenience me any more. I consider your conduct a piece of unparalleled clumsiness, and your language little short of impertinent. What you have said now you should have said in the letter which announced my uncle's death. Or you should have instructed Mr. Barker, who was abroad at the time and found me in Heidelberg, to make the necessary investigations. The evidence shall be forthcoming in proper season, and until then I do not desire the advantage of your company."

Mr. Screw was so much astonished with this mode of address from a man whom he had foolishly imagined to be good-natured that he stood a moment by the table hesitating what he should say. Claudius took up a book and began to read.

"Well," said he, perceiving that Mr. Screw was still in the room, "why don't you go?"

"Really, Dr. Claudius, I am not accustomed—" he began.

"Go," said Claudius, interrupting him; "it is not of the smallest interest to me to know what you are accustomed to. There is the door."

"Sir—"

"Do you prefer the window?" asked the Doctor, rising in great wrath and striding towards the unhappy lawyer. Mr. Screw instantly made up his mind that the door was preferable, and disappeared. When he was gone Claudius sat down again. He was very angry; but, in his own view, his anger was just. It was very clear to him, from the words Mr. Screw had inadvertently let fall, that some one had, for reasons unknown, undertaken to cause him a great deal of unpleasantness. What he had said to Screw was not to be denied. If there was any question as to his identity, full proof should have been required from the first. But his autograph letter from Heidelberg, attested by a notary, had been accepted as sufficient; and "Screw and Scratch" had answered the letter, and Claudius had received their answer in Baden. It had never entered his head that anything more would be required. So long as Screw had confined himself to stating his position, merely asking for further evidence, the Doctor had nothing to say. But at the suggestion that Claudius might want to draw money from the estate before his claims were fully established, he lost his temper. It was an imputation on his honour; and, however slight it might seem to Mr. Screw, Claudius was not the man to bear it.

Ten minutes later Mr. Barker walked in unannounced. It was natural enough that he should call, but Claudius did not want him. The Doctor had not had time to think over the situation, but he had, a vague impression that Barker had something to do with this sudden cloud of annoyance that had risen to darken his path. Barker, on his side, was prepared for storms, but he intended to play the part of confidential friend and consoler. Claudius, however, wanted neither friends nor consolation, and he was in the worst of tempers. Nevertheless, he rose and offered his guest a chair, and asked him how he did. Barker took the chair and said he was fairly well, on the way to recovery from the voyage.

"What have you been doing all day, Claudius?" he asked.

"I have been to a place called Greenwood, to see where they had buried my uncle," answered Claudius, and relapsed into silence.

"No wonder you look so gloomy. Whatever induced you to do such a thing?"

"I was not induced," said Claudius. "He was my last relation in the world, and I did the only thing I could to honour his memory, which was to go and see his grave."

"Yes, very proper, I am sure," replied Barker. "If my relations would begin and die, right away, I would trot around and see their graves fast enough!"

Claudius was silent.

"What on earth is the matter with you, Claudius? Have you got a headache, or are you going to be married?"

Claudius roused himself, and offered Barker a cigar.

"There is nothing the matter," he said; "I suppose my excursion has made me a little gloomy; but I shall soon get over that. There are matches on the mantelpiece."

"Thanks. Why did you not come down town to-day? Oh! of course you were away. It was very good fun. We had a regular bear garden."

"It looked like something of that sort yesterday when I was there."

"Yesterday? Oh! you had never been there before. Yes, it is always like that. I say, come and take a drive in the park before dinner."

"No, thanks. I am very sorry, but I have an appointment in a few minutes. I would like to go very much; you are very kind."

"Business?" asked the inquisitive Mr. Barker.

"Well—yes, if you like, business."

"Oh!" said Barker. "By the by, have you seen any of your lawyer people to-day?" Barker had expected that Claudius would confide to him the trouble Screw was raising. But as Claudius did not begin, Barker asked the question.

"Yes," answered the Doctor, "Screw has been here. In fact he is just gone."

"Anything wrong?" inquired the tormentor.

"No, nothing wrong that I know of," said Claudius. Then he suddenly turned sharply on Barker, and looked straight at him. "Did you expect to hear that there was anything wrong?" he asked quickly. Claudius had a very unpleasant way of turning upon his antagonist just a minute before the enemy was ready for him. Barker had found this out before, and, being now directly interrogated, he winced perceptibly.

"Oh dear, no," he hastened to say. "But lawyers are great bores sometimes, especially where wills are concerned. And I thought perhaps Screw might be wearying you with his formalities."

"No," said Claudius indifferently, "nothing to—" he was interrupted by a knock at the door. It was the Duke's servant, a quiet man in gray clothes and gray whiskers. He had a bald head and bright eyes.

"His Grace's compliments, sir, and can you see him now, sir?"

"Yes, I will come in a moment," said Claudius.

"I think, sir," said the man, "that his Grace is coming to your rooms."

"Very good. My compliments, and I shall be glad to see him." The gray servant vanished.

Barker rose to go; but Claudius was begging him not to hurry, when there was another knock, and the Duke entered. He shook hands with Claudius, and spoke rather coldly to Barker. The latter was uneasy, and felt that he was in the way. He was. Barker had fallen into a singular error of judgment in regard to the relations existing between the Duke and Claudius. He had imagined it in his power to influence the Duke's opinion, whereas in trying to effect that object he had roused the Englishman's animosity. Besides, Mr. Barker was to the Duke a caprice. He found the quick-thinking man of business amusing and even useful, but for steady companionship he did not want him. A passage across the Atlantic was more than enough to satisfy his desire for Mr. Barker's society, even if Barker had not managed to excite his indignation. But Claudius was different. The honest nobleman could not tell why it was, but it was true, nevertheless. He looked upon the Doctor more as an equal than Barker. The Duke was a very great man in his own country, and it was singular indeed that he should find a man to his liking, a man who seemed of his own caste and calibre, in the simple privat-docent of a German university. Perhaps Barker felt it too. At all events, when the Duke sat himself down in Claudius's room, after begging permission to ring for lights, and made himself most evidently at home, Mr. Barker felt that he was in the way; and so, promising to call on Claudius again in the morning, he departed. Claudius stood by the mantelpiece while the servant lit the gas.

"I am very glad to see you," he said, when the man had gone.

"I am glad of that, for I want your society. The Countess Margaret has a headache, and Lady Victoria has gone to dine in her rooms, and to spend the evening with her."

"I am very sorry to hear that the Countess is not well," said Claudius, "but I am very glad of anything that brings you here to-night. I am in trouble—that is, I have been very much annoyed."

"Ah, very sorry," said the Duke.

"It so happens that you are the only person in America, as far as I know, who can help me."

"I?" The Duke opened his eyes wide. Then he reflected that it might be something concerning the Countess, and waited.

"You are a gentleman," said Claudius reflectively, and hardly addressing his visitor as he said it.

"Quite so," said the Duke. "It's a very fine word that."

"And a man of honour," continued Claudius in a meditative tone.

"The deuce and all, it's the same thing," said the Duke, rather puzzled.

"Yes; in some countries it is. Now, what I want to ask you is this. Could you, as a gentleman and a man of honour, swear in a court of law that you know me, and that I am the person I represent myself to be? That is the question."

The Duke was too much surprised to answer directly. He made a great fuss over his cigar, and got up and shut the window. Then he sat down in another chair.

"I don't know what you mean," he said at last, to gain time.

"I mean what I say," said Claudius. "Could you swear, before the Supreme Court of the United States, for instance, that I am Claudius, sometime student, now Doctor of Philosophy of the University of Heidelberg in Germany? Could you swear that?"

"My dear boy," said the other, "what in the world are you driving at?" The Duke realised that he could not conscientiously swear to any such statement as that proposed by Claudius; and, liking him as he did, he was much distressed at being put into such a corner.

"I will tell you afterwards what it is about, Duke," said Claudius. "I am serious, and I would like you to answer the question, though I foresee that you will say you could not swear to anything of the kind."

"Honestly, Claudius, though there is not the slightest doubt in my mind that you are what you appear to be, I could not conscientiously swear it in evidence. I do not know anything about you. But Barker could."

"No, he could not. He knows no more about me than you do, saving that he met me two or three days sooner. He met me in Heidelberg, it is true, but he made no inquiries whatever concerning me. It never entered his head that I could be anything but what I professed to be."

"I should think not, indeed," said the Duke warmly.

"But now that I am here in the flesh, these lawyers are making trouble. One of them was here a little while since, and he wanted documentary evidence of my identity."

"Who was the lawyer?"

"A Mr. Screw, one of the executors of the will."

"Who is the other executor?" asked the Duke quickly.

"Barker's father."

The Englishman's face darkened, and he puffed savagely at his cigar. He had been angry with Barker the day before. Now he began to suspect him of making trouble.

"What sort of evidence did the man want?" he asked at length.

"Any sort of documentary evidence would do. He asked me for my certificate of birth, and I told him he could not have it. And then he went so far as to remark in a very disagreeable way that he could not authorise me to draw upon the estate until I produced evidence."

"Well, that is natural enough."

"It would have been so at first. But they had accepted the mere signature to my letter from Heidelberg as proof of my existence, and I got word in Baden in July that I might draw as much as I pleased. And now they turn upon me and say I am not myself. Something has happened. Fortunately I have not touched the money, in spite of their kind permission."

"There is something very odd about this, Claudius. Have you got such a thing as a birth certificate to show?"

"Yes," answered Claudius, after a pause. "I have everything in perfect order, my mother's marriage and all."

"Then why, in Heaven's name, can you not show it, and put all these rascally lawyers to flight?"

"Because—" Claudius began, but he hesitated and stopped. "It is a curious story," he said, "and it is precisely what I want to talk to you about."

"Is it very long?" asked the Duke; "I have not dined yet."

"No, it will not take long, and if you have nothing better to do we will dine together afterwards. But first there are two things I want to say. If I prove to you that I am the son of my uncle's sister, will you tell Mr. Screw that you know it for a fact, that is, that if it had to be sworn to, you would be willing to swear to it?"

"If you prove it to me so that I am legally sure of it, of course I will."

"The other thing I will ask you is, not to divulge what I shall tell you, or show you. You may imagine from my being unwilling to show these papers, even to a lawyer, when my own fortune is concerned, that I attach some importance to secrecy."

"You may trust me," said the Duke; "you have my word," he added, as if reluctantly. People whose word is to be trusted are generally slow to give it. Claudius bowed his head courteously, in acknowledgment of the plighted promise. Then he opened a trunk that stood in a corner of the room, and took from it the iron box in which he had deposited the lawyer's letter on that evening three months before, when his destiny had roused itself from its thirty years' slumber. He set the box on the table, and having locked the door of the room sat down opposite his guest. He took a key from his pocket.

"You will think it strange," he said with a smile, "that I should have taken the liberty of confiding to you my secret. But when you have seen what is there, you will perceive that you are the most fitting confidant in this country—for general reasons, of course; for I need not say there is nothing in those papers which concerns you personally." Claudius unlocked the box and took out a few letters that were lying on the top, then he pushed the casket across the table to the Duke.

"Will you please examine the contents for yourself?" he said. "There are only three or four papers to read—the rest are letters from my father to my mother—you may look at them if you like; they are very old."

All this time the Duke looked very grave. He was not accustomed to have his word of honour asked for small matters, and if this were some trivial question of an assumed name, or the like, he was prepared to be angry with Claudius. So he silently took the little strong box, and examined the contents. There were two packages of papers, two or three morocco cases that might contain jewels, and there was a string of pearls lying loose in the bottom of the casket. The Duke took the pearls curiously in his hand and held them to the light. He had seen enough of such things to know something of their value, and he knew this string might be worth anywhere from eight to ten thousand pounds. He looked graver than ever.

"Those are beautiful pearls, Dr. Claudius," he said; "too beautiful for a Heidelberg student to have lying about among his traps." He turned them over and added, "The Duchess has nothing like them."

"They belonged to my mother," said Claudius simply. "I know nothing of their value."

The Duke took the papers and untied the smaller package, which appeared to contain legal documents, while the larger seemed to be a series of letters filed in their envelopes, as they had been received.

"My mother's name was Maria Lindstrand," said Claudius. He leaned back, smoking the eternal cigarette, and watched the Duke's face.

Before the Englishman had proceeded far he looked up at Claudius, uttering an exclamation of blank amazement. Claudius merely bent his head as if to indorse the contents of the paper, and was silent. The Duke read the papers carefully through, and examined one of them very minutely by the light. Then he laid them down with a certain reverence, as things he respected.

"My dear Claudius—" he rose and extended his hand to the young man with a gesture that had in it much of dignity and something of pride. "My dear Claudius, I shall all my life remember that you honoured me with your confidence. I accepted it as a token of friendship, but I am now able to look upon it as a very great distinction."

"And I, Duke, shall never forget that you believed in me on my own merits, before you were really able to swear that I was myself." Claudius had also risen, and their hands remained clasped a moment. Then Claudius applied himself to rearranging the contents of his box; and the Duke walked up and down the room, glancing from time to time at the Doctor. He stopped suddenly in his walk.

"But—goodness gracious! why have you kept this a secret?" he asked, as if suddenly recollecting himself.

"My mother," said Claudius, "was too proud to come forward and claim what my father, but for his untimely death, would have given her in a few months. As for me, I have been contented in my life, and would have been unwilling to cause pain to any one by claiming my rights. My mother died when I was a mere child, and left these papers sealed, directing me not to open them until I should be twenty-one years old. And so when I opened them, I made up my mind to do nothing about it."

"It is not easy to understand you, Claudius; but I will swear to anything you like."

"Thank you; I am very grateful."

"Do not speak of that. I am proud to be of service. By the by, the present—the present incumbent is childless, I believe. He must be your father's brother?"

"Yes," said Claudius. "Should he die, I would not hesitate any longer."

"No indeed, I hope not. It is a shame as it is."

"By the by," said Claudius, who had put away his box; "why did you not go to Newport to-day? I meant to go on to-morrow and meet you there. This business had put it out of my head."

"Lady Victoria and the Countess both wanted to stay another day."

"Is the Countess ill?" asked Claudius. "Or do you think she would see me this evening?"

"I do not think there is anything especial the matter. She will very likely see you after dinner. As for me, I am hungry; I have walked all over New York this afternoon."

"Very well, let us dine. You know New York, and must select the place."

Arm-in-arm they went away together, and the Duke introduced Claudius to the glories of Delmonico's.

CHAPTER XIII

Troubles never come singly; moreover, they come on horseback, and go away on foot. If Claudius had passed an unpleasant afternoon, the Countess's day had been darkened with the shadow of a very serious difficulty. Early in the morning her maid had brought her coffee, and with it a note in a foreign hand. The maid, who was French, and possessed the usual characteristics of French maids, had exhausted her brain in trying to discover who the sender might be. But the missive was sealed with wax, and a plain "N" was all the impression. So she adopted the usual expedient of busying herself in the room, while her mistress opened the note, hoping that some chance exclamation, or even perhaps an answer, might give her curiosity the food it longed for. But Margaret read and reread the note, and tore it up into very small pieces, thoughtfully; and, as an afterthought, she burned them one by one over a wax taper till nothing was left. Then she sent her maid away and fell to thinking. But that did not help her much; and the warm sun stole through the windows, and the noise in the street prevented her from sleeping, for she was unused to the sound of wheels after the long weeks at sea. And so she rang for her maid again. The maid came, bringing another note, which, she said, had been given her by "Monsieur Clodiuse;" and would there be an answer?

It was simply a few lines to say he was going to be away all day, and that he hoped to have the pleasure of seeing the Countess in Newport to-morrow. But for some reason or other Margaret was not pleased with the note, and merely said there would be no answer.

"Madame would she dress herself to go out, or to keep the lodging?"

Madame would not go out. Was it warm? Oh yes, it was very warm. In fact it was hébétant. Would Madame see Monsieur le Duc if he called at eleven? Monseigneur's Monsieur Veelees had charged her to inquire of Madame. No, Madame would not see Monsieur le Duc this morning. But if any one called, Madame desired to be informed. Madame would be served. And so the toilet proceeded.

It was not very long before some one called. There was a knock at the door of the bedroom. Clémentine left the Countess's hair, which she was busy combing and tressing, and went to the door. It was old Vladimir, Margaret's faithful Russian servant.

"At this hour!" exclaimed the Countess, who was not in the best of tempers. "What does he want?"

Vladimir ventured to make a remark in Russian, from the door, which produced an immediate effect. Margaret rose swiftly, overturning her chair and sweeping various small articles from the table in her rapid movement. She went very quickly to the door, her magnificent black hair all hanging down. She knew enough Russian to talk to the servant.

"What did you say, Vladimir?"

"Margareta Ivanowna"—Margaret's father's name had been John—"Nicolaï Alexandrewitch is here," said Vladimir, who seemed greatly surprised. His geographical studies having been purely experimental, the sudden appearance of a Russian gentleman led him to suppose his mistress had landed in some outlying part of Russia, or at least of Europe. So she bade the old servant conduct the gentleman to her sitting-room and ask him to wait. She was not long in finishing her toilet. Before she left the room a servant of the hotel brought another box of flowers from Mr. Barker. Clémentine cut the string and opened the pasteboard shell. Margaret glanced indifferently at the profusion of roses and pink pond-lilies—a rare variety only found in two places in America, on Long Island and near Boston—and having looked, she turned to go.

Clémentine held up two or three flowers, as if to try the effect of them on Margaret's dress.

"Madame would she not put some flowers in her dress?"

No. Madame would not. Madame detested flowers. Whereat the intelligent Clémentine carefully examined the name of the sender, inscribed on a card which lay in the top of the box. Mr. Barker knew better than to send flowers anonymously. He wanted all the credit he could get. The Countess swept out of the room.

At the door of the sitting-room she was met by a young man, who bent low to kiss her extended hand, and greeted her with a manner which was respectful indeed, but which showed that he felt himself perfectly at ease in her society.

Nicolaï Alexandrewitch, whom we will call simply Count Nicholas, was the only brother of Margaret's dead husband. Like Alexis, he had been a soldier in a guard regiment; Alexis had been killed at

Plevna, and Nicholas had succeeded to the title and the estates, from which, however, a considerable allowance was paid to the Countess as a jointure.

Nicholas was a handsome man of five or six and twenty, of middle height, swarthy complexion, and compact figure. His beard was very black, and he wore it in a pointed shape. His eyes were small and deep-set, but full of intelligence. He had all the manner and appearance of a man of gentle birth, but there was something more; an indescribable, undefinable air that hung about him. Many Russians have it, and the French have embodied the idea it conveys in their proverb that if you scratch a Russian you will find the Tartar. It is rather a trait of Orientalism in the blood, and it is to be noticed as much in Servians, Bulgarians, Roumanians, and even Hungarians, as in Russians. It is the peculiarity of most of these races that under certain circumstances, if thoroughly roused, they will go to any length, with a scorn of consequence which seems to the Western mind both barbarous and incomprehensible. Margaret had always liked him. He was wild; but he was a courteous gentleman, and could always be depended upon.

"Mon cher," said Margaret, "I need not tell you I am enchanted to see you, but what is the meaning of the things you wrote me this morning? Are you really in trouble?"

"Hélas, yes. I am in the worst kind of trouble that exists for a Russian. I am in political trouble—and that entails everything else."

"Tell me all about it," said she. "Perhaps I may help you."

"Ah no! you cannot help. It is not for that I am come. I have a confession to make that concerns you."

"Well?" said she, with a smile. She did not suppose it could be anything very bad.

"You will be angry, of course," he said, "but that is nothing. I have done you an injury that I cannot repair."

"Enfin, my dear Nicholas, tell me. I do not believe anything bad of you."

"You are kindness itself, and I thank you in advance. Wait till you have heard. I am 'suspect,'—they think I am a Nihilist I am exiled to the mines, and everything is confiscated. Voilà! Could it be worse?"

Margaret was taken off her guard. She had herself been in more than easy circumstances at the time of her marriage, but the financial crisis in America, which occurred soon after that event, had greatly crippled her resources. She had of late looked chiefly to her jointure for all the luxuries which were so necessary to her life. To find this suddenly gone, in a moment, without the slightest preparation, was extremely embarrassing. She covered her eyes with one hand for a moment to collect her thoughts and to try and realise the extent of the disaster. Nicholas mistook the gesture.

"You will never forgive me, I know. I do not deserve that you should. But I will do all in my power to repair the evil. I will go to Siberia if they will consider your rights to the estate."

Margaret withdrew her hand, and looked earnestly at the young man.

"Forgive you?" said she. "My dear Nicholas, you do not suppose I seriously think there is anything to forgive?"

"But it is true," he said piteously; "in ruining me they have ruined you. Mon Dieu, mon Dieu! If I only had a friend—"

"Taisez vous donc, mon ami. It is everything most bête what you say. You have many friends, and as for me, I do not care a straw for the money. Only if I had known I would not have left Europe. Voilà tout."

"Ah, that is it," said Nicholas. "I escaped the police and hurried to Baden. But you were gone. So I took the first steamer and came here. But I have waited ten days, and it was only last night I saw in the papers that you had arrived yesterday morning. And here I am."

Margaret rose, from a feeling that she must move about—the restless fiend that seizes energetic people in their trouble. Nicholas thought it was a sign for him to go. He took his hat.

"Believe me—" he began, about to take his leave.

"You are not going?" said Margaret. "Oh no. Wait, and we will think of some expedient. Besides you have not told me half what I want to know. The money is of no consequence; but what had you done to lead to such a sentence? Are you really a Nihilist?"

"Dieu m'en garde!" said the Count devoutly. "I am a Republican, that is all. Seulement, our Holy Russia does not distinguish."

"Is not the distinction very subtle?"

"The difference between salvation by education and salvation by dynamite; the difference between building up and tearing down, between Robespierre and Monsieur Washington."

"You must have been indiscreet. How could they have found it out?"

"I was bête enough to write an article in the Russki Mir—the mildest of articles. And then some of the Nihilist agents thought I was in their interests and wanted to see me, and the police observed them, and I was at once classed as a Nihilist myself, and there was a perquisition in my house. They found some notes and a few manuscripts of mine, quite enough to suit their purpose, and so the game was up."

"But they did not arrest you?"

"No. As luck would have it, I was in Berlin at the time, on leave from my regiment, for I was never suspected before in the least. And the Nihilists, who, to tell the truth, are well organised and take good care of their brethren, succeeded in passing word to me not to come back. A few days afterwards the Russian Embassy were hunting for me in Berlin. But I had got away. Sentence was passed in contempt, and I read the news in the papers on my way to Paris. There is the whole history."

"Have you any money?" inquired Margaret after a pause.

"Mon Dieu! I have still a hundred napoleons. After that the deluge."

"By that time we shall be ready for the deluge," said Margaret cheerfully. "I have many friends, and something may yet be done. Meanwhile do not distress yourself about me; you know I have something of my own."

"How can I thank you for your kindness? You ought to hate me, and instead you console!"

"My dear friend, if I did not like you for your own sake, I would help you because you are poor Alexis's brother." There was no emotion in her voice at the mention of her dead husband, only a certain reverence. She had honoured him more than she had loved him.

"Princesse, quand même," said Nicholas in a low voice, as he raised her fingers to his lips.

"Leave me your address before you go. I will write as soon as I have decided what to do." Nicholas scratched the name of a hotel on his card.

When he was gone Margaret sank into a chair. She would have sent for Claudius—Claudius was a friend—but she recollected his note, and thought with some impatience that just when she needed him most he was away. Then she thought of Lady Victoria, and she rang the bell. But Lady Victoria had gone out with her brother, and they had taken Miss Skeat. Margaret was left alone in the great hotel. Far off she could hear a door shut or the clatter of the silver covers of some belated breakfast service finding its way up or down stairs. And in the street the eternal clatter and hum and crunch, and crunch and hum and clatter of men and wheels; the ceaseless ring of the tram-cars stopping every few steps to pick up a passenger, and the jingle of the horses' bells as they moved on. It was hot—it was very hot. Clémentine was right, it was hébétant, as it can be in New York in September. She bethought herself that she might go out and buy things, that last resource of a rich woman who is tired and bored.

Buy things! She had forgotten that she was ruined. Well, not quite that, but it seemed like it. It would be long before she would feel justified in buying anything more for the mere amusement of the thing. She tried to realise what it would be like to be poor. But she failed entirely, as women of her sort always do. She was brave enough if need be; if it must come, she had the courage to be poor. But she had not the skill to paint to herself what it would be like. She could not help thinking of Claudius. It would be so pleasant just now to have him sitting there by her side, reading some one of those wise books he was so fond of.

It was so hot. She wished something would happen. Poor Nicholas! He need not have been so terribly cut up about the money. Who is there? It was Vladimir. Vladimir brought a card. Yes, she would see the gentleman. Vladimir disappeared, and a moment after ushered in Mr. Horace Bellingham, commonly known as "Uncle Horace."

"I am so glad to see you, Mr. Bellingham," said Margaret, who had conceived a great liking for the old gentleman on the previous evening, and who would have welcomed anybody this morning.

Mr. Bellingham made a bow of the courtliest, most ancien-régime kind. He had ventured to bring her a few flowers. Would she accept them? They were only three white roses, but there was more beauty in them than in all Mr. Barker's profusion. Margaret took them, and smelled them, and fastened them at her waist, and smiled a divine smile on the bearer.

"Thank you, so much," said she.

"No thanks," said he; "I am more than repaid by your appreciation;" and he rubbed his hands together and bowed again, his head a little on one side, as if deprecating any further acknowledgment. Then he at once began to talk a little, to give her time to select her subject if she would; for he belonged to a class of men who believe it their duty to talk to women, and who do not expect to sit with folded hands and be amused. To such men America is a revelation of social rest. In America the women amuse the men, and the men excuse themselves by saying that they work hard all day, and cannot be expected to work hard all the evening. It is evidently a state of advanced civilisation, incomprehensible to the grosser European mind—a state where talking to a woman is considered to be hard work. Or—in fear and trembling it is suggested—is it because they are not able to amuse their womankind? Is their refusal a testimonium paupertatis ingenii? No—perish the thought! It may have been so a long time ago, in the Golden Age. This is not the Golden Age; it is the Age of Gold. Messieurs! faites votre jeu!

By degrees it became evident that Margaret wanted to talk about Russia, and Mr. Bellingham humoured her, and gave her a good view of the situation, and told anecdotes of the Princess Dolgorouki, and drew the same distinction between Nihilists and Republicans that Count Nicholas had made an hour earlier in the same room. Seeing she was so much interested, Mr. Bellingham took courage to ask a question that had puzzled him for some time. He stroked his snowy beard, and hesitated slightly.

"Pardon me, if I am indiscreet, Madam," he said at last, "but I read in the papers the other day that a nobleman of your name—a Count Nicholas, I think—had landed in New York, having escaped the clutches of the Petersburg police, who wanted to arrest him as a Nihilist. Was he—was he any relation of yours?"

"He is my brother-in-law," said Margaret, rather startled at seeing the point to which she had led the conversation. But she felt a strong sympathy for Mr. Bellingham, and she was glad to be able to speak on the subject to any one. She stood so much in need of advice; and, after all, if the story was in the papers it was public property by this time. Mr. Bellingham was a perfect diplomatist, and, being deeply interested, he had soon learned all the details of the case by heart.

"It is very distressing," he said gravely. But that was all. Margaret had had some faint idea that he might offer to help her—it was absurd, of course—or at least that he might give her some good advice. But that was not Mr. Bellingham's way of doing things. If he intended to do anything, the last thing he would think of would be to tell her of his intention. He led the conversation away, and having rounded it neatly with a couple of anecdotes of her grandmother, he rose to go, pleading an engagement. He really had so many appointments in a day that he seldom kept more than half of them, and his excuse was no polite invention. He bowed himself out, and when he was gone Margaret felt as though she had lost a friend.

She wearied of the day—so long, so hot, and so unfortunate. She tried a book, and then she tried to write a letter, and then she tried to think again. It seemed to her that there was so little to think about, for she had a hopeless helpless consciousness that there was nothing to be done that she could do. She might have written to her friends in Petersburg—of course she would do that, and make every possible representation. But all that seemed infinitely far off, and could be done as well to-morrow as to-day. At last Lady Victoria came back, and at sight of her Margaret resolved to confide in her likewise. She had so much common sense, and always seemed able to get at the truth. Therefore, in the afternoon Margaret monopolised Lady Victoria and carried her off, and they sat together with their work by the open window, and the Countess was "not at home."

In truth, a woman of the world in trouble of any kind could not do better than confide in Lady Victoria. She is so frank and honest that when you talk to her your trouble seems to grow small and your heart big. She has not a great deal of intellect; but, then, she has a great deal of common sense. Common sense is, generally speaking, merely a dislike of complications, and a consequent refusal on the part of the individual to discover them. People of vivid imagination delight in magnifying the difficulties of life by supposing themselves the centre of much scheming, plotting, and cheap fiction. They cheerfully give their time and their powers to the study of social diplomacy. It is reserved for people intellectually very high or very low in the scale to lead a really simple life. The average mind of the world is terribly muddled on most points, and altogether beside itself as regards its individual existence; for a union of much imagination, unbounded vanity, and unfathomable ignorance can never take the place of an intellect, while such a combination cannot fail to destroy the blessed vis inertiæ of the primitive fool, who only sees what is visible, instead of evolving the phantoms of an airy unreality from the bottomless abyss of his own so-called consciousness. Fortunately for humanity, the low-class unimaginative mind predominates in the world, as far as numbers are concerned; and there are enough true intellects among men to leaven the whole. The middle class of mind is a small class, congregated together chiefly within the boundaries of a very amusing institution calling itself "society." These people have scraped and varnished the aforesaid composition of imagination, ignorance, and vanity, into a certain conventional thing which they mendaciously term their "intelligence," from a Latin verb intelligo, said to mean "I understand." It is a poor thing, after all the varnishing. It is neither hammer nor anvil; it cannot strike, and, if you strike it, dissolution instantly takes place, after which the poor driveller is erroneously said to have "lost his mind," and is removed to an asylum. It is curious that the great majority of lunatics should be found in "society." Society says that all men of genius are more or less mad; but it is a notable fact that very few men of genius have ever been put in madhouses, whereas the society that calls those men crazy is always finding its way there. It takes but little to make a lunatic of poor Lady Smith-Tompkins. Poor thing! you know she is so very "high-strung," such delicate sensibilities! She has an idée fixe—so very sad. Ah yes! that is it. She never had an idea before, and now that she has one she cannot get rid of it, and it will kill her in time.

Now people whose intellect is of a low class are not disturbed with visions of all that there is to be known, nor with a foolish desire to appear to know it. On the other hand, they are perfectly capable of understanding what is honourable or dishonourable, mean or generous, and they are very tenacious of these principles, believing that in the letter of the law is salvation. They are not vain of qualities and powers not theirs; and, consequently, when they promise, they promise what they are able to perform. Occasionally such characters appear in "society,"—rare creatures, in whom a pernicious education has not spoiled the simplicity and honesty which is their only virtue. They fall naturally into the position of confessors to the community, for the community requires confessors of some sort. In them confides the hardened sinner bursting with evil deeds and the accumulation of petty naughtiness. To them comes the beardless ass, simpering from his first adventure, and generally "afraid he has compromised" the mature woman of the world, whom he has elected to serve, desiring to know what he ought to do about it. To them, too, comes sometimes the real sufferer with his or her little tale of woe, hesitatingly told, half hinted, hoping to be wholly understood. They are good people, these social confessors, though they seldom give much advice. Nevertheless, it is such a help to tell one's story and hear how it sounds!

Lady Victoria was not a woman of surpassing intellect; perhaps she had no intellect at all. She belonged to the confessors above referred to. She was the soul of honour, of faith, and of secrecy. People were always making confidences to her, and they always felt the better for it—though she herself could not imagine why. And so even Margaret came and told her troubles. Only, as Margaret was really intelligent, she did not hesitate or make any fuss about telling, when once she had made up her mind. The story was, indeed, public property by this time, and Lady Victoria was sure to know it all before long from other people. When Margaret had finished, she laid down her work and looked out of the window, waiting.

"I need not tell you I am sorry," said Lady Victoria. "You know that, my dear. But what will you do? It will be so very awkward for you, you know."

"I hardly can tell yet—what would you do in my place?"

"Let me see," said the English girl. "What would I do? You must have a Russian minister here somewhere. I think I would send for him, if I were you."

"But it takes so long—so dreadfully long, to get anything done in that way," said Margaret. And they discussed the point in a desultory fashion. Of course Lady Victoria's suggestion was the simplest and most direct one. She was quite certain that Margaret would get her rights very soon.

"Of course," said she, "they must do it. It would be so unjust not to." She looked at Margaret with a bright smile, as if there was no such thing as injustice in the world. But the Countess looked grave; and as she leaned back in her deep arm-chair by the window, with half-closed eyes, it was easy to see she was in trouble. She needed help and sympathy and comfort. She had never needed help before, and it was not a pleasant sensation to her; perhaps she was dissatisfied when she realised whose help of all others she would most gladly accept. At least it would be most pleasant that he should offer it. "He"—has it come to that? Poor Margaret! If "he" represented a sorrow instead of a happiness, would you confide that too to Lady Victoria? Or would you feel the least shadow of annoyance because you miss him to-day? Perhaps it is only habit. You have schooled yourself to believe you ought to do without him, and you fancy you ought to be angry with yourself for transgressing your rule. But what avails your schooling against the little god? He will teach you a lesson you will not forget. The day is sinking. The warm earth is drinking out its cup of sunlight to the purple dregs thereof. There is great colour in the air, and the clouds are as a trodden wine-press in the west. The old sun, the golden bowl of life, is touching earth's lips, and soon there will be none of the wine of light left in him. She will drink it all. Yet your lover tarries, Margaret, and comes not.

Margaret and Lady Victoria agreed they would dine together. Indeed, Margaret had a little headache, for she was weary. They would dine together, and then read something in the evening— quite alone; and so they did. It was nearly nine o'clock when the servant announced Claudius and the Duke. The latter, of course, knew nothing about Margaret's troubles, and was in high spirits. As for Claudius, his momentary excitement, caused by Mr. Screw's insinuations, had long since passed away, and he was as calm as ever, meditating a graphic description of his day's excursion to Greenwood Cemetery for Margaret's benefit. It was a lugubrious subject, but he well knew how to make his talk interesting. It is the individual, not the topic, that makes the conversation; if a man can talk well, graveyards are as good a subject as the last novel, and he will make tombstones more attractive than scandal.

No one could have told from Claudius's appearance or conversation that night that there was anything in the world to cloud his happiness. He talked to the woman he loved with a serene contempt for everything else in the world—a contempt, too, which was not assumed. He was perfectly happy for the nonce, and doubly so in that such a happy termination to a very long day was wholly unexpected. He had thought that he should find the party gone from New York on his return from Greenwood, and this bit of good luck seemed to have fallen to him out of a clear sky. Margaret was glad to see him too; she was just now in that intermediate frame of mind during which a woman only reasons about a man in his absence. The moment he appears, the electric circuit is closed and the quiescent state ceases. She was at the point when his coming made a difference that she could feel; when she heard his step her blood beat faster, and she could feel herself turning a shade paler. Then the heavy lids would droop a little to hide what was in her dark eyes, and there were many voices in her ear, as though the very air cried gloria, while her heart answered in excelsis. But when he was come the gentle tale seemed carried on, as from the hour of his last going; and while he stayed life seemed one long day.

She had struggled hard, but in her deepest thoughts she had foreseen the termination. It is the instinct of good women to fight against love—he comes in such a questionable shape. A good woman sees a difference between being in love and loving—well knowing that there is passion without love, but no love without passion. She feels bound in faith to set up a tribunal in her heart, whereby to judge between the two; but very often judge and jury and prisoner at the bar join hands, and swear eternal friendship on the spot. Margaret had feared lest this Northern wooer, with his mighty strength and his bold eyes, should lead her feelings whither her heart would not. Sooner than suffer that, she would die. And yet there is a whole unspoken prophecy of love in every human soul, and his witness is true.

All this evening they sat side by side, welding their bonds. Each had a secret care, but each forgot it utterly. Claudius would not have deigned to think of his own troubles when he was with her; and she never once remembered how, during that morning, she had longed to tell him all about her brother-in-law. They talked of all sorts of things, and they made up their minds to go to Newport the next day.

Miss Skeat asked whether Newport was as romantic as Scarborough.

CHAPTER XIV

There were odours of Russian cigarettes in Mr. Horace Bellingham's room, and two smokers were industriously adding to the fragrant cloud. One was the owner of the dwelling himself, and the other was Claudius. He sat upon the sofa that stood between the two windows of the room, which was on the ground floor, and looked out on the street. The walls were covered with pictures wherever they were not covered with books, and there was not an available nook or corner unfilled with scraps of bric-à-brac, photographs, odds and ends of reminiscence, and all manner of things characteristic to the denizen of the apartment. The furniture was evidently calculated more for comfort than display, and if there was an air of luxury pervading the bachelor's quiet rez-de-chaussée, it was due to the rare volumes on the shelves and the good pictures on the walls, rather than to the silk or satin of the high-art upholsterer, or the gilding and tile work of the modern decorator, who ravages upon beauty as a fungus upon a fruit tree. Whatever there was in Mr. Bellingham's rooms was good; much of it was unique, and the whole was harmonious. Rare editions were bound by famous binders, and if the twopenny-halfpenny productions of some little would-be modern poet, resplendent with vellum and æsthetic greenliness of paper, occasionally found their way to the table, they never travelled as far as the shelves. Mr. Bellingham had fools enough about him to absorb his spare trash.

On this particular occasion the old gentleman was seated in an arm-chair at his table, and Claudius, as aforesaid, had established himself upon the sofa. He looked very grave and smoked thoughtfully.

"I wish I knew what to do," he said. "Mr. Bellingham, do you think I could be of any use?"

"If I had not thought so, I would not have told you—I could have let you find it out for yourself from the papers. You can be of a great deal of use."

"Do you advise me to go to St. Petersburg and see about it then?"

"Of course I do. Start at once. You can get the necessary steps taken in no time, if you go now."

"I am ready. But how in the world can I get the thing done?"

"Letters. Your English friend over there will give you letters to the English Ambassador; he is Lord Fitzdoggin—cousin of the Duke's. And I will give you some papers that will be of use. I know lots of people in Petersburg. Why, it's as plain as a pikestaff. Besides, you know the proverb, mitte sapientem et nihil dicas. That means then when you send a wise man you must not dictate to him."

"You flatter me. But I would rather have your advice, if that is what you call 'dictating.' I am not exactly a fool, but then, I am not very wise either."

"No one is very wise, and we are all fools compared to some people," said Mr. Bellingham. "If anybody wanted a figurehead for a new Ship of Fools, I sometimes think a portrait of myself would be singularly appropriate. There are times when I should fix upon a friend for the purpose. Mermaid—half fish—figurehead, half man, half fool. That's a very good idea."

"Very good—for the friend. Meanwhile, you know, it is I who am going on the errand. If you do not make it clear to me it will be a fool's errand."

"It is perfectly clear, my dear sir," insisted Mr. Bellingham. "You go to St. Petersburg; you get an audience—you can do that by means of the letters; you lay the matter before the Czar, and request justice. Either you get it or you do not. That is the beauty of an autocratic country."

"How about a free country?" asked Claudius.

"You don't get it," replied his host grimly. Claudius laughed a cloud of smoke into the air.

"Why is that?" he asked idly, hoping to launch Mr. Bellingham into further aphorisms and paradoxes.

"Men are everywhere born free, but they—"

"Oh," said Claudius, "I want to know your own opinion about it."

"I have no opinion; I only have experience," answered the other. "At any rate in an autocratic country there is a visible, tangible repository of power to whom you can apply. If the repository is in the humour you will get whatever you want done, in the way of justice or injustice. Now in a free country justice is absorbed into the great cosmic forces, and it is apt to be an expensive incantation that wakes the lost elementary spirit. In Russia justice shines by contrast with the surrounding corruption, but there is no mistake about it when you get it. In America it is taken for granted everywhere, and the consequence is that, like most things that are taken for granted, it is a myth. Rousseau thought that in a republic like ours there would be no more of the 'chains' he was so fond of talking about. He did not anticipate a stagnation of the national moral sense. An Englishman who has made a study of these things said lately that the Americans had retained the forms of freedom, but that the substance had suffered considerably."

"Who said that?" asked Claudius.

"Mr. Herbert Spencer. He said it to a newspaper reporter in New York, and so it was put into the papers. It is the truest thing he ever said, but no one took any more notice of it than if he had told the reporter it was a very fine day. They don't care. Tell the first man you meet down town that he is a liar; he will tell you he knows it. He will probably tell you you are another. We are all alike here. I'm a liar myself in a small way—there's a club of us, two Americans and one Englishman."

"You are the frankest person I ever met, Mr. Bellingham," said Claudius, laughing.

"Some day I will write a book," said Mr. Bellingham, rising and beginning to tramp round the room. "I will call it—by the way, we were talking about Petersburg. You had better be off."

"I am going, but tell me the name of the book before I go."

"No, I won't; you would go and write it yourself, and steal my thunder." Uncle Horace's eyes twinkled, and a corruscation of laugh-wrinkles shot like sheet-lightning over his face. He disappeared into a neighbouring room, leaving a trail of white smoke in his wake, like a locomotive. Presently he returned with a Bullinger Guide in his hand.

"You can sail on Wednesday at two o'clock by the Cunarder," he said. "You can go to Newport to-day, and come back by the boat on Tuesday night, and be ready to start in the morning." Mr. Bellingham prided himself greatly on his faculty for making combinations of times and places.

"How about those letters, Mr. Bellingham?" inquired Claudius, who had no idea of going upon his expedition without proper preparations.

"I will write them," said Uncle Horace, "I will write them at once," and he dived into an address-book and set to work. His pen was that of the traditional ready-writer, for he wrote endless letters, and his correspondence was typical of himself—the scholar, the wanderer, and the Priest of Buddha by turns, and sometimes all at once. For Mr. Bellingham was a professed Buddhist and a profound student of Eastern moralities, and he was a thorough scholar in certain branches of the classics. The combination of these qualities, with the tact and versatile fluency of a man of the world, was a rare one, and was a source of unceasing surprise to his intimates. At the present moment he was a diplomatist, since he could not be a diplomat, and to his energetic suggestion and furtherance of the plan he had devised the results which this tale will set forth are mainly due.

Claudius sat upon the sofa watching the old gentleman, and wondering how it was that a stranger should so soon have assumed the position of an adviser, and with an energy and good sense, too, which not only disarmed resistance, but assubjugated the consent of the advised. Life is full of such things. Man lives quietly like a fattening carp in some old pond for years, until some idle disturber comes and pokes up the mud with a stick, and the poor fish is in the dark. Presently comes another destroyer of peace, less idle and more enterprising, and drains away the water, carp and all, and makes a potato-garden of his old haunts. So the carp makes a new study of life under altered circumstances in other waters; and to pass the time he wonders about it all. It happens even to men of masterful character, accustomed to directing events. An illness takes such a man out of his sphere for a few months. He comes back and finds his pond turned into a vegetable-garden and his ploughed field into a swamp; and then for a time he is fain to ask advice and take it, like any other mortal. So Claudius, who felt himself in an atmosphere new to him, and had tumbled into a very burning bush of complications, had fallen in with Mr. Horace Bellingham, a kind of professional bone-setter, whose province was the reduction of society fractures, speaking medically. And Mr. Bellingham, scenting a patient, and moreover being strongly attracted to him on his own merits, had immediately broached the subject of the Nihilist Nicholas, drawing the conclusion that the man of the emergency was Claudius, and Claudius only. And the bold Doctor weighed the old gentleman's words, and by the light of what he felt he knew that Uncle Horace was right. That if he loved Margaret his first duty was to her, and that first duty was her welfare. No messenger could or would be so active in her interests as himself; and in his anxiety to serve her he had not thought it strange that Mr. Bellingham should take it for granted he was ready to embark on the expedition. He thought of that later, and wondered at the boldness of the stranger's assumption, no less than at the keenness of his wit. Poor Claudius! anybody might see he was in love.

"There; I think that will draw sparks," said Mr. Bellingham, as he folded the last of his letters and put them all in a great square envelope. "Put those in your pocket and keep your powder dry."

"I am really very grateful to you," said Claudius. Uncle Horace began to tramp round the room again, emitting smoky ejaculations of satisfaction. Presently he stopped in front of his guest and turned his eyes up to Claudius's face without raising his head. It gave him a peculiar expression.

"It is a very strange thing," he said, "but I knew at once that you had a destiny, the first time I saw you. I am very superstitious; I believe in destiny."

"So would I if I thought one could know anything about it. I mean in a general way," answered Claudius, smiling.

"Is generalisation everything?" asked Mr. Bellingham sharply, still looking at the young man. "Is experience to be dismissed as empiricism, with a sneer, because the wider rule is lacking?"

"No. But so long as only a few occupy themselves in reducing empiric knowledge to a scientific shape they will not succeed, at least in this department. To begin with, they have not enough experience among them to make rules from."

"But they contribute. One man will come who will find the rule. Was Tycho Brahé a nonentity because he was not Kepler? Was Van Helmont nothing because he was not Lavoisier? Yet Tycho Brahé was an empiric—he was the last of the observers of the concrete, if you will allow me the phrase. He was scientifically the father of Kepler."

"That is very well put," said Claudius. "But we were talking of destiny. You are an observer."

"I have very fine senses," replied Mr. Bellingham. "I always know when anybody I meet is going to do something out of the common run. You are."

"I hope so," said Claudius, laughing. "Indeed I think I am beginning already."

"Well, good luck to you," said Mr. Bellingham, remembering that he had missed one engagement, and was on the point of missing another. He suddenly felt that he must send Claudius away, and he held out his hand. There was nothing rough in his abruptness. He would have liked to talk with Claudius for an hour longer had his time permitted. Claudius understood perfectly. He put the letters in his pocket, and with a parting shake of the hand he bade Mr. Horace Bellingham good-morning, and good-bye; he would not trouble him again, he said, before sailing. But Mr. Bellingham went to the door with him.

"Come and see me before you go—Wednesday morning; I am up at six, you know. I shall be very glad to see you. I am like the Mexican donkey that died of congojas ajenas—died of other people's troubles. People always come to me when they are in difficulties." The old gentleman stood looking after Claudius as he strode away. Then he screwed up his eyes at the sun, sneezed with evident satisfaction, and disappeared within, closing the street door behind him.

"Some day I will write my memoirs," he said to himself, as he sat down.

Claudius was in a frame of mind which he would have found it hard to describe. The long conversation with Mr. Bellingham had been the first intimation he had received of Margaret's disaster, and the same interview had decided him to act at once in her behalf—in other words, to return to Europe immediately, after a week's stay in New York, leaving behind all that was most dear to him. This resolution had formed itself instantaneously in his mind, and it never occurred to him, either then or later, that he could have done anything else in the world. It certainly did not occur to him that he was doing anything especially praiseworthy in sacrificing his love to its object, in leaving Margaret for a couple of months, and enduring all that such a separation meant, in order to serve her interests more effectually. He knew well enough what he was undertaking—the sleepless nights, the endless days, the soul-compelling heaviness of solitude, and the deadly sinking at the heart, all which he should endure daily for sixty days—he could not be back before that. He knew it all, for he had suffered it all, during those four and twenty hours on the yacht that followed his first wild speech of love. But Claudius's was a knightly soul, and when he served he served wholly, without reservation. Had the dark-browed Countess guessed half the nobleness of purpose her tall lover carried in his breast, who knows but she might have been sooner moved herself. But how could she know? She suspected, indeed, that he was above his fellows, and she never attributed bad motives to his actions, as she would unhesitatingly have done with most men; for she had learned lessons of caution in her life. Who steals hearts steals souls, wherefore it behoves woman to look that the lock be strong and the key hung high. Claudius thought so too, and he showed it in every action, though unconsciously enough, for it was a knowledge natural and not acquired, an instinctive determination to honour where honour was due. Call it Quixotism if need be. There is nothing ridiculous in the word, for there breathes no truer knight or gentler soul than Cervantes's hero in all the pages of history or romance. Why cannot all men see it? Why must an infamous world be ever sneering at the sight, and smacking its filthy lips over some fresh gorge of martyrs? Society has non-suited hell to-day, lest peradventure it should not sleep o' nights.

Thomas Carlyle, late of Chelsea, knew that. How he hit and hammered and churned in his wrath, with his great cast-iron words. How the world shrieked when he wound his tenacious fingers in the glory of her golden hair and twisted and wrenched and twisted till she yelled for mercy, promising to be good, like a whipped child. There is a story told of him which might be true.

It was at a dinner-party, and Carlyle sat silent, listening to the talk of lesser men, the snow on his hair and the fire in his amber eyes. A young Liberal was talking theory to a beefy old Conservative, who despised youth and reason in an equal degree.

"The British people, sir," said he of the beef, "can afford to laugh at theories."

"Sir," said Carlyle, speaking for the first time during dinner, "the French nobility of a hundred years ago said they could afford to laugh at theories. Then came a man and wrote a book called the Social Contract. The man was called Jean-Jacques Rousseau, and his book was a theory, and nothing but a theory. The nobles could laugh at his theory; but their skins went to bind the second edition of his book[1]."

[Footnote 1: There was a tannery of human skins at Meudon during the Revolution.]

Look to your skin, world, lest it be dressed to morocco and cunningly tooled with gold. There is much binding yet to be done.

Claudius thought neither of the world nor of Mr. Carlyle as he walked back to the hotel; for he was thinking of the Countess Margaret, to the exclusion of every other earthly or unearthly consideration. But his thoughts were sad, for he knew that he was to leave her, and he knew also that he must tell her so. It was no easy matter, and his walk slackened, till, at the corner of the great thoroughfare, he stood still, looking at a poor woman who ground a tuneless hand-organ. The instrument of tympanum torture was on wheels, and to the back of it was attached a cradle. In the cradle was a dirty little baby, licking its fist and listening with conscientious attention to the perpetual trangle-tringle-jangle of the maternal music. In truth the little thing could not well listen to anything else, considering the position in which it was placed. Claudius stood staring at the little caravan, halted at the corner of the most aristocratic street in New York, and his attention was gradually roused to comprehend what he saw. He reflected that next to being bound on the back of a wild horse, like Mazeppa, the most horrible fate conceivable must be that of this dirty baby, put to bed in perpetuity on the back of a crazy grind-organ. He smiled at the idea, and the woman held out a battered tin dish with one hand, while the other in its revolution ground out the final palpitating squeaks of "Ah, che la morte ognora." Claudius put his hand into his pocket and gave the poor creature a coin.

"You are encouraging a public nuisance," said a thin gentlemanly voice at his elbow. Claudius looked down and saw Mr. Barker.

"Yes," said the Doctor, "I remember a remark you once made to me about the deserving poor in New York—it was the day before yesterday, I think. You said they went to the West."

"Talking of the West, I suppose you will be going there yourself one of these days to take a look at our 'park'—eh?"

"No, I am going East."

"To Boston, I suppose?" inquired the inquisitive Barker. "You will be very much amused with Boston. It is the largest village in the United States."

"I am not going to Boston," said Claudius calmly.

"Oh! I thought when you said you were going East you meant—"

"I am going to sail for Europe on Wednesday," said the Doctor, who had had time to reflect that he might as well inform Barker of his intention. Mr. Barker smiled grimly under his moustache.

"You don't mean that?" he said, trying to feign astonishment and disguise his satisfaction. It seemed too good to be true. "Going so soon? Why, I thought you meant to spend some time."

"Yes, I am going immediately," and Claudius looked Barker straight in the face. "I find it is necessary that I should procure certain papers connected with my inheritance."

"Well," said Barker turning his eyes another way, for he did not like the Doctor's look, "I am very sorry, any way. I suppose you mean to come back soon?"

"Very soon," answered Claudius. "Good-morning, Barker."

"Good morning. I will call and see you before you sail. You have quite taken my breath away with this news." Mr. Barker walked quickly away in the direction of Elevated Road. He was evidently going down town.

"Strange," thought Claudius, "that Barker should take the news so quietly. I think it ought to have astonished him more." Leaving the organ-grinder, the dirty baby, and the horse-cars to their fate, Claudius entered the hotel. He found the Duke over a late breakfast, eating cantelopes voraciously. Cantelopes are American melons, small and of sickly appearance, but of good vitality and unearthly freshness within, a joy to the hot-stomached foreigner. Behold also, his Grace eateth the cantelope and hath a cheerful countenance. Claudius sat down at the table, looking rather gloomy.

"I want you to give me an introduction to the English Ambassador in Petersburg. Lord Fitzdoggin, I believe he is."

"Good gracious!" exclaimed the peer; "what for?"

"I am going there," answered Claudius with his habitual calm, "and I want to know somebody in power."

"Oh! are you going?" asked the Duke, suddenly grasping the situation. He afterwards took some credit to himself for having been so quick to catch Claudius's meaning.

"Yes. I sail on Wednesday."

"Tell me all about it," said the Duke, who recovered his equanimity, and plunged a knife into a fresh cantelope at the same moment.

"Very well. I saw your friend, Mr. Horace Bellingham, this morning, and he told me all about the Countess's troubles. In fact, they are in the newspapers by this time, but I had not read about them. He suggested that some personal friend of the Countess had better proceed to headquarters at once, and see about it; so I said I would go; and he gave me some introductions. They are probably good ones; but he advised me to come to you and get one for your ambassador."

"Anything Uncle Horace advises is right, you know," said his Grace, speaking with his mouth full. "He knows no end of people everywhere," he added pensively, when he had swallowed.

"Very well, I will go; but I am glad you approve."

"But what the deuce are you going to do about that fortune of yours?" asked the other suddenly. "Don't you think we had better go down and swear to you at once? I may not be here when you get back, you know."

"No; that would not suit my arrangements," answered Claudius. "I would rather not let it be known for what purpose I had gone. Do you understand? I am going ostensibly to Heidelberg to get my papers from the University, and so, with all thanks, I need not trouble you." The Duke looked at him for a moment.

"What a queer fellow you are, Claudius," he said at last. "I should think you would like her to know."

"Why? Suppose that I failed, what a figure I should cut, to be sure." Claudius preferred to attribute to his vanity an action which was the natural outcome of his love.

"Well, that is true," said the Duke; "but I think you are pretty safe for all that. Have some breakfast—I forgot all about it."

"No, thanks. Are you going to Newport to-day? I would like to see something outside of New York before I go back."

"By all means. Better go at once—all of us in a body. I know the Countess is ready, and I am sure I am."

"Very good. I will get my things together. One word—please do not tell them I am going; I will do it myself.

"All right," answered the Duke; and Claudius vanished. "He says 'them,'" soliloquised the Englishman, "but he means 'her.'"

Claudius found on his table a note from Mr. Screw. This missive was couched in formal terms, and emitted a kind of phosphorescent wrath. Mr. Screw's dignity was seriously offended by the summary ejectment he had suffered at the Doctor's hands on the previous day. He gave the Doctor formal notice that his drafts would not be honoured until the executors were satisfied concerning his identity; and he solemnly and legally "regretted the position Dr. Claudius had assumed towards those whose sacred duty it was to protect the interests of Dr. Claudius." The cunning repetition of name conveyed the idea of two personages, the claimant and the real heir, in a manner that did not escape the Doctor. Since yesterday he had half regretted having lost his temper; and had he known that Screw had been completely duped by Mr. Barker, Claudius would probably have apologised to the lawyer. Indeed, he had a vague suspicion, as the shadow of a distant event, that Barker was not altogether clear of the business; and the fact that the latter had shown so little surprise on hearing of his friend's sudden return to Europe had aroused the Doctor's imagination, so that he found himself piecing together everything he could remember to show that Barker had an interest of some kind in removing him from the scene. Nevertheless, the burden of responsibility for the annoyance he was now suffering seemed to rest with Screw, and Screw should be taught a great lesson; and to that end Claudius would write a letter. It was clear he was still angry.

The Doctor sat down to write; and his strong, white fingers held the pen with unrelenting determination to be disagreeable. His face was set like a mask, and ever and anon his blue eyes gleamed scornfully. And this is what he said—

"SIR—Having enjoyed the advantage of your society, somewhat longer than I could have wished, during yesterday afternoon, I had certainly not hoped for so early a mark of your favour and interest as a letter from you of to-day's date. As for your formal notice to me that my drafts will not be honoured in future, I regard it as a deliberate repetition of the insulting insinuation conveyed to me by your remarks during your visit. You are well aware that I have not drawn upon the estate in spite of your written authorisation to do so. I consider your conduct in this matter unworthy of a person professing the law, and your impertinence is in my opinion only second to the phenomenal clumsiness you have displayed throughout. As I fear that your ignorance of your profession may lead you into some act of folly disastrous to yourself, I will go so far as to inform you that on my return from Europe, two months hence, your proceedings as executor for the estate of the late Gustavus Lindstrand will be subjected to the severest scrutiny. In the meantime, I desire no further communications from you.

CLAUDIUS."

This remarkable epistle was immediately despatched by messenger to Pine Street; and if Mr. Screw had felt himself injured before, he was on the verge of desperation when he read Claudius's polemic. He repeated to himself the several sentences, which seemed to breathe war and carnage in their trenchant brevity; and he thought that even if he had been guilty of any breach of trust, he could hardly have felt worse. He ran his fingers through his thick yellow-gray hair, and hooked his legs in and out of each other as he sat, and bullied his clerks within an inch of their lives. Then, to get consolation, he said to himself that Claudius was certainly an impostor, or he would not be so angry, or go to Europe, or refuse any more communications. In the midst of his rage, Mr. Barker the younger opportunely appeared in the office of Messrs. Screw and Scratch, prepared to throw any amount of oil upon the flames.

"Well?" said Mr. Barker interrogatively, as he settled the flower in his gray coat, and let the paper ribband of the "ticker" run through his other hand, with its tale of the tide of stocks. Yellow Mr. Screw shot a lurid glance from his brassy little eyes.

"You're right, sir—the man's a humbug."

"Who?" asked Barker, in well-feigned innocence.

"Claudius. It's my belief he's a liar and a thief and a damned impostor, sir. That's my belief, sir." He waxed warm as he vented his anger.

"Well, I only suggested taking precautions. I never said any of these things," answered Barker, who had no idea of playing a prominent part in his own plot. "Don't give me any credit, Mr. Screw."

"Now, see here, Mr. Barker; I'm talking to you. You're as clever a young man as there is in New York. Now, listen to me; I'm talking to you," said Mr. Screw excitedly. "That man turned me out of his house—turned me out of doors, sir, yesterday afternoon; and now he writes me this letter; look here, look at it; read it for yourself, can't you? And so he makes tracks for Europe, and leaves no address behind. An honest man isn't going to act like that, sir—is he, now?"

"Not much," said Barker, as he took the letter. He read it through twice, and gave it back. "Not much," he repeated. "Is it true that he has drawn no money?"

"Well, yes, I suppose It Is," answered Screw reluctantly, for this was the weak point In his argument. "However, it would be just like such a leg to make everything sure in playing a big game. You see he has left himself the rear platform, so he can jump off when his car is boarded."

"However," said Barker sententiously, "I must say it is in his favour. What we want are facts, you know, Mr. Screw. Besides, if he had taken anything, I should have been responsible, because I accepted him abroad as the right man."

"Well, as you say, there is nothing gone—not a red. So if he likes to get away, he can; I'm well rid of him."

"Now that's the way to look at it. Don't be so down in the mouth, sir; it will all come straight enough." Barker smiled benignly, knowing it was all crooked enough at present.

"Well, I'm damned anyhow," said Mr. Screw, which was not fair to himself, for he was an honest man, acting very properly according to his lights. It was not his fault if Barker deceived him, and if that hot-livered Swede was angry.

"Never mind," answered Barker, rather irrelevantly; "I will see him before he sails, and tell you what I think about it. He is dead sure to give himself away, somehow, before he gets off."

"Well, sail in, young man," said Screw, biting off the end of a cigar. "I don't want to see him again, you can take your oath."

"All right; that settles it. I came about something else, though. I know you can tell me all about this suit against the Western Union, can't you?"

So the two men sat in their arm-chairs and talked steadily, as only Americans can talk, without showing any more signs of fatigue than if they were snoring; and it cost them nothing. If the Greeks of the time of Pericles could be brought to life in America, they would be very like modern Americans in respect of their love of talking and of their politics. Terrible chatterers in the market-place, and great wranglers in the council—the greatest talkers living, but also on occasion the greatest orators, with a redundant vivacity of public life in their political veins, that magnifies and inflames the diseases of the parts, even while it gives an unparalleled harmony to the whole. The Greeks had more, for their activity, hampered by the narrow limits of their political sphere, broke out in every variety of intellectual effort, carried into every branch of science and art. In spite of the whole modern school of impressionists, æsthetes, and aphrodisiac poets, the most prominent features of Greek art are its intellectuality, its well-reasoned science, and its accurate conception of the ideal. The resemblance between Americans of to-day and Greeks of the age of Pericles does not extend to matters of art as yet, though America bids fair to surpass all earlier and contemporary nations in the progressive departments of science. But as talkers they are pre-eminent, these rapid business men with their quick tongues and their sharp eyes and their millions.

When Barker left Screw he had learned a great deal about the suit of which he inquired, but Screw had learned nothing whatever about Claudius.

As for the Doctor, as soon as he had despatched his letter he sent to secure a passage in Wednesday's steamer, and set himself to prepare his effects for the voyage, as he only intended returning from Newport in time to go on board. He was provided with money enough, for before leaving Germany he had realised the whole of his own little fortune, not wishing to draw upon his larger inheritance until he should feel some necessity for doing so. He now felt no small satisfaction in the thought that he was independent of Mr. Screw and of every one else. It would have been an easy matter, he knew, to clear up the whole difficulty in twenty-four hours, by simply asking the Duke to vouch for him; and before hearing of Margaret's trouble he had had every intention of pursuing that course. But now that he was determined to go to Russia in her behalf, his own difficulty, if he did not take steps for removing it, furnished him with an excellent excuse for the journey, without telling the Countess that he was going for the sole purpose of recovering her fortune, as he otherwise must have told her. Had he known the full extent of Barker's intentions he might have acted differently, but as yet his instinct against that ingenious young gentleman was undefined and vague.

CHAPTER XV

The cliff at Newport—the long winding path that follows it from the great beach to the point of the island, always just above the sea, hardly once descending to it, as the evenly-gravelled path, too narrow for three, though far too broad for two, winds by easy curves through the grounds, and skirts the lawns of the million-getters who have their tents and their houses therein—it is a pretty place. There the rich men come and seethe in their gold all summer; and Lazarus comes to see whether he cannot marry Dives's daughter. And the choleric architect, dissatisfied with the face of Nature, strikes her many a dread blow, and produces an unhealthy eruption wherever he strikes, and calls the things he makes houses. Here also, on Sunday afternoon, young gentlemen and younger ladies patrol in pairs, and discourse of the most saccharine inanities, not knowing what they shall say, and taking no thought, for obvious reasons. And gardeners sally forth in the morning and trim the paths with strange-looking instruments—the earth-barbers, who lather and shave and clip Nature into patterns, and the world into a quincunx.

It is a pretty place. There is nothing grand, not even anything natural in Newport, but it is very pretty for all that. For an artificial place, destined to house the most artificial people in the world during three months of the year, it is as pleasing as it can be in a light-comedy-scenery style. Besides, the scenery in Newport is very expensive, and it is impossible to spend so much money without producing some result. It cost a hundred thousand to level that lawn there, and Dives paid the money cheerfully. Then there is Croesus, his neighbour, who can draw a cheque for a hundred millions if he likes. His house cost him a pot of money. And so they build themselves a landscape, and pare off the rough edges of the island, and construct elegant landing-stages, and keep yachts, and make to themselves a fashionable watering-place; until by dint of putting money into it, they have made it remarkable among the watering-places of the world, perhaps the most remarkable of all.

But there are times when the cliff at Newport is not an altogether flippant bit of expensive scene-painting, laid out for the sole purpose of "effect." Sometimes in the warm summer nights the venerable moon rises stately and white out of the water; the old moon, that is the hoariest sinner of us all, with her spells and enchantments and her breathing love-beams, that look so gently on such evil works. And the artist-spirits of the night sky take of her silver as much as they will, and coat with it many things of most humble composition, so that they are fair to look upon. And they play strange pranks with faces of living and dead. So when the ruler of the darkness shines over poor, commonplace Newport, the aspect of it is changed, and the gingerbread abominations wherein the people dwell are magnified into lofty palaces of silver, and the close-trimmed lawns are great carpets of soft dark velvet; and the smug-faced philistine sea, that the ocean would be ashamed to own for a relation by day, breaks out into broken flashes of silver and long paths of light. All this the moonlight does, rejoicing in its deception.

There is another time, too, when Newport is no longer commonplace, when that same sea, which never seems to have any life of its own, disgorges its foggy soul over the land. There is an ugly odour as of musty salt-water in men's nostrils, and the mist is heavy and thick to the touch. It creeps up to the edge of the cliff, and greedily clings to the wet grass, and climbs higher and over the lawns, and in at the windows of Dives's dining-room, and of Croesus's library, with its burden of insidious mould. The pair of trim-built flirtlings, walking so daintily down the gravel path, becomes indistinct, and their forms are seen but as the shadows of things dead—treading on air, between three worlds. The few feet of bank above the sea, dignified by the name of cliff, fall back to a gaping chasm, a sheer horror of depths, misty and unfathomable. Onward slides the thick cloud, and soon the deep-mouthed monotone of the fog-horns in the distance tells it is in the bay. There is nothing commonplace about the Newport cliff in a fog; it is wild enough and dreary enough then, for the scene of a bad deed. You might meet the souls of the lost in such a fog, hiding before the wrath to come.

Late on Tuesday afternoon Claudius and Margaret had taken their way towards the cliff, a solitary couple at that hour on a week-day. Even at a distance there was something about their appearance that distinguished them from ordinary couples. Claudius's great height seemed still more imposing now that he affected the garb of civilisation, and Margaret had the air of a woman of the great world in every movement of her graceful body, and in every fold of her perfect dress. American women, when they dress well, dress better than any other women in the world; but an American woman who has lived at the foreign courts is unapproachable. If there had been any one to see these two together on Tuesday afternoon, there would have been words of envy, malice, and hatred. As it was, they were quite alone on the cliff walk.

Margaret was happy; there was light in her eyes, and a faint warm flush on her dark cheek. A closed parasol hung from her hand, having an ivory handle carved with an "M" and a crown—the very one that three months ago had struck the first spark of their acquaintance from the stones of the old Schloss at Heidelberg—perhaps she had brought it on purpose. She was happy still, for she did not know that Claudius was going away, though he had brought her out here, away from every one, that he might tell her. But they had reached the cliff and had walked some distance in the direction of the point, and yet he spoke not. Something tied his tongue, and he would have spoken if he could, but his words seemed too big to come out. At last they came to a place where a quick descent leads from the path down to the sea. A little sheltered nook of sand and stones is there, all irregular and rough, like the lumps in brown sugar, and the lazy sea splashed a little against some old pebbles it had known for a long time, never having found the energy to wash them away. The rocks above overhung the spot, so that it was entirely shielded from the path, and the rocks below spread themselves into a kind of seat. Here they sat them down, facing the water—towards evening—not too near to each other, not too far,—Margaret on the right, Claudius on the left. And Claudius punched the little pebbles with his stick after he had sat down, wondering how he should begin. Indeed it did not seem easy. It would have been easier if he had been less advanced, or further advanced, in his suit. Most people never jump without feeling, at the moment of jumping, that they could leap a little better if they could "take off" an inch nearer or further away.

"Countess," said the Doctor at last, turning towards her with a very grave look in his face, "I have something to tell you, and I do not know how to say it." He paused, and Margaret looked at the sea, without noticing him, for she half fancied he was on the point of repeating his former indiscretion and saying he loved her. Would it be an indiscretion now? She wondered what she should say, what she would say, if he did—venture. Would she say "it was not right" of him now? In a moment Claudius had resolved to plunge boldly at the truth.

"I am obliged to go away very suddenly," he said; and his voice trembled violently.

Margaret's face lost colour in answer, and she resisted an impulse to turn and meet his eyes. She would have liked to, but she felt his look on her, and she feared lest, looking once, she should look too long.

"Must you go away?" she asked with a good deal of self-possession.

"Yes, I fear I must. I know I must, if I mean to remain here afterwards. I would rather go at once and be done with it." He still spoke uncertainly, as if struggling with some violent hoarseness in his throat.

"Tell me why you must go," she said imperiously. Claudius hesitated a moment.

"I will tell you one of the principal reasons of my going," he said. "You know I came here to take possession of my fortune, and I very naturally relied upon doing so. Obviously, if I do not obtain it I cannot continue to live in the way I am now doing, on the slender resources which have been enough for me until now."

"Et puis?" said the Countess, raising her eyebrows a little.

"Et puis," continued the Doctor, "these legal gentlemen find difficulty in persuading themselves that I am myself—that I am really the nephew of Gustavus Lindstrand, deceased."

"What nonsense!" exclaimed Margaret. "And so to please them you are going away. And who will get your money, pray?"

"I will get it," answered Claudius, "for I will come back as soon as I have obtained the necessary proofs of my identity from Heidelberg."

"I never heard of anything so ridiculous," said Margaret hotly. "To go all that distance for a few papers. As if we did not all know you! If you are not Dr. Claudius, who are you? Why, Mr. Barker went to Heidelberg on purpose to find you."

"Nevertheless, Messrs. Screw and Scratch doubt me. Here is their letter—the last one. Will you look at it?" and Claudius took an envelope from his pocket-book. He was glad to have come over to the argumentative tack, for his heart was very sore, and he knew what the end must be.

"No." The Countess turned to him for the first time, with an indescribable look in her face, between anger and pain. "No, I will not read it."

"I wish you would," said Claudius, "you would understand better." Something in his voice touched a sympathetic chord.

"I think I understand," said the Countess, looking back at the sea, which was growing dim and indistinct before her. "I think you ought to go."

The indistinctness of her vision was not due to any defect in her sight. The wet fog was rising like a shapeless evil genius out of the sluggish sea, rolling heavily across the little bay to the lovers' beach, with its swollen arms full of blight and mildew. Margaret shivered at the sight of it, and drew the lace thing she wore closer to her throat. But she did not rise, or make any sign that she would go.

"What is the other reason for your going?" she asked at length.

"What other reason?"

"You said your inheritance, or the evidence you require in order to obtain it, was one of the principal reasons for your going. I suppose there is another?"

"Yes, Countess, there is another reason, but I cannot tell you now what it is."

"I have no right to ask, of course," said Margaret,—"unless I can help you," she added, in her soft, deep voice.

"You have more right than you think, far more right," answered Claudius. "And I thank you for the kind thought of help. It is very good of you." He turned towards her, and leaned upon his hand as he sat. Still the fog rolled up, and the lifeless sea seemed overshed with an unctuous calm. They were almost in the dark on their strip of beach, and the moisture was already clinging in great, thick drops to their clothes, and to the rocks where they sat. Still Claudius looked at Margaret, and Margaret looked at the narrow band of oily water still uncovered by the mist.

"When are you going?" she asked slowly, as if hating to meet the answer.

"To-night," said Claudius, still looking earnestly at her. The light was gone from her eyes, and the flush had long sunk away to the heart whence it had come.

"To-night?" she repeated, a little vaguely.

"Yes," he said, and waited; then after a moment, "Shall you mind when I am gone?" He leaned towards her, earnestly looking into her face.

"Yes," said Margaret, "I shall be sorry." Her voice was kind, and very gentle. Still she did not look at him. Claudius held out his right hand, palm upward, to meet hers.

"Shall you mind much?" he asked earnestly, with intent eyes. She met his hand and took it.

"Yes, I shall be very sorry." Claudius slipped from the rock where he was sitting, and fell upon one knee before her, kissing the hand she gave as though it had been the holy cross. He looked up, his face near hers, and at last he met her eyes, burning with a startled light under the black brows, contrasting with the white of her forehead, and face, and throat. He looked one moment.

"Shall you really mind very much?" he asked a third time, in a strange, lost voice. There was no answer, only the wet fog all around, and those two beautiful faces ashy pale in the mist, and very near together. One instant so—and then—ah, God! they have cast the die at last, for he has wound his mighty arms about her, and is passionately kissing the marble of her cheek.

"My beloved, my beloved, I love you—with all my heart, and with all my soul, and with all my strength"—but she speaks no word, only her arms pass his and hang about his neck, and her dark head lies on his breast; and could you but see her eyes, you would see also the fair pearls that the little god has formed deep down in the ocean of love—the lashes thereof are wet with sudden weeping. And all around them the deep, deaf fog, thick and muffled as darkness, and yet not dark.

"Ugh!" muttered the evil genius of the sea, "I hate lovers; an' they drown not, they shall have a wet wooing." And he came and touched them all over with the clamminess of his deathly hand, and breathed upon them the thick, cold breath of his damp old soul. But he could do nothing against such love as that, and the lovers burned him and laughed him to scorn.

She was very silent as she kissed him and laid her head on his breast. And he could only repeat what was nearest, the credo of his love, and while his arms were about her they were strong, but when he tried to take them away, they were as tremulous as the veriest aspen.

The great tidal wave comes rolling in, once in every lifetime that deserves to be called a lifetime, and sweeps away every one of our landmarks, and changes all our coast-line. But though the waters do not subside, yet the crest of them falls rippling away into smoothness after the first mad rush, else should we all be but shipwrecked mariners in the sea of love. And so, after a time, Margaret drew away from Claudius gently, finding his hands with hers as she moved, and holding them.

"Come," said she, "let us go." They were her first words, and Claudius thought the deep voice had never sounded so musical before. But the words, the word "go," sounded like a knell on his heart. He had forgotten that he must sail on the morrow. He had forgotten that it was so soon over.

They went away, out of the drizzling fog and the mist, and the evil sea-breath, up to the cliff walk and so by the wet lanes homewards, two loving, sorrowing hearts, not realising what had come to them, nor knowing what should come hereafter, but only big with love fresh spoken, and hot with tears half shed.

"Beloved," said Claudius as they stood together for the last time in the desolation of the great, dreary, hotel drawing-room—for Claudius was going—"beloved, will you promise me something?"

Margaret looked down as she stood with her clasped hands on his arm.

"What is it I should promise you—Claudius?" she asked, half hesitating.

Claudius laid his hand tenderly—tenderly, as giants only can be tender, on the thick black hair, as hardly daring, yet loving, to let it linger there.

"Will you promise that if you doubt me when I am gone, you will ask of the Duke the 'other reason' of my going?"

"I shall not doubt you," answered Margaret, looking proudly up.

"God bless you, my beloved!"—and so he went to sea again.

CHAPTER XVI

When Mr. Barker, who had followed the party to Newport, called on the Countess the following morning, she was not visible, so he was fain to content himself with scribbling a very pressing invitation to drive in the afternoon, which he sent up with some flowers, not waiting for an answer. The fact was that Margaret had sent for the Duke at an early hour—for her—and was talking with him on matters of importance at the time Barker called. Otherwise she would very likely not have refused to see the latter.

"I want you to explain to me what they are trying to do to make Dr. Claudius give up his property," said Margaret, who looked pale and beautiful in a morning garment of nondescript shape and of white silken material. The Duke was sitting by the window, watching a couple of men preparing to get into a trim dogcart. To tell the truth, the dogcart and the horse were the objects of interest. His Grace was not aware that the young men were no less personages than young Mr. Hannibal Q. Sniggins and young Mr. Orlando Van Sueindell, both of New York, sons of the "great roads." Either of these young gentlemen could have bought out his Grace; either of them would have joyfully licked his boots; and either of them would have protested, within the sacred precincts of their gorgeous club in New York, that he was a conceited ass of an Englishman. But his Grace did not know this, or he would certainly have regarded them with more interest. He was profoundly indifferent to the character of the people with whom he had to do, whether they were catalogued in the "book of snobs" or not. It is generally people who are themselves snobs who call their intimates by that offensive epithet, attributing to them the sin they fall into themselves. The Duke distinguished between gentlemen and cads, when it was a question of dining at the same table, but in matters of business he believed the distinction of no importance. He came to America for business purposes, and he took Americans as he found them. He thought they were very good men of business, and when it came to associating with them on any other footing, he thought some of them were gentlemen and some were not—pretty much as it is everywhere else. So he watched the young men getting into their dogcart, and he thought the whole turn-out looked "very fit."

"Really," he began, in answer to the Countess's question, "—upon my word, I don't know much about it. At least, I suppose not."

"Oh, I thought you did," said Margaret, taking up a book and a paper-cutter. "I thought it must be something rather serious, or he would not have been obliged to go abroad to get papers about it."

"Well, you know, after all, he—aw—" the Duke reddened—"he—well yes, exactly so."

"Yes?" said Margaret interrogatively, expecting something more.

"Exactly," said the Duke, still red, but determined not to say anything. He had not promised Claudius not to say he could have vouched for him, had the Doctor stayed; but he feared that in telling Margaret this, he might be risking the betrayal of Claudius's actual destination. It would not do, however.

"I really do not understand just what you said," said Margaret, looking at him.

"Ah! well, no. I daresay I did not express myself very clearly. What was your question, Countess?"

"I asked who it was who was making so much trouble for the Doctor;" said Margaret calmly.

"Oh, I was sure I could not have understood you. It's the executors and lawyer people, who are not satisfied about his identity. It's all right, though."

"Of course. But could no one here save him the trouble of going all the way back to Germany?"

The Duke grew desperate. He was in a corner where he must either tell a lie of some sort or let the cat out of the bag. The Duke was a cynical and worldly man enough, perhaps, as the times go, but he did not tell lies. He plunged.

"My dear Countess," he said, facing towards her and stroking his whiskers, "I really know something about Dr. Claudius, and I will tell you all I am at liberty to tell; please do not ask me anything else. Claudius is really gone to obtain papers from Heidelberg as well as for another purpose which I cannot divulge. The papers might have been dispensed with, for I could have sworn to him."

"Then the other object is the important one," said the Countess pensively. The Duke was silent. "I am greatly obliged to you," Margaret continued, "for what you have told me."

"I will tell you what I can do," said the Englishman after a pause, during which an unusual expression in his face seemed to betoken thought. "I am going to the West for a couple of months to look after things, and of course accidents may happen. Claudius may have difficulty in getting what he wants, and I am the only man here who knows all about him. He satisfied me of his identity. I will, if you like, sign a statement vouching for him, and leave it in your hands in case of need. It is all I can do."

"In my hands?" exclaimed Margaret, drawing herself up a little. "And why in my hands, Duke?" The Duke got very red indeed this time, and hesitated. He had put his foot into it through sheer goodness of heart and a desire to help everybody.

"Aw—a—the—the fact is, Countess," he got out at last, "the fact is, you know, Claudius has not many friends here, and I thought you were one of them. My only desire is—a—to serve him."

Margaret had quickly grasped the advantage to Claudius, if such a voucher as the Duke offered were kept in pickle as a rod for his enemies.

"You are right," said she, "I am a good friend of Dr. Claudius, and I will keep the paper in case of need."

The Duke recovered his equanimity.

"Thank you," said he. "I am a very good friend of his, and I thank you on his behalf, as I am sure he will himself. There's one of our Foreign Office clerks here for his holiday; I will get him to draw up the paper as he is an old friend of mine—in fact, some relation, I believe. By Jove! there goes Barker." The latter exclamation was caused by the sudden appearance of the man he named on the opposite side of the avenue, in conversation with the two young gentlemen whom the Duke had already noticed as preparing to mount their dogcart.

"Oh," said Margaret indifferently, in response to the exclamation.

"Yes," said the Duke, "it is he. I thought he was in New York."

"No," said the Countess, "he has just called. It was his card they brought me just as you came. He wants me to drive with him this afternoon."

"Indeed. Shall you go?"

"I think so—yes," said she.

"Very well. I will take my sister with me," said the Duke. "I have got something very decent to drive in." Margaret laughed at the implied invitation.

"How you take things for granted," said she. "Did you really think I would have gone with you?"

"Such things have happened," said the Duke good-humouredly, and went away. Not being in the least a ladies' man, he was very apt to make such speeches occasionally. He had a habit of taking it for granted that no one refused his invitations.

At four o'clock that afternoon Silas B. Barker junior drew up to the steps of the hotel in a very gorgeous conveyance, called in America a T-cart, and resembling a mail phaeton in build. From the high double box Mr. Barker commanded and guided a pair of showy brown horses, harnessed in the most approved philanthropic, or rather philozooic style; no check-rein, no breeching, no nothing apparently, except a pole and Mr. Barker's crest. For Mr. Barker had a crest, since he came from Salem, Massachusetts, and the bearings were a witch pendant, gules, on a gallows sinister, sable.

Behind him sat the regulation clock-work groom, brought over at considerable expense from the establishment of Viscount Plungham, and who sprang to the ground and took his place at the horses' heads as soon as Barker had brought them to a stand. Then Barker, arrayed in a new hat, patent-leather boots, a very long frock-coat, and a very expensive rose, descended lightly from his chariot and swiftly ascended the steps, seeming to tread half on air and half on egg-shells. And a few minutes later he again appeared, accompanied by the Countess Margaret, looking dark and pale and queenly. A proud man was dandy Silas as he helped her to her place, and going to the other side, got in and took the ribbands. Many were the glances that shot from the two edges of the road at the unknown beauty whom Silas drove by his side, and obsequious were the bows of Silas's friends as they passed. Even the groggy old man who drives the water-cart on Bellevue Avenue could scarce forbear to cheer as she went by.

And so they drove away, side by side. Barker knew very well that Claudius had taken his leave the day before, and to tell the truth, he was a good deal surprised that Margaret should be willing to accept this invitation. He had called to ask her, because he was not the man to let the grass grow under his feet at any time, much less when he was laying siege to a woman. For with women time is sometimes everything. And being of a reasonable mind, when Mr. Barker observed that he was surprised, he concluded that there must be some good reason for his astonishment, and still more that there must be some very good reason why Margaret should accept his first invitation to a tête-à-tête afternoon. From one reflection to another, he came at last to the conclusion that she must be anxious to learn some details concerning the Doctor's departure, from which again he argued that Claudius had not taken her into his confidence. The hypothesis that she might be willing to make an effort with him for Claudius's justification Mr. Barker dismissed as improbable. And he was right. He waited, therefore, for her to broach the subject, and confined himself, as they drove along, to remarks about the people they passed, the doings of the Newport summer, concerning which he had heard all the gossip during the last few hours, the prospect of Madame Patti in opera during the coming season, horses, dogs, and mutual friends—all the motley array of subjects permissible, desultory, and amusing. Suddenly, as they bowled out on an open road by the sea, Margaret began.

"Why has Dr. Claudius gone abroad," she asked, glancing at Barker's face, which remained impenetrable as ever. Barker changed his hold on the reins, and stuck the whip into the bucket by his side before he answered.

"They say he has gone to get himself sworn to," he said rather slowly, and with a good show of indifference.

"I cannot see why that was necessary," answered Margaret calmly "It seems to me we all knew him very well."

"Oh, nobody can understand lawyers," said Barker, and was silent, knowing how strong a position silence was, for she could know nothing more about Claudius without committing herself to a direct question. Barker was in a difficult position. He fully intended later to hint that Claudius might never return at all. But he knew too much to do anything of the kind at present, when the memory of the Doctor was fresh in the Countess's mind, and when, as he guessed, he himself was not too high in her favour. He therefore told a bit of the plain truth which could not be cast in his teeth afterwards, and was silent.

It was a good move, and Margaret was fain to take to some other subject of conversation, lest the pause should seem long. They had not gone far before the society kaleidoscope was once more in motion, and Barker was talking his best. They rolled along, passing most things on the road, and when they came to a bit of hill, he walked his horses, on pretence of keeping them cool, but in reality to lengthen the drive and increase his advantage, if only by a minute and a hairbreadth. He could see he was amusing her, as he drew her away from the thing that made her heavy, and sketched, and crayoned, and photographed from memory all manner of harmless gossip—he took care that it should be harmless—and such book-talk as he could command, with such a general sprinkling of sentimentalism, ready made and easy to handle, as American young men affect in talking to women.

Making allowance for the customs of the country, they were passing a very innocently diverting afternoon; and Margaret, though secretly annoyed at finding that Barker would not talk about Claudius, or add in any way to her information, was nevertheless congratulating herself upon the smooth termination of the interview. She had indeed only accepted the invitation in the hope of learning something more about Claudius and his "other reason." But she also recognised that, though Barker were unwilling to speak of the Doctor, he might have made himself very disagreeable by taking advantage of the confession of interest she had volunteered in asking so direct a question. But Barker had taken no such lead, and never referred to Claudius in all the ramblings of his polite conversation.

He was in the midst of a description of Mrs. Orlando Van Sueindell's last dinner-party, which he had unfortunately missed, when his browns, less peaceably disposed than most of the lazy bean-fed cattle one sees on the Newport avenue, took it into their heads that it would be a joyous thing to canter down a steep place into the sea. The road turned, with a sudden dip, across a little neck of land separating the bay from the harbour, and the descent was, for a few yards, very abrupt. At this point, then, the intelligent animals conceived the ingenious scheme of bolting, with that eccentricity of device which seems to characterise overfed carriage-horses. In an instant they were off, and it was clear there would be no stopping them—from a trot to a break, from a canter to a gallop, from a gallop to a tearing, breakneck, leave-your-bones-behind-you race, all in a moment, down to the sea.

Barker was not afraid, and he did what he could. He was not a strong man, and he knew himself no match for the two horses, but he hoped by a sudden effort, repeated once or twice, to scare the runaways into a standstill, as is sometimes possible. Acting immediately on his determination, as he always did, he wound one hand in each rein, and half rising from his high seat, jerked with all his might. Margaret held her breath.

But alas for the rarity of strength in saddlers' work! The off-rein snapped away like a thread just where the buckle leads half of it over to the near horse, and the strain on the right hand being thus suddenly removed, the horses' heads were jerked violently to the left, and they became wholly unmanageable. Barker was silent, and instantly dropped the unbroken rein. As for Margaret, she sat quite still, holding to the low rail-back of her seat, and preparing for a jump. They were by this time nearly at the bottom of the descent, and rapidly approaching a corner where a great heap of rocks made the prospect hideous. To haul the horses over to the left would have been destruction, as the ground fell away on that side to a considerable depth down to the rocks below. Then Barker did a brave thing.

"If I miss him, jump off to the right," he cried; and in a moment, before Margaret could answer or prevent him, he had got over the dashboard, and was in mid-air, a strange figure, in his long frock-coat and shiny hat. With a bold leap—and the Countess shivered as she saw him flying in front of her—he alighted on the back of the off horse, almost on his face, but well across the beast for all that. Light and wiry, a mere bundle of nerves dressed up, Mr. Barker was not to be shaken off, and, while the animal was still plunging, he had caught the flying bits of bridle, and was sawing away, right and left, with the energy of despair. Between its terror at being suddenly mounted by some one out of a clear sky, so to say, and the violent wrenching it was getting from Barker's bony little hands, the beast decided to stop at last, and its companion, who was coming in for some of the pulling too, stopped by sympathy, with a series of snorts and plunges. Barker still clung to the broken rein, leaning far over the horse's neck so as to wind it round his wrist; and he shouted to Margaret to get out, which she immediately did; but, instead of fainting away, she came to the horses' heads and stood before them, a commanding figure that even a dumb animal would not dare to slight—too much excited to speak yet, but ready to face anything.

A few moments later the groom, whose existence they had both forgotten, came running down to them, with a red face, and dusting his battered hat on his arm as he came. He had quietly slipped off behind, and had been rolled head over heels for his pains, but had suffered no injury. Then Barker got off. He was covered with dust, but his hat was still on his head, and he did not look as though he had been jumping for his life. Margaret turned to him with genuine gratitude and admiration, for he had borne himself as few men could or would have done.

"You have saved my life," she said, "and I am very grateful. It was very brave of you." And she held out her hand to meet his, now trembling violently from the fierce strain.

"Oh, not at all; it was really nothing," he said, bowing low. But the deep wrinkle that scored Barker's successes in life showed plainly round his mouth. He knew what his advantage was, and he had no thought of the danger when he reflected on what he had gained. Not he! His heart, or the organ which served him in place of one, was full of triumph. Had he planned the whole thing with the utmost skill and foresight he could not have succeeded better. Such a victory! and the very first day after Claudius's departure—Ye gods! what luck!

And so it came to pass that by the time the harness had been tied together and the conveyance got without accident as far as the first stable on the outskirts of the town, where it was left with the groom, Barker had received a goodly meed of thanks and praise. And when Margaret proposed that they should walk as far as the hotel, Barker tried a few steps and found he was too lame for such exercise, his left leg having been badly bruised by the pole of the carriage in his late exploit; which injury elicited a further show of sympathy from Margaret. And when at last he left her with a cab at the door of her hotel, he protested that he had enjoyed a very delightful drive, and went away in high spirits. Margaret, in her gratitude for such an escape, and in unfeigned admiration of Barker's daring and coolness, was certainly inclined to think better of him than she had done for a long time. Or perhaps it would be truer to say that he was more in her thoughts than he had been; for, in the reign of Claudius, Barker had dwindled to a nearly insignificant speck in the landscape, dwarfed away to nothing by the larger mould and stronger character of the Swede.

Margaret saw the Duke in the evening. He gave her a document, unsealed, in a huge envelope, bidding her keep it in a safe place, for the use of their mutual friend, in case he should need it. She said she would give it to Claudius when he came back; and then she told the Duke about her drive with Barker and the accident. The Duke looked grave.

"Of course," he said, "I introduced Barker to you, and it would seem very odd if I were to warn you against him now. All the same, Countess, I have had the honour of being your friend for some time, and I must say I have sometimes regretted that I brought him to your house." He reddened a little after he had spoken, fearing she might have misunderstood him. "I wish," he added, to make things clearer, "that I could have brought you Claudius without Barker." Then he reddened still more, and wished he had said nothing. Margaret raised her eyebrows. Perhaps she could have wished as much herself, but she dropped the subject.

"When are you coming back from the West, Duke," she asked, busying herself in arranging some books on her table. The hotel sitting-room was so deadly dreary to the eye that she was trying to make it look as if it had not been lately used as a place of burial.

"It may be two months before I am here again. A—about the time Claudius comes over, I should think."

"And when do you go?"

"Next week, I think."

"I wish you were going to stay," said Margaret simply, "or Lady Victoria. I shall be so lonely."

"You will have Miss Skeat," suggested his Grace.

"Oh, it's not that," said she. "I shall not be alone altogether, for there is poor Nicholas, you know. I must take care of him; and then I suppose some of these people will want to amuse me, or entertain me—not that they are very entertaining; but they mean well. Besides, my being mixed up in a Nihilist persecution adds to my social value." The Duke, however, was not listening, his mind being full of other things—what there was of it, and his heart had long determined to sympathise with Margaret in her troubles; so there was nothing more to be said.

"Dear me," thought Miss Skeat, "what a pity! They say she might have had the Duke when she was a mere child—and to think that she should have refused him! So admirably suited to each other!" But Miss Skeat, as she sat at the other end of the room trying to find "what it was that people saw so funny" in the Tramp Abroad, was mistaken about her patroness and the very high and mighty personage from the aristocracy. The Duke was much older than Margaret, and had been married before he had ever seen her. It was only because they were such good friends that the busybodies said they had just missed being man and wife.

But when the Duke was gone, Margaret and Miss Skeat were left alone, and they drew near each other and sat by the table, the elder lady reading aloud from a very modern novel. The Countess paid little attention to what she heard, for she was weary, and it seemed as though the evening would never end. Miss Skeat's even and somewhat monotonous voice produced no sensation of drowsiness to-night, as it often did, though Margaret's eyes were half-closed and her fingers idle. She needed rest, but it would not come, and still her brain went whirling through the scenes of the past twenty-four hours, again and again recurring to the question "Why is he gone?" unanswered and yet ever repeated, as the dreadful wake-song of the wild Irish, the "Why did he die?" that haunts the ear that has once heard it for weeks afterwards.

She tried to reason, but there was no reason. Why, why, why? He was gone with her kiss on his lips and her breath in his. She should have waited till he came back from over the sea before giving him what was so very precious. More than once, as she repeated the words he had spoken at parting, she asked herself whether she doubted him after all, and whether it would not be wiser to speak to the Duke. But then, the latter so evidently believed in Claudius that it comforted her to think of his honest faith, and she would dismiss every doubt again as vain and wearying. But still the eternal question rang loudly in her soul's ears, and the din of the inquisitive devil that would not be satisfied deafened her so that she could not hear Miss Skeat. Once or twice she moved her head nervously from side to side, as it rested on the back of the chair, and her face was drawn and pale, so that Miss Skeat anxiously asked whether she were in any pain, but Margaret merely motioned to her companion to continue reading, and was silent. But Miss Skeat grew uneasy, feeling sure that something was the matter.

"Dear Countess," she said, "will you not retire to rest? I fear that this horrid accident has shaken you. Do go to bed, and I will come and read you to sleep." Her voice sounded kindly, and Margaret's fingers stole out till they covered Miss Skeat's bony white ones, with the green veins and the yellowish lights between the knuckles.

Miss Skeat, at this unusual manifestation of feeling, laid down the book she held in her other hand, and settled her gold-rimmed glasses over her long nose. Then her eyes beamed across at Margaret, and a kindly, old-fashioned smile came into her face that was good to see, and as she pressed the hot young hand in hers there was a suspicion of motherliness in her expression that would have surprised a stranger. For Miss Skeat did not look motherly at ordinary times.

"Poor child!" said she softly. Margaret's other hand went to her eyes and hid them from sight, and her head sank forward until it touched her fingers, where they joined Miss Skeat's.

"I am so unhappy to-night," murmured Margaret, finding at last, in the evening hours, the sympathy she had longed for all day. Miss Skeat changed her own position a little so as to be nearer to her.

"Poor child!" repeated Miss Skeat almost in a whisper, as she bent down to the regal head that lay against her hand, smoothing the thick hair with her worn fingers. "Poor child, do you love him so very dearly?" She spoke almost inaudibly, and her wrinkled eyelids were wet. But low as was her voice, Margaret heard, and moved her head in assent, without lifting it from the table.

Ah yes—she loved him very, very much. But she could not bear to confess it, for all that, and a moment afterwards she was sitting upright again in her chair, feeling that she had weathered the first storm. Her companion, who was not ignorant of her ways, contented herself then with patting Margaret's hand caressingly during the instant it remained in her own, before it was drawn away. There was a world of kindness and of gentle humanity in the gaunt gentlewoman's manner, showing that the heart within was not withered yet. Then Miss Skeat flattened the book before her with the paper-cutter, and began to read. Reading aloud had become to her a second nature, and whether she had liked it or not at first, she had learned to do it with perfect ease and indifference, neither letting her voice drag languidly and hesitatingly when she was tired, nor falling into that nerve-rending fault of readers who vainly endeavour to personate the characters in dialogue, and to give impressiveness in the descriptive portions. She never made a remark, or asked her hearer's opinion. If the Countess was in the humour to sleep, the reading was soporific; if she desired to listen, she felt that her companion was not trying to bias her judgment by the introduction of dramatic intonation and effect. With an even, untiring correctness of utterance, Miss Skeat read one book just as she read another—M. Thiers or Mr. Henry James, Mark Twain or a Parliamentary Report—it was all one to her. Poor Miss Skeat!

But to Margaret the evening seemed long and the night longer, and many days and evenings and nights afterwards. Not that she doubted, but that she thought—well—perhaps she thought she ought to doubt. Some cunning reader of face and character, laughing and making love by turns, had once told her she had more heart than head. Every woman knows she ought to seem flattered at being considered a "person of heart," and yet every woman cordially hates to be told so. And, at last, Margaret began to wonder whether it were true. Should she have admitted she loved a man who left her a moment afterwards in order to make a voyage of two months for the mere furthering of his worldly interest? But then—he told her he was going before he kissed her. What could be the "other reason"?

CHAPTER XVII

It is not to be supposed that a man of Barker's character would neglect the signal advantage he had gained in being injured, or at least badly bruised, while attempting to save Margaret from destruction. That he had really saved her was a less point in his favour than that he had barked his shins in so doing. The proverbial relationship between pity and love is so exceedingly well known that many professional love-makers systematically begin their campaigns by endeavouring to move the compassion of the woman they are attacking. Occasionally they find a woman with whom pity is akin to scorn instead of to love—and then their policy is a failure.

The dark Countess was no soft-hearted Saxon maiden, any more than she was a cold-blooded, cut-throat American girl, calculating her romance by the yard, booking her flirtations by double-entry and marrying at compound interest, with the head of a railway president and the heart of an Esquimaux. She was rather one of those women who are ever ready to sympathise from a naturally generous and noble nature, but who rarely give their friendship and still more seldom their love. They marry, sometimes, where there is neither. They marry—ye gods! why do people marry, and what reasons will they not find for marrying? But such women, if they are wedded where their heart is not, are generally very young; far too young to know what they are doing; and though there be little inclination to the step, it always turns out that they had at least a respect for the man. Margaret had been married to Count Alexis because it was in every way such a plausible match, and she was only eighteen then, poor thing. But Alexis was such an uncommonly good fellow that she had honestly tried to love him, and had not altogether failed. At least she had never had any domestic troubles, and when he was shot at Plevna, in 1876, she shed some very genuine tears and shut herself away from the world for a long time. But though her sorrow was sincere, it was not profound, and she knew it from the first, never deceiving herself with the idea that she could not marry again. She had sustained many a siege, however, both before her husband's untimely death and since; and though a stranger to love, she was no novice in love-making. Indeed few women are; certainly no beautiful women.

Margaret, then, though a pure-hearted and brave lady, was of the world, understanding the wiles thereof; and so, when Mr. Barker began to come regularly to see her, and when she noticed how very long the slight lameness he had incurred from the runaway accident seemed to last, and when she observed how cunningly he endeavoured to excite her sympathy towards him, she began to suspect that he meant something more than a mere diversion for himself. He spoke so feelingly of his lonely position in the world; to accentuate which, he spoke of his father without any feeling whatever. He represented himself as so drearily lonely and friendless in this hard-hearted, thorny world. Quite a little lamb was Silas, leaving shreds of his pure white wool rent off and clinging to the briars of his solitary life-journey. He was very patient in his sufferings, he said, for he so keenly felt that coarser natures could not suffer as he did; that troubles glided from their backs like water from the feathers of the draggled but happy goose, whereas on his tender heart they struck deep like a fiery rain. Was it not Danty who told of those poor people who were exposed to the molten drizzle? Ah yes! Danty knew, of course, for he had been a great sufferer. What a beautiful, yet sad, word is that, "to suffer"! How gentle and lovely to suffer without complaint! Had the Countess ever thought of it? To suffer silently—and long—(here Silas cast a love-sick glance out of his small dark eyes)—with the hope of gaining an object infinitely far removed, but—(another glance)—infinitely beautiful and worth obtaining. Oh! Silas would suffer for ever in such a hope! There was nothing Silas would not do that was saintly that he might gain heaven.

After a time, Margaret, who disliked this kind of talk intensely, began to look grave, an omen which Barker did not fail to interpret to his advantage, for it is a step gained when a woman begins to be serious. Only a man ignorant of Margaret's real character, and incapable of appreciating it, could have been so deceived in this case. She had felt strongly that Barker had saved her life, and that he had acted with a boldness and determination on that occasion which would have merited her admiration even had it not commanded her gratitude. But she was really grateful, and, wishing to show it, could devise no better plan than to receive his visits and to listen politely to his conversation.

One day, late in the afternoon, they were sitting together over a cup of tea, and Barker was pouring out his experiences, or what he was pleased to call by that name, for they were not genuine. Not that his own existence would have been a dull or uninteresting chapter for a rainy afternoon, for Barker had led a stirring life of its kind. But as it was necessary to strike the pathetic key, seeing that Claudius had the heroic symphony to himself, Barker embroidered skilfully a little picture in which he appeared more sinned against than sinning, inasmuch as he had been called upon to play the avenging angel. He had succeeded, he admitted, in accomplishing his object, which in his opinion had been a justifiable one, but it had left a sore place in his heart, and he had never quite recovered from the pain it had given him to give so much pain—wholesome pain indeed, but what of that?—to another.

"It was in New York, some years ago," he said. "A friend of mine, such a dear good fellow, was very much in love with a reigning beauty, a Miss—; well, you will guess the name. She threw him over, after a three months' engagement, in the most heartless manner, and he was so broken-hearted that he drank himself to death in six months at the club. He died there one winter's evening under very painful circumstances."

"A noble end," said Margaret, scornfully. "What a proud race we Americans are!" Barker sighed skilfully and looked reproachfully at Margaret.

"Poor chap!" he ejaculated, "I saw him die. And that night," continued Mr. Barker, with a mournful impressiveness, "I determined that the woman who had caused so much unhappiness should be made to know what unhappiness is. I made up my mind that she should suffer what my friend had suffered. I knew her very well,—in fact she was a distant connection; so I went to her at a ball at the Van Sueindells'. I had engaged her to dance the German[2], and had sent her some very handsome roses. I had laid my plan already, and after a little chaff and a few turns I challenged her to a set flirtation. 'Let us swear,' I said, 'to be honest, and let us make a bet of a dozen pairs of gloves. If one of us really falls in love, he or she must acknowledge it and pay the gloves.' It was agreed, for she was in great spirits that night, and laughed at the idea that she could ever fall in love with me—poor me! who have so little that is attractive. At first she thought it was only a joke, but as I began to visit her regularly and to go through all the formalities of love-making, she became interested. We were soon the talk of the town, and everybody said we were going to be married. Still the engagement did not come out, and people waited, open-mouthed, wondering what next. At last I thought I was safe, and so, the first chance I had at a party in Newport, I made a dead set at a new beauty just arrived from the South—I forget where. The other—the one with whom I was betting—was there, and I watched her. She lost her temper completely, and turned all sorts of colours. Then I knew I had won, and so I went back to her and talked to her for the rest of the evening, explaining that the other young lady was a sister of a very dear friend of mine.

[Footnote 2: American for the cotillon.]

"The next day I called on my beauty, and throwing myself at her feet, I declared myself vanquished. The result was just as I expected. She burst into tears and put her arms round my neck, and said it was she who lost, for she really loved me though she had been too proud to acknowledge it. Then I calmly rose and laughed. 'I do not care for you in the least,' I said; 'I only said so to make you speak. I have won the gloves.' She broke down completely, and went abroad a few days afterwards. And so I avenged my friend."

There was a pause when Barker had finished his tale. He sipped his tea, and Margaret rose slowly and went to the window.

"Don't you think that is a very good story, Countess?" he asked. "Don't you think I was quite right?" Still no answer. Margaret rang the bell, and old Vladimir appeared.

"Mr. Barker's carriage," said she; then, recollecting herself, she repeated the order in Russian, and swept out of the room without deigning to look at the astonished young man, standing on the hearthrug with his tea-cup in his hand. How it is that Vladimir succeeds in interpreting his mistress's orders to the domestics of the various countries in which she travels is a mystery not fathomed, for in her presence he understands only the Slav tongue. But however that may be, a minute had not elapsed before Mr. Barker was informed by another servant that his carriage was at the door. He turned pale as he descended the steps.

You have carried it too far, Mr. Barker. That is not the kind of story that a lady of Countess Margaret's temper will listen to; for when you did the thing you have told her—if indeed you ever did it, which is doubtful—you did a very base and unmanly thing. It may not be very nice to act as that young lady did to your friend; but then, just think how very much worse it would have been if she had married him from a sense of duty, and made him feel it afterwards. Worse? Ay, worse than a hundred deaths. You are an ass, Barker, with your complicated calculations, as the Duke has often told you; and now it is a thousand to one that you have ruined yourself with the Countess. She will never take your view that it was a justifiable piece of revenge; she will only see in it a cruel and dastardly deception, practised on a woman whose only fault was that, not loving, she discovered her mistake in time. A man should rejoice when a woman draws back from an engagement, reflecting what his life might have been had she not done so.

But Barker's face was sickly with disappointment as he drove away, and he could hardly collect himself enough to determine what was best to be done. However, after a time he came to the conclusion that a letter must be written of humble apology, accompanied by a few very expensive flowers, and followed after a week's interval by a visit. She could not mean to break off all acquaintance with him for so slight a cause. She would relent and see him again, and then he would put over on the other tack. He had made a mistake—very naturally, too—because she was always so reluctant to give her own individual views about anything. A mistake could be repaired, he thought, without any serious difficulty.

And so the next morning Margaret received some flowers and a note, a very gentlemanly note, expressive of profound regret that anything he could have said, and so forth, and so forth. And Margaret, whose strong temper sometimes made her act hastily, even when acting rightly, said to herself that she had maltreated the poor little beast, and would see him if he called again. That was how she expressed it, showing that to some extent Barker had succeeded in producing a feeling of pity in her mind—though it was a very different sort of pity from what he would have wished. Meanwhile Margaret returned to New York, where she saw her brother-in-law occasionally, and comforted him with the assurance that when his hundred napoleons were at an end, she would take care of him. And Nicholas, who was a gentleman, like his dead brother, proud and fierce, lived economically in a small hotel, and wrote magazine articles describing the state of his unhappy country.

Then Barker called and was admitted, Miss Skeat being present, and his face expressed a whole volume of apology, while he talked briskly of current topics; and so he gradually regained the footing he had lost. At all events he thought so, not knowing that though Margaret might forgive she could never forget; and that she was now forewarned and forearmed in perpetuity against any advance Barker might ever make.

One day the mail brought a large envelope with an English postage stamp, addressed in a strong, masculine hand, even and regular, and utterly without adornment, but yet of a strikingly peculiar expression, if a handwriting may be said to have an expression.

"CUNARD S.S. Servia, Sept. 15th.

"My Beloved Lady—Were it not for the possibility of writing to you, this voyage would be an impossible task to me; and even as it is, the feeling that what I write must travel away from you for many days before it travels towards you again makes me half suspect it is a mockery after all. After these wonderful months of converse it seems incredible that I should be thus taken out of your hearing and out of the power of seeing you. That I long for a sight of your dear face, that I hunger for your touch and for your sweet voice, I need not tell you or further asseverate. I am constantly looking curiously at the passengers, vainly thinking that you must appear among them. The sea without you is not the sea, any more than heaven would be heaven were you not there.

"I cannot describe to you, my dear lady, how detestable the life on board is to me. I loathe the people with their inane chatter, and the idiotic children, and the highly-correct and gentlemanly captain, all equally. The philistine father, the sea-sick mother, the highly-cultured daughter, and the pipe-smoking son, are equally objects of disgust. When I go on deck the little children make a circle round me, because I am so big, and the sailors will not let me go on to forecastle under three shillings—which I paid cheerfully, however, because I can be alone there and think of you, without being contemplated as an object of wonder by about two hundred idiots. I have managed to rig a sort of table in my cabin at last, and here I sit, under the dubious light of the port-hole, wishing it would blow, or that we might meet an iceberg, or anything, to scare the people into their dens and leave me a little open-air solitude.

"It seems so strange to be writing to you. I never wrote anything but little notes in the old days at Baden, and now I am writing what promises to be a long letter, for we cannot be in under six days, and in all that time there is nothing else I can do—nothing else I would do, if I could. And yet it is so different. Perhaps I am incoherent, and you will say, different from what? It is different from what it used to be, before that thrice-blessed afternoon in the Newport fog.

"The gray mist came down like a curtain, shutting off the past and marking where the present begins. It seems to me that I never lived before that moment, and yet those months were happy while they lasted, so that it sometimes seemed as though no greater happiness could be possible. How did it all happen, most blessed lady?

"The lazy, good-natured sea, that loves us well, washes up and glances through my port-hole as I write, as if in answer to my question. The sea knows how it happened, for he saw us, and bore us, and heard all the tale; and even in Newport he was there, hidden under the fog and listening, and he is rejoicing that those who loved are now lovers. It is not hard to see how it happened. They all worship you, every human being that comes near you falls down and acknowledges you to be the queen. For they must. There is no salvation from that, and it is meet and right that it should be so. And I came, like the others, to do homage to the great queen, and you deigned to raise me up and bid me stand beside you.

"You are my first allegiance and my first love. I thank Heaven that I can say it honestly and truly, without fear of my conscience pricking. You know too, for I have told you, how my boyhood and manhood have been passed, and if there is anything you do not know I will tell you hereafter, for I would always hate to feel that there was anything about me you did not know—I could not feel it. But then, say you, he should have told me what he was going to do abroad. And so I have, dear lady; for though I have not explained it all to you, I have placed all needful knowledge in safe hands, where you can obtain it for the asking, if ever the least shadow of doubt should cross your mind. Only I pray you, as suing a great boon, not to doubt—that is all, for I would rather you did not know yet.

"This letter is being written by degrees. I have not written all this at once, for I find it as hard to express my thoughts to you on paper as I find it easy by word of mouth. It seems a formal thing to write, and yet there should be nothing less marred by formality than such a letter as mine. It is only that the choice is too great. I have too much to say, and so say nothing. I would ask, if I were so honoured by Heaven, the tongues of men and of angels, and all the mighty word-music of sage and prophet, that I might tell you how I love you, my heart's own. I would ask that for one hour I might hold in my hand the bâton of heaven's choir. Then would I lead those celestial musicians through such a grand plain chant as time has never dreamt of, nor has eternity yet heard it; so that rank on rank of angels and saints should take up the song, until the arches of the outer firmament rang again, and the stars chimed together; and all the untold hierarchy of archangelic voice and heavenly instrument should cry, as with one soul, the confession of this heart of mine—'I love.'

"Another day has passed, and I think I have heard in my dreams the bursts of music that I would fain have wafted to your waking ears. Verily the lawyers in New York say well, that I am not Claudius. Claudius was a thing of angles and books, mathematical and earthy, believing indeed in the greatness of things supernal, but not having tasted thereof. My beloved, God has given me a new soul to love you with, so great that it seems as though it would break through the walls of my heart and cry aloud to you. This new Claudius is a man of infinite power to rise above earthly things, above everything that is below you—and what things that are in earth are not below you, lady mine?

"Again the time has passed, in a dull reluctant fashion, as if he delighted to torment, like the common bore of society. He lingers and dawdles through his round of hours as though it joyed him to be sluggish. It has blown a little, and most of the people are sea-sick. Thank goodness! I suppose that is a very inhuman sentiment, but the masses of cheerful humanity, gluttonously fattening on the ship's fare and the smooth sea, were becoming intolerable. There is not one person on board who looks as though he or she had left a human being behind who had any claim to be regretted. Did any one of these people ever love? I suppose so. I suppose at one time or another most of them have thought they loved some one. I will not be uncharitable, for they are receiving their just punishment. Lovers are never sea-sick, but now a hoarse chorus, indescribable and hideous, rises from hidden recesses of the ship. They are not in love, they are sea-sick. May it do them all possible good!

"Here we are at last. I hasten to finish this rambling letter that it may catch the steamer, which, I am told, leaves to-day. Nine days we have been at sea, and the general impression seems to be that the last part of the passage has been rough. And now I shall be some weeks in Europe—I cannot tell how long, but I think the least possible will be three weeks, and the longest six. I shall know, however, in a fortnight. My beloved, it hurts me to stop writing—unreasonable animal that I am, for a letter must be finished in order to be posted. I pray you, sweetheart, write me a word of comfort and strength in my journeying. Anything sent to Baring's will reach me; you cannot know what a line from you would be to me, how I would treasure it as the most sacred of things and the most precious, until we meet. And so, à bientôt, for we must never say 'goodbye,' even in jest. I feel as though I were launching this letter at a venture, as sailors throw a bottle overboard when they fear they are lost. I have not yet tested the post-office, and I feel a kind of uncertainty as to whether this will reach you.

"But they are clamouring at my door, and I must go. Once more, my own queen, I love you, ever and only and always. May all peace and rest be with you, and may Heaven keep you from all harm!"

This letter was not signed, for what signature could it possibly need? Margaret read it, and read it again, wondering—for she had never had such a letter in her life. The men who had made love to her had never been privileged to speak plainly, for she would have none of them, and so they had been obliged to confine themselves to such cunning use of permissible words and phrases as they could command, together with copious quotations from more or less erotic poets. Moreover, Claudius had never been in a position to speak his heart's fill to her until that last day, when words had played so small a part.

It was a love-letter, at least in part, such as a man might have written a hundred years ago—not such as men write nowadays, thought Margaret; certainly not such as Mr. Barker would write—or could. But she was glad he had written; and written so, for it was like him, who was utterly unlike any one else. The letter had come in the morning while Clémentine was dressing her, and she laid it on her writing-desk. But when the maid was gone, she read it once again, sitting by her window, and when she had done she unconsciously held it in her hand and rested her cheek against it. A man kisses a letter received from the woman he loves, but a woman rarely does. She thinks when he is away that she would hardly kiss him, were he present, much less will she so honour his handwriting. But when he himself comes the colour of things is changed. Nevertheless, Margaret put the folded letter in her bosom and wore it there unseen all through that day; and when Mr. Barker came to offer to take her to drive she said she would not go, making some libellous remark about the weather, which was exceeding glad and sunshiny in spite of her refusal to face it. And Mr. Barker, seeing that he was less welcome than usual, went away, for he was mortally afraid of annoying her.

Margaret was debating within herself whether she should answer, and if so, what she should say. In truth, it was not easy. She felt herself unable to write in the way he did, had she wished to. Besides, there was that feminine feeling still lurking in her heart, which said, "Do not trust him till he comes back." It seemed to her it must be so easy to write like that—and yet, she had not thought so at the first reading. But she loved him, not yet as she would some day, but still she loved, and it was her first love, as it was his.

She had settled herself in the hotel for the present, and to make it more like home—like her pretty home at Baden—she had ordered a few plants and growing flowers, very simple and inexpensive, for she felt herself terribly pinched, although she had not yet begun actually to feel the restrictions laid on her by her financial troubles. When Barker was gone, she amused herself with picking off the dried leaves and brushing away the little cobwebs and spiders that always accumulate about growing things. In the midst of this occupation she made up her mind, and rang the bell.

"Vladimir, I am not at home," she said solemnly, and the gray-haired, gray-whiskered functionary bowed in acknowledgment of the fact, which was far from evident. When he was gone she sat down to her desk and wrote to Dr. Claudius. She wrote rapidly in her large hand, and before long she had covered four pages of notepaper. Then she read it over, and tore it up. The word "dear" occurred once too often for her taste. Again the white fingers flew rapidly along the page, but soon she stopped.

"That is too utterly frigid," she said half aloud, with a smile. Then she tried again.

"DEAR DR. CLAUDIUS—So many thanks for your charming letter, which I received this morning. Tell me a great deal more, please, and write at once. Tell me everything you do and say and see, for I want to feel just as though you were here to talk everything over.

"Mr. Barker has been here a good deal lately, and the other day he told me a story I did not like. But I forgave him, for he seemed so penitent. Please burn my letters.

"It is very cold and disagreeable, and I really half wish I were in Europe. Europe is much pleasanter. I have not read a word of Spencer since you left, but I have thought a great deal about what you said the last time we did any work together.

"Let me know positively when you are coming back, and let it be as soon as possible, for I must see you. I am going to see Salvini, in Othello, to-night, with Miss Skeat. He sent me a box, in memory of a little dinner years ago, and I expect him to call. He did call, but I could not see him.

"I cannot write any more, for it is dinner-time. Thanks, dear, for your loving letter. It was sweet of you to post it the same day, for it caught the steamer.

—In tearing haste, yours, M.

"P.S.—Answer all my questions, please."

There was an indistinctness about the last word; it might have been "your," or "yours." The "tearing haste" resolved itself into ringing the bell to know what time it was, for Margaret had banished the hideous hotel clock from the room. On finding it was yet early, she sat down in a deep chair, and warmed her toes at the small wood fire, which was just enough to be enjoyable and not enough to be hot. It was now the beginning of October, for Claudius's letter, begun on the 15th of September, had not been posted until the 21st, and had been a long time on the way. She wondered when he would get the letter she had just written. It was not much of a letter, but she remembered the last paragraph, and thought it was quite affectionate enough. As for Claudius, when he received it he was as much delighted as though it had been six times as long and a hundred times more expansive. "Thanks, dear, for your loving letter,"—that phrase alone acknowledged everything, accepted everything, and sanctioned everything.

In the evening, as she had said in writing to the Doctor, she went with Miss Skeat and sat in the front box of the theatre, which the great actor had placed at her disposal. The play was Othello. Mr. Barker had ascertained that she was going, and had accordingly procured himself a seat in the front of the orchestra. He endeavoured to catch a look from Margaret all through the first part of the performance, but she was too entirely absorbed in the tragedy to notice him. At length, in the interval before the last act, Mr. Barker took courage, and, leaving his chair, threaded his way out of the lines of seats to the entrance. Then he presented himself at the door of the Countess's box.

"May I come in for a little while?" he inquired with an affectation of doubt and delicacy that was unnatural to him.

"Certainly," said Margaret indifferently, but smiling a little withal.

"I have ventured to bring you some marrons glacés," said Barker, when he was seated, producing at the same time a neat bonbonnière in the shape of a turban. "I thought they would remind you of Baden. You used to be very fond of them."

"Thanks," said she, "I am still." And she took one. The curtain rose, and Barker was obliged to be silent, much against his will. Margaret immediately became absorbed in the doings on the stage. She had witnessed that terrible last act twenty times before, but she never wearied of it. Neither would she have consented to see it acted by any other than the great Italian. Whatever be the merits of the play, there can be no question as to its supremacy of horror in the hands of Salvini. To us of the latter half of this century it appears to stand alone; it seems as if there could never have been such a scene or such an actor in the history of the drama. Horrible—yes! beyond all description, but, being horrible, of a depth of horror unrealised before. Perhaps no one who has not lived in the East can understand that such a character as Salvini's Othello is a possible, living reality. It is certain that American audiences, even while giving their admiration, withhold their belief. They go to see Othello, that they may shudder luxuriously at the sight of so much suffering; for it is the moral suffering of the Moor that most impresses an intelligent beholder, but it is doubtful whether Americans or English, who have not lived in Southern or Eastern lands, are capable of appreciating that the character is drawn from the life.

The great criticism to which all modern tragedy, and a great deal of modern drama, are open is the undue and illegitimate use of horror. Horror is not terror. They are two entirely distinct affections. A man hurled from a desperate precipice, in the living act to fall, is properly an object of terror, sudden and quaking. But the same man, reduced to a mangled mass of lifeless humanity, broken to pieces, and ghastly with the gaping of dead wounds—the same man, when his last leap is over and hope is fled, is an object of horror, and as such would not in early times have been regarded as a legitimate subject for artistic representation, either on the stage or in the plastic or pictorial arts.

It may be that in earlier ages, when men were personally familiar with the horrors of a barbarous ethical system, while at the same time they had the culture and refinement belonging to a high development of æsthetic civilisation, the presentation of a great terror immediately suggested the concomitant horror; and suggested it so vividly that the visible definition of the result—the bloodshed, the agony, and the death-rattle—would have produced an impression too dreadful to be associated with any pleasure to the beholder. There was no curiosity to behold violent death among a people accustomed to see it often enough in the course of their lives, and not yet brutalised into a love of blood for its own sake. The Romans presented an example of the latter state; they loved horror so well that they demanded real horror and real victims. And that is the state of the populations of England and America at the present day. Were it not for the tremendous power of modern law, there is not the slightest doubt that the mass of Londoners or New Yorkers would flock to-day to see a gladiatorial show, or to watch a pack of lions tearing, limb from limb, a dozen unarmed convicts. Not the "cultured" classes—some of them would be ashamed, and some would really feel a moral incapacity for witnessing so much pain—but the masses would go, and would pay handsomely for the sport; and, moreover, if they once tasted blood they would be strong enough to legislate in favour of tasting more. It is not to the discredit of the Anglo-Saxon race that it loves savage sports. The blood is naturally fierce, and has not been cowed by the tyranny endured by European races. There have been more free men under England's worst tyrants than under France's most liberal kings.

But, failing gladiators and wild beasts, the people must have horrors on the stage, in literature, in art, and, above all, in the daily press. Shakspere knew that, and Michelangelo, who is the Shakspere of brush and chisel, knew it also, as those two unrivalled men seem to have known everything else.

And so when Michelangelo painted the Last Judgment, and Shakspere wrote Othello (for instance), they both made use of horror in a way the Greeks would not have tolerated. Since we no longer see daily enacted before us scenes of murder, torture, and public execution, our curiosity makes us desire to see those scenes represented as accurately as possible. The Greeks, in their tragedies, did their slaughter behind the scenes, and occasionally the cries of the supposed victims were heard. But theatre-goers of to-day would feel cheated if the last act of Othello were left to their imagination. When Salvini thrusts the crooked knife into his throat, with that ghastly sound of death that one never forgets, the modern spectator would not understand what the death-rattle meant, did he not see the action that accompanies it.

"It is too realistic," said Mr. Barker in his high thin voice when it was over, and he was helping Margaret with her silken wrappings.

"It is not realistic," said she, "it is real. It may be an unhealthy excitement, but if we are to have it, it is the most perfect of its kind."

"It is very horrible," said Miss Skeat; and they drove away.

Margaret would not stay to see the great man after the curtain fell. The disillusion of such a meeting is too great to be pleasurable. Othello is dead, and the idea of meeting Othello in the flesh ten minutes later, smiling and triumphant, is a death-blow to that very reality which Margaret so much enjoyed. Besides, she wanted to be alone with her own thoughts, which were not entirely confined to the stage, that night. Writing to Claudius had brought him vividly into her life again, and she had caught herself more than once during the evening wondering how her fair Northern lover would have acted in Othello's place. Whether, when the furious general takes Iago by the throat in his wrath, the Swede's grip would have relaxed so easily on one who should dare to whisper a breath against the Countess Margaret. She so lived in the thought for a moment that her whole face glowed in the shade of the box, and her dark eyes shot out fire. Ah me! Margaret, will he come back to stand by your side and face the world for you? Who knows. Men are deceivers ever, says the old song.

Home through the long streets, lighted with the pale electric flame that gives so deathly a tinge to everything that comes within the circling of its discolour; home to her rooms with the pleasant little fire smouldering on the hearth, and flowers—Barker's flowers—scenting the room; home to the cares of Clémentine, to lean back with half-closed eyes, thinking, while the deft French fingers uncoil and smooth and coil again the jet-black tresses; home to the luxury of sleep unbroken by ill ease of body, though visited by the dreams of a far-away lover—dreams not always hopeful, but ever sweet; home to a hotel! Can a hostelry be dignified with that great name? Yes. Wherever we are at rest and at peace, wherever the thought of love or dream of lover visits us, wherever we look forward to meeting that lover again—that is home. For since the cold steel-tipped fingers of science have crushed space into a nut-shell, and since the deep-mouthed capacious present has swallowed time out of sight, there is no landmark left but love, no hour but the hour of loving, no home but where our lover is.

The little god who has survived ages of sword-play and centuries of peace-time, survives also science the leveller, and death the destroyer.

And in the night, when all are asleep, and the chimes are muffled with the thick darkness, and the wings of the dream-spirits caress the air, then the little Red Mouse comes out and meditates on all these things, and wonders how it is that men can think there is any originality in their lives or persons or doings. The body may have changed a little, men may have grown stronger and fairer, as some say, or weaker and more puny, as others would have it, but the soul of man is even as it was from the beginning.

CHAPTER XVIII

A month has passed since Margaret went to see Othello, and New York is beginning to wake to its winter round of amusements. There are dinners and dances and much leaving of little pasteboard chips with names and addresses.

Mr. Barker had made progress, in his own opinion, since the day when he so unfortunately roused Margaret's anger by his story. He bethought him one day that Claudius's influence had begun with the reading of books, and he determined to try something of the kind himself. He was no scholar as Claudius was, but he knew men who were. He cultivated the acquaintance of Mr. Horace Bellingham, and spent studious hours in ascertaining the names of quaint and curious volumes, which he spared no expense in procuring. He read books he had never heard of before, and then talked about them to Margaret; and when he hit upon anything she did not know he was swift to bring it to her, and sometimes she would even listen while he read a few pages aloud.

Margaret encouraged Barker in this new fancy unconsciously enough, for she thought it an admirable thing that a man whose whole life was devoted to business pursuits should develop a taste for letters; and when he had broken the ice on the sea of literature she talked more freely with him than she had ever done before. It was not Barker who interested her, but the books he brought, which were indeed rare and beautiful. He, on the other hand, quick to assimilate any knowledge that might be of use to him, and cautious of exposing the weaker points of his ignorance, succeeded in producing an impression of considerable learning, so that by and by he began to think he was taking Claudius's place in her daily pursuits, as he hoped to take it in her heart.

Meanwhile no one had heard from the Doctor, for his correspondence with Margaret was unknown to Barker, and the latter began to cherish a hope that, after all, there might be overwhelming difficulties in the way of proving Claudius's right to the estate. He had more than once talked over the matter with Mr. Screw, and they came to the conclusion that this silence was prognostic of the Doctor's defeat. Screw thought it probable that, had Claudius immediately obtained from Heidelberg the necessary papers, he would have sent a triumphant telegram over the cable, announcing his return at the shortest possible interval. But the time was long. It was now the first week in November and nearly two months had passed since he had sailed. Mr. Barker had avoided speaking of him to the Countess, at first because he did not wish to recall him to her memory, and later because he observed that she never mentioned the Doctor's name. Barker had inquired of Mr. Bellingham whether he knew anything of his friend's movements, to which Uncle Horace had replied, with a grim laugh, that he had quite enough to do with taking care of distinguished foreigners when they were in New York, without looking after them when they had gone elsewhere.

One evening before dinner Vladimir brought Margaret a telegram. She was seated by the fire as usual and Miss Skeat, who had been reading aloud until it grew too dark, was by her side warming her thin hands, which always looked cold, and bending forward towards the fire as she listened to Margaret's somewhat random remarks about the book in hand. Margaret had long since talked with Miss Skeat about her disturbed affairs, and concerning the prospect that was before her of being comparatively poor. And Miss Skeat, in her high-bred old-fashioned way, had laid her hand gently on the Countess's arm in token of sympathy.

"Dear Countess," she had said, "please remember that it will not make any difference to me, and that I will never leave you. Poverty is not a new thing to me, my dear." The tears came into Margaret's eyes as she pressed the elder lady's hand in silence. These passages of feeling were rare between them, but they understood each other, for all that. And now Margaret was speaking despondently of the future. A few days before she had made up her mind at last to write the necessary letters to Russia, and she had now despatched them on their errand. Not that she had any real hope of bettering things, but a visit from Nicholas had roused her to the fact that it was a duty she owed to him as well as to herself to endeavour to recover what was possible of her jointure.

At last she opened the telegram and uttered an exclamation of surprise.

"What in the world does it mean?" she cried, and gave it to Miss Skeat, who held it close to the firelight.

The message was from Lord Fitzdoggin, Her British Majesty's Ambassador at St. Petersburg, and was an informal statement to the effect that his Excellency was happy to communicate to the Countess Margaret the intelligence that, by the untiring efforts and great skill of a personal friend, the full payment of her jointure was now secured to her in perpetuity. It stated, moreover, that she would shortly receive official information of the fact through the usual channels.

Miss Skeat beamed with pleasure; for though she had been willing to make any sacrifice for Margaret, it would not have been an agreeable thing to be so very poor again.

"I never met Lord Fitzdoggin," said Margaret, "and I do not understand in the least. Why should he, of all people, inform me of this, if it is really true?"

"The Duke must have written to him," said Miss Skeat, still beaming, and reading the message over again.

Margaret paused a moment in thought, then lighting the gas herself, she wrote a note and despatched Vladimir in hot haste.

"I have asked Mr. Bellingham to dine," she said, in answer to Miss Skeat's inquiring look. "He will go to the party with me afterwards, if he is free."

It chanced that Mr. Bellingham was in his rooms when Margaret's note came, and he immediately threw over an engagement he had previously made, and sent word he would be at the Countess's disposal. Punctual to the minute he appeared. Margaret showed him the telegram.

"What does this mean, Mr. Bellingham?" she asked, smiling, but scrutinising his face closely.

"My dear Countess," cried the old gentleman, delighted beyond measure at the result of his policy, and corruscating with smiles and twinkles, "my dear Countess, allow me to congratulate you."

"But who is the 'personal friend' mentioned? Is it the Duke? He is in the far West at this moment."

"No," answered Mr. Bellingham, "it is not the Duke. I am inclined to think it is a manifestation of some great cosmic force, working silently for your welfare. The lovely spirits," continued the old gentleman, looking up from under his brows, and gesticulating as though he would call down the mystic presence he invoked—"the lovely spirits that guard you would be loth to allow anything so fair to suffer annoyance from the rude world. You are well taken care of, Countess, believe me."

Margaret smiled at Uncle Horace's way of getting out of the difficulty, for she suspected him of knowing more than he would acknowledge. But all she could extract from him was that he knew Lord Fitzdoggin slightly, and that he believed the telegram to be perfectly genuine. He had played his part in the matter, and rubbed his hands as though washing them of any further responsibility. Indeed he had nothing to tell, save that he had advised Claudius to get an introduction from the Duke. He well knew that the letters he had given Claudius had been the real means of his success; but as Margaret only asked about the telegram, he was perfectly safe in denying any knowledge of it. Not that such a consideration would have prevented his meeting her question with a little fib, just to keep the secret.

"Will you not go to this dance with me this evening?" asked Margaret after dinner, as they sat round the fireplace.

"What ball is that?" inquired Mr. Bellingham.

"I hardly know what it is. It is a party at the Van Sueindell's and there is 'dancing' on the card. Please go with me; I should have to go alone."

"I detest the pomp and circumstance of pleasure," said Uncle Horace, "the Persian appurtenances, as my favourite poet calls them; but I cannot resist so charming an invitation. It will give me the greatest pleasure. I will send word to put off another engagement."

"Do you really not mind at all?"

"Not a bit of it. Only three or four old fogies at the club. Est mihi nonum superantis annum plenus Albani cadus," continued Mr. Bellingham, who never quoted Horace once without quoting him again in the next five minutes. "I had sent a couple of bottles of my grandfather's madeira to the club, 1796, but those old boys will enjoy it without me. They would talk me to death if I went."

"It is too bad," said Margaret, "you must go to the club. I would not let you break an engagement on my account."

"No, no. Permit me to do a good deed without having to bear the infernal consequences in this life, at all events. The chatter of those people is like the diabolical screaming of the peacock on the terrace of the Emir's chief wife, made memorable by Thackeray the prophet." He paused a moment, and stroked his snowy pointed beard. "Forgive my strong language," he added; "really, they are grand adjectives those, 'diabolical' and 'infernal.' They call up the whole of Dante to my mind." Margaret laughed.

"Are you fond of Dante?" asked she.

"Very. I sometimes buy a cheap copy and substitute the names of my pet enemies all through the Inferno wherever they will suit the foot. In that way I get all the satisfaction the author got by putting his friends in hell, without the labour of writing, or the ability to compose, the poem." The Countess laughed again.

"Do you ever do the same thing with the Paradiso?"

"No," answered Uncle Horace, with a smile. "Purgatory belonged to an age when people were capable of being made better by suffering, and as for paradise, my heaven admits none but the fair sex. They are all beautiful, and many of them are young."

"Will you admit me, Mr. Bellingham?"

"St. Margaret has forestalled me," said he gallantly, "for she has a paradise of her own, it seems, to which she has admitted me."

And so they passed the evening pleasantly until the hour warned them that it was time to go to the great Van Sueindell house. That mansion, like all private houses in America, and the majority of modern dwellings in other parts of the world, is built in that depraved style of architecture which makes this age pre-eminent in the ugliness of brick and stone. There is no possibility of criticism for such monstrosity, as there also seems to be no immediate prospect of reform. Time, the iron-fisted Nihilist, will knock them all down some day and bid mankind begin anew. Meanwhile let us ignore what we cannot improve. Night, the all-merciful, sometimes hides these excrescences from our sight, and sometimes the moon, Nature's bravest liar, paints and moulds them into a fugitive harmony. But in the broad day let us fix our eyes modestly on the pavement beneath us, or turn them boldly to the sky, for if we look to the right or the left we must see that which sickens the sense of sight.

On the present occasion, however, nothing was to be seen of the house, for the long striped canvas tent, stretching from the door to the carriage, and lined with plants and servants, hid everything else from view. There is probably no city in the world where the business of "entertaining" is so thoroughly done as in New York. There are many places where it is more agreeable to be "entertained;" many where it is done on a larger scale, for there is nothing in America so imposing as the receptions at Embassies and other great houses in England and abroad. To bring the matter into business form, since it is a matter of business, let us say that nowhere do guests cost so much by the cubic foot as in New York. Abroad, owing to the peculiar conditions of court-life, many people are obliged to open their houses at stated intervals. In America no one is under this necessity. If people begin to "entertain" they do it because they have money, or because they have something to gain by it, and they do it with an absolute regardlessness of cost which is enough to startle the sober foreigner.

It may be in bad taste, but if we are to define what is good taste in these days, and abide by it, we shall be terribly restricted. As an exhibition of power, this enormous expenditure is imposing in the extreme; though the imposing element, being strictly confined to the display of wealth, can never produce the impressions of durability, grandeur, and military pomp so dear to every European. Hence the Englishman turns up his nose at the gilded shows of American society, and the American sniffs when he finds that the door-scraper of some great London house is only silverplated instead of being solid, and that the carpets are at least two years old. They regard things from opposite points of view, and need never expect to agree.

Margaret, however, was not so new to American life, seeing she was American born, as to bestow a thought or a glance on the appointments of Mr. and Mrs. Van Sueindell's establishment; and as for Mr. Bellingham, he had never cared much for what he called the pomp and circumstance of pleasure, for he carried pleasure with him in his brilliant conversation and his ready tact. All places were more or less alike to Mr. Bellingham. At the present moment, however, he was thinking principally of his fair charge, and was wondering inwardly what time he would get home, for he rose early and was fond of a nap in the late evening. He therefore gave Margaret his arm, and kept a lookout for some amusing man to introduce to her. He had really enjoyed his dinner and the pleasant chat afterwards, but the prospect of piloting this magnificent beauty about till morning, or till she should take it into her head to go home, was exhausting. Besides, he went little into society of this kind, and was not over-familiar with the faces he saw.

He need not have been disturbed, however, for they had not been many minutes in the rooms before a score of men had applied for the "pleasure of a turn." But still she held Mr. Bellingham's arm, obdurately refusing to dance. As Barker came up a moment later, willing, perhaps, to show his triumph to the rejected suitors, Margaret thanked Mr. Bellingham, and offered to take him home if he would stay until one o'clock; then she glided away, not to dance but to sit in a quieter room, near the door of which couples would hover for a quarter of an hour at a time waiting to seize the next pair of vacant seats. Mr. Bellingham moved away, amused by the music and the crowd and the fair young faces, until he found a seat in a corner, shaded from the flare of light by an open door close by, and there, in five minutes, he was fast asleep in the midst of the gaiety and noise and heat— unnoticed, a gray old man amid so much youth.

But Barker knew the house better than the most of the guests, and passing through the little room for which every one seemed fighting, he drew aside a heavy curtain and showed a small boudoir beyond, lighted with a solitary branch of candles, and occupied by a solitary couple. Barker had hoped to find this sanctum empty, and as he pushed two chairs together he eyed the other pair savagely.

"What a charming little room," said Margaret, sinking into the soft chair and glancing at the walls and ceiling, which were elaborately adorned in the Japanese fashion. The chairs also were framed of bamboo, and the table was of an unusual shape. It was the "Japanese parlour[3]," as Mrs. Van Sueindell would have called it. Every great house in New York has a Japanese or a Chinese room. The entire contents of the apartment having been brought direct from Yokohama, the effect was harmonious, and Margaret's artistic sense was pleased.

[Footnote 3: Parlour or parlor, American for "sitting-room."]

"Is it not?" said Barker, glad to have brought her to a place she liked. "I thought you would like it, and I hoped," lowering his voice, "that we should find it empty. Only people who come here a great deal know about it."

"Then you come here often?" asked Margaret, to say something. She was glad to be out of the din, for though she had anticipated some pleasure from the party, she discovered too late that she had made a mistake, and would rather be at home. She had so much to think of, since receiving that telegram; and so, forgetting Barker and everything else, she followed her own train of thought. Barker talked on, and Margaret seemed to be listening—but it was not the music, muffled through the heavy curtains, nor the small voice of Mr. Barker that she heard. It was the washing of the sea and the creaking of cordage that were in her ears—the rush of the ship that was to bring him back— that was perhaps bringing him back already. When would he come? How soon? If it could only be to- morrow, she would so like to—what in the world is Mr. Barker saying so earnestly? Really, she ought to listen. It was very rude. "Conscious of my many defects of character—" Oh yes, he was always talking about his defects; what next? "—conscious of my many defects of character," Mr. Barker was saying, in an even, determined voice, "and feeling deeply how far behind you I am in those cultivated pursuits you most enjoy, I would nevertheless scorn to enlarge upon my advantages, the more so as I believe you are acquainted with my circumstances."

Good gracious! thought Margaret, suddenly recovering the acutest use of her hearing, what is the man going to say? And she looked fixedly at him with an expression of some astonishment.

"Considering, as I was saying," he continued steadily, "those advantages upon which I will not enlarge, may I ask you to listen to what I am going to say?"

Margaret, having lost the first part of Barker's speech completely, in her fit of abstraction, had some vague idea that he was asking her advice about marrying some other woman.

"Certainly," she said indifferently; "pray go on." At the moment of attack, however, Barker's heart failed him for an instant. He thought he would make one more attempt to ascertain what position Claudius held towards Margaret.

"Of course," he said, smiling and looking down, "we all knew about Dr. Claudius on board the Streak."

"What did you know about him?" asked Margaret calmly, but her face flushed for an instant. That might have happened even if she had not cared for Claudius; she was so proud that the idea of being thought to care might well bring the colour to her cheek. Barker hardly noticed the blush, for he was getting into very deep water, and was on the point of losing his head.

"That he proposed to you, and you refused him," he said, still smiling.

"Take care, sir," she said quickly, "when Dr. Claudius comes back he—" Barker interrupted her with a laugh.

"Claudius coming back?" he answered, "ha! ha! good indeed!"

He looked at Margaret. She was very quiet, and she was naturally so dark that, in the shadow of the fan she held carelessly against the light, he could not see how pale she turned. She was intensely angry, and her anger took the form of a preternatural calm of manner, by no means indicative of indifferent reflection. She was simply unable to speak for the moment. Barker, however, whose reason was in abeyance for the moment, merely saw that she did not answer; and, taking her silence for consent to his slighting mention of Claudius, he at once proceeded with his main proposition. At this juncture the other couple slowly left the room, having arranged their own affairs to their satisfaction.

"That being the case," he said, "and now that I am assured that I have no rivals to dread, will you permit me to offer you my heart and my hand? Countess Margaret, will you marry me, and make me the happiest of men? Oh, do not be silent, do not look as if you did not hear! I have loved you since I first saw you—will you, will you marry me?" Here Mr. Barker, who was really as much in love as his nature allowed him to be, moved to the very edge of his chair and tried to take her hand.

"Margaret!" he said, as he touched her fingers.

At the touch she recovered her self-possession, too long lost for such a case. She had tried to control her anger, had tried to remember whether by any word she could have encouraged him to so much boldness. Now she rose to all her haughty height, and though she tried hard to control herself, there was scorn in her voice.

"Mr. Barker," she said, dropping her hands before her and standing straight as a statue, "you have made a mistake, and if through any carelessness I have led you into this error I am sorry for it. I cannot listen to you, I cannot marry you. As for Dr. Claudius, I will not permit you to use any slighting words about him. I hold in my possession documents that could prove his identity as well as any he can obtain in Germany. But I need not produce them, for I am sure it will be enough for you to know that I am engaged to be married to him—I am engaged to be married to Dr. Claudius," she repeated very distinctly in her deep musical tones; and before Barker could recover himself, she had passed from the room into the lights and the sound of music beyond.

What do you think, reader? Was it not a brave and noble action of hers to vindicate Claudius by taking upon herself the whole responsibility of his love rather than by going home and sending Mr. Barker documentary evidence of the Doctor's personality? Claudius had never asked her to marry him, the very word had never been mentioned. But he had told her he loved her and she had trusted him.

Start not at the infinity of social crime that such a doubt defines. It is there. It is one thing for a woman to love a man at arm's length conditionally; it is another for her to take him to her heart and trust him. Does every millionaire who makes love to a penniless widow mean to marry her? for Margaret was poor on that Tuesday in Newport. Or reverse the case; if Claudius were an adventurer, as Barker hinted, what were the consequences she assumed in declaring herself engaged to marry him?

In spite of her excitement, Margaret was far too much a woman of the world to create a sensation by walking through the rooms alone. In a moment or two she saw a man she knew, and calling him to her by a look, took his arm. She chatted pleasantly to this young fellow, as proud as need be of being selected to conduct the beauty whither she would, and after some searching she discovered Mr. Bellingham, still asleep behind the swinging door.

"Thanks," she said to her escort. "I have promised to take Mr. Bellingham home." And she dropped the young man's arm with a nod and a smile.

"But he is asleep," objected the gallant.

"I will wake him," she answered. And laying her hand on Mr. Bellingham's, she leaned down and spoke his name. Instantly he awoke, as fresh as from a night's rest, for he had the Napoleonic faculty for catching naps.

"Winter awaking to greet the spring," he said without the slightest hesitation, as though he had prepared the little speech in his sleep. "Forgive me," he said, "it is a habit of mine learned long ago." He presented his arm and asked her what was her pleasure.

"I am going home," she said, "and if you like I will drop you at your door."

Mr. Bellingham glanced at a great enamelled clock, half-hidden among flowers and fans, as they passed, and he noticed that they had not been in the house much more than three quarters of an hour. But he wisely said nothing, and waited patiently while Margaret was wrapped in her cloaks, and till the butler had told the footman, and the footman had told the other footman, and the other footman had told the page, and the page had told the policeman to call the Countess Margaret's carriage. After which the carriage appeared, and they drove away.

Uncle Horace chatted pleasantly about the party, admitting that he had dreamed more than he had seen of it. But Margaret said little, for the reaction was coming after the excitement she had passed through. Only when they reached Mr. Bellingham's rooms, and he was about to leave her, she held his hand a moment and looked earnestly in his face.

"Mr. Bellingham," she said suddenly, "I trust you will always be my friend—will you not?" The old gentleman paused in his descent from the carriage, and took the hand she offered.

"Indeed I will, my dear child," he said very seriously. Then he bent his knee to the sill of the door and kissed her fingers, and was gone. No one ever resented Mr. Bellingham's familiarity, for it was rare and honest of its kind. Besides, he was old enough to be her grandfather, in spite of his pretty speeches and his graceful actions.

Margaret passed a sleepless night. Her anger with Mr. Barker had not been so much the mere result of the words he had spoken, though she would have resented his sneer about Claudius sharply enough under any circumstances. It was rather that to her keen intelligence, rendered still more acute by her love for the Doctor, the whole scene constituted a revelation. By that wonderful instinct which guides women in the most critical moments of their lives, she saw at last the meaning of Barker's doings, of his silence concerning Claudius, and of his coolness with the latter before he had got rid of him. She saw Barker at the bottom of the plot to send Claudius to Europe; she saw him in all the efforts made by the Duke and Barker to keep Claudius and herself apart on board the yacht; she saw his hand in it all, and she understood for the first time that this man, whom she had of late permitted to be so much with her, was her worst enemy, while aspiring to be her lover. The whole extent of his faithlessness to Claudius came before her, as she remembered that it had doubtless been to serve the Doctor that Barker had obtained an introduction to her at Baden; that he had done everything to throw them together, devoting himself to Miss Skeat, in a manner that drove that ancient virgin to the pinnacle of bliss and despair, while leaving Claudius free field to make love to herself. And then he had suddenly turned and made up his mind that he should have her for his own wife. And her anger rose higher and hotter as she thought of it.

Then she went over the scene of the evening at Mrs. Van Sueindell's house—how she had not listened and not understood, until she was so suddenly roused to the consciousness of what he was saying—how she had faced him, and, in the inspiration of the moment, had boldly told him that she loved his rival. In that thought she found satisfaction, as well she might, for her love had been put to the test, and had not failed her.

"I am glad I said it," she murmured to herself, and fell asleep. Poor Claudius, far away over the sea, what a leap his heart would have given could he have known what she had done, and that she was glad of it.

And Mr. Barker? He felt a little crushed when she left him there alone in the Japanese boudoir, for he knew at once that he might as well throw up the game. There was not the least chance for him any longer. He might indeed suspect that the documents Margaret spoke of were a myth, and that her declaration of the engagement was in reality the only weapon she could use in Claudius's defence. But that did not change matters. No woman would "give herself away," as he expressed it, so recklessly, unless she were perfectly certain. Therefore Mr. Barker went into the supper-room, and took a little champagne to steady his nerves; after which he did his best to amuse himself, talking with unusual vivacity to any young lady of his acquaintance whom he could allure from her partner for a few minutes. For he had kept himself free of engagements that evening on Margaret's account, and now regretted it bitterly. But Mr. Barker was a great match, as has been said before, and he seldom had any difficulty in amusing himself when he felt so inclined. He had not witnessed Margaret's departure, for, not wishing to be seen coming out of the boudoir alone, a sure sign of defeat, and being perfectly familiar with the house, he had found his way by another door, and through circuitous passages to the pantry, and thence to the supper-room; so that by the time he had refreshed himself Margaret and Mr. Bellingham had gone.

Do people of Mr. Barker's stamp feel? Probably not. It requires a strong organisation, either animal or intellectual, to suffer much from any shock to the affections. Englishmen, on those occasions when their passion gets the better of their caution, somewhat a rare occurrence nowadays, are capable of loving very strongly, and of suffering severely if thwarted, for they are among the most powerful races in the animal kingdom. Their whole history shows this, moulded as it has generally been by exceptional men, for the most part Irish and Scotch, in whom the highest animal and intellectual characteristics were united. Germans, in whom the intellectual faculties, and especially the imagination, predominate, are for the most part very love-sick for at least half their lives. But Americans seem to be differently organised; meaning, of course, the small class, who would like to be designated as the "aristocracy" of the country. The faculties are all awake, acute, and ready for use; but there is a lack of depth, which will rouse the perpetual wonder of future generations. While the mass of the people exhibits the strong characteristics of the Saxon, the Celtic, and the South German races, physical endurance and occasionally intellectual pre-eminence,—for, saving some peculiarities of speech, made defects merely by comparison, there are no such natural orators and statesmen in the world as are to be found in Congress; at the same time, the would-be aristocracy of the country is remarkable for nothing so much as for the very unaristocratic faculty of getting money—rarely mingling in public questions, still more rarely producing anything of merit, literary or artistic. Therefore, being so constituted that the almighty dollar crowns the edifice of their ambitions as with a coronet of milled silver, they are singularly inapt to suffer from such ills as prick the soul, which taketh no thought for the morrow, what it shall eat or what it shall drink.

Truly, a happy people, these American aristocrats.

CHAPTER XIX

When Margaret awoke the next morning her first impulse was to go away for a time. She was disgusted with New York, and desired nothing so much as the sensation of being free from Mr. Barker. A moment, however, sufficed to banish any such thoughts. In the first place, if she were away from the metropolis it would take just so many hours longer for the Doctor's letters to reach her. There had been a lacuna in the correspondence of late, and it seemed to her that the letters she had received were always dated some days before the time stamped on the Heidelberg postmark. He spoke always of leaving very soon; but though he said many loving and tender things, he was silent as to his own doings. She supposed he was occupied with the important matter he described as the "other reason," and so in the two or three short notes she wrote him she abstained from questioning any more.

Furthermore, she reflected that however much she might wish to be away, it was most emphatically not the thing to do. On the whole, she would stay where she was.

She was roused from her reverie by Clémentine, who entered in a halo of smiles, as though she were the bearer of good news. In the first place she had a telegram, which proved to be from Claudius, dated Berlin, and simply announcing the fact that he would sail at once. Margaret could hardly conceal her great satisfaction, and the colour came so quickly to her face as she read the flimsy bit of paper from the cable office that Clémentine made the most desperate efforts to get possession of it, or at least to see the signature. But Margaret kept it under her pillow for half an hour, and then burned it carefully by the taper, to Clémentine's inexpressible chagrin.

Meanwhile, however, there were other news in the wind, and when the artful Frenchwoman had succeeded in opening the window just so that a ray of light should fall on madam's face, she fired her second shot.

"Monsieur le Duc is of return, Madame," she said, suddenly turning towards her mistress.

"The Duke?" repeated Margaret innocently. "When did he come?"

"Ah, Madame," said the maid, disappointed at having produced so little effect, "it is precisely what I do not know. I come from meeting Monsieur Veelees upon the carrefour. He has prayed me to present the compliments of Monsieur le Duc and to ask at what hour Madame la Comtesse would be in disposition to see him."

"Ah, very well," said the Countess. "I will get up, Clémentine."

"Si tôt, Madame? it is yet very morning," argued the girl with a little show of polite surprise.

"That is indifferent. Go, Clémentine, and tell Monsieur le Duc I will see him at once."

"At once, Madame? I run," said Clémentine, going slowly to the door.

"Enfin—when I am dressed. Don't you understand?" said Margaret impatiently.

"Parfaitement, Madame. I will speak with Monsieur Veelees." And she vanished.

It was a bright November morning, and though there had been a slight frost daring the night, it was fast vanishing before the sun. Margaret went to the window and breathed the cool air. An indescribable longing seized her to be out, among trees and plants and fresh growing things—to blow away the dark dreams of the night, the visions of Barker and Screw, and of the ballroom, and of that detestable Japanese boudoir. She hurried her toilet in a manner that completely aroused Clémentine's vigilant suspicion.

"Hélas," Clémentine used to say to Willis the Duke's servant, "Je ne lui ai jamais connu d'amant. I had pourtant much hoped of Monsieur Clodiuse." But she never ventured such remarks when old Vladimir was at hand.

When the Countess was dressed she went out into her little drawing-room, and found the Duke looking more sunburnt and healthy than ever, though a trifle thinner. The rough active Western life always agreed with him. He came forward with a bright smile to meet her.

"Upon my word, how well you look!" he exclaimed as he shook hands; and indeed she was beautiful to see, for if the sleepless night had made her pale, the good news of Claudius's coming had brought the fire to her eyes.

"Do I?" said she. "I am glad; and you look well too. Your run on the prairies has done you good. Come," said she, leading him to the window, "it is a beautiful day. Let us go out."

"By all means: but first I have some good news for you. Fitzdoggin has telegraphed me that Claudius—I mean," he said, interrupting himself and blushing awkwardly, "I mean that it is all right, you know. They have arranged all your affairs beautifully." Margaret looked at him curiously a moment while he spoke. Then she recognised that the Duke must have had a hand in the matter, and spoke very gratefully to him, not mentioning that she had received news direct, for she did not wish to spoil his pleasure in being the first to tell her. To tell the truth, the impulsive Englishman was rather in doubt whether he had not betrayed the Doctor's secret, and seemed very little inclined to say anything more about it.

"I wish," she said at last, "that we could ride this morning. I have not been on a horse for ever so long, and I want the air."

"By Jove," cried the Duke, overjoyed at the prospect of breaking an interview which seemed likely to lead him too far, "I should think so. I will send and get some horses directly. The very thing, by Jove!" And he went to the door.

"How are you going to get anything fit to ride in New York, at such short notice?" asked Margaret, laughing at his impetuosity.

"There's a fellow here lends me anything in his stable when I am in New York," he answered, half out of the room. "I'll go myself," he called back from the landing, and shut the door behind him. "Upon my word," he said to himself as he lighted a cigarette in the cab, and drove away to his friend's stable, "she is the most beautiful thing I ever saw. I almost let the cat out of the bag, just to please her. I don't wonder Claudius is crazy about her. I will talk about the West when we are riding, and avoid the subject." With which sage resolution his Grace seemed well satisfied. When he returned, he found Margaret clad in a marvellous habit, that reminded him of home.

"The horses will be at the Park by the time we have driven there," he said. "We will drive up." He made no toilet himself, for being English and to the saddle born, he cared not a jot how he looked on horseback. In half an hour they were mounted, and walking their horses down the broad bend of the road where it enters the Central Park. Margaret asked about Lady Victoria, and the Duke, to make sure of not getting off the track, immediately began talking about the journey they had just made. But Margaret was not listening.

"Do you know?" she said, "it is very pleasant to feel I am not poor any longer. I suppose it is a very low sentiment."

"Of course," said the Duke. "Beastly thing to have no money."

"Do you know—" she began again, but stopped.

"Well," said the Duke, following her first train of thought, "it always seems to me that I have no money myself. I don't suppose I am exactly poor, though."

"No," laughed Margaret, "I was not thinking of that."

"What is it?" he asked.

"I think I will confide in you a little, for you have always been such a good friend to me. What do you know of Mr. Barker?"

"I am sure I don't know," said the Englishman, taken off his guard by the question. "I have known him some time—in this sort of way," he added vaguely.

"I believe," said the Countess bluntly, "that it was Mr. Barker who made all this trouble for Dr. Claudius."

"I believe you are right," answered the Duke suddenly turning in his saddle and facing her. "I wonder how he could be such a brute?"

Margaret was silent. She was astonished at the readiness with which her companion assented to her proposition. He must have known it all along, she thought.

"What makes you think so?" he asked presently.

"What are your reasons for believing it?" she asked, with a smile.

"Really," he began; then shortly, "I believe I don't like his eyes."

"Last night," said Margaret, "I was talking with him at a party. I chanced to speak of the Doctor's coming back, and Mr. Barker laughed and sneered, and said it was ridiculous."

The Duke moved angrily in his saddle, making the horse he rode shake his head and plunge a little.

"He is a brute," he said at last.

"Your horse?" inquired Margaret sweetly.

"No—Barker. And pray what did you answer him? I hope you gave him a lesson for his impertinence."

"I told him," said she, "that I had documents in my possession that would establish his right as well as any he could get in Germany."

"Barker must have been rather taken aback," said the other in high glee. "I am glad you said that."

"So am I. I do not imagine I shall see much of Mr. Barker in future," she added demurely.

"Um! As bad as that?" The Duke was beginning to catch the drift of what Margaret was saying. She had no intention of telling him any more, however. Bitterly as she felt towards Barker, she would not allow herself the triumph of telling her friend she had refused to marry him.

"I know it is a very womanly fancy," she said, "but I want to ride fast, please. I want exercise."

"All right," said the Duke, and they put their horses into a canter. The Countess felt safe now that her friends had returned and that Claudius had telegraphed he was about to sail. She felt as though her troubles were over, and as if the world were again at her feet. And as they galloped along the roads, soft in the warm sun to the horses' feet, breathing in great draughts of good clean air, the past two months seemed to dwindle away to a mere speck in the far distance of her life, instead of being entangled with all the yesterdays of the dark season just over.

And Claudius—the man who made all this change in her life, who had opened a new future for her—how had he passed these months, she wondered? To tell the truth, Claudius had been so desperately busy that the time had not seemed so long. If he had been labouring in any other cause than hers it would have been insupportable. But the constant feeling that all he did was for her, and to her advantage, and that at the same time she was ignorant of it all, gave him strength and courage. He had been obliged to think much, to travel far, and to act promptly; and for his own satisfaction he had kept up the illusion that he was in Heidelberg by a cunning device. He wrote constantly, and enclosed the letters to the old notary at the University, who, with Teutonic regularity, stamped and posted them. And so it was that the date of the letter, written in St. Petersburg, was always two or three days older than that of the postmark. For Claudius would not put a false date at the head of what he wrote, any more than, if Margaret had written to ask him whether he were really in Heidelberg or not, he would have deceived her in his answer. Probably he would not have answered the question at all. The letters were merely posted in Heidelberg; and Margaret had trusted him enough not to notice or be willing to comment upon the discrepancy.

And, by dint of activity and the assistance of the persons to whom he had letters, he had succeeded in bringing the Countess's business to a satisfactory conclusion. He found it just as Mr. Bellingham had told him. In an autocratic country, if you are to have justice at all, you will have it quickly. Moreover, it was evident to the authorities that a man coming all the way from America, and presenting such credentials as Claudius brought, deserved to be attended to at once—the more so when his whole appearance and manner were such as to create a small furore, in the Embassy circles. Claudius went everywhere, saw every one, and used every particle of influence he could obtain to further the object of his visit. And so it was that, at the end of a month or so, a special ukase provided for the payment in perpetuity to herself and her heirs for ever of the jointure-money first decreed to the Countess Margaret for life only from the estates of her late husband, Count Alexis of the Guards. This was even more than Claudius had hoped for—certainly more than Margaret had dreamt of. As for Nicholas, Claudius cared nothing what became of him, for he probably thought him a foolish Nihilist, and he knew enough of the Countess's character to be sure she would never let her brother suffer want, whatever his faults.

So when he had concluded the affair he hastened to Berlin, telegraphing from thence the news of his immediate return. In less than a fortnight, at all events, he ought to be in New York. The thought gave him infinite relief; for, since he had finished his business in Petersburg, the reaction which in strong natures is very sure to follow a great effort, for the very reason that strong natures tax their powers to the utmost, recklessly, began to make itself felt. It seemed to him, as he looked back, that he had heard so little from her. Not that he complained; for he was fully sensible of her goodness in writing at all, and he treasured her letters as things sacred, even to the envelopes, and whatsoever had touched her hand. But he felt keenly that he was in total ignorance of her doings; and one or two references to Barker troubled him. He too had his suspicions that the scheming American had been concerned in the sudden fit of caution developed by Messrs. Screw and Scratch. He too had suspected that his quondam friend had been insincere, and that everything was not as it should be. But he was neither so wise as Margaret, who would have told him not to soil his hands with pitch, nor so supremely indifferent as the Duke, who would have said that since he had got the money it didn't matter in the least if Barker were a brute or not. On the contrary, Claudius promised himself to sift the evidence; and if he discovered that Barker was guilty of any double-dealing, he would simply break his neck. And as Claudius thought of it, his teeth set, and he looked capable of breaking any number of necks, then and there.

But for all his wrath and his suspicions, the real cause of Barker's strange behaviour never presented itself to his mind. It never struck him that Barker could aspire to Margaret's hand; and he merely concluded that the young man had laid a plot for getting his money. If any one had related to Claudius the scene which took place at Mrs. Van Sueindell's the very night when he sent his telegram, he would have laughed the story to scorn in perfect good faith, for he could not have believed it possible. Nor, believing it, would he have cared. And so he rushed across Europe, and never paused till he had locked himself into his stateroom on board the steamer, and had begun a long letter to Margaret. He knew that he would see her as soon as a letter could reach her, but that made no difference. He felt impelled to write, and he wrote—a letter so tender and loving and rejoicing that were it to appear in these pages no lover would ever dare write to his lady again, lest she chide him for being less eloquent than Claudius, Phil.D. of Heidelberg. And he wrote on and on for many days, spending most of his time in that way.

Meanwhile, the Duke and Margaret cantered in the Park, and talked of all kinds of things; or rather, the Duke talked, and Margaret thought of Claudius. Before they returned, however, she had managed to let the Duke know that the Doctor was on his way back; whereat the Englishman rejoiced loudly. Perhaps he would have given a great deal to know whether they were engaged, to be married; but still Margaret gave no sign. It was far from her thoughts; and the fact had only presented itself in that form to her on the spur of the moment, the preceding evening, as likely to prove a crushing blow at once to Mr. Barker's plotting and Mr. Barker's matrimonial views. But while the Duke talked, she was thinking. And as the situation slowly unfolded its well-known pictures to her mind, she suddenly saw it all in a different light.

"I must be mad," she thought. "Barker will tell every one; and the Duke ought not to know it except from me!"

"Speaking of Dr. Claudius—" she began; the Duke was at that moment talking earnestly about the Pueblo Indians, but that was of no importance. "Speaking of the Doctor, you ought to know—I would rather that no one else told you—we are going to be married."

The Duke was so much surprised—not so much at the information as at her manner of imparting it—that he pulled up short. Seeing him stop, she stopped also.

"Are you very much astonished?" she asked, pushing the gray veil up to her hat, and looking at him smilingly out of her deep, dark eyes. The Duke spoke no word, but leapt from his horse, which he left standing in the middle of the path, surprised into docility by the sudden desertion. There were a few wild-flowers growing by the road, which here led through a wooded glade of the Park; they were the flowers called Michaelmas daisies, which bloom until November in America. He picked a great handful of them, and came running back.

"Let me be the first to congratulate you, my dear friend," he said, standing bareheaded at her stirrup, and offering the flowers with a half-bashful smile that sat strangely on a man of his years. It was a quick, impulsive action, such as no one could have expected from him who did not know him intimately well—and few could boast that they did. Margaret was touched by his look and manner.

"Thanks," she said, bending over her saddle-bow, and taking the daisies as he held them up to her. "Yes, you are the first—to congratulate me," which was true. He still stood looking at her, and his hand would hardly let go the flowers where his fingers touched hers. His face grew pale, then ashy-white and he steadied himself against her horse's neck.

"What is the matter? are you ill? have you hurt yourself?" asked Margaret in real alarm, for he looked as though he were going to faint, and it was a full minute since he had come back to her from the roadside. Then he made a great effort and collected himself, and the next instant he had dashed after his horse, which was wandering away towards the trees.

"I did feel queer for a minute," he said when he was once more in the saddle and by her side. "I dare say it is the heat. It's a very hot day, now I think of it. Would you allow me a cigarette? I hate to smoke in public, you know, but it will make me all right again." Margaret assented, of course, to the request; it was morning, in the recesses of the Park, and nobody would see. But she looked strangely at him for a minute, wondering what could have produced his sudden dizziness.

They rode more slowly towards the entrance of the Park, and the Countess's thoughts did not wander again. She talked to her companion on every subject he broached, showing interest in all he said, and asking questions that she knew would please him. But the latter part of the ride seemed long, and the drive home interminable, for Margaret was in haste to be alone. She was not sure that the Duke's manner had changed since he had turned so strangely pale, but she fancied he spoke as if making an effort. However, they reached the hotel at last, and separated.

"Thanks, so much," she said; "it has been such a delightful morning."

"It has indeed," said he, "and—let me congratulate you once more. Claudius is a gentleman in every way, and—I suppose he is as worthy of you as any one could be," he added quickly, in a discontented voice, and turned away, hat in hand. She stood looking after him a moment.

"I wonder," she said to herself as she entered her room and closed the door. "Poor man! it is not possible, though. I must be dreaming. Ah me! I am always dreaming now, it seems to me;" and she sank down in a chair to wait for Clémentine.

And so it is that some women go through life making far more victims than they know of. There are some honest men who will not speak, unless they have a right to, and who are noble enough to help those who have a right. The Duke had known Margaret ever since she had married Alexis, as has been said. Whether he had loved her or not is a question not so easily answered. Certain it is that when she told him she was going to be married to Claudius he turned very pale, and did not recover the entire use of his mind for a whole day.

Nevertheless, during the succeeding fortnight he devoted himself sedulously to Margaret's amusement, and many were the things that he and she and Lady Victoria, and the incomparable Miss Skeat, who always enjoyed everything, planned and carried out together. Margaret did not shun society or shut herself up, and more than once she saw Barker in the street and in the crowds at parties. The houses in America are so small that parties are always crowded. But he had the good sense to avoid her, and she was not troubled by any communication from him. Clémentine, indeed, wondered that so few flowers came, for a day or two, and old Vladimir pondered on the probable fate of Mr. Barker, who, he supposed, had been sent to Canada in chains for some political offence, seeing that he called no longer. But these faithful servitors could not ask questions, and sources of information they had none. Barker, however, as Margaret had anticipated, had been active in spreading the news of her engagement; for, before very long, callers were plenty, and flowers too, and many were the congratulations that poured in. Then she saw the wisdom of having informed the Duke of her position before any officious acquaintance could do it for her. The Duke, indeed, saw very few people in New York, for he hated to be "entertained," but he knew a great many men slightly, and some one of them would probably have obliged him with the information.

One morning as he and the Countess were about to drive up to the Park for their daily ride, which had become an institution, the servant presented a card, saying the gentleman was anxious to see her ladyship at once, if possible. The card was that of Mr. Screw, of Screw and Scratch.

"Very well," said the Countess, who was pulling on her gloves, and holding her riding-stick under one arm as she did so. "Ask him to come up." The Duke moved to withdraw.

"Don't go, please," said Margaret; and so he remained. A moment later Mr. Screw's yellow head and small eyes appeared at the door.

"The Countess Margaret?" he inquired deferentially.

"Yes. Mr. Screw, I believe?"

"The same, Madam. A—pardon me, but—I desired to speak with you alone," stammered the lawyer, seeing that the Duke did not move.

"I have asked the—this gentleman, who is my friend, to remain," said Margaret calmly. "You may speak freely. What is your business with me, sir?" She motioned him to a chair, and he sat down opposite her, hat in hand. He would have liked to hook his legs into each other and put his hands into his pockets, but he was too well bred for that. At last he took courage.

"Frankly, Madam, I have come to discharge a moral duty, and I will speak plainly. I am informed on credible authority that you are engaged to marry a gentleman, calling himself Dr. Claudius—a—a tall man—fair beard?"

"Your information is correct, Mr. Screw," said Margaret haughtily, "I am engaged to be married to Dr. Claudius."

"As one of the executors of the late Mr. Gustavus Lindstrand, deceased," proceeded Mr. Screw slowly, "I feel it my duty, as an honest man, to inform you that there are serious doubts as to whether the gentleman who calls himself Dr. Claudius is Dr. Claudius at all. The person in question disappeared two months ago, and has not been heard of since, as far as I can make out. I have no interest in the matter as far as it concerns yourself, as you may well imagine, but I have thought it right to warn you that the gentleman whom you have honoured with a promise of marriage has not established his claim to be the person he represents himself."

Margaret, who, after the first words, had foreseen what Mr. Screw had come to say, and who believed that very respectable and honest man to be concerned in the plot against Claudius, was naturally angry, but she had the good sense to do the right thing.

"Mr. Screw," she said in her commanding voice, icily, "I am deeply indebted to you for your interference. Nevertheless, I am persuaded that the gentleman to whom I am engaged is very really and truly the person he represents himself to be. A fact of which my friend here will probably be able to persuade you without difficulty." And she forthwith left the room. The Duke turned upon the lawyer.

"Look here, Mr. Screw," he said sharply, "I am the—well, never mind my name, you can find out from the people downstairs. I am an English gentleman, and I know who Dr. Claudius is. I knew his father; I brought him to this country in my yacht. I am prepared to go into court this minute and swear to the identity of the gentleman you are slandering. Slandering, sir! Do you hear me?" The ducal anger was hot. "And except for the fact that Dr. Claudius will be here to speak for himself the day after to-morrow morning, I would take you into court now by main force and make you hear me swear to him. Do you hear me, sir?"

"My dear sir," began Mr. Screw, who was somewhat taken aback by this burst of wrath.

"Don't call me 'your dear sir,'" said the nobleman, moving towards Screw.

"Sir, then," continued the other, who had not an idea to whom he was speaking, and perhaps would not have cared had he known, being such an honest man, "I cannot conceive why, if you are so certain, you have not come forward before, instead of allowing your friend to go to Europe in order to procure evidence he might have obtained here."

"I am not going to argue with you," said the Duke. "Dr. Claudius would have gone to Europe in any case, if that is any satisfaction to you. What did you come here for?"

"Because I thought it right to warn an unsuspecting lady of her danger," answered Mr. Screw boldly.

"Is that true? Do you really believe Claudius is not Claudius?" asked the Duke, coming close to the lawyer and looking him in the eyes.

"Certainly, I believe him to be an impostor," said the other returning his gaze fearlessly.

"I suppose you do," said the Duke, tolerably satisfied. "Now then, who sent you here?"

"No one sent me," answered Screw with some pride. "I am not in the habit of being sent, as you call it. It was in the course of a conversation I had with Mr. Barker, the other day—"

"I thought so," interrupted the Englishman. "I thought Mr. Barker was at the bottom of it. Will you please to deliver a message to Mr. Barker, with my compliments?" Screw nodded solemnly, as under protest.

"Then be kind enough to tell him from me that he is a most infernal blackguard. That if he attempts to carry this abominable plot any further I will post him at every one of his clubs as a liar and a cheat, and—and that he had better keep out of my way. As for you, sir, I would advise you to look into his character, for I perceive that you are an honest man."

"I am obliged to you, sir," said Mr. Screw, with something of a sneer. "But who are you, pray, that ventures to call my clients by such ugly names?"

"There is my card—you can see for yourself," said the Duke. Screw read it. His anger was well roused by this time.

"We have small respect for titles in this country, my Lord Duke," said he stiffly. "The best thing I can say is what you said to me, that you impress me as being an honest man. Nevertheless you may be mistaken."

"That is a matter which will be decided the day after to-morrow," said the other. "Meanwhile, in pursuance of what I said, I thank you very sincerely indeed"—Mr. Screw smiled grimly—"no, I am in earnest, I really thank you, on behalf of the Countess Margaret, for the honourable part you have endeavoured to perform towards her; and I beg your pardon for having mistaken you, and supposed you were in the plot. But give my message to Mr. Barker—it is actionable, of course, and he may take action upon it, if he likes. Good-morning, sir."

"Good-morning," said Screw shortly, somewhat pacified by the Duke's frank apology.

"I think I settled him," said the peer to Margaret, as they got into the cab that was to drive them to the Park. And they cantered away in royal spirits.

CHAPTER XX

Whatever reason may say, whatever certainty we may feel, the last hours of waiting for an ocean steamer are anxious ones. The people at the office may assure us twenty times that they feel "no anxiety whatever"—that is their stock phrase; our friends who have crossed the ocean twice a year for a score of years may tell us that any vessel may be a few hours, nay, a few days, behind her reckoning; it may seem madness to entertain the least shadow of a doubt—and yet, until the feet we love are on the wharf and the dear glad hands in ours, the shadow of an awful possibility is over us, the dreadful consciousness of the capacity of the sea.

The Duke, who, but for his anxiety to see the end, would have long since been on his way to England, had taken every precaution to ascertain the date of the ship's arrival. He took it for granted that Claudius would sail in the Cunard steamer, and he found out the vessel which sailed next after the Doctor had telegraphed. Then he made arrangements to be informed so soon as she was sighted, determined to go down in the Custom-House tug and board her at the Quarantine, that he might have the satisfaction of being first to tell Claudius all there was to be told.

"The day after to-morrow," he had said to Margaret, "we may safely expect him," and he watched, with a sort of dull pleasure, the light that came into her eyes when she heard the time was so near.

The first disappointment—alas, it was only the first—came on the evening before the appointed day. The Duke received a note from the office to the effect that late arrivals having reported very heavy weather, it was feared that the steamer might be delayed some hours. He at once inquired for the Countess, but found to his annoyance that both she and his sister had gone to the theatre. He had been out when they went, and so they had taken Miss Skeat as a sort of escort, and were doubtless enjoying themselves mightily. It was necessary, however, that Margaret should know the news of the delay before she went to bed, for it would have been cruel to allow her to wake in the morning with the assurance that Claudius might arrive at any moment.

"If I wait for them, and make a fuss, she will think it is something serious," reflected the Duke with more than usual tact. So he wrote a note, simply stating that he had news of a delay in the arrival of some hours,—perhaps a whole day, he added, wishing to be on the safe side. He gave the note to Vladimir, and went away to his rooms.

Margaret and Lady Victoria came home together in great spirits, laughing and rustling in their silk cloaks as they entered the little drawing-room, and sat down by the fire for a chat. Then Vladimir brought the Duke's note. Margaret read it by the firelight, and her face fell suddenly.

"What is it, dear?" asked Lady Victoria affectionately, as she noticed her companion's distressed look.

"Nothing—I suppose I ought not to be anxious. The steamer is delayed, that is all," and she gave the English girl her brother's note.

"Oh, if it had been anything serious he would have sat up for us. It will probably be in in the afternoon instead of in the morning." But Margaret's eyes were heavy and her gladness was gone from her.

"Do you ever have presentiments?" she asked, as they separated half an hour later.

"Never," answered Lady Victoria cheerily, "and if I ever do they never come true."

"I do," said Margaret, "I have a feeling that I shall never see him again." Poor Countess! She looked very miserable, with her white face and weary eyes.

Early the next morning Lady Victoria told her brother what had been the effect of his note. He was very angry with himself for not having put it into better shape, and he determined to repair his error by devoting himself entirely to watching for the steamer. With this object, he went down to the Cunard office and established himself with a novel and a box of cigarettes, to pass the day. He refused to move, and sent out in the afternoon for something to eat. The people in the office did not know him, and he felt free to be as Bohemian as he pleased. Once in the course of the day he was told that a French steamer had come in and had met with very heavy weather, losing a boat or two. It was possible, they said, that the Cunarder, which had sailed on the day following this vessel's departure, though from a nearer point, might be delayed another twenty-four hours. For his part, he felt no fear of the safe arrival of the ship, in due time. The odds are a thousand to one that a company which has never lost a vessel at sea will not lose any particular one you name. Nevertheless, he arranged to be called up in the night, if her lights were sighted, and he returned somewhat disconsolately to the hotel. Again he bethought him that if he told the Countess he had passed the day in the steamer office she would overrate his anxiety and so increase her own.

Margaret was really very unreasonable. There was not the slightest doubt that the steamer was safe, but she had become possessed, as Lady Victoria expressed it, by this unaccountable presentiment, that her fair-haired lover was gone from her for ever. Hideous things came up before her, poor drowned faces in the green swirl of the waves, men dead, and dying men grasping frantically at the white water-crests breaking over them, as though the rushing foam were a firm thing and could save them. She heard the wild thin wind screeching across the ocean furrows, breathless in his race with death. And then all seemed quiet, and she could see a grand form of a man, stiff-limbed and stark, the yellow hair all hanging down and the broad white throat turned up in death, floating solemnly through the deep green water, and seaweed, and ooze, far down below the angry waves.

She struggled hard against these dark thoughts; but it was no use. They would come back, and all through the evening she sat by her fire, with eyes wide, and parted lips, staring at the embers and straining her hearing to catch the sound of some one coming to the door—some one bearing the welcome news that the good ship was sighted at last. But no sound came, all through that weary evening, nor any message of comfort. Lady Victoria sat with her, and Miss Skeat, pretending not to notice her distressed mood; and once or twice the Duke came in and spoke cheerfully of what they would do "when Claudius came back." But Margaret went to her room at last with a heavy heart, and would not be comforted.

To tell the truth, the Duke firmly expected to receive the news of the ship's arrival during the night, and so great was his anxiety to relieve Margaret that he insisted upon Willis and Vladimir sitting up all night, so as to be sure of having the message delivered the moment it arrived. The Russian and the English servants hated each other, and he was certain they would not give each other any rest. But the Duke slept soundly, and waking at daybreak yelled viciously for Willis.

"Well?" he said, "I suppose you went to sleep. Where is the telegram?"

"There's no telegraph been yet, your Grace;" said the gray man-servant, who looked as though he had been up several nights instead of one.

"Oh!" said the Duke with a change of voice. He was not given to bullying his servants, and always regretted being hasty with them, but his conviction had been strong that the message ought to have come in the night.

Having spent the day previous in the office, he felt in duty bound not to relinquish his post until the Countess's doubts were set at rest. So he got into a cab; for, like many foreigners, he hated the Elevated Road, and was driven down town to the Bowling-Green.

It rained heavily all the morning, and the Duke, who, as may be imagined, was not generally given to spending his days in steamboat offices, was wonderfully and horribly bored. He smoked and kicked the chairs and read his novel, and was generally extremely uneasy, so that the clerks began to find him a nuisance, not having any idea that he was a real living swell. And still it rained, and the newspaper vendors looked in, all drizzly and wet, and the gay feathers of New York business seemed draggled.

Suddenly—it might have been at two o'clock—there was a stir in the office, a rattling of feet on the board floor, and a sort of general revival.

"She's in sight," a clerk called out to the Duke. His Grace stretched himself and departed. He had ascertained that the Custom-House tug did not start for two hours after the ship was sighted. So he sent a telegram to Margaret to announce that her waiting was over, and then, to pass the time, he went, and got something to eat. In due season he was seated in the single cabin of the little high-pressure boat, as it ploughed its way bravely through the waves and the rain to meet the great ocean monster. The Custom-House officials, cheery well-fed men, who know the green side of a XX[4], and are seldom troubled with gloomy forebodings, chatted and chaffed merrily together. One of them was very bald, and appeared to be a perpetual laughing-stock for the rest.

[Footnote 4: Twenty dollars.]

"Well, Ike," shouted one of his companions between two pulls of a small black bottle, "you hev got a skatin' rink on to the top of your head, and no mistake". The other grinned, and retorted to the effect that it was better to have the outside smooth than the inside soft.

"Well, I guess you got both, like a water-melon," returned the first speaker.

There are seldom more than one or two passengers on the Custom-House tug, and on this occasion the Duke was alone. He could not stand the atmosphere of tobacco and whisky in the cabin, and made his way along the side to the engine-room, leaving the Custom-House men to their smoke and their repartee.

It was almost five o'clock, and already nearly dark, when they came up with the great steamer. In five minutes the Duke was over the side, hurrying down to find his friend. Not seeing him anywhere, he found the bursar and inquired for Dr. Claudius. The officer replied that he had not made his acquaintance on the voyage, but offered the Duke a list of the passengers, remarking that the ship was unusually crowded for the time of year.

The Duke ran his finger down the list, then thinking he had missed the name he sought, he held the paper close to the lamp. But there was no "Dr. Claudius" there. His face fell and his heart beat fast, for he had been so positively certain. Poor Margaret! What would she do? How foolish of Claudius not to telegraph the day he sailed!

"You are quite sure there are no omissions here?" asked the Duke of the bursar.

"Quite sure, sir," answered he. "Wait a minute, though," he said, as the Duke dropped the list, "there was a passenger taken ashore at Queenstown very ill. A tall man, I should say, though they carried him. He had not registered on board, and he was so ill he gave up the passage. I could not tell you his name."

"Had he a light beard?" asked the Duke in great alarm.

"Um! yes; a large beard at all events. I remember how he looked as they carried him past. He was awfully pale, and his eyes were closed."

"My God!" exclaimed the Duke; "it must have been he! Does no one know his name?"

"The captain may. He would not see you now, just going into port, but I will go and ask him," added the officer kindly, seeing how much distressed the other seemed to be.

"Do—thanks—please ask him—yes!" he ejaculated, and sank into a chair. The bursar returned in a quarter of an hour.

"I am sorry to say, sir," he said, "that no one seems to have known his name. It sometimes happens. I am very sorry."

The Duke saw there was nothing to be done. It was clear that Claudius was not on board; but it was by no means clear that Claudius was not lying ill, perhaps dead, in Queenstown. The poor Englishman bit his lips in despair, and was silent. He could not decide how much he ought to tell Margaret, and how much he ought to keep to himself. The sick passenger seemed to answer the description, and yet he might not have been the Doctor for all that. Tall man—pale—he would be pale anyhow if he were ill—fair beard—yes, it sounded like him.

"I wish Vick were here," said the Duke to himself; "she has so much sense." Immediately the idea of consulting with his sister developed itself in his mind. "How can I get ashore?" he asked suddenly.

"I am afraid you will have to wait till we are in," said the friendly officer. "It will not be more than an hour now."

Impelled by some faint hope that the Doctor's name might have been omitted by some accident, the Duke rose and threaded his way among the crowding passengers, as they got their traps together and moved about the great saloons. He pursued every tall man he saw, till he could catch a glimpse of his face. At last he met a towering figure in a darkened passage way.

"My dear Claudius!" he cried, holding out his hand. But the stranger only paused, muttered something about a "mistake" and passed on. The excitement grew on the Duke, as it became certain that Claudius was not on board, and never in the whole of his very high and mighty life had he been in such a state of mind. Some of the passengers noted his uneasy movements and exchanged remarks in an undertone, as he passed and repassed.

"He is probably crazy," said an Englishman.

"He is probably drunk," said an American.

"He is probably a defaulting bank cashier," said a Scotchman.

"He looks very wild," said a New York mamma.

"He looks very unhappy," said her daughter.

"He is very well dressed," said her son, who got his clothes half yearly from Smallpage.

But the time passed at last, and the great thing came up to her pier, and opened her jaws and disgorged her living freight down a steep plank on to dry earth again; and the Duke, with a final look at the stream of descending passengers, forced his way ashore, and jumped into the first cab he saw.

"Drive to the nearest Elevated station," he shouted.

"Which avenue?" inquired the driver with that placidity which cabmen assume whenever one is in a hurry.

"Oh, any avenue—damn the avenue—Sixth Avenue of course!" cried the Duke in a stew.

"Very good, sir—Sixth Avenue Elevated, did you say?" and he deliberately closed the door and mounted to his box.

"What shall I tell her—what shall I say?" were the questions that repeated themselves with stunning force in his ear as he rattled through the streets, and slid over the smooth Elevated Road, swiftly towards his hotel. He had still some few hundred yards to walk from the station when he got out. His courage failed him, and he walked slowly, with bent head and heavy heart, the bearer of bad news.

Leisurely he climbed the steps, and the few stairs to his room. There stood Lady Victoria under the gaslight, by the fire, looking at the clock.

"At last," she cried, "how did you miss him?"

"Whom?" asked her brother dejectedly.

"Why, Claudius, of course!"

"Claudius is not come," he said in a low voice.

"Not come?" cried Lady Victoria, "not come? Why he has been here these two hours, with Margaret!"

The Duke was fairly overpowered and worn-out with excitement, and he fell back into a chair.

"How the—" he began, but checked the expletive, which found vent elsewhere, as expletives will. "Where the devil did he come from?"

"From Europe, I believe," said she. "Don't swear about it."

"Excuse me, Vick, I am bowled out; I was never so taken aback in my life. Tell me all about it, Vick." And he slowly recovered his senses enough to appreciate that Claudius had really arrived, and that he, the friend who had taken so much trouble, had somehow missed him after all. But he was honestly glad.

"I only saw him a moment, and I came in to your room to wait. Of course I let him go in there alone."

"Of course," assented her brother gravely.

"Margaret was waiting for him, for she got your telegram that the ship was in sight at three o'clock, and he got here at five; I thought it was very quick."

"Devilish quick, indeed," said her profane brother under his breath. "Tell me all about it," he added aloud.

It was easily enough explained, and before they went to bed that night every one understood it all. It was simply this—Claudius had come by another steamer, one of the German line, and had chanced to arrive a couple of hours before the Cunarder. Margaret had received the Duke's message, as Lady Victoria had said, and, as Claudius appeared soon afterwards, she saw no discrepancy.

The tall Doctor left his slender luggage to the mercy of the Custom House, and, hailing a cab, paid the man double fare in advance to hurry to the hotel. He could hardly wait while the servant went through the formality of taking up his name to the Countess, and when the message came back that he would "please to step up upstairs," as the stereotyped American hotel phrase has it, he seemed indeed to make of the stairway but a single step.

One moment more, and he was kneeling at her feet, trembling in every limb and speechless, but kissing the fair white hands again and again, while she bent down her flushed dark cheek till it touched his yellow hair. Then he stood up to his height and kissed her forehead and clasped his fingers about her waist and held her up to the length of his mighty arms before him, unconscious, in his overmastering happiness, of the strength he was exerting. But she laughed happily, and her eyes flashed in pride of such a man.

"Forgive me, my beloved," he said at last. "I am beside myself with joy." She hid her face on his breast as they stood together.

"Are you very glad to come back?" she asked at last, looking up to him with a smile that told the answer.

"Glad is too poor a word, my dear, dear lady," he said simply.

Two hours later they were still seated side by side on the deep sofa. Claudius had told her everything, for, now that he had accomplished his mission, there were to be no more secrets; and there were tears in Margaret's dark eyes as she heard, for she knew what it had cost him to leave her, knowing how he loved. And then they talked on.

"If it is to be so soon, dear," she said, "let it be on Christmas Day."

"So be it. And, beloved, where shall we go?" he asked.

"Oh, away—away from New York, and—and Mr. Barker and Mr. Screw and all these horrid people," she cried; for she too had confessed and told him all.

"Yes," he said; and was silent for a moment. "Dear one," he began again, "there is one thing more that you ought to know—" he stopped.

"Yes?" she said interrogatively.

"My blessed lady, I have told you the story of my birth for the first time to-day. I thought you ought to know it."

"That would never have made any difference, Claudius," she answered half reproachfully.

"My uncle—my father's brother—died a week before I sailed."

"I am sorry, dear," said she in ready sympathy; "were you fond of him?" She did not realise what he meant.

"I never remember to have seen him," he replied; "but—he died childless. And I—I am no longer a privat-docent." Margaret turned quickly to him, comprehending suddenly.

"Then you are the heir?" she asked.

"Yes, darling," he said softly. "It is a great name, and you must help me to be worthy of it. I am no longer Dr. Claudius." He added the last sentence with a shade of regret.

"And you need never have taken any trouble about this stupid money, after all? You are independent of all these people?"

"Yes," he answered, with a smile, "entirely so."

"I am so glad,—so glad, you do not know," said she, clasping her hands on his shoulder. "You know I hated to feel you were wrangling with those lawyers for money;" and she laughed a little scornfully.

"We will have it, all the same," said Claudius, smiling, "and you shall do as you like with it, beloved. It was honestly got, and will bring no ill luck with it. And now I have told you, I say, let us go to my father's house and make it ours." He spoke proudly and fondly. "Let me welcome my dear lady where her match was never welcomed before."

"Yes, dear, we will go there."

"Perhaps the Duke will lend us the yacht?" said Claudius.

"Yes," said Margaret, and there was a tinge of sadness in her voice, "yes, perhaps the Duke will lend us the yacht."

Francis Marion Crawford was born in Bagni di Lucca, Italy on 2nd August, 1854, the only son of the American sculptor Thomas Crawford and Louisa Cutler Ward. His aunt was Julia Ward Howe, the American poet, most famous for the words to 'The Battle Hymn of the Republic'.

After his father's death in 1857, his mother remarried to Luther Terry, with whom she had Crawford's half-sister, Margaret Ward Terry.

Crawford's education began at St Paul's School, Concord, New Hampshire and then went on to Cambridge University, the University of Heidelberg and finally the University of Rome.

In 1879, Crawford went to India to study the ancient language of Sanskrit and to edit Allahabad, The Indian Herald.

Returning to America in February 1881, he enrolled at Harvard University for a year to continue his studies in Sanskrit. Crawford had no real career path at this time although for two years he contributed to various periodicals, mainly The Critic.

Early in 1882, Crawford established a close, lifelong friendship with Isabella Stewart Gardner, a noted and eccentric heiress from Boston who over the years built up a large and eclectic collection of art.

Crawford lived most of his time in Boston with his Aunt Julia and Uncle Sam. The family were concerned by his lack of ambition, prospects in general, and his financial ones in particular.

His mother had hoped he might train in Boston for a career as an operatic baritone based on his private renditions of Schubert lieder. With that in mind it was, in January 1882, that George Henschel, the conductor of the Boston Symphony Orchestra, was called in to assess young Crawford's talents. Henschel was direct and to the point. Crawford would 'never be able to sing in perfect tune'. His Uncle Sam, knowing that Crawford was keen on literary pursuits, proposed that his years in India might be good source material to write about. Crawford agreed. He set to work. Uncle Sam also set about developing contacts with a number of New York publishers.

Events moved very quickly. By December of that year Crawford had completed his first novel, 'Mr Isaacs', based on modern Anglo-Indian life flavoured with a touch of Oriental mystery. It was an immediate success. Crawford set about writing a second novel and the result was 'Dr Claudius' in 1883.

In October 1884 he married Elizabeth Berdan, the daughter of the Civil War Union General Hiram Berdan. The marriage would produce two sons; Harold and Bertram, and two daughters; Eleanor and Clara.

Crawford, buoyed by his excellent start, now decided to return to Italy and to live there permanently.
The couple initially went to Sorrento and lived at the historic Hotel Cocumella during 1885 before moving permanently to Sant' Agnello, where the purchase of the Villa Renzi would now be rededicated as Villa Crawford.

As a writer Crawford had more than his fair share of detractors but, perhaps due to the physical distance between author and these detractors, they did not distract from his prolific output.

Each year seemed to bring a new F. Marion Crawford novel. His popularity was evident although some works, such as 1896's offering 'Adam Johnstone's Son', was described by his left-wing English contemporary, George Gissing, as "rubbish". Over half of his novels are set in Italy. He also wrote three long historical studies of Italy and was nearing completion on a history of Rome in the Middle Ages when he died.

His 'Saracinesca' series are considered his best works. The third in the series, 'Don Orsino' (1892) was told against the background of a real estate bubble and is especially effective. The volume immediately after was 'Corleone' (1897), and the first major treatment of the Mafia in literature.

Crawford himself was fondest of 'Khaled: A Tale of Arabia' (1891), a story of a genie who becomes human. 'A Cigarette-Maker's Romance' (1890) was dramatized, and had considerable popularity on the stage as well as in its novel form.

Towards the end of the 1890's Crawford ventured down another path with his writing. He began his historical works. 'Ave Roma Immortalis' was published in 1898, followed by 'Rulers of the South' (1900), and 'Gleanings from Venetian History' (1905). Most were re-titled with longer more explanatory titles for the American market. Within them all his careful and precise knowledge of the local Italian history together with his literary talents combined to great effect.

Whilst on an American Lecture tour in the winter of 1897-1898 Crawford was researching and gathering technical information for his historical work 'Marietta' (published 1901), that describes glass-making in late medieval Venice. Whilst visiting a glass-smelting plant in Colorado he suffered a severe lung injury when he inhaled toxic gasses. This would eventually contribute to his death a decade or so later.

Crawford's commercial popularity and appeal at the time was such that in 1901, the American Macmillan firm began a deluxe uniform edition of his novels as his works came up for re-printing. In 1904 the P. F. Collier Company in New York was authorized to publish a 25-volume edition (which was later expanded to 32 volumes).

In 1902 he wrote a stage play 'Francesca da Rimini', that was produced in Paris by his friend and legendary actress Sarah Bernhardt.

Towards the end of his life Hollywood had begun to realise that his works were a valuable source of stories and ideas and several were turned into movies and continued to be so for decades after his death.

Crawford also had a gift for pulling off excellent short stories. Several, such as 'The Upper Berth' (1886), 'For the Blood Is the Life' (1905, a vampiress tale), 'The Dead Smile' (1899), and 'The Screaming Skull' (1908), are among the most anthologized classics of the horror genre. After his death several collected volumes were published from various sources.

After most of his fictional works had been published, most had the view that he was a gifted narrator; and his books of fiction, were full of historic vitality and energy as well as dramatic characterization. He was widely popular among readers to whom literature was more for escapism than a confrontation with reality or pages of subjective analysis. In 'The Novel: What It Is' (1893), Crawford was both resolute and disarming in defending his literary approach, self-conceived as a combination of romanticism and realism, defining the art form in terms of its marketplace and audience. The novel, he wrote, is "a marketable commodity" and "intellectual artistic luxury" that "must amuse, indeed, but should amuse reasonably, from an intellectual point of view .... Its intention is to amuse and please, and certainly not to teach and preach; but in order to amuse well it must be a finely-balanced creation ...."

Francis Marion Crawford died at Sorrento on Good Friday 1909 at Villa Crawford of a heart attack.

F. Marion Crawford – A Concise Bibliography

Novels

Mr. Isaacs: A Tale of Modern India (1882)
Dr. Claudius (1883)
To Leeward (1884)
A Roman Singer (1884)
An American Politician (1884)
Zoroaster (1885)
A Tale of a Lonely Parish (1886)
Saracinesca (1887)
Marzio's Crucifix (1887)
Paul Patoff (1887)
With the Immortals (1888)
Greifenstein (1889)
Sant' Ilario (1889); sequel to Saracinesca
A Cigarette-Maker's Romance (1890)
Khaled: A Tale of Arabia (1891)
The Witch of Prague (1891)
The Three Fates (1892)
Don Orsino (1892); sequel to Sant' Ilario
The Children of the King (1893)
Pietro Ghisleri (1893)
Marion Darche (1893)
Katharine Lauderdale (1894)
The Upper Berth (1894); with "By the Waters of Paradise"
Love in Idleness (1894)
The Ralstons (1894); sequel to Katharine Lauderdale
Casa Braccio (1895); related to Katharine Lauderdale and The Ralstons.
Adam Johnstone's Son (1896)
Taquisara (1896)
A Rose of Yesterday (1897)
Corleone (1897)
Via Crucis (1899)
In the Palace of the King (1900)
Marietta (1901)
Cecilia (1902)
Man Overboard! (1903)
The Heart of Rome (1903)
Whosoever Shall Offend (1904)
Soprano (1905); U.S. title: Fair Margaret.
A Lady of Rome (1906)
Arethusa (1907)

The Little City of Hope (1907)
The Primadonna (1908); sequel to Soprano/Fair Margaret
The Diva's Ruby (1908); sequel to The Primadonna
The White Sister (1909)
Stradella (1909)
The Undesirable Governess (1910)
Wandering Ghosts; British title: Uncanny Tales.

Non-fiction

Our Silver (1881)
The Novel: What It Is (1893)
Constantinople (1895)
Bar Harbor (1896)
Ave Roma Immortalis (1898)
Rulers of the South (1900; 1905 in the U.S. as Southern Italy and Sicily and The Rulers of the South)
Gleanings from Venetian History (1905; in the U.S. as Salvae Venetia and in 1909 as Venice; the People and the Place)

Drama

In the Palace of the King (1900) with Lorrimer Stoddard.
Francesca da Rimini (1902) The piece was adapted into an opera by Franco Leoni in 1904.
Evelyn Hastings (1902) Unpublished typescript discovered in 2008.
The White Sister (1909) with Walter C. Hackett.

Filmography

A Cigarette-Maker's Romance, directed by Frank Wilson (UK, 1913, based on the novella)
The White Sister, directed by Fred E. Wright [it] (1915, based on the novel)
In the Palace of the King [it], directed by Fred E. Wright [it] (1915, based on the novel)
Whosoever Shall Offend, directed by Arrigo Bocchi (UK, 1919, based on the novel)
Il cuore di Roma, directed by Edoardo Bencivenga (Italy, 1919, based on the novel)
A Cigarette-Maker's Romance, directed by Tom Watts (UK, 1920, based on the novella)
Saracinesca [it], directed by Gaston Ravel (Italy, 1921, based on the novel)
Sant' Ilario [it], directed by Henry Kolker (Italy, 1923, based on the novel)
The White Sister, directed by Henry King (1923, based on the novel)
In the Palace of the King, directed by Emmett J. Flynn (1923, based on the novel)
Son of India, directed by Jacques Feyder (1931, based on the novel Mr. Isaacs)
The White Sister, directed by Victor Fleming (1933, based on the novel)
The Screaming Skull, directed by Alex Nicol (1958, named after the short story)
The White Sister, directed by Tito Davison (Mexico, 1960, based on the novel)